T0129254

Winning the lottery is the biggest ticket to freedom Greer Hawthorne's ever had. Until her best friend's brother comes to town . . .

Greer Hawthorne's winning lottery ticket doesn't just bring her wealth, it also means her chance at a long-postponed education. She's finally on the cusp of proving to her big, overprotective family that she's independent—until a careless mistake jeopardizes her plan to graduate. Lucky for her, there's someone in town who may be able to help . . .

Alex Averin plans to show up for his sister's wedding, then quickly get back to his job as a world-renowned photojournalist. But when gorgeous, good-hearted Greer needs an assist with a photography project, he's powerless to say no. Showing Greer his professional passion ignites a new one, and rouses instincts in Alex he thought he'd long set aside.

Can a ceaseless wanderer find a stopping place alongside a woman determined to set out on her own . . . or are Alex and Greer both pushing their luck too far?

Books by Kate Clayborn

A Chance of a Lifetime
Beginner's Luck
Luck of the Draw
Best of Luck

Published by Kensington Publishing Corporation

Best of Luck

A Chance of a Lifetime

Kate Clayborn

LYRICAL PRESS
Kensington Publishing Corp.
www.kensingtonbooks.com

Lyrical Press books are published by
Kensington Publishing Corp. 119 West 40th Street New York, NY 10018

Copyright © 2018 by Kate Clayborn

All Kensington titles, imprints, and distributed lines are available at special quantity discounts for bulk purchases for sales promotion, premiums, fundraising, and educational or institutional use.

Special book excerpts or customized printings can also be created to fit specific needs. For details, write or phone the office of the Kensington Special Sales Manager:
Kensington Publishing Corp.
119 West 40th Street
New York, NY 10018
Attn. Special Sales Department. Phone: 1-800-221-2647.
Kensington and the K logo Reg. U.S. Pat. & TM Off.
LYRICAL PRESS Reg. U.S. Pat. & TM Off.
Lyrical Press and the L logo are trademarks of Kensington Publishing Corp.

First Electronic Edition: November 2018
eISBN-13: 978-1-5161-0514-4
eISBN-10: 1-5161-0514-1

First Print Edition: November 2018
ISBN-13: 978-1-5161-0515-1
ISBN-10: 1-5161-0515-X

Printed in the United States of America

To best friends:
all and sundry, old and new, far and near.
The luckiest charms there are in this world.

Prologue

Greer

When I first see him there, I think I must still be dreaming.

I'd woken up at 3:13 a.m.—unlucky, that—the sharp planes of his face still fresh in my mind, my skin still flushed, the sheets tangled around my legs, and I'd nearly gasped in embarrassment over it. Dreaming about *him*, of all people, a man I'd only met hours ago. A man so handsome I could barely look him in the eye without flushing. A man who wore all his vast experience in the rangy, confident movements of his body. A man whose friendly, innocent hug at the end of the night had felt like electricity to me, like being shocked awake after a long, unnatural slumber.

My best friend's brother, Alex Averin.

Now he pauses as he steps across the threshold of Boneshaker's, my favorite coffee shop not two blocks from Kit's house, where he's supposed to be staying for the weekend—where, I've decided, I'll avoid until he leaves, since I'd basically gone acutely nonverbal in his presence. Between me and Zoe and Kit, my two closest friends, I've always been the quiet one, but last night I'd brought shyness to new heights, barely managing three full sentences over the course of dinner and dessert. I'd watched as Kit had beamed over him, proud of everything about her brother, and proud of everything that she was getting to show and tell him about her life here: her job, her newly purchased house, even her budding friendship with Ben Tucker, a guy who I could already tell was more than half in love with her. And I'd watched as Zoe—cool and funny and unflappable—had traded stories with Alex of travel to Europe, to South America, even to Australia, where they'd both, apparently, visited the same koala refuge.

I'd just *watched*.

Watching. My specialty. For years, the only habit I was healthy enough to cultivate.

I return to that specialty now—so familiar, like I'm a wayward, crooked drawer that's been pushed back into its track and now can slide easily into place, flush with its surroundings, barely noticeable. I turn my body in my chair slightly so I'm not directly facing the door, arranging my book in a way that makes it seem like I'm reading, though I'm still 100 percent tracking him. As he moves toward the counter, the heads of all three women at a table beside me turn to watch him, one of them actually letting her mouth fall open a little.

I can't say I blame her. He's beautiful, that's the thing—not just handsome, not just a strong jaw and a tall, fit leanness, broad shoulders and narrow hips, not just thick, jet-black hair that's gorgeously messy, exactly as it was in my dream, exactly as I'd *made* it in my dream. He's actually *beautiful*—smooth olive skin underneath his heavy stubble, and high, cut cheekbones that transform into something softer and kinder when he smiles. Full lips, white teeth, his right-side incisor slightly crooked. Clear, bright green eyes that you can see across a room, framed with long, black lashes that leave a shadow on his skin when he lowers them.

From where I sit I watch him order, watch his mouth move: *coffee, black*. He pays in cash, shoves a dollar in the tip jar, and the barista looks like she wants to propose marriage. He smiles at her, and I try to telegraph her a message: *Oh, I know. It* hurts *when he smiles like that.*

He moves down the counter to wait for his coffee, and I curve my shoulders and look down to my book again, hoping he doesn't see me. Without the cover of Kit and Zoe, my awkwardness will seem worse— either panicked silence or a blurting non sequitur, and I don't think I could face his quizzical brow, his gentle smile of pitying encouragement, the same one he offered up last night across the table after I'd stumbled over answering a question as simple as *Where did you grow up?*

In my dream, though. . .he looked at me with total concentration. With desire.

I shake my head, force my eyes to focus, training them back at the top of the page of my textbook so I can start reading all over again. I'm sure I've lost every bit of information I read over in the minutes before he walked in.

"Hey," comes a quiet, deep, already familiar voice from above me, and for a second I keep my eyes down, hoping I've somehow developed actual powers of invisibility, rather than standard wallflower syndrome.

But I can feel him there watching me, those thick black brows probably arranging themselves into the most charming little furrow. *This again,* he's probably thinking.

When I turn to face him, to look up to meet those sea-glass eyes, my elbow knocks my textbook from the table, and Alex reaches a hand out, catching it easily at the spine, not even disrupting the steaming coffee he's holding in his left hand. I think I let out a small groan of frustration, or of exasperation—I'm sure at any moment, after seeing that display of his reflexes, either the barista or the open-mouthed latte drinker will just toss her panties across the room at him.

"*Cultural Anthropology,*" he says, looking down at the book he's just rescued, his lips tipping up wryly in some ironic recognition. This renowned photojournalist who's traveled the entire world, has seen it and so many of its cultures through his own eyes—who's shaped, through his lens, the way other people see it—holding my little college textbook, my little lottery-induced dream of a college degree. It must seem—

"I always wanted to take a class like this," he says, smiling down at me, and for a second I think about throwing *my* panties at him.

It feels like a good two and a half minutes of me simply *blinking* at him, adjusting to the handsome glare his face gives off, but in actuality I'm pretty sure it's only a few startled seconds before I manage a weak, "It's a good class."

He nods, gestures to the seat across from me. "Mind if I sit?"

"Oh," I say, pulling my papers toward me, clearing space for him on the table. "Sure." Inside my head there's a tattoo of a thought: *Don't think about the dream.*

"Thanks." He sinks into his chair. "Didn't get much sleep last night."

Don't think about it, I tell myself again, hopelessly.

"Did you and Kit have a late night?" I feel ludicrously pleased at how normal and casual I've managed to sound. Now that the shock has worn off—or I guess now that my eyes have adjusted to his presence—I feel a bit more settled, ready to converse like a normal person.

"Sort of." When he shifts in his seat I notice something for the first time. He has a bag with him—a sun-bleached canvas rucksack, one of its straps duct-taped, and as my eyes settle on it he reaches a hand down, tries to tuck it more tightly under the table.

"Are you—are you leaving already?" The disbelief in my voice—it seems to lash him like a whip. He snaps his head to the side to look out the window, inhaling sharply through his nose. "You're supposed to stay for the whole weekend," I add. Kit's been preparing for Alex's visit for days, ever since his quick, unexpected call to let her know he'd be in town—a call she'd greeted with such genuine excitement and hope that I'd immediately felt a prickle of unease. Never good luck, I'd thought, to look forward to something that much.

He looks back at me then, and I'm tempted to lower my eyes.

But Kit—Kit must be so *disappointed*.

"I got called in for a job," he says, and it could be true. Alex shoots for the *New York Times*, for the AP, once, even, for *National Geographic*, photographs that Zoe and I oohed and aahed over when Kit had shown them to us last year.

But because I'm good—I'm so, so good at seeing every single thing, at *watching*—I notice it. I notice the way the corner of his mouth, right there on the left side, twitches. Barely a split second of movement, a pull of his lips that'd be entirely hidden from the casual observer.

"You're lying." I stare right into those eyes, those sea-glass eyes I'd avoided looking at last night, and I hope mine are burning right into his. I hope I've put into them all the accusation I mean to level at him. Kit's heart is probably broken—all her plans for him this weekend, all the things she meant to show him about her new home. All the time she's been waiting for him to come.

I remember: I can do more than just watch. When it comes to the people I love, I can do anything. "You can't do this to her. You can't leave."

The look he gives me—it's nothing like what I saw in his face last night, nothing like the gentle, indulgent smiles he gave to Kit, nothing like the low, laughing surprise he'd had for Zoe's bold sense of humor. Nothing even like the open curiosity in his eyes when he'd seen me for the first time.

It looks like anger.

"I can," he says, and his voice is forceful. Unapologetic. So, so *confident*.

There's a thick silence between us, the sounds of the café tinkling and vague. But I hear his voice like an echo.

I can.

It sounds so—it sounds so *true*. There isn't anything stopping Alex—he's healthy, he's successful, he's made his own way in the world. Someone— his sister, me, anyone, probably—may tell him *you can't*, but he doesn't have to listen.

He could get up and leave right now. He could pick up his rucksack and take his coffee with him, walk out this coffee shop's doors. There'd be a trail of women's undergarments in his wake.

Instead he shifts in his seat, puts his elbows on the table, and holds his to-go cup between his hands. The movement puts him closer to me, the steam from his coffee wafting between us, warming the space between our bodies. For a split second I'm back in that dream, and I drop my eyes to the table. There's a stray penny, tail side up, beside his right forearm.

"Out there," he says, nodding toward the door, his voice softer now, a still-rough texture to it that now doesn't sound quite so unapologetic. "Out there is the thing I waited for my whole life."

I press my lips together, roll them inward, a habit I seem to have picked up since I started my college classes. Trying not to over-participate, trying not to get a reputation as the eager adult degree student while the slackers in the back roll their eyes at me, hoping for an early release from class.

Alex's eyes dip to my mouth, and suddenly I don't care so much about seeming eager. I use a fingernail to tap out the curiosity I feel building in my shoulders, my elbows, my wrists. I hear the *plink, plink* of it against the ceramic. "What's that?" I ask, my voice hardly above a whisper.

And then he smiles. He smiles like he—like he somehow *knows*, like he heard me make that wish six months ago, the night Kit and Zoe and I had all joked about our possible lottery win, a win that became a shocking, I'm-still-not-over-it reality. The night I'd told my friends that all I'd want was an education.

"Freedom," he says, and he could not have cut me deeper if he'd held a hot knife against my body.

My secret wish, the one I'd made silently that same night our numbers came up, the one I'm working so hard to make come true—with my winnings, with my college classes, with every small effort I make to be stronger, healthier, more independent.

I lean back in my seat, lengthening the distance between us. I let the moment stretch a beat too long, my eyes on my mug, my book, the penny. Strangely, even though we don't know each other well—at all, really—I can feel him waiting for me to argue, to push back. And when I finally meet his eyes, that's what I see there.

Expectation. Anticipation.

Maybe not quite what I saw in my dream, but maybe not all that different either.

But Alex isn't who I thought he was, not if he'll leave Kit this way. And his freedom isn't the same as mine, not if it looks like this—a beat-up bag, a faraway look, no limitations, no attachments, no debts, no thought to who or what you leave behind.

I let go of that electric, curious heat he makes me feel. I replace it with all the disappointment I feel on behalf of my friend. I pull my book closer to me.

"I'd better get back to studying." I keep my gaze level, uninterested, aloof—the corollary gift of my shyness for moments like these.

He doesn't wait long. Maybe a few seconds of taut silence before he stands again and hoists his bag over one shoulder, his cup of coffee still steaming in his hand. Oblivious, clearly, to the way so many eyes in the café are newly drawn to him.

"Greer," he says, tipping his chin down in some old-fashioned gesture of acknowledgment that—despite my new opinion of him—feels like a brand on my skin. His smile is different now: smaller, sadder. "Maybe I'll meet you again sometime."

And then he's gone, ducking out the same door he came in, and I don't see him again. Not for almost two whole years.

Not even in my dreams.

Chapter 1

Greer

"He's right. You can't leave."

At first I don't process what the bureaucrat in the statement necklace across the desk from me is saying. After all, I'm three minutes deep in a daydream about that necklace, which is so aggressively big and multicolored that I've pictured the bureaucrat in a kind of medieval fairy tale/ancient war epic mashup in which it figures heavily as some kind of magical token of her as yet undiscovered powers. I'm trying to find a way to work in a unicorn, but so far, no dice.

"What?" I say, once her punch-to-the-gut words sink in.

She looks over the rim of her plastic-framed glasses, primary school red, two teeny-tiny rhinestones on each winged tip. It's too much, what with the statement necklace. Plus someone who accessorizes this much should be more fun than this.

"You," she begins, stretching out that one syllable before continuing. "Cannot. Graduate." It's the kind of tone that I'll bet she has to use a lot on panicked, desperate undergraduates, the ones who come in here looking for a reprieve about their unacceptable GPA or some honor code violation that'll keep them from their diploma. She's got to enunciate every single thing. She's got to speak slowly to cut through their narcissism or their naïveté or their general unwillingness to accept reality.

Says the twenty-seven-year-old woman who was just thinking about a unicorn.

"There has to be some kind of mistake," I say, repeating words I've already said once today, barely an hour ago, when I'd sat in a similarly uncomfortable chair across from my academic advisor. He'd looked at me with a gentle, consoling expression, handed me my three-page degree application, and said, "We've got a problem here, Greer." I'd stared down at that slim stack of paperwork with a thudding sense of shock.

"There's no way," I'd said to him as I'd taken it with a shaking hand, already gathering my bag. "I'll go check at the registrar's office. There's no way I've gotten this wrong."

If there's one thing I've gotten good at in the two and a half years since I won the lottery, it's paperwork. The lottery itself involves a fair amount of paperwork, sure: disclosures and waivers and verifications of all kinds. Yes, you can use my name or image to promote the state lottery. Yes, I sign verifying that I am who I say I am. No, I do not dispute the other two claimants to this ticket. Yes, I can provide an authenticating letter from my bank; no, I don't owe any back taxes or child support.

But what I'd chosen to do with my winnings—that too had been paperwork city. Some of it had involved an accountant (four pages of paperwork just to meet with him, by the way), some of it had involved an attorney (no paperwork for that, since Zoe had done all her work for me for free), and some of it, *most* of it—the paperwork connected to my getting this long-postponed college education—had only involved me. Applications and essays, overload permission slips, internship filings, independent study proposals. Regular tracking of my coursework, to show I was right on schedule for...*this*.

This degree application. The one that verifies I'm walking across a stage at the end of the summer, diploma in hand with a full-time, health-insurance and retirement-plan supported professional job waiting.

The one that says I'm finally *free*.

"There's no mistake," Necklace says, setting the application on her desk and folding her hands on top of it. "You need an art credit."

"But I took—"

"You took two art *history* courses," she says, cutting me off. She's probably heard a version of my story a million times. Students lost in the bureaucracy of the university, little scheduling mistakes that mean trouble later. "One of those needed to be a studio art. The practice of art, not just the study of it."

"Okay, but—"

She cuts me off with a palm-out gesture before I can make a case for myself. Before I can show her the records I kept from every meeting with my advisor, including the one in which I'd selected the second art history course to fill a requirement. Shouldn't he have warned me? Shouldn't he have stopped me, pointed me in a different direction? Even as I think it, I know I'm wrong. Maybe he could've done a better job, but I know the buck stops with me. I know this is my mistake, my responsibility.

"Ms. Hawthorne. You have managed to very nearly complete a degree program in social work with a minor in social welfare in"—she looks down again at my application, scanning the top—"about two and a half years, which is an incredibly impressive feat. This is a minor hiccup, one you can remedy with a single semester of per-credit-hour payment."

She breaks off here to give me a pointed look at the word *payment*, and I wonder if maybe she's one of the few people in this city who saw the frozen, shocked smiles on my and Zoe's faces when we'd taken that paperwork-approved promotional photograph for the lottery, sans publicity-shy Kit. Of course Necklace wouldn't know how little I have left of the cardboard check I'd held that day. "I know this is a disappointment," she says, "but you shouldn't feel at all ashamed."

Ashamed? That's the least of it. I feel like a failure. I feel stupid and careless, and worst of all, I feel *weak*. I've done everything right the last two years, but all of a sudden I feel like the Greer who's never been able to see things through, who's been too tired or too sick to finish what I start, the Greer who needs help with even the smallest tasks.

"I *have* to graduate," I say, hating the way my voice has risen to a desperate, almost keening pitch. "I have a job waiting for me."

She sighs, cuts a glance over to the clock that I know is hanging on the wall above me. The lobby outside her office is packed with students, and I sympathize. The timing for me couldn't be worse either. That I had to find this out on *this* Friday, of all possible Fridays, feels like particularly bad luck.

I squint at her necklace, trying to work out the stones in there. If there are any opals stuck in between what look mostly like acrylic, oven-baked blobs, there's a bad luck reason for this, maybe.

Necklace lets out a gusty sigh. "Your job requires that you have the degree at your start date?"

I don't see a single opal in there.

"Yes." It's not a lie. It's part of my contract, in fact, another piece of paperwork I've recently signed. I'm giving her a look like *I'm* the unicorn, the never-before-seen student creature she's going to make an exception for. *Use your undiscovered powers on me,* I'm thinking. *I'll even wear that necklace.*

She grabs a pen out of a cup on her desk, flips my degree application over, and scribbles a few lines of text before handing it over. "This is the name of the chair of the studio art department. Below that is the name of the chair of our academic standards committee. You might be able to make an appeal."

Inside my bag, my phone pings with a text, and I know I'm out of time, at least for today. Waiting in my car I've got a suitcase, a garment bag, and a small wooden box of good luck charms—borrowed, blue, new—for Kit. I don't know how I'm going to empty my head enough of this problem to get through the weekend.

"I'll get in touch with them right away," I tell her, standing from my chair. My knees feel like they're made of jelly donuts. "Thank you."

Before I can turn away, hustle out the door, and take out my phone to address whatever logistical crisis related to this weekend has come up in the last hour, she clears her throat. She lowers her red glasses, so now they're resting on a thin gold chain on top of the statement necklace. My eyes blur with the garishness of it. I couldn't picture a unicorn if I tried.

"He's a photographer," she says, and everything in my line of sight is replaced with an image in my mind, one I try not to think about all that often.

Sea-glass eyes and a sad smile. A broad back carrying a beat-up rucksack, walking out the door.

"The chair of the department, I mean," she says. "Try that as your way in, if you're looking to get in his good graces."

"Right." For a second, I'm frozen stock still there, a living embodiment of *you can't leave*, even though my phone pings with three more messages. On any other day I'd say it was only my mother who'd have such persistence, but today I'm guessing it's my fellow maid of honor, because I'm supposed to be at a pedicure across town in ten minutes and there's about three thousand other errands to run before my best friend gets married tomorrow.

But standing across from Not-Bad-Luck Necklace and clutching my stack of Bad Luck Paperwork, I can only think about one thing.

I know a photographer.

And this weekend, I'm going to see him for the first time in a long time.

* * * *

He breezes in the same way he'd done two years ago.

He's windblown and stubbled along his jaw, sporting a sheepish grin as he ducks through the front door of Betty's restaurant, closed down for the night in honor of Kit and Ben's rehearsal dinner. "Oh, thank *God*," Zoe says, nudging me as though I haven't noticed him come in, as though I didn't sense a change in the air even before that door opened. Across the room, where she's standing with Ben, Kit says, "Finally!," but there's a laugh in her voice. She crosses the room to her brother, holding out her arms for a hug that I drop my eyes to avoid seeing.

I'm not going to forgive him so easily.

His first call had come mid-pedicure, while all three of us had had our feet soaking in warm, bubbling water and while I'd been doing a bang-up job of not revealing a thing about my impending graduation crisis. I'd shown up to that nail salon with a sunny disposition and a can-do attitude, and I'd intended to keep it that way. When Kit disconnected the call she'd shrugged and said, "Weather out of LaGuardia," and I'd been ready to fully engage my sunny disposition to explain how we were going to can-do this rehearsal even if her brother didn't show up.

But Kit had surprised me, barely batting an eye at either of the next two calls—one when we were checking into the Crestwood Hotel for our pre-wedding girls' sleepover, the other when we were driving to the rehearsal itself.

"He'll get here," Kit had said, confident in Alex's eventual arrival or else so blissed out by her impending wedding and three-week honeymoon trip through Europe that she hadn't allowed herself to consider the possibility that the man who'd basically raised her might not make it. I'd felt the tension that'd been gathering in my neck since this afternoon ratchet up to near painful levels.

Alex has moved further inside the warm, wainscoted interior of the main dining room, usually full of Betty's diverse crowd of bearded or barrel-roll-hair hipsters, young professionals, and the few old-timers who still remember when her bar was a smoke-filled fish and chips place and who grudgingly allow her food is better. He and Ben are shaking hands, one of Alex's coming up to clutch Ben's elbow in a gesture of casual affection and approval that suggests he knows the groom is forgiving too. Zoe's already crossed the room, leaving me behind the bar where I'm checking the Sterno cans under the chafing dishes like I work here. From the other side of the bar Betty gives me a skeptical look, and I pretend not to see her making a shooing motion at me.

Why wouldn't he have flown in earlier, I'm thinking, *to avoid exactly this kind of thing? Why wouldn't he have made Kit's wedding his top priority? Why wouldn't he have put her needs, her special day, first in his mind and his plans?*

That's what I'm *doing, after all.*

"Greer, look who's here," says Kit, interrupting my very intense self-congratulatory monologue, and I nearly burn my hands on a dish of garlic-parmesan green beans. When I look up I see Kit and Alex, arms linked in the same way they would've been had Alex actually showed up for his part in the rehearsal, Kit a full two heads shorter than her brother and wearing a smile of relief and pride.

As for Alex? Up close he's more handsome than I remember, even if he's grossly underdressed in a faded black T-shirt and wrinkled, army-green chinos and beat-up hiking boots. He runs a hand through his hair, slightly longer than it'd been last time he was here, and smiles as though the last words we exchanged weren't harsh ones. He looks like he's never been felled by a piece of paperwork in his whole life. The casual nomad with no permanent address. Reckless and strong and no strings attached.

Over his shoulder I see the familiar strap of his bag.

"Good of you to stop by." As soon as it's out of my mouth, my own eyes are widening in shock at the same time as Kit's, and at the same time as Zoe's, who's returned just in time to see me act like a jerk.

One question about my reunion with Alex is answered, then: his face is still a wire cutter for my brain-mouth synapse. I open it again, trying to rally my sunny disposition, but I'm interrupted by Betty, who probably caught the scent of awkward.

"Alex, welcome. Can I put your bag behind the bar?" She gives me another pointed look, one that says *This is why I work here, and you don't.* I back away from the chafing dishes and away from the gaze Alex has leveled at me.

He's still watching me when he answers Betty. "I'm going to make a stop in your restroom and change my clothes."

Betty and Kit usher him away, Kit giving me a brief, puzzled glance over her shoulder, and Zoe looks at me. "Everything all right?"

I sink onto the stool behind me, try for a casual wave of the hand, a self-deprecating eye roll. "I guess I'm being a bit intense about our maid of honor duties."

The look I get in return tells me Zoe's not buying what I'm selling. "You've been a little off today." I know her well enough to know she won't leave me alone about it. She'll cross-examine me until I've spilled it, and then she'll probably take out her phone and call the registrar's office at the university and leave a legalese-packed voice mail that'd make the statement necklace rattle right off the bureaucrat's neck.

I look over my shoulder, make sure Kit's nowhere nearby. For all my self-congratulation, I guess I haven't done a great job setting my worries aside if Zoe and I are having this conversation, and the least I can do is keep Kit far away from it today of all days. "There's a problem with my graduation."

Zoe's gold-brown eyes immediately sharpen, her posture lengthening. "What kind of problem?" In spite of the fact that I don't want to be doing this here, I love the way Zoe knows already—that this is serious, that I'd be freaked out about it. She and Kit have had tickets reserved for the graduation ceremony since February. They want to wear T-shirts with my face printed on them.

I tell her a short version—a missing fine arts credit, an appeal I have to make to the chair of the department to see if I can get an exception. "I'll get it taken care of Monday," I say, trying to project all the confidence I don't feel.

"How? Like, what's the plan?"

I clear my throat, shift my feet in the yellow flats that are supposed to match my sunny disposition. "I don't know yet. I'll think it through, once we get past tomorrow."

Just then Alex steps back into the dining room, wearing a gray dress shirt with the sleeves rolled up to his elbows, a slim-cut pair of black dress pants that look newly pressed, and a pair of what have to be freshly shined black shoes. The stubble seemed like carelessness before, but now it only seems like maximum *I-belong-in-a-cologne-ad* effect.

In his left hand, he's got ahold of that damned bag.

I stand from my stool, smooth the front of my dress, avoiding Zoe's eyes and Alex's—everything. His whole presence here. I know already that part of the plan is to not look his way again.

Because even if Alex Averin were the kind of person who could help you with an art department chair who holds your fate in his hands, he wouldn't be the kind of person who'd stick around to do it.

* * * *

Dinner's a hit, the conversation around the room easy and flowing, a general feeling of giddy excitement about tomorrow's wedding. I don't participate much, which isn't all that unusual, but this time it's less about my shyness than it is about my continued distraction. I've done my best to stick to the plan and avoid Alex, but right about the time everyone's starting in on plates of the miniature lava cakes Betty's brought out from the kitchen, something—some heavy, inevitable feeling—draws my eyes his way, and I forget all about the plan.

He's stiff backed and quiet, looking a bit pale in the bar's soft light, his mouth set in a tense line, so unlike the easy smile he wore when he arrived. It's such an uncomfortable posture that I can't help but feel worse about how I handled our encounter. I'm sure he's tired, after all. I'm sure he didn't mean to be late. I'm sure it's hard, balancing your time, when you're out there photographing things most people don't even have the stomach to look at on the morning news.

When Ben stands up to thank everyone for coming, I decide I'll take a chance and smile at him if he looks over at me, a peace offering that'll get us through the weekend. But what's odd is that Alex's eyes aren't landing on anything or anyone long enough to notice much at all. They're bouncing from Ben to the door to the kitchen, to Kit sitting beside him, to their dad over at another table, to his plate, to his own hand, which he's using to turn his butter knife over and over. When he finally stops, it's to reach up to his collar and hook a finger on the edge, tugging slightly. The move draws my attention to the line of his throat, and it's—well, not quite *convulsing*, but he's certainly swallowing more than any person who's not even managed a bite of the cake sitting in front of him should.

If there's anyone else watching as closely as I am, they might think Alex is sick. But for me, there's something different about the way he's moving, the ceaseless, mindless way his body is betraying him, even as he tries to control it. I've seen this before, have watched someone cycle through this same grueling adrenaline rush.

I straighten in my chair, wait for Ben to encourage everyone to lift their glasses. I've missed whatever the last part of his toast was, but Kit stands from her seat and presses her lips against his at the same time she clinks his glass with her own, so I'm sure it was something typically lovely and loving, the way Ben always is with Kit. Alex, I can tell, knows this is his opportunity, and in one swift movement while Kit's back is turned, he pushes back his chair and turns to head down the rear hall toward the bathrooms, the only exit strategy available to him without crossing into Kit's sight line.

I barely wait two full seconds before I follow him.

At first I think I'll only linger, wait for him to come out from the bathroom and ask if he's all right, if he maybe wants me to whisper a discreet request for help from Zoe's boyfriend Aiden, a paramedic who probably knows actual medical treatment for what I think might be ailing him. But as soon as I pass into the hallway, I see Alex's tall, lanky form ducking through the heavy back door, the one with a neon red *EXIT* sign above, a loud thunk echoing behind him.

For a few seconds I just stand there, a tremor of memory tinkling along my spine—that morning he left the coffee shop, confident and defiant, all *I can* swagger. I'm almost afraid to go out there and see a different version of him. But behind me, the sounds of Kit and Ben's party are laughing, joyous, anticipatory. I don't want him to miss it. And I don't want her to miss him. Also, that door locked behind him.

I duck into one of the bathrooms, grab a bottle of soap from the edge of the sink that I can use to keep the door propped open, and take one deep breath before I slip outside.

He's against the brick wall directly across from me, the alley behind Betty's damp and dimly lit and smelling faintly of cigarette smoke. Not a good place to lose your shit, I'm guessing, and Alex really, really looks like he is—ass against the wall, shoulders and chest pitched forward with his hands resting on his thighs, like he's just finished running miles and miles. Even from where I stand I can hear him breathing—it's a hissing, reedy-sounding thing, as though his airways aren't all the way open. *Maybe I should get Aiden,* I think, and take a small step back toward the door.

"Don't," he says, stopping me, his voice low and pained. "I'm okay. I'll be okay."

"You're not sick?"

It feels like forever before he answers, me listening to the *drip drip drip* of Betty's AC unit draining onto the pavement.

"No," he finally says. "I'm—I'm having..." He takes another breath, and I cross the alley and turn, leaning beside him, my back to the wall. Against my bare shoulder blades, it's hard and roughly textured, but it's been warmed all day by the hot sun, and it feels soothing, comfortable.

"A panic attack?" I say, quietly.

He keeps his hands on his thighs, stays hunched over. But he turns his head toward me, looks up at me from the side of his eyes.

I shrug, feel that warm-brick roughness against my skin. "I recognized it. My brother Humphrey used to get them."

There's another long, loaded silence while he seems to hitch against some outer limit of his panting, one of his hands reaching up to press against his sternum. "Your brother's name is Humphrey?"

"Yeah." A rare occasion where I'm happy about my mother's strange taste, if it'll serve as a distraction for Alex. "Humphrey Bogart Hawthorne. I'm Greer Garson Hawthorne. My sister is Ava Gardner Hawthorne. My oldest brother, Cary—well. I'm guessing you've got the gist of it, now."

"That is...wow." He gusts out the *wow*, as if the stricture around his chest has been loosened slightly. Both of his hands have dropped to his sides, his body straightening slightly from where he leans over. "Greer Garson Hawthorne," he repeats, and *Lord*. I've never heard my name sound quite like *that* before. I shift slightly, feel the rough brick behind me scrape across my skin.

"My mom's an actress," I say, distracting myself now. "Or, she was an actress, when she was young. She has a flair for the dramatic." Understatement. If my mother were here, she'd have called an ambulance—big voiced, urgent. She'd have been doing a very beautiful brow-wrinkle while waiting for it to arrive. She would have enfolded Alex in a perfectly posed hug, one that ensured the skin of her arms didn't smoosh in an unflattering way. "My dad's really normal, though," I say—to keep saying *something*, anything. "Ultranormal. Only-wears-three-colors-of-dress-shirts normal. I think he probably wanted to name us—I don't know. Jennifer and Brian, that kind of thing."

He moves his hand across his sternum now, back and forth, as though he's trying to massage out the thudding pulse I can see beating out of his heart, showing along the side of his neck. "What's his name? Your dad, I mean."

"Michael."

"Ah." Still rubbing, breathing through his nose now. You can tell it's an effort, but it's progress.

"Want to know something funny?"

He only nods, concentrating as hard on his breathing as he is on my idle chatter.

"My mom's name is Susan. So it's, you know. Michael and Susan, and then their four really dramatically named kids."

I think the sound he makes is a laugh, or at least an approximation of one. Maybe the best he can do under the circumstances.

"I'm sorry about this." His head lifts again, and he looks at the narrow strip of light coming from the back door. Then, like a switch has been flipped, his body seems to curl into itself again, his breathing kicking back up into that staccato rhythm.

Without thinking, I reach out and take his hand, my fingers sliding between his. My palm pressed all the way against his. My wrist, my forearm—all touching his. It was instinct, this touch, some way for me to be with him during this awful, grasping thing. Some way to tell him that I have a hold on him too, not just this panic he's trying to wrestle free of.

But I still have to close my eyes against the feel of it. Against how big his hand feels against mine, how calloused and rough it is compared to the soft vulnerability of his wrist. We stand like that for so long, or at least it feels long, out in the weird time capsule that is this back alley. At one point, I squeeze his hand—firmly, pointedly—and take a deep, sucking inhale through my nose, then let it gust out from my mouth noisily. I do it twice more before he starts to match me, and after a while we're just holding hands and deep breathing in tandem, hurricaning out the sound of that AC drip.

By unspoken, mutual agreement, we gust out one final breath, and then it's quiet, his breathing better, though not back to normal, pre-panic levels.

"I have to get back in there," he says, and he's made that sound so *impossible.* So *difficult.* There's something stunning about it—him out here, against this wall, holding on to my hand like it's a lifeline—when I've seen the pictures he's taken. It seems like no one who's taken those pictures, pictures that freeze tense, explosive moments of conflict, could ever be panicked about anything.

But maybe it should seem like someone who's taken those pictures should be panicked about everything.

"Does this happen a lot?"

Instead of answering, he disentangles his hand from mine, and I feel blood rush painfully back into my fingers. I hadn't realized we were clinging to each other so hard. I twist my wrist but stay where I am—where that brick wall feels warm and solid behind me. Alex pushes himself off, though, his back to me now, and I watch the long line of his spine straighten so beautifully, so easily, his shoulders widening like wings spreading for flight. He reaches up, runs both of his hands through his hair, and then tucks them in his pockets before turning back to me. He looks as gorgeous as he always looks. He looks like the last ten minutes haven't even happened.

Maybe I'll meet you again sometime, I think, the echo of the last words he spoke to me two years ago ringing loud in my head.

"Don't tell Kit." Then, maybe realizing the sharpness of his tone, he adds a genuine, soft-eyed, "Please."

There's a few seconds where we look at each other, where I try and work out the calculus of his request: My loyalty to Kit. My knowing how important Alex is to her, and how much she'd want to know he was struggling. My genuine hope that everything about this weekend is perfect and happy and stress-free for her. My reaction to that look in his eyes, the one that keeps saying *please.*

"Okay," I finally say, a little robotically.

"You want to go back in first?"

I look toward the door, and for the first time, I hear the muted beat of music coming from inside. "You go ahead. I'll make a stop in the restroom." A lie, but the truth is, *I* need a minute now, and I take one more deep breath as he ducks back into Betty's, making sure he leaves the door propped open behind him.

And I think: *That didn't look like relaxed, easy charm. That didn't look like casual nomadism, no strings attached, no permanent address, no cares in the world. That didn't look like freedom.*

That didn't look like the Alex I'd met two years ago at all.

Chapter 2

Alex

You're not going to panic.

I stand a bit straighter and move to check my reflection in the huge, elaborately framed mirror that stands in the foyer of the Ursinus Mansion, my sister's choice of venue for her and Ben's big day, their own place too small for the number of family and friends and coworkers they've got between them. It's ten minutes until go time, and outside guests are already in their seats, Ben and his dad and their buddy River already milling around near the flowered arch at the end of the aisle. I'm hoping the scent of it isn't too strong, remembering the way the air inside the restaurant had felt thick and close and too fragrant last night....

No. I make the voice in my head stern, scolding. *It's not going to happen again.*

I take a deep breath through my nose—the same kind Greer wordlessly coaxed me into last night, and rally a new determination. I've made mistakes with Kit, especially in the last few years, but I can't be anything other than perfect for her on her wedding day. I can't be anything other than her calm, resolutely in-control brother, no matter what the fuck happened last night, no matter what's been happening with increasing, frightening frequency.

In the mirror, the expression I see reflected back at me is blandly calm, smooth as a lake in the early morning, not even a ripple of the nerves lying beneath. For a second I have a disturbing flash of how I must've looked last night in that alley, clutching Greer's hand, the back of my neck bathed in a hot, prickling sweat. Her small, cool palm had been a strange antidote, my blood slowing in time to the pulse I'd felt under her skin, and when the whining, white noise in my head had faded, the thing I'd wanted most in the world, only for a second, was to bring her body against mine, to feel that steady pulse everywhere.

It's not going to happen again. Not now.

I look down, adjust the cuffs of my dress shirt beneath my suit jacket, slowly inhale through my nose. But when I look up again it's an effort not to jolt as I see an older version of me, to the left of my shoulder—still tall, still lean, though with a more desperate, hungry quality than what I see in my own reflection.

Dad.

It's hard not to feel a pang of resentment at his appearance now, when I'm spending so much energy trying to stay calm, trying to keep my head about me for this day. It's Dad, after all, who I associate with these—I think of Greer saying it, her brows lowered, a question in her voice—*panic attacks*, my first one coming in the middle of the night while I'd sat alone beside his hospital bed, only a half day after he'd had the stroke that'd brought me back to Ohio for the first time in years. That night, barely two years ago now, I'd felt trapped, held in place against my will, my heart thudding against the bones in my chest. I'd felt my body swing wildly between hot and cold. I'd thought I'd die there in that room, sterile and close, all the equipment keeping my father alive mockingly useless to me.

I clear my throat and set my jaw, my eyes scanning his face. I can tell by the look in his dark eyes—one physical quality we don't share—that he's irritated, and I straighten my shoulders in preparation for whatever shit he's about to fling at me, so long as he doesn't get it anywhere near Kit. The tiny barometer for panic I've had living inside me dips low, nearly nonexistent, my brain and body steeling themselves in preparation.

I turn away from the mirror and face him, spotting his girlfriend Candace at his side, who greets me with a friendly smile. Candace—a recovering addict herself who met my dad early on in his recovery efforts—has her own share of ugly family baggage, and she's admirably, consistently immune to any tension that my dad and I give off when we're around each other.

"Nice to see you, Candace," I tell her. "You look great."

She blushes, fingers at the corsage she wears around her wrist, a gift from Kit that matches the boutonniere my dad's wearing. "I'm just so glad to be here," she says in her raspy, smoke-scraped voice, her eyes welling up. Candace and my sister aren't close, not really, but I gather Kit's kindness to her means a lot, given that Candace is pretty estranged from her own kids.

"Dad." I shift my eyes toward him, as much an acknowledgment as it is a warning for whatever that look is in his.

"Guess we'll be going to our seats." His jaw tightens determinedly against the slight sag that persists on his left side, his still-dark brows now slashing resentment on his face. Not for the first time I wish Kit had left him off the invite list. He's better, no one could deny that—not drinking, not betting, and he's got a good thing going with Candace, who's kept him off cigarettes and natters on about heart-healthy recipes every time I call for a check-in, as much a nursemaid and mother to him as a girlfriend.

But he's still my dad, which means he's been defensive and lazily cruel about Kit's choice to have me walk her down the aisle instead of him. Last night as we'd left dinner, my nerves still jangled and my palm still tingling from Greer's touch, he'd stiffly endured a hug from Kit and said, "Nice of you to invite me to this, even though I didn't have anything to rehearse for."

I'd watched, a familiar mix of anger and shame coursing through my veins, as she'd blinked away a split-second well of tears. Ben's hand on the nape of her neck and the steady look of censure he'd directed at my dad had at least reminded me that I'm walking Kit down the aisle to a guy who understands her. Kit wouldn't want a scene—some ugly, ultimately useless effort to curb my father's worst instincts—but she would want to know someone's there for her, sharing the sting of his flailing, childish complaints.

I don't have to worry about making a scene, don't have to worry about being so unflappable for Kit, who's happily ensconced somewhere upstairs with her friends, and at the moment, I'm grateful.

"Dad," I say to him, my voice pitched low to avoid the chance of anyone overhearing embarrassing Averin family drama—a skill I perfected over years of dodging the prying eyes and open ears of neighbors, teachers, social workers. "I'll say this to you one time. You do anything to fuck this day up for Kit, and this is the end for you and me. When she walks by you going up that aisle, the only thing you do is smile and tell her she's beautiful. You understand me?"

The sad thing is, this works on my dad, who looks—well, if not chastened, exactly, then at least resigned. It's the one and only ace up my sleeve I've ever held against my gambler father, and given the precarious nature of my childhood, I've never felt all that guilty about daring him to take that bet. I know—from the one worn, creased photograph of my mother I keep in my wallet—that I'm his best living memory of her, that he looks at me and sees her green eyes. It's the worst advantage of my youth, that my dad always saw me as a generous but painful last gift from my mother, when he's always seen Kit as something else—an unfortunate reminder of his basest impulses in the wake of my mother's death. When Dad was at his lowest, debts so deep he couldn't recount them all, drowning in booze, I could always shock him into too-brief periods of sobriety with little more than an uttered warning: *All's I need is a bus ticket, Dad. One bus ticket and you'd never see my face again.*

I'd never have done it, of course, not without Kit. I wasn't stupid enough to think the two of us—me only five and a half years older than her—could ever make it out on our own without the buffer of a legal guardian keeping us out of the system. And while I might've had a chance out there once I got old enough, there was no way I'd leave her. My sister had been my heartbeat ever since the day her mother, looking glassy eyed and uninterested, had set Kit's warm, damp-diapered body next to mine on the couch and walked out the front door for good.

I'd loved Kit before that, in the kind of simple, little-boy way that came from seeing her tiny fingernails and her rare, gummy smile, almost always saved up for me. But that day, I'd known something different about my responsibility to Kit, and the rhythm of my life and heart had changed accordingly, a *pat pat pat* that sounded like her name, quick and pressured and full of the many things I needed to do to keep her safe and healthy. For the first few years after her mom had gone, that'd mostly meant keeping my dad upright enough to do the basics while I grew tall enough and smart enough and just criminal enough to do more and more on my own—operate a stove, forge Dad's signature, steal a can of SpaghettiOs from a 7-Eleven.

Later, it'd meant keeping her from the very worst of his behaviors. It'd meant adding extra spray starch to the dress shirt he'd need to wear for a parent-teacher conference, masking the smell of alcohol that would seep out of his pores. It'd meant breaking the ribs of a loan shark I'd caught lurking outside our apartment building. It'd meant controlling his temper the same way I'm doing now.

He nods, offers Candace his arm, then heads outside toward their seats, leaving me alone again. My head is quieter now, more focused, and I know, I *know* it's fucked up. Maybe I could solve all my current problems by taking my father on the job with me. Maybe I'd stop sabotaging shoots with shaking hands and a sloppy, impatient eye if I had him there, if I had some external motivator to keep my shit together.

I hear a footstep on the stairs behind me and mentally slap myself, remembering the true external motivator for calmness today. I'll turn and see her now—Kit, my baby sister, my baby sister on her *wedding* day, and shit, however hard I'm riding myself about not showing any panic, I know already I'm not going to be able to hide the tears that are coming, pressing tight in my throat.

But it's not Kit there.

It's Greer.

I try to tell myself that the flush of heat I feel is some remembered shame from last night. But with all the effort it's taking me to stay even-keeled, I can't summon the energy to really believe that this feeling is anything other than exactly the same one I'd had when I'd first seen her two years ago, rushing into Kit's front door like an actual breath of fresh air, something about her voice like a song to me. My hand had twitched at my side, searching for my camera. Some way to freeze her in my mind.

It does the same thing now as I watch her come down the stairs, wearing a long dress of the palest blue, the layers of fabric thin and flowing, the shape of her legs beneath them a teasing curve every time she takes a step. She's got a small gardenia tucked behind her left ear, tiny silver earrings dancing at her lobes, a matching necklace, and paths of perfect skin dappled with freckles that make me swallow in suppressed desire. *Jesus Christ.*

"Let's get this show on the road," says a clear, sharp voice that breaks the spell. Zoe, right behind Greer, tall and blond and like she walked out of a magazine in that same dress Greer's wearing, but I didn't even notice her. "I need a glass of champagne and a piece of that cake I saw in the dining room. Hi, Alex," she says, patting my arm as she walks toward the doorway.

I snap my mouth shut, only now realizing it'd been open. Fucking *great.*

Greer stops beside me, and—hell. That gardenia in her hair. I want to know how that smells, mixed with her skin.

"You're okay?" she asks, barely a whisper. She's not looking at me; she's keeping her eyes toward the door, focused on the guests who await. If Kit's back there, she wouldn't even know about this exchange, same as she doesn't know about the morning Greer handed me my ass two years ago, same as she doesn't know I hyperventilated in the alley of her favorite bar last night. I want to say something to thank her for her discretion, for keeping the promise she made to me, but when I hear the sound of Kit's throat clearing behind us at the top of the steps, I know it's not the time.

"I'm okay." She nods and walks to Zoe, leaving me and Kit alone.

She's beautiful in her dress, the same fabric that her friends are wearing, but a bright cream, simply cut, and I wouldn't be surprised if Kit—unfussy as she's always been—let her friends do the picking. I know already that nothing really matters to her about today but who's at the end of that aisle. It's a silly, backward, sexist tradition, "giving the bride away," and we

both know it, but I'm suddenly so glad she asked. Glad that I've got this
moment with her on such a big day.

"I don't know why I'm nervous," she says, those big black eyes of hers
turned up to me, full of everything unfathomable about her—how smart
she always was, how much trust she had in me, how much she needed me.
How much that had filled me up and emptied me out, all at the same time.
"Same as you used to be, every first day of school."

She smiles, probably remembering the same thing I am—how she'd
fidget with her backpack straps, her lunchbox handle, the hem of her shirt,
whatever—at the thought of walking up the steps to whatever new school
she was starting. But every time, she did fine. Better than fine. She'd always
needed me less than she thought.

She looks down, fidgets with the ribbon around her bouquet. "Alex."
It's so quiet I have to tip my head down to hear her better. "You gave me
every good thing in my life when we were kids, you know. You don't know
what it means to me, having you here to do this."

I clear my tight throat—too many times for it to be anything other
than what it is, which is my attempt to keep this from getting messy—and
crook my arm for her to take. No panic now, not even a trace of it, and I
thank all the gods in the universe for that—that I'm exactly who I need
to be for her today.

"Tool Kit," I say to her now, using her old nickname, my voice in the
patient, steady register I recognize from years of practice, years of practice
at being her calm in the eye of whatever storm our childhood inflicted
upon us. "Let's go get you married, huh?"

And I take the first step to give her away.

* * * *

I'd like to say it lasts.

I make it through the ceremony; I sit in my front row seat and keep
my hands clasped loosely in my lap, watch my sister and Ben exchange
tearful vows and a kiss that makes me drop my eyes. I stand from my seat
and clap with all the other guests, walk behind the wedding party when
it's time to file out, my hands tucked in my pockets, my smile feeling easy
and natural on my face, my breath even and relieved at having made it
through the most important part.

But soon enough I feel the tension inside me rise again. Before we head
to the large, peaked white tent for the reception, the photographer Kit's

hired—barely in his twenties, by my estimate, with pants cut to show his dress socks and a shitty Sony and too-busy hands on his lens—gathers us for various posed pictures, and my palms start to sweat. Part of it is garden-variety professional judgment—I'm probably going to think every one of these pictures is garbage, especially since this guy doesn't seem to understand how the actual sun works—but most of it is all too familiar fear. *I'm trapped here. I'll panic, and everyone will see.*

If there's a bright spot, it's when I'm standing with Kit for a picture, Greer beside me and Zoe beside Kit, and Ben's stepmother Sharon loudly announces that she'll never wear a pair of Spanx again while reaching a hand into her waistband and snapping the fabric against her skin. I feel the tremor of Greer's soft laugh all along the left side of my body, and for a second, my mind goes quiet.

But it's short lived, that quiet, and by the time we're into the dancing portion of the evening, I feel like I've spent most of this wedding in a state of clenched-teeth, white-knuckled preparation for the worst. At the most strained moments, I think longingly about my camera, about the heavy weight of it in my hands. I think about the pictures I could be taking—Henry Tucker at the end of his toast, the glow from a candle winking off the very edge of his glasses, a small, stunning highlight of the tear in his eye. Kit and Zoe laughing their way through the Electric Slide, Zoe's updo listing a little to the right and her boyfriend Aiden watching her from the corner of the dance floor, his crooked smile a charming visual parallel. Candace seated at a round table near the wedding party's, still touching her corsage, her head inclined toward my dad and one of the Tucker cousins, all three of them dappled with light from an arc of water glasses sitting in front of them.

Twice I'd almost approached the kid with the Sony to ask if I could take over. But both times, as if she'd had a homing device on my ambition, my obsession with work, Kit had cut me a quelling glance across the room.

Almost as if it's mocking me, my phone vibrates from where it rests inside my jacket pocket, pressed right up against my heart. I tell myself I can't take a work call at a wedding, at *this* wedding especially, but the vibration there is a buzzy reminder of the panic lingering under my skin, and I tuck my hand inside to pull it out, promising myself I'll simply shut it off, not look at the screen.

But there's that saying about old habits, I guess, and when I glimpse my agent's name, I get a familiar pulse of curiosity, more comfortable than almost any other feeling I've had today. Before I've even thought about it,

I've slid my finger across the screen, ducking out from under the tent to find a quiet spot in the fading twilight.

"Jae," I say, once I've raised the phone to my ear, already wincing at what I've done, tonight of all nights. "I can't take any work this weekend."

"Shit, I didn't even think you'd answer." I know Jae-Sung Shin's voice so well, know it even better than his face, since I don't think we've been in a room together more than a dozen times since he started representing me six years ago, after I'd had a feature in the *Times* magazine that'd broken my career wide open. If it were up to Jae, I'd give up chasing breaking news shit entirely and start getting all my work directly from him—commissions that news agencies or magazines or nonprofits want for editorial spreads, longer-form stuff where the photos are going to be a centerpiece. In his mind, it'd be a win-win: he makes more money from his cut, and I stay safer and work less.

"Aren't you at your sister's wedding?"

"Yes," I say, and it's clipped. Because I am a fucking dirtbag for answering this phone.

"I'm not calling with a job." For the first time I notice his voice sounds a little slurred, like he's been out drinking. I take a look at my watch—8:15, Saturday night. Not outside the realm of possibility, though it's early. Jae likes a party, is always trying to drag me to something whenever I'm in the city for longer than two days. "I ran into Deidre Gaskell tonight."

Fuck. Heat spreads up my neck—part panic, part foreboding. Deidre Gaskell does publicity for UNHCR, giving me some of my most regular work over the last few years photographing various refugee crises. I'd seen her last week at one of the largest camps on the Pakistan-Afghanistan border.

And I hadn't been in good shape. I'd been in back alley shape, same as I had been last night.

"She said you—" Jae breaks off, and I hear the clink of ice in a glass. When he continues, he sounds sober as a judge. "She said you had some trouble shooting one day."

"Conditions were rough. I had a fever."

I didn't have a fever. I'd had shaky hands and a pounding heart rate and an inability to focus on anything except for how I could calm the fuck down, how I could keep everyone from seeing what was happening to me. I open my mouth to say that I'd shot six days in a row, that I'd sent Deidre a set of photos that were as good as anything I've ever done. So what if I'd had trouble one day? Who'd blame anyone for having a bad day with a job like this? *You would,* my conscience nudges, remembering all the times I'd snapped at young, green reporters, telling them to get their shit together, to focus, to do the job.

"Listen, Alex," Jae says, before I can speak. "She's going to send someone else out to Turkey next week."

"Not an issue." I'm hoping my quick response covers the sick feeling of embarrassment I have. "I've been needing a change from the longer-term stuff. Let's see what they've got at the *Times*." Somewhere behind me, a new bass rhythm starts up from the sound system, and a cheer goes up from the crowd. It's probably some widely recognized pop song that I'm unlikely to have ever heard if it's come out in the last ten years.

"Alex." I can tell already I'm not going to like what he says next. "I'm not sending any more work for a while."

"You don't pick where I go." My voice is sharp, overloud. I take another few steps away from the tent. "I can check the feeds. I can be on a plane tomorrow. I can pick the story."

There's a deliberate, heavy pause on the other end. He's letting me replay those words back to myself, so I can hear exactly how they sound. Petulant, defensive. Ungrateful. I run a hand through my hair, tug at my starched collar, open my mouth to offer the apology I owe him.

But then a throat clears behind me, and even that small noise—it's cool water over all the parts of me that have been infused with unpleasant warmth.

"Jae," I say into the phone. "I'm sorry. I'll call you Monday, all right?" I hang up with a wince.

Out here in the waning light, Greer's skin is dewy, the skin under her eyes faintly purpled either with fatigue or smudgy makeup. Her dress is wrinkled, and the gardenia is drooping slightly in her hair. She's somehow more gorgeous than when she came down those steps, somehow more herself than she was before. There's a constellation of expression on her face: part concern, part disappointment, and a hundred other nuances I wish I knew well enough to decode.

"I was just heading back in."

"I thought I'd—" she begins, setting her hands at the sides of her dress, tangling her fingers in the layers of fabric. "I was checking to see that it hadn't happened again."

"No." I'm embarrassed, but it's different. There's another texture to this rough shame, like if I rub in another direction, I'll feel the soft gratification of her checking on me. "I'm not having an easy time in there, though."

"Is it crowds?"

I shrug, wishing there was an easy answer. "Sometimes. Sometimes it's being in one place. Being stuck. Being—obligated." As soon as it's out of my mouth, I can hardly believe I've said it. Something so true, but also something that makes me sound like such a selfish asshole. A new wave of heat flushes to my neck.

The sound she makes, her chin tipped down, is a soft, knowing *hmm*, a lower register than her speaking voice, and I feel that flush of heat transform into something different. I clear my throat, seize on a safer subject.

"How's school?"

She lifts her eyes to mine, and it's not so safe, I guess, because a shadow passes over her face. I hate that it's dark enough out here to keep me from seeing the blue of her eyes. The music in the tent thumps louder, and she lowers them again. "I graduate in August."

"A summer graduation, huh?"

"It's a smaller ceremony. They'll actually call my name."

"Greer Garson Hawthorne," I say, and the side of her mouth curls upward, a sneak preview smile that's gone as quickly as it came.

"You're leaving tomorrow?" She gestures toward my phone, the movement of her hand making the gauzy top layer of her dress lift gently before settling again. I watch every frame of that movement. I wish I'd stayed in the tent to see if she'd have danced to this pop song I know nothing about.

"I don't know," I answer, which is—absurd. Absolutely absurd. Basically, no matter where I am in the world, I'm *always* leaving tomorrow.

"Maybe—" she begins, then stops, tunneling her fingers back into her dress. "Never mind."

"No. What?" I think about that morning in the café, her face like it is now, half-shuttered, but a whole room, a whole *house* of meaning behind it. I was so damned greedy for her to talk to me that morning. To say anything at all, even if it was more of what I didn't want to hear.

The thumping song ends, the muffled, microphoned voice of the deejay barely audible to us out here before a slower strand of music starts up. Greer turns her head toward the tent, her chin still tipped down, and in profile, I get to see the way her nose turns up a little at the end, a fine, delicate slope. She wears her hair so short that you can see everything about her face if you're paying attention. You can see all the sharp angles and all the soft curves.

When she speaks again, she's quieter, adjusting her voice to the new sounds in the air, blending in. "Maybe if you did stay in one place for a little while. If you stayed here, since you're already in town. It might—help."

There's a trace of something in what she's said—something simultaneously needful and accusatory. From anyone else, the suggestion would annoy me. It *has* annoyed me, in the past.

"My sister," I say, running a hand through my hair. "I don't want her to think—" There's too many complicated things to account for. I don't want my sister to think something's wrong with me. I don't want my sister to think my staying in town, even for a little while, could turn into something permanent. She's wanted that for years.

"Kit'll be on her honeymoon," Greer says, as though she's heard my thoughts. No doubt she knows all about the arguments Kit and I have had about my rare visits, my trouble staying put. No doubt after that morning at Boneshaker's she heard all about my refusing Kit's offer of a share of her lottery money, my explosive reaction to the suggestion I make this place my home base. "No obligation."

"Like a test, you mean." I tuck my phone back into my pocket.

"I didn't say that," she says quickly, almost guiltily. "It doesn't work like that." I think of her brother, the one she'd said had panic attacks too. She probably knows all about how this works. "But maybe getting some rest would be good. The pace you work at, I'm sure it doesn't help with this. You might be better able to handle things if you had some time off."

"Time off," I repeat, like I'm trying out how to pronounce something in a brand-new language. "I don't much like not having anything to do."

I've made it sound casual, almost as though I'm making a joke at my own expense. But the truth is, I *hate* not having anything to do, which is why I've continued to take jobs over and over again, when I know I'm not at my best. It's why I've lied about rough conditions and fevers and hangovers I never really have. It's why *I'm not sending any more work for a while* feels like a damning sentence from a judge rather than support from someone who cares. Right now, the tension that's been stalking me all night ratchets up to a breath-shortening degree.

But across this small patch of grass between us, Greer stays quiet for a long moment, her own chest rising and falling evenly. Beautifully, hypnotically. When she speaks again, it's on one of her delicate exhales.

"Well," she says, her eyes meeting mine. "I might be able to help you with that."

Chapter 3

Greer

"The thing is, you can't be afraid to ask for help."

From my spot beside Dennise, I shift uncomfortably in my orthotic-supported flats, move my tablet from one hand to the other, subtly tilt my head from side to side in hopes of flushing out some of the tightness that's gathered there. It's been about forty-five minutes of me standing here on the pale yellow linoleum of the hospital room floor, taking notes while my boss talks to Mr. Morgan, who's been admitted to Holy Cross for the third time in the last two months, another minor fall that's nevertheless resulted in ten stitches across his forehead and three broken fingers. Mr. Morgan is eighty-seven years old and suffers from occasional vasovagal syncope, and he absolutely needs to hire the in-home care his insurance will pay for.

So far, he's resisted, stubborn about strangers in his house and even more stubborn about the fact that he's never going to get any steadier on his feet, no matter how careful he is. Dennise has already spent an hour this morning back in our basement offices on the phone with his daughter in Seattle, who keeps promising to fly in for a visit as soon as things slow down at her job, but I don't think Dennise or Mr. Morgan is counting on it.

"The little button," Mr. Morgan says, gesturing toward the spot on his chest where his Life Alert would normally rest, and I feel my heart clench in empathy. Never mind that I'm not eighty-seven years old, never mind that I don't have vasovagal syncope. I know how it feels, not being in control of your body, and I know how it feels not to want to give up the control you do have. "It worked. I pressed it and the squad came."

In the five and a half months I've been working as an intern in the Care Coordination Office of the hospital, I've come to learn Dennise's tells. They're subtle, because she's an absolute pro, hardly ever betraying a whiff of impatience, but they're there—a little movement whereby she brings her thumb and her ring finger together, making two taps, a slight shift in the way she says *mmm-hmm*, a bit more emphasis on the *mmm* part. She does both now, then slides her brown eyes toward me before looking back to Mr. Morgan. "We don't want you to have to press that button, though," she says, and for the next five minutes it's more of the same.

By the time we say our goodbyes, Dennise has sheen of sweat on her hairline and I'm frantically tapping out the last of my notes one-handed. When I finish, I crane my neck from side to side a bit, feel a familiar dull throb that tells me a headache is coming on. Out in the fluorescent-lit corridor, Dennise shakes her head and clucks her tongue at the nurse that's headed into Mr. Morgan's room, promising she'll be back down later to try again.

"You're still pretty quiet in there," says Dennise as we head to the elevators, and I feel my ears heat as I close the cover of the tablet. *You're still pretty quiet* would be a decent inscription for my tombstone, actually. "Starting in a couple of months, you'll be on your own with consults like this."

"I know." But the thing is, I don't know, not anymore, and I've been distracted all morning here thinking about it. Getting hired for a full-time position under Dennise was already a major coup, since most of her staff already have a master's in social work. I've benefited from being older, more mature, and unfortunately way, way more familiar with this hospital than most of the interns who get sent her way, but if she finds out that even my undergraduate degree is in jeopardy, I can forget all about being employed while I try and go for that master's degree myself in a couple of years. I swallow, thinking back to Saturday night, to the afternoon I have ahead of me.

To Alex and the promise he's made me.

"I'm a little tired from this weekend," I add.

"Oh, your friend's wedding, right? How was it?"

For a split second I picture myself blurting it all out, everything I haven't managed to say to anyone since Alex and I returned to the tent the night of the reception—me first, this time—a tentative agreement between us that we're set to carry out as soon as my shift here is done. I'd sit in the stiffly upholstered chair in this elevator bay and look up at Dennise's kind, open face and tell her the whole thing.

It was amazing except for the part where I asked a tired, vulnerable man to help me graduate and keep this job. I wore a gorgeous dress with silver heels that two days later are still making my back ache, but it was worth it for the way he looked at me. He promised me he'd stay, at least for a few days, but I'm already afraid he'll go.

"It was nice," I say instead. "She left for her honeymoon yesterday afternoon." A little reluctantly, actually, once Alex had asked her at Sunday morning brunch if she'd mind him staying in her place for a vague "couple of days." Never much one for the unexpected, Kit had reacted with a mixture of shock and concern, and she'd cornered Zoe and me in the lobby of the Crestwood once the party had broken up. "Do you think he's all right?" she'd asked, a quaver in her voice, and at that moment I'd understood everything Alex had been worried about when I'd suggested he stay in town.

"I'm sure he's fine," I'd said, and then I'd thought about where I could buy a hair shirt. A church gift shop? A fetish store? TJ Maxx?

"Well, you deserve a break," Dennise says, and even as I'm smoothing the front of my dress—my lucky dress, actually, worn especially for today—my imaginary hair shirt scratches uncomfortably. "You did so much to prepare for that wedding."

"Just the usual bridesmaid stuff." Mental health triage followed by some light manipulation to save my own sorry ass. I need two hair shirts. Or a shirt-skirt combination.

The bell for the elevator dings, and Dennise and I wait for a couple with furrowed brows and tense mouths to hustle out before we go in. I look after them sympathetically, tuck a hand in the pocket of my dress to run my thumb over the fake, synthetic fur rabbit's foot I've had on my keychain for years, sending the couple a silent wish for good news.

"Are you headed out now?" Dennise is already looking down at her phone to see where her next appointment is. In what's supposed to be my last semester, I work half days here four days a week as part of my practicum experience for the social work program. On a regular Monday, though, I'd have the rest of the afternoon free, and I might even stay on with Dennise for that appointment. To help out, to get more experience. To make myself indispensable.

But of course, today's not a regular Monday.

"Yes. I've got some—uh. Some work to take care of on campus."

Dennise looks up from her phone and over at me. "Everything all right there? I sent a good progress report over to your advisor on Friday."

God, this hair shirt is hot. "Everything's perfect. Just tying up loose ends."

"Well," she says, smiling at me as the elevator doors open. She steps out onto the critical care floor, a few stops up from where I'll be getting off, and looks back at me. "It's like I said to Mr. Morgan. Don't be afraid to ask for help if you need it."

"Absolutely," I say cheerfully, even as the doors close. I know she's right; I know I can't be afraid to ask for help.

But is it okay to be afraid of what'll happen now that I have?

* * * *

I've asked Alex to meet me outside of the main library, my favorite spot on campus, standing tall and big windowed at the end of a long, wide sidewalk that's lined with Bradford pear trees, snowballed with white blooms in the springtime and cheerfully bright green at this time of year. About twenty yards from the front doors, there's a bronze statue of Socrates that I'm pretty sure cannot be accurate unless Socrates didn't know how to drape his toga over his top half and also looked like Triton from *The Little Mermaid.* Since I've been going here—spending quite a lot of time inside the library between my classes, before my classes, after my classes—I've been asked to take no fewer than five photos of students with Triton-Socrates, who looks stern and forbidding with his hand on his chin and his mouth turned down, a moue of frustration that generally makes the photos of laughing, dramatically posed undergraduates even funnier.

Standing in the shadow of that statue now, though, the frustration feels pointed, specific—a bronzed reflection of my own mood at being in this mess. So close to the finish here, so close to my freedom, and once again I haven't been able to see something through, to cross that threshold that gives me my independence. I close my eyes and hear familiar words, words that live in my head like stitching on clothes—unremarkable, almost invisible—until something tears and you realize just how important they are.

Greer, you're not cut out for this kind of thing
Greer, you know your body can't handle so much
Greer, you always take on more than you're capable of
"Hi."

So that is…probably not Socrates talking to me.

I open my eyes, find Alex standing a few feet away, wearing a version of what he'd been wearing when he showed up on Friday—black T-shirt, this one less faded, a pair of army-green utility pants, boots. His beard is back, two days since he'd been clean shaven at the ceremony, already shadowed when I'd met him outside of the tent. Over his eyes, he wears a pair of dark sunglasses, and sure, they look movie star cool and all, but I absolutely hate what they hide from me.

"I was—uh, you know. Resting my eyes," I say, straightening and adjusting the strap of my bag. "How've you been?"

"Restless." His voice is a little dull, closed off, though as soon as he's said it something in his face softens. He takes off his sunglasses and tucks them in the collar of his shirt, fixing me with the full force of that sea-glass stare. "Glad to be out of the house."

Even though I first met Alex in Kit's house, it's not easy for me to picture him there now, not easy for me to imagine him doing simple, domestic things like wiping down counters or flipping through television channels or—*cartoonish gulp*—sleeping in a bed.

"Me too. I mean, I was not in my house. I was at work. Which is at the hospital. My house is somewhere else." Socrates is judging me, I can feel it.

Alex quirks an eyebrow and entirely ignores 75 percent of the nonsense I have just released into the air. "You work at a hospital?"

"Yes, I'm a—I'm in training to be a social worker there. Helping people find care placements for when they leave the hospital."

"That must be difficult. Hospitals are hard."

I blink across the sidewalk at him. "You photograph war zones."

"That is—" He breaks off, an oddly thoughtful expression on his face, as though he had to be reminded. "True," he finishes. After a beat, he takes a deep breath, clasps his hands together at his waistline and wrings them together once before tucking them back into his pockets. "So. You figure out your plan?"

"Right, the plan." I don't want to say this in front of Socrates, so I gesture toward the sidewalk, start heading toward north campus, where all the fine arts buildings are clustered. On Saturday, all I'd really known—after some frantic, secretive googling during my Friday pedicure—was that the professor I need to appeal to is a photographer whose particular area of specialty means that he's almost certainly heard of Alex. But since I spent most of Sunday afternoon doing more research, I also know that this professor is soliciting submissions from photographers who are willing to have a print in the charity auction he's running to raise money for his department's scholarship fund. Given that the appeals on his social media have grown increasingly desperate, I'm guessing he doesn't have a lot in the kitty yet. I tell Alex that as we walk, and he keeps his eyes ahead, his hands still tucked loosely in his pockets.

"So I offer to donate a photograph, and—?"

"You might not have to," I say quickly, hopefully. As desperate as I am, I'd still like to go it alone; I'd still like to walk into Peter Hiltunen's office and handle this myself. I'd still like to avoid being an obligation for Alex, no matter that he'd like to have something to do for however long he's here.

I feel him look over at me, but I only grip my bag more tightly. Walking toward us on the quad's pathway is a young woman I did a group project with in a Sociology of the Family course last semester. She's got her phone pressed to her ear, and she's talking loudly about being "*literally* dead of embarrassment." When she raises her eyes I lift a hand to give her a small wave, but she doesn't notice. Instead she stumbles over her words and her eyes go wide as she looks at Alex.

Typical.

When she passes us—I'd have had to slap her *literal* face to have gotten her to return my wave, I guess—I finally work up the courage to look his way. As usual, he doesn't seem to notice the effect he's had on passing strangers. "It may be that you only have to show your face," I tell him.

"Show my face? What good is that going to do?"

I suppress a smile. "Your face is pretty effective."

He stops on the path, and I'm a couple of steps ahead before I do too, turning back to look at him.

"So's yours," he says. Simply. As though it's the most obvious thing in the world to him.

I think my mouth does that open-close thing a few times, or maybe it's mostly open before I finally compose myself enough to get words out again. When I do, it is clear I have handled the compliment by replacing my personality with someone else's.

"There's a coffee cart in that building, to the left of the one where I'm headed," I say, pointing to the sign that stands outside the squat, concrete box that houses the Department of Photography and Film. No wonder there's a fund-raising effort under way. "Go there, order two cups, to go. Wait five minutes and then come find me, office number seventeen. Just stand outside the door and wait. If you hear me cough"—I break off, do the little *uch uch* sound that's going to be our signal—"find a reason to knock on the door. Maybe you say we're running late, or that you need to borrow my wallet. The point is, we know each other, right?"

"We do know each other." His eyes are bright, interested.

"If I don't cough, then just keep waiting. That means I'm handling it myself. Which is what I prefer."

"What's the coffee for?"

"It's a diversion. You'll look weird standing around with nothing in your hands."

There's a pause while Alex blinks those long, black lashes. "You're like James Bond. I feel like your Moneypenny."

I smooth the front of my dress again. It's a dark green shirt dress with tiny gray arrows printed all over it. I've got on a skinny, pale pink belt that matches my shoes. I'm no one's James Bond, but Alex does make me feel like I'm wearing everything that's on the inside of myself—all my weird, imagination-brain thoughts—right on the outside. Right where he can see it.

"Moneypenny would've been the one giving the directions, probably," I say, and his low chuckle is like fireworks in my bloodstream. "Just look casual. Relaxed." *Groan.* I'm pretty sure I wince. "I wasn't referring to your—thing. I only meant you should look like this was part of your day all along."

"No problem. There are currently no other parts of my day."

"Right." *Restless*, he'd said, but you'd never know he's struggling now, the way he stands there. I don't suppose I'll ever really be able to see what's on the inside of him, not completely. I don't suppose he stays anywhere long enough for that to happen. "Wish me luck, I guess."

He smiles at me, a closed-lipped, crooked thing, the lines around his eyes somehow deeper as he watches me. I wait and wait.

But he doesn't wish me anything before I go.

* * * *

Peter Hiltunen is definitely what I would categorize as a "cool prof," quotations and abbreviation an essential part of the moniker. He's got a reddish brown beard that he's manicured into a slight point at the chin, a pair of unrimmed, sharply rectangular glasses, and one of those tiny-print plaid dress shirts that every man who's ever hit on me at Betty's is always wearing. His office is also minimalist in the way that makes a point, the way that suggests he's not the kind of plebeian to have problems figuring out where to put an extension cord. I'm sitting in a red plastic chair that seems like it's modeled on an internal organ. A kidney, maybe, or a diseased lung.

I'm also doing a really bad job of convincing him. It's not my shyness that's ruining this; if anything, it's my over-preparation, my wholehearted willingness to make this case. I'd started by showing him my completed degree application, hoping to sway him with my very impressive course list; then I'd passed him a copy of my offer letter from Holy Cross, signed by Dennise and her direct superior. I'd folded my hands on top of my lap and explained that I've completed several of my courses in overload, independent study format, that I'm very self-directed, self-motivated. That I could meet any challenge he might give me.

"It's not that I don't believe you," he says, and my stomach gets that horrible, hollow feeling, not unlike the one I had on Friday afternoon. *I'm not going to graduate.* He's already handed my paperwork back to me, but my signal cough is stuck right at the base of my throat. "It's that I'm *used* to you."

Used to me? I don't know if I imagine it, but I hear movement outside the half-ajar door. A shuffle, maybe. I clear my throat, but hold the cough for now.

When he speaks again, his voice is slow, scolding in tone. "Listen, Greta—"

"It's Greer."

"Pardon?"

"It must be Greta that you're used to. My name's Greer."

"Yes, sorry. Anyways, listen. You're not the first one to come in here thinking you can get away with forgetting about the requirement, and I'm not—"

The knock on the door is so forceful that the door opens a little.

"Excuse me," comes Alex's voice, different than I've ever heard it before. Gruff, impatient. Also, hot in a way that makes me shift slightly in this diseased-lung chair, which is very gross.

Professor Hiltunen stands from his own chair, pulling the door fully open, and for a second I can almost feel the shock that goes through him, a beat of stunned silence that seems to radiate off his back. "Aleksandr Averin," he says, sticking his hand out for Alex to shake. In the frame of the doorway, Alex stands tall, one hand by his side, one hand holding two to-go cups of coffee, one stacked on top of the other. He doesn't even look at Hiltunen.

He looks at me, top to bottom, as though he's checking me for injuries. *Only my pride,* I try to tell him with my eyes.

"I met your sister once at a gallery opening we had here," the professor continues, deftly withdrawing the hand Alex didn't shake. "I couldn't believe it, that we were one degree away from the likes of you. I've taught your photo-essay on the Arab Spring for a few semesters now. In fact I asked your sister if she'd consider—"

Alex has shifted his eyes back to Hiltunen, his expression quizzical, as though he's just spotted a foreign object in his salad.

"I'm here for Greer." His voice is laced with such annoyance that I don't know how Hiltunen's glasses don't melt off his face.

The professor looks back over his shoulder at me, his brow lowered. Maybe he forgot Greta was here for a minute. Unsurprising, since I don't think I've moved a muscle since I heard that knock.

"She's a friend of mine," Alex says, and I wonder where he learned to pitch his voice that way. That way that brooks no argument. That way that say it's about to be punching time. I give him a weak smile that's meant to be placating, calming, but it doesn't seem to work. His fingers on that to-go cup look strangly.

"Hi, Alex," I say, another attempt to calm the temper that's pulsing off him. He moves to stand beside the chair I'm in, handing me a coffee. "Hi," he says, almost through his teeth. "I—need to borrow your wallet?" God. He's a terrible Moneypenny. Moneypenny never looked like she wanted to dismantle a desk with her bare hands.

"Sure." I fumble with the bag I've held in my lap, knowing I've got to take it from here. Hiltunen is sufficiently starstruck, but I've got to smooth the way. "Sorry for the interruption, Professor. I'm showing Alex around while he's in town." I hand Alex the wallet, and for a half second he only stares down at it. He is comically bad at subterfuge. I look back at Hiltunen, ready to do some more way-smoothing, but he speaks before I can.

"I'm doing a charity auction for a scholarship program we have here." He's speaking only to Alex now. "Collecting pieces from artists in the area and beyond. I don't suppose you'd—"

"I can donate something." I can tell by the way he's said it he expects this to be over now. He wants out of this office, and my stomach is sinking in dread. If this triggers another panic attack for him, I will need more than the skirt-shirt combo. I will need undergarments. A face mask. Aside from my own disappointment in myself at needing a save, this is exactly why I was afraid to ask for help. I wasn't just afraid of what it would cost me.

I was afraid of what it would cost him.

"You know," Hiltunen says, rubbing a hand over his beard in a very "cool prof" way, "if you're going to be around for a few days, maybe I could convince you to visit my documentary photography class? I could put an honorarium together quickly. It'd be a real—"

"Maybe," Alex says, and when I look up at him, I can see he's letting the set of his shoulders do the talking. He's letting his position in relation to me do the talking. This is a negotiation, not a sure thing. He looks at Hiltunen long enough that it's as though he's casting a spell on him.

The professor sits down in his chair, which is not shaped like an internal organ. "Now, Greer," he says, and my fingers clutch the coffee cup Alex brought, ignoring the patronizing tone. Whatever Hiltunen thinks of me personally, the spell from Alex is *working*. "You *did* neglect to take the fine arts—"

"Sounds like you went over that point already," Alex says, and I look up at him sharply, a warning he takes seriously, tucking my wallet in his back pocket in a move that looks like retreat. Even if I have asked him for help, I don't need to be the meat in a patronizing sandwich. I focus back on Hiltunen.

"I'm sorry," I say. "Go on."

"I'm doing a five-week adult education course on digital photography right now. It's Thursday nights from six to nine—"

"I can do that." Maybe that was a little too eager. Hiltunen gives me a long-suffering look, and I think I can smell a fresh puff of testosterone waft off of Alex.

"You've already missed the first week, everything about mechanics and camera function and some basics on manipulating light. But perhaps you could still participate. And if you do well—" He pauses dramatically, strokes his beard again, and I really hope this isn't what his lecture style is like, or I'm going to hate all twelve remaining hours of this class. "If you do *very* well, I'll write a letter of support to the exception committee."

"I'll do well. I'll do my absolute best. Thank you." I'm clutching my bag again, ready to stand and get out of here before he can change his mind.

But the professor clears his throat, looks up briefly at Alex before returning his eyes to me.

"The students in this course participate in a public showcase in one month." Dramatic pause. "Not all that long, I suppose, before your planned graduation." He says *planned* with a slight but pointed emphasis.

"Public showcase, sure. I can do that."

"Student work, faculty work, and—ah. Some guest artist work, when we can find it. In past years, we've had local guest artists present. It can really raise our profile, especially if the artist makes—uh—himself available leading up to it. Interviews around town, help curating the showcase. That kind of thing."

There's a thick pause in the air, Alex still and tense beside me. Both of us know what Hiltunen is insinuating here. One *month*? Talk about an obligation. Donating the photograph is the work of a few minutes; he doesn't even really need to be in town to send one in. The heavily hinted visit to a class is maybe a half day's work later this week.

But one month? Part of me expects Alex to simply disappear into the air at this moment. He'll never do it, never. And the stony silence from beside me tells me so. I pushed my luck, I guess. If this is the professor's condition, I can forget about walking across that stage. I think of Dennise this morning, leaving me in that elevator, her face briefly concerned before she smiled at me, all the confidence in me that's made me feel, for the first time in my life, like I could really and truly be on my own. I think about my family, when I break the news. I know just what they'll say.

Well, Greer, you expected so much of yourself
It's not the first time you've dealt with a little delay
You have to be careful about pushing so hard

Hiltunen covers the awkward silence by rustling papers he pulls from a drawer in his desk, handing a few packets over. Great, more paperwork. His tone has changed after his obvious volley was met with silence, and now he halfheartedly explains to me the enrollment forms and the additional fees, the printout of his lecture from the first week. When he urges me to "review the course expectations on my own time," I can tell he's trying to get rid of me, to forget that he offered me what's probably a vaguely unethical solution to my problem in hopes that he could solve one of his. My confidence in his commitment to writing that letter of exception takes another steep, sad plunge.

"I don't really know if you'll be able to catch up from the first class you missed. It's a lot to take on," he says.

"I'll catch her up," Alex says, even before Hiltunen's finished speaking. I look up at him, see his chest rise as he takes a silent breath through his nose. With his free hand he reaches into the front pocket of his pants, taking out his phone. From a thin sleeve on the back of its case he slides a steel-gray business card out, using only his thumb. A white knight unsheathing his sword.

For the first time since Alex entered the room, I feel more kinship with the professor than I do with him. It's as though we're both waiting to see what Alex will do with that sharp, deadly weapon. When he slides his phone back into his pocket and extends the card to Hiltunen, his arm, his hand, everything about him is steady. But I see the way his jaw clenches before he speaks. I see the way the skin around the collar of his T-shirt is flushed slightly. I see that whatever he's about to say, it won't be easy, and that tremor of fear—what this means for me, what this means for him—rattles through my body.

Talk about a dramatic pause.

"I'll stay for the showcase."

Chapter 4

Alex

"Obviously you don't need to stay for the showcase," Greer says—or blurts, rather, almost as soon as we're out of the front door of the building. The sun feels blinding, overwarm. A weather-directed mockery of my shock.

I said I'd stay for a *month*.

"The point is," she continues, walking briskly ahead, tugging a pair of huge, tortoiseshell sunglasses out of her purse and sliding them on, "now I've got a foot in the door. I'll do the class and—well. I'm a really good student. He'll write the letter. I'll say you got called away. Breaking news somewhere. That's obviously not a stretch for anyone to believe. He'll be disappointed, but—"

"Greer." I say it not because I have anything to offer, certainly not a reassuring word to tell her that it's fine, that one month is no problem. I say it because I imagine that for Greer—Greer who chooses her words carefully, Greer who often chooses not to say any words at all—talking so much means she's maybe feeling as shocked as I am. I say it because I like the sound of her name. I say it because maybe she needs a minute too.

A *month*.

This morning, even before the sun had been up, I'd woken in a cold sweat, and that had been new—a panic attack coming out of sleep. It'd mostly been the same as the others—racing heart, waves of nausea, a whole body and brain restlessness that had made me roll from the bed to stand. I'd set my hands low on my hips and stared at the polished wood floors of Kit's guest room, feeling trapped and stuck, trying to catch my breath and knowing already that I'd made a mistake, telling my sister I'd stay for a couple of days.

The day had stretched out in front of me, long and formless, and while it's true that the panic attacks have started coming during shoots, taking a real break from work—*time off*—means that all the ways I generally keep from getting too trapped in my head are unavailable to me. Out there, I'm either shooting or scouting places to shoot, and if I have free time, it's the kind of free time spent doing the shit you have to do to figure out your life in a brand-new place—finding a decent shop to get food or buy clean drinking water, working out where you can get a good internet connection, preferably close to a place where you can get your clothes washed. If I'm on my own in a hotel, I may stay up late, sorting through and editing images, writing captions from the notes I have scribbled in my Moleskine, sending emails to editors who have hired me. If I'm staying in a group house with other journalists, I may defer to the collective schedule—still up late, but probably trading stories and tips, sometimes casting a paternal eye on newcomers who are flush with adrenaline and too much alcohol, often looking for bad-idea hookups with colleagues that are as likely to fuck up their professional cred as they are to provide relief from homesickness or fear or the sometimes crushing, painful fatigue.

But in Kit's house? In Kit's house, everything is easy, her fridge stocked with food she sent Ben to get—even in the midst of honeymoon packing—once she'd known I'd be staying, her water sources plentiful in the way I sometimes forget is possible when I've been away for a long time, her internet fast and her washer and dryer brand new. The rooms are quiet—too full and cozy to have an echo, too set back from the street to have much traffic noise.

It's exactly the life I wanted for her, and exactly the one that isn't for me.

I'd looked at my phone on the nightstand and known with certainty that at some point today, I'd check my news feeds and book a flight out of here, Jae's approval or not, Kit's disappointment or not. All I needed to do first was help Greer. One afternoon, that's what she'd asked me for, and I'd wanted to help. I just hadn't known I'd offer quite this much of it. *A month.*

So, yeah—I need a minute. A minute to think through how I'll keep my sanity and this promise to Greer. How I'll keep her from looking like she had when I'd stood in the doorway of the professor's office—young and small in an aggressively uncomfortable-looking chair, her shoulder bag a sullen lump on her lap and her pale hands clutched together in tense pleading on top. Her blue eyes had looked to mine with such desperate, imploring hope that for a second I thought it wouldn't be the panic attacks that'd end my career; it'd be the murder of the person making her look that way.

"I'm so sorry," she says now, one of her hands clenched around the strap of her bag, something she's done on and off since I first saw her today, standing by that statue in a prim hipster dress, a tiny line between her eyebrows as she stood, as quiet and still and thoughtful as the bronze man looming over her. "I thought it would only be the donation, but he kept…I mean, I'm surprised he didn't ask for a selfie. He's probably making you a friendship bracelet right now," she mutters, a bit under her breath.

"A what?"

"Oh," she says, turning her face toward me. In those sunglasses she looks like a movie star, or like the superspy you wouldn't see coming. James Bond to my Moneypenny, or the other way around, whichever.

"You know, one of those woven bracelets you make for your friends?" She takes in my expression, which I'm guessing reflects the curiosity I always feel around her, at the secret liveliness that seems to hide within her. "Never mind. The point is, I'll fix this. If you donate the photo, and maybe consider doing the guest lecture—"

"Let's sit for a minute." I gesture to a bench that's tucked beneath a huge, leafy maple off the path. We've transitioned into a more photo-ready part of the campus, well-manicured and obviously well-funded, with big, red brick and white columned buildings that probably look good in a brochure. Across the quad there's a small group of students playing Frisbee, laughing and shouting. It's a place I can't picture staying in, but right now, watching Greer and hearing the nervous thread to her speech, I also can't picture leaving.

"I'll take a look at what he's given you there." I nod my head toward the paperwork she clutches in one hand, and though she heads to the bench and sits, she clings tightly to the stack of papers.

After a tense minute of us both staring blankly at the group in the distance, she speaks. "I think I'll pass. On showing you the paperwork."

"It'll help me get a sense of what you missed the first—"

"No," she interrupts, her voice as firm as I've ever heard it. "What I mean is—the course, the showcase. I'll handle that myself. You really, really don't have to stay."

A warm breeze rustles through the canopy above us, and a split second later I catch a smell of something pleasantly sharp. An herby, flowery camphor. Lavender, I think. "I said I would."

She shifts, turns her knees my way, keeping her ankles crossed tidily, and uses the hand that's not death-gripping her paperwork to push her sunglasses up into her hair. Right now, she doesn't look any kind of young and small. She looks like she's about to lay into me.

"*This*," she says, holding up the papers and shaking them slightly, "is important to me. I need to graduate. It's better if Professor Hiltunen doesn't have the idea in mind that you'll be here for his showcase when we both know—"

"We both know what?"

She takes a deep breath, closes her eyes briefly before opening them again, her gaze softer this time. The sympathy is worse, honestly.

"Alex." Her voice is quiet, as though she's worried someone will overhear. She leans forward slightly, and I know the lavender smell comes from her. "I meant what I said on Saturday. If you're doing this—making yourself... *obligated* to me—as some kind of test for yourself, for your problem—"

"I'm not. I'm doing it because I want to help you." I've said it with all the conviction I didn't feel this morning, standing in that guest bedroom, thinking about my way out.

Her mouth sets into a line, firm and unforgiving. "I don't believe you."

The sigh I let out is gusty, frustrated. I lower my head, run a hand through my hair, and feel a disquieting sense of familiarity settle at the back of my neck. I look over at her, and find her as still and self-contained as ever, and for a few seconds we simply stare at each other, until I remember what that familiar feeling is.

"You said that to me before."

Her forehead wrinkles, that hair-thin line between her brows again.

"The morning I left here—the night after we first met. I told you I got called for a job, and you said I was lying."

"Oh," she says, shrugging. "Well, you were, weren't you?" The confidence with which she says it—it pierces me. Shames me. It'd been hard for me to leave that day—I'd fucked up with Kit, had said hurtful things to her, had ruined a weekend that meant a lot to her. Later, I'd apologized, and she'd forgiven me, but I don't think I've really forgiven myself.

So Greer's not wrong, and the look I give her is part smile, part grimace, all embarrassment. "I was. I called myself in for that job."

She puts a hand out, palm up, a gesture that says, *See?* Then she looks back down at her lap, her eyes scanning blankly over the papers she doesn't want me to look at. Why would she trust them with me, after all?

I clear my throat, lower my head again. I offer her the honesty she deserves. "I thought about doing the same thing this morning."

For a long minute, she says nothing. It's only the sound of the leaves shaking above us, the boisterous Frisbee players in the distance, the occasional birdcall or buzzing insect.

"I didn't even do the cough," she says, finally. "I only cleared my throat."

"I'm not a great Moneypenny, I guess." I wouldn't say she's smiling, but she's not frowning either. After another long pause, she sets the stack of papers between us on the bench. And then she slowly, deliberately, pushes them my way.

Within seconds, she's replaced the paperwork she'd been holding with a set of keys she's pulled from her purse. The keychain is what I'm guessing is a fake rabbit's foot, pink synthetic fur that's worn in one spot, the exact spot where she sets her thumb, worrying it slightly. I raise an eyebrow at her, but she only nods down at the paperwork.

The first few pages I skip—everything about enrollments, all the waivers—and get right into the first week material, all easy enough, stuff I can probably show Greer in a few hours. The final packet in the stack is about the showcase itself, about what Greer has to do to participate. Slowly, I start to get the feeling like I'm working out where to buy food, where to get water, where to use the internet, where to do laundry. The feeling like I've got something immediate to take care of. I think idly back to the weeks after my dad had his stroke, how I'd only managed the strange hum of anxiety in my blood by managing the immediacies of his care.

"Says here you've got to end up with four photos, all linked by theme. 'Variations on an idea that intrigues you,'" I quote, and she makes that small *hmm* noise again. "A photo-essay. I can do thi—"

I'm interrupted because she's snatched the papers back from me, the most forceful move she's ever made in my presence. It's worse than the *hmm* for all it makes me aware of her.

"*I* can do this," she says.

"Right, of course." I give her what I hope looks like an innocent, understanding smile, and she blinks owlishly at me.

"You can *help* me. Not do it for me."

"Of course," I repeat, and for the first time since I met her by the library this morning, things feel lighter, more playful between us. *A month.* Maybe it won't be so bad.

"On one condition."

I feel my smile transform slightly, change into something closed lipped and tentative. She's got that James Bond look about her again.

"You go see a therapist while you're here. About your panic attacks."

My lips flatten.

"I know a good one," she continues, as if she hasn't seen me turn as still as the statue that started this afternoon. I don't object to therapy, not in principle, but in practice the idea terrifies me—the trash of my past, available to a stranger. The chaos of my present laid bare.

"Greer—" My voice is unsure, unsteady.

"She's got an office not far from Kit's place. She used to see my brother." She looks down, strokes her rabbit's foot again. "One time," she adds, looking up at me, and despite the unsteadiness I feel, I'm grounded somehow by the lightness in her gaze, a slight sparkle that tells me she knows something I don't. That she doesn't think it'll just be one time.

"That's all I ask."

* * * *

"I don't get it," says Jae.

I'm sitting at Kit's dining room table, headphones for my phone in and eyes on my computer, where I've got a set of about fifteen photographs open, the best options for Peter Hiltunen's charity auction. I've given to auctions like this before, and in general, there's an art to choosing your piece: nothing too grim, nothing too newsy, nothing that requires too much context. It feels good to scan through the images, to keep my eyes and mind on what feels easy to me—pictures from all over, pictures from all kinds of situations. It's possible—*possible*—that I've been hiding in work for the last few hours, emails and edits and whatever else I can do to keep my mind off what I've agreed to.

"I don't really get it either," I say. It's late, after ten, but it's not unusual for Jae and me to catch up at strange hours, given that we're rarely in the same time zone. Jae mostly works from home these days, the office in his apartment tucked into a corner of his guest bedroom, where I've often crashed on short stints in the city.

"Once I asked you to do a panel discussion on stress and photojournalism for the New School and you said—and I quote—'I don't need a whole room of people psychoanalyzing me.' And now you're going to therapy?"

"One time. That's all I promised." I lean forward in my chair, scan my eyes over an image I took in Goma, a woman with her back to me wearing a brightly patterned wrap skirt that falls just above her ankles, an oversized crewneck sweatshirt tucked bulkily into it. Her head is wrapped in royal-blue-and-tan fabric; she's a bright column on the dusty road that surrounds her. This one's a contender, even if it's a little spare.

"But—" Jae begins, and then he stops, starts over. He's still adjusting, I'm guessing, to the fact that I've told him this at all, that I called him twenty minutes ago and told him I'd be taking a month off to help a friend and to deal with—I'd paused thickly—*panic attacks.* There'd been five seconds of silence on the other end of the phone and then he'd said, "Alex?" as though it might be someone crank calling him.

"I'm glad about it; don't get me wrong," he continues. "But I'm not sure I understand the deal. She gets a world-renowned photojournalist to help her with her school project—"

"It's not really a school project," I correct, but of course it *is* a school project. I just don't like the little inflection in Jae's voice, the one that suggests I'm out here robbing a cradle. "She's twenty-seven years old."

"She gets a world-renowned photojournalist," he repeats, ignoring me, "and you—go to therapy?"

I lean back in my chair, scrub a hand over my face, images still bright behind my eyelids—the ones on my screen, sure. But also ones of Greer today, dappled with the sunlight that'd been peeking through the maple.

"She's good at negotiation." Quiet but deadly. Like an assassin, but for your feelings.

"Is she going to be a lawyer? Some kind of businesswoman?"

"No. A social worker."

Jae's silent on the other end of the phone again. I open my eyes, focus back on the computer screen, narrow my eyes at another image featuring dozens of circular canopies draped in gauzy, orange-yellow fabric, shot through with twinkle lights, white-silk-draped tables and chairs beneath. Wedding season in Bangladesh, a story I shot for a travel magazine when I'd been in the area. Pretty, but too touristy for the auction, and not really on brand for me. I close it, slide my eyes over to another image from the day before, a baburchi in a short-sleeved plaid shirt, the pattern not unlike the one Peter Hiltunen had on today. He stands over a long counter, chopping an onion, but what's striking is the looming pile of translucent rings already stacked beside him, a tiny mountain of flavor that had made my eyes stream with tears as I'd shot. In the photo, the cook laughs at me, his eyes bright and dry. Maybe this one for the auction.

"Quit multitasking," Jae says, and I drop my eyes, embarrassed at how well he knows me through the phone alone. The truth is, aside from Kit, Jae's the closest thing to a best friend I've ever really had. Given that he takes 22 percent of my income, it maybe should feel odd—but it doesn't, not really. "This'll be good for you. Why not think about—"

"Aw, Jae," I say, scratching a hand over my scalp, knowing we're about to tread well-worn ground. Usually I can put him off by saying my connection's bad, or that my battery's dying. "Don't bring this up again." "Hey, listen. Do I call you when you're in the middle of a job and tell you to—I don't know what. Take more pictures of kids or dogs, or do more black and whites? To stop doing that thing where you kneel, put the subject above you?"

"Hey," I say, offended. But he has a point; I *do* tend to do that, an early trick I'd learned to manipulate scale, to make an easily overlooked subject seem giant, impossible to ignore. For a second I think about the prints hung outside of Hiltunen's office, student work that was so technically skilled I'd felt a small pang of jealousy, or maybe longing. The last couple of years, whenever I've had young photographers out in the field with me, I'm always a little surprised by their native intelligence looking through a lens. No matter what the purists say, these kids have been carrying around decently high-quality cameras in the palms of their hands for years, loading up their social media sites with pictures of everything from food to family.

Shit, maybe I should choose a different picture for the auction. I reach out to reopen my screen, but pull my hand back when Jae speaks again.

"The point is, I don't tell you how to do your job. This is mine. I tell you where there's an opportunity, and this is a good one. You've basically got someone barking at you to sign a book deal, a nice retrospective of your career so far, and now you've got a whole month to consider it. I can send you over some paperwork."

"One thing at a time," I tell him, standing from my chair and making my way into the kitchen. Now that I've shut the computer, my stomach rumbles, and I realize I haven't had anything since the coffee from this afternoon. On top of everything else, my eating habits are garbage, not unhealthy but recklessly sporadic, especially when I'm in the field. Probably something else I should work on while I'm here. "It's been a big day for me."

"Oh, sure. Getting hosed by a coed."

"She's not a coed. And I didn't get hosed." Much.

"I'll send the book stuff, but you don't have to look at it. You can put it in the same place you store all my Evites, the ones you never RSVP to."

"I don't like those things. Too many animations. Lots of clicking." Also I'm usually too busy working for whatever stuff Jae invites me to.

I open Kit's pantry, pull down a carton of ready-to-heat soup she's put there—it used to be our favorite, tomato soup. A treat when we'd have it with grilled cheese. I smile now, looking at the carton, so different from the small cans of Campbell's I'd buy. This one says *Organic*. *Flavored with basil. Non-GMO.* There's a picture on the front, creamy red soup in a sleek white bowl, a few thin twirls of cheese on top, a single basil leaf tucked artfully in between. Good for Kit, buying this nice carton of soup. I set it down on the counter, and for a second feel strangely unsure about whether I should eat it. I feel a little tremor of anxiety—not quite the onset of a panic attack. But a tiny warning bell, maybe. *Jesus, what the fuck is* wrong *with me?*

"You sound a hundred years old," Jae says. "I'll also send you an AARP subscription."

"No address," I deadpan, staring at that carton of soup. Jae chuckles nonchalantly, and I *feel* a hundred years old. "I gotta make some dinner."

"Alex, listen. I'm glad I'm not in the room for this part, because you'd probably do that thousand-yard stare you always do when I try to talk to you about something other than the business. Hell, you might hang up on me in the next three seconds. But I just want to say—I think it'll be good for you. Even if it is just one month. Even if it's just one time."

One month. One time.

I swallow, mumble out a brief "Thanks, man," a promise to keep him posted. When I hang up the phone, I set it next to the carton of soup, and for a few long, silent seconds, I think I might end this day like I began it—hands on my hips, sucking wind, freaking the fuck out about nothing I can put a finger on. Soup, for Christ's sake.

But then the screen of my phone lights, a white message box with a name I like to say. When I slide my finger across the screen, her message is two separate lines: first, a phone number, followed by a name—*Dr. Patricia Garrett-Lynch.*

Second, an address, followed by an instruction: *Tomorrow, 10 a.m.*

My brow lowers, and then another message pops up: *That's the kind of text James Bond would send, I think. The point is, it's a camera store and I need a camera.*

My mouth curves into a smile, my breath and blood slowing in pleasant relief. Just as I'm about to reply, I see she's typing again, so I wait.

I hope you're okay tonight.

Quiet but deadly.

I go ahead and make the soup.

Chapter 5

Greer

I wake up at my usual time—6:27 a.m.—and wait.

My second-floor bedroom is overly warm, a consequence not so much of the summer heat as of my sleeping with the door closed, a necessity when Ava has her boyfriend Doug sleep over, which these days is basically all the time. They were quiet last night, mostly, Doug keeping the volume abnormally low on his game of Mass Effect, and Ava murmuring lines to herself beside him on the couch, her script in her lap and a glass of rosé in her hand. Maybe they'd sensed something, all that hair shirt tension radiating off me when I'd come home last night after stopping off to have dinner with Zoe and Aiden at their place.

"So he's going to be your private tutor?" Zoe had said, one of her dark blond eyebrows raised, emphasis on *private*, and Aiden had nudged her hand with his. "Leave her alone, Zo," he'd said, giving me a sympathetic smile that somehow suggested he knew I was nervous about asking for Alex's help.

Shy people, we stick together.

Of course I hadn't told Zoe and Aiden the whole thing—nothing about Alex's panic attacks, nothing about how I'd basically coerced him into therapy in exchange for a task to complete while he's stuck here, trying to white-knight rescue me from the ivory tower I've trapped myself in. All that I'd kept to myself to ruminate over, and the quiet in this townhouse last night only served to keep me thinking about the next month, about how much help Alex needs and how much help *I* need, about how both of us will get through this when I can barely stop thinking about whether his mouth feels as good as it looks.

I'm okay, he'd texted back, late last night, and I'd held my phone in my hand for a long time, absolutely *not* thinking about anything battery operated in my nightstand.

I kick off the covers, slide my eyes over to the clock. 6:28. Plenty of time to do the usual, what I've done for most mornings since I was a teenager, which is to take a quick inventory of my body, letting myself feel every single thing. When I was younger, when it all first started and when it was all still a mystery, the inventory was decidedly more terrifying: I might open my eyes and find my vision slightly blurred. I might try to speak and find my voice oddly hoarse, my throat feeling half-closed. I might even have a tingling sensation in my hands or feet, faint in the mornings but worsening through the day.

These days, the inventory is pretty benign: maybe some soreness or tension, maybe a slight headache I can almost always manage with a few Advil and some extra time on my isometrics. Today might be one of those days, my body still smarting at me from the weekend—the heels, the dancing. And the stress and sleeplessness probably hasn't helped. Slowly, I crane my neck back and forth, then tip my chin up, feel an answering pinch before I tip it back down toward my chest. Definitely some extra exercises today, and maybe a long walk to loosen me up before I meet Alex—

My phone vibrates on my nightstand, which means it's 6:30 exactly, and I reach for it. "Hi, Mom," I say, not bothering to look at the screen.

"Hi, Greens. Doing okay this morning?"

"Doing great." My voice is bright, cheerful. I've learned that waking up a few minutes before the call helps with this, keeps my mom from worrying over any garden-variety grogginess.

Our exchange—it's a script I'd never need to study, for a performance we've been doing together from the first morning I woke up here in the suburban townhouse Ava and I share, not even two full miles away from my parents' house. Before that, it'd been a routine Mom and I had done in person, her knocking softly on the door of my childhood bedroom each morning, her voice falsely cheerful but her eyes heavy with concern, tracking over my body as though she'd somehow be able to *see* something wrong this time.

"You're sure?" The follow-up was an addition to our dialogue, a lean-in to the fact that she can't see my face when she asks. Mom hadn't wanted me to move out, even though I was twenty-one when I finally did, even though I'd been working consistently for a year by then, even though I'd still be under the watchful eye of Ava, who—always eager to please my mom—could be counted on to report to her about anything she thought might be going on with me. I often wonder what we'll add when I move downtown like I've planned, closer to my new job—

If. If I move downtown. *If* I start my new job. I swallow, thinking of Alex. Suit of armor Alex, helping me get free.

"Completely sure. Feeling good today."

"Okay," she says, but if I don't stop her now, there'll be follow-ups. *Have you been doing your exercises? Are you getting enough sleep? They're not making you work too hard there at the hospital, are they?*

"I can't talk this morning, Mom. I've got an—appointment at ten. For school," I clarify, in case she assumes something medical. "You have a busy day ahead?"

"Oh, you know me." That means she absolutely has a busy day ahead, probably enough social commitments to put a normal person in a stress coma. In addition to the volunteer work she does for the community theater—the same one Ava's the star player of most seasons—Mom's also a member of four book clubs, three charity committees, two community arts boards, and one neighborhood watch. I smile, my heart full with something like pride. My mom can do all these things now, can have so much freedom with her time, in part because of me and that lucky ticket.

"I'll check in tonight." We both know that means I'll call at exactly 8 p.m., same as I do every night, to let her know I'm okay. We both know, too, that she'll text me before that, probably around midday, with some small, unimportant question that's a smokescreen for checking in, and that I'll still respond to within five minutes. "Love you, Mom."

Downstairs in the kitchen, I move through my routine quietly, careful not to wake Ava or Doug. He does freelance lighting work, including at the theater where he and Ava met, so his workdays generally don't start until late, and Ava—a hairstylist who moonlights with her stage roles in the spring and summer seasons—never goes to work before ten. My cat, Kenneth, slinks in from the living room, where he sleeps in the warmer summer months, and purrs gently as he circles twice through my feet, his version of a good morning greeting. I feed him first, then reach for my box of Cheerios in the pantry, which are—

Almost gone.

I suppress a sigh, knowing that Doug's struck again, and hope there's at least an egg or two in the fridge. Doug's a nice enough guy, I guess, but he never asks to eat my cereal and he never replenishes it when he does. He also uses up all our wall plugs with his gaming console, and he sleeps in Game of Thrones boxer shorts, a fact I know because he walks around this place in them like I won't mind at all seeing an image of the Iron Throne emblazoned across his crotch.

Maybe Doug *isn't* a nice enough guy, actually.

At my feet, Kenneth meows in solidarity. "New place for us, soon, Kenny boy," I whisper. "Just the two of us."

"Greens?" comes Ava's voice from the stairway, and a few seconds later she comes in the kitchen, her freshly dyed auburn hair piled on top of her head, her face shiny from the special mask she puts on before bed. Ava's four years older than me, but she looks as fresh faced as a teenager, obsessed with beauty treatments and, I suspect in the last year or so, Botox.

"Sorry if I woke you."

She waves a hand. "You didn't. Doug's snoring, as usual. Anyways, glad I caught you." She pulls a mug from the cabinet above the coffee machine, pours herself a cup. "Your graduation," she says, and I wish I'd already taken that Advil I was thinking about. "That's still on, right?"

I blink at her. "Yes, it's still on." I hope she can't hear the hitch in my voice, the fear that it's not. "Why would you ask me that?"

She shrugs, pulling creamer from the fridge and adding it to her coffee. "Oh, you know," she says, then trails off with a light laugh, but we both know what comes after that *you know.*

You know Greer can't always follow through

You never know what might go wrong, when it comes to Greer

For the barest of seconds I imagine replacing all her wrinkle cream with mayonnaise.

"Why, Ava?" I repeat.

"It's no biggie. I'll have my understudy go on that day. I just wanted to make sure."

Her *understudy.* There's nothing so official happening in the theater where Ava does her shows, but I wouldn't say so. I know it's special to her, the thing she looks forward to most every year. "It's okay if you can't make it." I'm still holding the Cheerios box; I've tugged it toward my chest like it's a teddy bear.

Ava's unlined face compresses in a moue of disbelief. "Don't be silly," she says, and I know she means it. I know she wouldn't miss it. She's never missed anything for me, anytime I've needed her, and I hope over the last couple of years I've shown her how grateful I am for that. As she moves to leave the kitchen, she squeezes my shoulder and leans in, giving me a smacking kiss on the cheek. When she pulls back, she pauses, looking so like my mom that I lower my eyes. "You doing your exercises?"

"Yep. Feeling good today."

She drifts past me, moving down the hall to head upstairs. "Greens," she calls back, her voice light, musical. Ava used to sing me to sleep sometimes, when I'd had a bad day. Britney Spears's "Lucky," which is probably the most embarrassing minor personal fact I can think of about myself. "You'll let me know if anything changes, yeah?"

I look down at Kenneth, who's staring up at me, eyes narrowed in judgment, though whether it's at me or at Ava or our dynamic together is another of his private, feline mysteries. "Yeah," I say. "Of course I will."

* * * *

Barden Camera is a narrow, cramped store, slightly mildewy in smell and buzzy with the sound of an overworked air conditioner. The lone salesclerk is a man named Bart who is talkative in a way that suggests an undercurrent of loneliness; behind the glass case counters he's got a small television turned on, muted, a twenty-four-hour news station flashy with images and tickers and talking heads.

For a guy who doesn't like being in one place, being stuck—this must be a panic attack petri dish.

"I could show you something else too," Bart says loudly, setting his hands on his hips and looking down at the two cameras he has set out on top of the glass case that functions as a countertop. "I've got a used D500 in the back that'd—"

Beside me, I hear rather than see Alex scrape a hand over the edge of his jaw, thickly stubbled this morning. I'd shown up five minutes early, but he'd already been outside, leaning casually against the brick wall of a neighboring storefront. Even with the beard coming in he'd looked better rested, had smiled at me and said, "Hello, Greer," as though it was the most natural thing in the world for us to meet on a Tuesday morning in my hometown.

I'm too afraid to look over at him, to see the effect this must be having on him.

"No, that's okay," I say, sending Bart what I hope is a placating smile and not a clenched-teeth nervous grimace. "I think it's going to be between these two. Can we have a minute? I promise I'll decide really fast."

"No problem, no problem," Bart says, because he's the kind of guy who fills the space up with talk, even if it's repetition. "Time for my medicine, anyway." He mimes drinking something. "I mean coffee, of course! Four cups before noon, that's how I do it—"

"Thanks, Bart," says Alex, the first time he's spoken in a while. It's gentler, kinder than the way he spoke to the professor on Monday, but there's the same quiet quality of command to it, and Bart nods happily and ducks through a dingy maroon curtain into the back of the store.

"Oh, God," I whisper, putting a hand to my forehead. "I'm sorry. Do you want to wait outside?"

"No."

I finally get up the courage to look over at him, expecting the worst, a fluorescent-lit version of Alex on Friday night, but instead he looks calm, a little teasing, one dark eyebrow raised and a crooked smile on his lips, less white knight and more dashing rogue. He drops his eyes to the counter, where he's got the spec sheet I gave him on the way in, and taps it once with his index finger. He lowers his voice, leans down to me slightly, I guess so Bart can't hear him, or else so he can remind me of his magnetic face, voice, everything.

"I just—you don't need a D500." He leans back, speaks at a normal volume again. "Either one of these'll get you what you need for your class, but frankly it's bullshit your professor wants this kind of equipment for beginners."

I suppress a smile at this, Alex's continued hostility toward Hiltunen, which seems entirely borne out of the way he'd treated me. "How'd you learn?" I ask him.

"Nothing so fancy as this." He briefly lifts and then sets down the older model Nikon Bart's put out for me. It hadn't taken me long to realize the used cameras were more in my price range; in fact I'm pretty sure I hiccupped in shock at the price of the first one Bart offered, and for all his blustering energy, he'd taken the hint quickly. "I had a teacher who gave me an old FG. Thirty-five millimeter, if you can believe it. Actual film."

"That's the one you used for the picture at Kit's?" She loves that picture, the one above her fireplace—ice-encased branches of a tree set against a clear blue sky, so bright and sharp that you can feel the cold coming off it.

He lowers his eyes again, and jeez, his eyelashes. Maybe it's Maybelline. "Yeah. I shot with that camera for years before switching to digital. I still have it." He looks a little wistful, and my heart tugs.

I set the tip of my finger on the Nikon, surely imagining that it's still warm from the heat of Alex's hand. "This is the brand you use?"

"Yeah. Different model, but I've always shot with Nikons." He shifts on his feet, his brow furrowing. "The Canon wouldn't be bad either. It'd be a bit lighter in your hand."

I purse my lips, not liking that suggestion. I don't need it to be *lighter*. I pick it up, feel the solid weight of it. I sense I don't have the right hold on it, that there's something unnatural in the way it shapes to me, and I can feel Alex's eyes on my hands. For the first time since this whole thing started, I'm excited about the possibility of this camera, this course. Sure, this is a massive roadblock to my major goal, but I wanted to go to college for just that kind of experience. I wanted to learn as much as I could, wanted to take as many classes as I could fit into a day. It's its own type of freedom, learning something new. "I'm going to get this one."

"Okay," he says, and raps his knuckles once on the glass.

Bart emerges from the back, coffee in hand, big smile on his face. "Great choice. How about a camera bag?" He points to a display behind him. "I'll give you half off, a nice couple like you."

Now I have basically died, and my ghost is standing here with this camera. Maybe Bart's into that spectral photography I'm always hearing about. He could snap a quick photo and I'll just be an orb, or a smudgy white blob no one will notice because Alex's eyelashes and cheekbones are so captivating.

"You ought to have a good bag," says Alex, completely ignoring Bart's assumption. "Keep your equipment safe."

"Okay," I say quickly. "The brown one." Bart makes a face, and that's because there is no brown one. "I mean the black one." *God.* Would that there had been more "Acting Normal" classes offered during my tenure at the university.

Bart chatters loudly while we check out, and lucky for me Alex takes it cheerfully; despite my earlier concerns, he seems to relish being in a shop like this, unrecognized by someone he's talking to as a fellow professional. Alex's face lights when Bart says he still develops film even though hardly anyone asks him to anymore, a comment Alex greets with a sort of sad, shaking head familiarity. *Nerd alert,* I think, gently, happily, not minding the cramped space and funny smell much at all.

There's only one glancing moment of tension, and that's when I slide my signed credit card slip back over to Bart and he looks up at both of us with his guileless smile. "See you both in here again soon," he drawls, and I can tell he's waiting for Alex, more than me, to respond. I think of myself the other day, asking Alex to wish me luck, the leaden weight of his non-answer.

"See you soon," I say, wishing I were speaking for the both of us.

* * * *

"I think we ought to put the paperwork away for a bit," says Alex, an hour later. We're sitting at a café table outside of Boneshaker's, under a thick canvas awning that keeps the noonday sun off our faces but also seals in the noonday heat. Beneath the cotton dress I'm wearing, my skin is dewy with sweat, but across the table Alex looks temperature neutral and comfortable. I should've picked a table inside, at least for my own sake, but the memory of the last time we were in there together—tentative and then tense—still feels too close.

"We're only on page twenty, though." I put my thumb on the corner of the packet I printed this morning, the PowerPoint Hiltunen loaded to the course website from the session I've missed, and lift to fan the pages. "There's a lot left to go." If it's possible, I'm even less temperature neutral now, hearing those pages shuffle like a card deck. There's so *much*, and I have my first class in two days, and I still have to complete my first assignment, and—

"This is too much about your equipment," he says, reaching a hand out, raising an eyebrow in question. I pass him the packet, and he flips through a few of the remaining pages and his mouth twitches in annoyance. "Metering system," he mumbles. "What a load of garbage."

I'm not sure if he meant for me to hear him, but I ask anyway. "You don't think I need to know that?"

He does that move over his beard again, but this time I watch it—the heel of his hand set first on the hinge of his jaw, dragging down, his fingers loose, slightly bent. I'm convinced that the sound of it can be heard from miles away, a siren call to single people everywhere.

He shrugs. "To take a good picture? No. I didn't know half this shit when I started. Are you going to have a quiz on it?" He says *quiz* like he's talking about a colonoscopy.

"I don't think so. I just need to have the assignment done." I make a move to take that piece of paperwork out of the folder I've brought, but Alex stops me with a shake of his head.

"We'll worry about the assignment tomorrow."

I blink across the table at him. *Tomorrow.* This is lots of days-in-a-row Alex. I wish I had a tiny cooling device in the waistband of this dress. He flips back through the packet, takes the paperclip off that's binding it all together, removing a few of the pages and setting them on the table between us.

"These three terms, that's what you need to know most. Basically, your exposure system. ISO, aperture, and shutter speed. Those are the most important functions on your camera."

I pull the pages toward me. They're ones we've already gone over, and while I understand them in the abstract, I also suspect it's the kind of thing you don't really get until you *do*. Dennise is always talking about that at work, the difference between theory and practice, between what's in your textbook and what's in the hospital room with you when you're talking to a patient. I look toward where I've set the camera on the table, wondering if we should experiment a little. There's a flare of excitement in my belly.

"Let's get you comfortable holding the thing first. The first teacher I had—the one who gave me the FG, that's what he taught me. Photography's not just about what your camera can do. It's about what your body can do."

The flare of excitement is replaced with a sinking feeling. Talk about starting with my weakness. I'm pretty sure Alex doesn't wake up every morning and do a scanning inventory of his aches and pains. Maybe I *should've* gotten the lighter camera. For a second, I sit, hands clasped in my lap, expecting that Alex demonstrate something for me—hold the camera himself, ask me to imagine my hands like his. But he doesn't do that. Instead he leans back in his chair, hands clasped loosely over his flat stomach—*gunh*—and waits, roguish eyebrow raised again.

I pick up the camera.

"First thing is, don't listen to what your teacher tells you. Listen to what your hands tell you. Me, I always shoot with my left hand under the lens, like this." He holds up one hand so that the back of it is facing me, his thumb pointed upward and his index, middle, and ring fingers straight. His pinky finger curves slightly inward, toward his body. "The lens sits right here," he says, stroking the index finger of his left hand, tracing the corner where it and his thumb make an L. "My right hand I use to operate the shutter, but the thing is, I like it so my pinky finger here"—he makes a small motion, waggling that curved-in digit—"is always touching my right hand. I don't know why. It's just what feels right."

I adjust my hands, shifting them in a way that mimics what he's just described, but I can already tell that won't work—my hands aren't big enough, my fingers feel stiff and awkward.

"Remember, my camera's bigger. I shoot with a longer lens." *Hey-oh,* thinks the dumbest, crudest part of my brain. My cheeks feel newly warm, and I'm grateful to have something to keep my eyes and hands on.

"This feels okay," I tell him finally, once I've settled on something—my left hand a more curving, cuplike shape than the one he made, my wrist turned more inward. The fingers on my right hand fit more easily to the camera body once I've figured out what my left hand is doing, though my pinky finger feels a little extraneous at the moment. I pay attention to how it feels, a different kind of inventory—not scanning for what I already know about my body, but scanning for how my body feels in a new situation.

"It'll start to feel more natural after a while. Like an extension of you. Now you've got to stand up."

"Uh," I say, casting an eye toward the windows beside us. Stand up? Alex sets his hands on the arms of his chair and stands first. Oh, sure. That'll keep people from watching us.

"Elbows, they've got to be tucked in to your sides, which will keep you sturdy," he says, and I see what he means by the whole "extension of your body" thing, because when he tucks his own elbows in close, he shapes his hands again, as though he has his camera with him now. I'm convinced that anyone looking out the windows, or walking by, would know exactly what he's miming. He *does* look sturdy, and he's—he's so confident in the way he holds himself, the way he doesn't mind anyone staring. I have a thudding, echoing memory of Alex's words to me in this café two years ago: *I can.*

He smiles down at me, something sheepish about it. "Don't leave me hanging here, now."

I like that so much, the way he says it. The way it evens things out a little between us.

I stand, mirroring his pose, listen to him tell me about placing my legs slightly apart, one foot in front of the other, my knees slightly bent. This would absolutely be the moment in a movie where he stands behind me, where he uses this as an excuse to touch me, where the male-gaze-obsessed director makes sure to get an angle on my heaving bosom. But neither of us is interested in a movie moment, and I like that too—how seriously he's taking it, how he lets me figure it out for myself. The most he moves is to step to the side of his chair, to tilt his head at my stance and nod his head in approval before moving back.

He tells me about brow contact, about how some photographers like to put the camera right up against the ridge of their eyebrow, another point of stability, but some keep a thin line of space between. Alex, he's a brow guy, and he tells me to try it both ways. I tell him brow contact is probably easier without mascara, and he laughs, and for the first time, it feels easy between us, friendly and fun.

He's still smiling when he pats his flat, firm stomach once and says, "Here matters." He pats again, a firm clap. "Stable here. Best-case scenario, you breathe out when you take a photo, but if you're shooting fast, you can't always. At the very least, you try to be regular about it. In, out."

In, out. He pauses, drops his hands to his side, and for a few seconds we simply look at each other, both of us aware of another echo this time— not of anything we've ever said to each other, but something we did once together, only a few days ago, our hands pressed together and our lungs moving in tandem. This time, Alex's cheeks flush slightly. He blinks, and then sits, clearing his throat.

"Of course you won't always be standing when you take a photo." His hands curl around the arms of his chair, his knuckles briefly going white before he looks up at me.

I set down my camera. For a second, I think about telling him why I wake up at 6:27 every morning. I think about saying, *Alex, I know how you feel. I know how it is, when you can't trust your body to do what you tell it to do.*

But just as quickly I think about what it would mean, to tell him. I think about my mom and Ava, my brothers and my dad, sometimes, even Kit and Zoe—how they ask me gently how I'm doing, how I'm feeling. I think about a different kind of brow contact—the lowered brow of concern, the *how's Greer holding up* expression. I think about how Alex—even though he's here, offering me help in a desperate situation of my own making—has never looked at me that way at all.

I sit down in my chair, tidy my paperwork. "You're still going to go to therapy, right?" I keep my eyes down, away from that sea-glass pleading in his.

There's a long moment of ambient noise—cars passing slowly on the street, the occasional *whoosh* of the espresso machine I can hear even from out here, the distant honk of a horn.

"Yes," he says finally, a little formally. "That was the deal, after all."

And that's lesson one, in the bag.

Chapter 6

Alex

You might think that a person who's spent the last decade surrounding himself with the unfamiliar, the far flung, the rarely seen and hardly ever acknowledged, would find it difficult to be surprised in a place like Barden, Virginia.

But then you probably haven't been inside the office of Dr. Patricia Garrett-Lynch.

It's Wednesday afternoon, not even a full two days since I made this deal with Greer, not much more than twenty-four hours since we'd sat outside of a café and I'd taught her how to hold her camera. All morning with her, I'd felt the kind of quiet, in-the-moment presence I've started to think I've lost the capability for. It's what had made me good at my job, that presence, and as Greer and I had walked side by side to Boneshaker's, I'd thought—*Maybe the easy pace is already making a difference. Maybe I'm getting the rest I need. Maybe I don't need the therapy.*

But one fleeting memory of a panic attack and the noise in my head was back, clanging and ceaseless. I'd thought, *Oh, fuck, it's happening again*, and I don't suppose I was present for much the rest of the day. When I'd left Greer, I'd pulled my phone from my pocket, desperate to check news alerts, but there'd only been two notifications: one message from Kit, asking how I was getting along, and one reminder—for this appointment, the one I'd made with reckless confidence only a few hours before.

Now that I'm in the small, cramped lobby, I'm dealing with a different sort of noise. I'm anxious as fuck, that's a given, but I've also just noticed that the music playing at a low volume out of the mounted speakers is not, in fact, the generic, supposedly soothing stuff you might hear in a spa or in any other doctor's office—it's Pink Floyd, *The Wall*. I'd ask someone about it, but there's no one out here with me. Instead of the southern-drawl receptionist I'd spoken to yesterday, there's a piece of printer paper folded in half with *OUT TO LUNCH* scribbled on it. The paper itself has a sort of pink, glowing quality to it, and that's because it's propped against a Himalayan salt lamp. There is stuff *everywhere*.

It's the walls, though, that really get me. I don't even bother sitting down to wait, because there's too much to look at. Almost every available inch of space is taken up, no seeming plan other than *where will this fit*. There's old cartoons from the *New Yorker*, a few framed finger paintings that I have to hope are from kids and not from adult patients who get asked to do bizarre art therapy shit back there with the good doctor, a grand total of ten of those feathered dream catchers, and too many postcards to even count. There is also a poster of David Bowie in his costume from *Labyrinth*, and someone has cut out pink paper hearts and stuck them all over it. One of the paper hearts has a lipstick print on it, and it's not like it's got clean lines. Someone really went for it on behalf of the Starman.

I almost take out my phone and text Greer: *Is this a joke?*

"Hey, take a picture. It'll last longer."

I startle away from the Bowie poster and turn, and even from across the room I've got to look down to meet the eyes of a woman who's probably four foot nine inches tall with an extra inch made up from the frothy, steel-gray curls rising out of her head. She's got a thick Brooklyn accent, and when she crosses the room to shake my hand, it's in a grip so unexpectedly forceful that I'm pretty sure she pulls me forward a step. "Get it?" she says. "Because you're a photographer!"

Her smile is as enthusiastic as her handshake, slightly gap toothed and so wide you can't concentrate on anything else about her face. When she releases my hand and turns away, heading back down the hallway from which she came, I stick a hand in my pocket and extract a piece of gum from the pack I bought on the walk over, shoving it in my mouth as I follow her.

When we cross the threshold to her office she stands with her hands on her hips and looks at me. "Aleksandr," she says, not like an acknowledgment but like she's trying to remind herself who she just picked up from the bus depot she calls an office lobby. "I know your work."

She spins away and moves to a low, particle-board bookshelf that's shoved against one wall, pulling a *National Geographic* from a disordered stack, immediately starting to flip through its pages. She doesn't need to, not really—I've only had one spread in there, a career highlight, photos I took at Dadaab refugee camp in Kenya three years ago. Even if it weren't for what I'd seen there, even if it weren't for the way I'd dreamed of that camp for months after, I remember every photograph I've ever had published. Because if it's been published, that means I probably studied it for hours—either before I sent it, if I had the time, or after. "Meticulous," Jae always says. "But also annoying."

"This is my favorite," she says, holding it out toward me, and I blink down at it quickly, pretty sure what I'll see. And yeah, that's the one, Jae's favorite, and the editor's favorite, and Kit's favorite too—three kids, all Somali refugees, dressed in brightly colored clothes, too-big polo shirts and swim trunks cinched tight at their waists. Two sit on the red-orange, dusty ground, a dirty soccer ball between them, looking up at the third, who's staring at the camera. Just after I shot it, the four of us kicked that soccer ball for almost two hours while they'd made me practice saying their names over and over, laughing when I'd intentionally confuse them. We'd played until a dust storm kicked up and drove us back into thin white tents.

"Good kids," I say blandly, already moving my eyes around the office. The walls aren't nearly as packed, but it's messy in here, absentminded-professor messy, halfway-to-hoarder messy. It smells vaguely of bacon. I have a pointed, entirely unexpected longing for the prison-cell spareness of Peter Hiltunen's office. "Where should I sit?" I ask, conscious of my height compared to hers. My lower back is dewy with sweat, and all I want is to get this over with.

She grabs a stack of papers off a battered leather club chair and waves a short arm at it. "It reclines. If you want this to feel like a real head-shrink."

When I sit in it, it creaks disturbingly, and it's so shallow and low to the ground that I feel like my knees are half-tucked into my armpits. She'd only mentioned her brother coming here, but I wonder whether Greer has sat in this chair. I'll bet it fits her body just so.

"I'll stay this way," I say, though she doesn't seem to be paying attention. She's getting herself settled in her own chair, some ergonomic thing that's positioned in front of her messy desk, an iPad and a stylus in her hand, and reading glasses lifted from a beaded cord around her neck to perch at the end of her nose.

"I don't like being called doctor, so you can call me Patricia. But not Patty, because I don't like it and because it makes me think of hamburgers."

I—what. The temptation to text Greer is overwhelming. "I prefer Alex."

"Sure, sure," she says, toeing off her shoes. I'm still staring at her mismatched socks—one pink, one black, when she speaks again. "Is it PTSD?" she asks, and I cough in surprise, thinking I had a few more seconds of her fidgeting and setting up over there, or at least some gentle lead-in. Maybe a *tell me about yourself* or a *what brings you here today.*

"I—no. No, I don't think it is."

"Because I googled you too. You've been in some dicey situations. War zones."

I shift, and the chair makes an elaborately flatulent sound. *Great.*

"Yes," I say, once I've controlled my urge to either groan or bolt from the room. "But not much time in combat situations for me." Barely any, actually, a choice I'd made after one too-close call in Afghanistan five years ago. One limit I'd put on my freedom since I'd started shooting internationally, and it'd been because of Kit, because I didn't ever want her to get a call about me, my death a world away from her.

Still, I'd found a lawyer the next time I was stateside, had drafted a will that left everything to her. Just in case.

"Well anyway, PTSD can come from all kinds of things, not necessarily combat or otherwise dangerous or traumatic events. All kinds of symptoms associated with it too."

"I have panic attacks," I blurt. Not because I want to, but because I feel like I have to somehow get a word in here. "Shortness of breath. Sweating. Heart racing. Trouble swallowing." I've listed it so mechanically, not like I'm a patient but like I'm the doctor, giving someone notes to transcribe or speaking into a recorder. "They've started recently."

"How recently?"

The only thing stopping me from shifting again, from releasing some of my restless energy, is the memory of the noises this chair is capable of. I'll probably break my jaw chewing this gum. "A couple of years ago." Patricia raises an eyebrow, makes a note with her stylus.

But she doesn't press me on it, at least not yet. "You chew the gum to help you?"

"What?"

She waves a hand, and there's got to be twenty ultraslim silver bangle bracelets on her wrist, jingling as they resettle along her forearm. "Often helps people with nausea."

"Oh." Oddly, I *do* feel less sick to my stomach than I did on the walk I took here. "Maybe?"

"Okay. So what helps so far?"

Greer, I think. The immediacy of it, the solidity of it, the *truth* of it surprises me. But I don't dare say it. "Time. I wait for it to pass."

"Do you drink? Take any medications?"

"No. Neither." I'm particular about both, no surprise as to why, given my dad's addictions. I open my mouth to say it, but close it again. Maybe we'll come around to family shit, eventually.

She asks me a few more questions—when my last physical was, whether I have trouble sleeping, whether I've ever been treated for mental health issues before. When she finishes—a quick volley given my brief answers— she sticks her stylus between her temple and the frame of her glasses and then clasps her hands over the top of her iPad. "Okay. Tell me what made you come here today."

Greer, I think again, but this time, it's not the whole truth. I could've said no, same as I could've left the day after the wedding, as I'd originally planned. I could've kept quiet in Hiltunen's office. I could've canceled anytime between when I made this appointment and now. But they've worn into me, these attacks. Beat me down. They've started coming when I don't expect them, when I'm supposed to be at my best.

"I need to fix this. I can't do my job if I'm this way."

Patricia gives me a long, steady look. "It's not like putting a new transmission in your car, you know. There's not one thing that's broken in there. Dealing with panic, with anxiety—it can be complicated. Medical and behavioral. If anything, it's like learning how to drive again."

"I taught myself how to drive," I say, ridiculously. I did, too. I drove my dad's car illegally until I was eighteen, when I could take the driver's test without having to go through the classes that cost, to my teenaged mind, a stupid, offensive amount of money.

She smiles, lifts her hands from where they rest to give a brief, palms-up gesture of question. "So?"

I take a deep breath, think about Greer's eyes on mine. I think about the promise I made her. And I think about my camera—my hands steady, my eyes focused, my head empty of everything except what's in the shot. I'd felt that yesterday. I want to feel it again.

"Complicated is fine."

"Complicated is my favorite," she says, and retrieves her stylus. "Let's get started."

* * * *

I'm only home from Patricia's office for an hour, staring blankly at a newspaper I'd picked up on the walk back, when Greer's soft knock sounds at the door. I'm immediately grateful she didn't ring the doorbell.

It's quaint, the old-fashioned-crank style of it, one of the many things Kit's proud of here, but I have to believe that even a person with a particularly calm temperament would find the shrill ring alarming.

I stand, my legs and back feeling creaky and stiff, my mind sluggish and tired. That was—that was fucking *hard*, that's the thing. It was hard to talk to Patricia, to tell her even the short version of my past. At first I'd tried to keep my responses brief, neutral: *I raised my sister after her mother left. My father has problems with addiction. I have spent most of the last ten years outside of the country.* But her follow-ups were somehow both gentle and pointed, questions that mixed up feelings in my mind, made me conceive of myself and everyone in my life differently. "Did you ever feel anger toward your father and sister?" she'd asked, sometime around the thirty-five-minute mark—and I'd answered snappishly, too quickly. "Why would I ever feel anger toward my sister?"

But then I'd thought about how I'd behaved here two years ago, how I'd so coldly and forcefully rejected her offer of money, of a home base to come back to between trips. I'd felt my face heat in shame, and I'd felt Patricia's eyes on me, not quite triumphant—but *knowing*.

So I can't decide, as I walk to the door, whether it's a good thing Greer and I are set to work on her first assignment now. On the surface of it, Greer and Patricia have about as much in common as a bicycle and a semi truck, but damn if Greer doesn't have that knowing look about her too, and I don't want her seeing everything messy and complicated about me while I'm teaching her about what I'm supposed to know best.

When I open the door, though, see Greer standing there with a shoebox tucked under her arm and her new bag slung across her body, her blue eyes wide and hopeful, her cheeks pink with summer heat, I think: *I don't care what she sees, so long as she comes in.*

"Hey. Let me take those things for you."

"Oh, that's okay." She holds the box a little more stiffly as she crosses the threshold. She's like this, I've noticed—tentative, a bit defensive at offers of help, protective of herself and what's hers.

I take a step back and reach an arm out, my attempt to welcome her to a home that isn't mine. It feels awkward, like putting on clothes that don't fit.

"It was that bad?" she asks, staying where she is. The shoebox deforms slightly under the press of her arm, and her forehead crinkles. In her face I can see the weight of this, the responsibility she feels. She'd wanted it to go well.

"It was—exhausting." Oddly so, not unlike the comedown after the adrenaline-packed panic attacks. I look at her, willing her not to ask me anything else about it, not now. I don't think I could get into it, even if I wanted to.

She nods once, as though I've made that request aloud. "Okay." She takes another step forward, sets the shoebox and her bag down on the trunk that sits inside the foyer. I look down at them both, feeling a small release of breath I must've been holding. The shoebox must have to do with the assignment, and I feel a spark of curiosity. "If you want," she says, "we could—loaf around for a while, start on the lesson later."

Loaf around? "I'm all right. We can get started—"

But she's already walked past me into the living room, her flats silent on the hardwoods as she passes into the dining room and then into the kitchen. When I get in there, she's already got Kit's pantry open. "Wow," she says quietly.

"What?" From my spot leaning in the doorway, I watch her stare inside the space. When she looks over at me, her eyes are bright with amusement.

"She must've cleaned for you. One time I was here making cookies and I found a stack of metallurgy journals and a pair of tweezers on the top shelf."

I snort a laugh of recognition. "There's a real mess in the upstairs closet. I refolded all the towels last night and it looked like maybe she'd shoved a bunch of junk in there in a rush before she took off. Probably the journals and tweezers are there now."

"You refolded all the towels?"

I shrug. "I taught Kit better than this. She's messy." She'd always tended to it, even when we were kids. Books and papers left out, detritus of half-done experiments she'd come up with on her own. After she'd go to bed at night I'd spend at least a half hour putting it all away.

Greer smiles at me, and I sense the laugh that lives inside her, the one she's trying to suppress for my benefit. She looks back into the pantry, rummages around, and when she emerges she's holding a plastic sleeve of microwave popcorn. "A-*ha*." She holds it up, victorious, and then like she's remembered I'm here, she lowers it again, her face resetting into something more neutral as she walks to the microwave over the stove. "Kit never has enough crunchy stuff. She likes candy for snacks. I thought we were going to have to settle for dry cereal."

I blink, a tiny effort at catching up to this—snacks with Greer in my sister's kitchen, some vague plan to *loaf around*. I cross to the refrigerator, pull out a couple of the fancy fruit sodas in glass bottles that I haven't tried yet. When the kernels start to pop, Greer turns to me again. "We could watch a bunch of Ina Garten. That always relaxes me."

"What's Ina Garten?"

For a long moment, there's only the hum of the microwave, the rising tide of tiny explosions inside it. Greer stares at me, her brow furrowed and her lips pursed. I feel like I've just asked her what a menstrual period is. "You mean *who*," she finally says. "You mean who?"

"So it's a person, then."

"Are you telling me you've never seen a show on the Food Network?" The look on her face is one of such naked disappointment that I have to press my lips together to keep from smiling.

"I didn't grow up with cable."

She blinks. "I mean, okay. That's too bad, but also you've stayed in like one million hotels in your life. You've *never* watched the Food Network?"

"I don't watch much television, I guess."

"What do you do when you take a sick day?"

"A—sick day? I don't really—I just don't shoot on a day that I'm sick. I sleep. Or read."

For a split second, her face lights, brows raising, eyes widening. "What do you like to read?"

"The—the newspaper?"

Damn, wrong answer. Her face falls. "That's not really sick day reading." She looks out into the dining room, spots the copy of the *Times* I have spread out there, and in a move that is inexplicably, ridiculously sexy, she presses up slightly onto her tiptoes so she can get a better look. I can see the line of her leg change, the slight flare of her contracted calf muscles in her cropped, skinny cut jeans. The microwave timer beeps annoyingly, a few kernels still popping. "You're reading an article about flooding in Vietnam."

My face heats again. I scrape a hand across my jaw, pull my mouth to one side. "That's probably a job I would've been doing. If I were doing jobs right now."

She drops her heels back to the ground, levels me with another long, clear-eyed stare. "That sounds soothing." Her nose crinkles slightly, as though she's not used to the sound of sarcasm from her own mouth. "For your panic, I mean."

"It used to be," I say without thinking, a moment of pure, unpressed response that had felt impossible to me back when I was in Patricia's office.

She tilts her head, and that fractional movement shifts the light behind her, a beam of bright sun passing through the back window limning the whole of her left side. I keep my eyes up, knowing what that light must be doing to the fabric of the white button-up she's wearing. My fingers twitch at my side.

"New coping mechanisms," she says, moving to open the microwave, not looking at me at all. She sounds remarkably like Patricia. No nonsense, no pretense. "You need them."

* * * *

Two hours later, I've watched Ina Garten make salmon tacos, lamb chops and couscous, two different kinds of pie, and a soup with so many ingredients I'd actually talked back to the television. I've also eaten half a bowl of Greer's popcorn, which was not finished when she took it out of the microwave. First she'd melted a small pat of butter and poured it on top, and then she'd added salt, a few shakes of cinnamon, and a handful of chocolate chips. "This is good comfort food," she'd said.

Now she sits beside me on the couch, the bowl between us, her legs stretched out onto the coffee table, feet crossed at the ankles. "This is the best show," she says, not even really to me. She's just quietly commenting for herself, delighting in her own enjoyment of this simple thing. I can't say for sure whether I'm enjoying this—the show, I mean—or if I'm just enjoying sitting with her, feeding off the strange, silent self-containment she has about her. It *should* be disconcerting; it seems like it would be with anyone else. But with Greer, the silence, the self-containment—it feels natural, comforting. She's presence and absence, all at the same time.

"Is this one episode?"

Greer turns her head from where she's had it resting against the back cushions of the couch. "What do you mean?"

"I mean—" I gesture a hand toward the flat-screen. "Is this—with the stew and then this fruit tart thing—has this been on the same episode?"

"No," she says, her brow furrowed again. She's had to do a lot of work for this sick day, I'll tell you what, basically explaining to me what cable television is. I'm pretty sure she put her feet up to stop me looking at the other newspaper I have there, yesterday's *Post*. On the back of one heel, she's got a dark smudge of newsprint that I'd like to set my thumb to. "Why would you ask that?"

I shrug. "I thought she was wearing the same clothes."

Her lips part slightly, her tongue peeking out to swipe across her bottom lip. I can see that lip quiver slightly, and I know she wants to laugh again. I shift against the cushions, wanting her to. "She likes button-up shirts. Mostly blue. Collar turned up. It's like—it's her *thing.*"

"Ah."

We're quiet again, but she's more restless now, noticing the smudge on her heel, and when she lifts her thumb to her mouth, another tiny swipe of her tongue before she rubs at the newsprint herself, I have to close my eyes to keep from thinking about what her tongue would feel like against mine.

"It's probably boring for you," she says, her head tipped down as she rubs at the stubborn spot. "Watching a food show. Lying around on the couch."

"It's not boring." I've maybe said it too hastily, so it sounds like I'm making up for something, when really I'm trying to stop my mind from unruly thoughts about what it'd mean to be *lying around* with her in another context. "I'm just not used to it. This is what you do, then, when you're sick?"

Something slight changes in her, a tightening in her body even as she curls in on herself, rubbing at that smudge. When she stops, setting her foot down on the floor, she keeps her head tipped down, looking at the newspaper.

"I don't take a lot of sick days." There's a line of tension in her voice. "I stay busy too."

She clears her throat and reaches for the remote, shutting off the television. Then she stacks her spine so she's sitting straight now, no casual slouching anymore. I feel oddly bereft, at sea. Also I want to see how the fruit tart turns out.

"Do you mind if we start the lesson?"

"Sure." Even before I've finished with the single syllable she's up. When she comes back with her camera bag and the shoebox, she sits, setting the bag between our feet and the box on the coffee table, which she opens after an almost imperceptible hesitation.

Inside she's got a collection of objects, some that immediately remind me of the pink rabbit's foot she keeps on her keychain. There's a four-leaf clover that's suspended, spring green and symmetrical, inside a flat glass oval. A small horseshoe, barely big enough for the palm of your hand. A bright copper penny.

Good luck charms, I guess, but some of the other objects are tiny mysteries about Greer I want the answers to. A scrap of pale blue fabric with small yellow stars printed on it. A silver medallion on a chain, embossed with something I can't see from here. A never-used pencil, the kind you don't see all that much anymore—marigold yellow topped with a shiny, aluminum sleeve holding a dark pink eraser. I lean forward to get a better look at what else she's got, but she passes a piece of pale green printer paper my way, blocking my view.

"That's the assignment," she says, reaching into the shoebox. I look down at the paper I'm holding, but feel my eyes stray up again to her busy hands. She takes out the clover and the horseshoe, sets them both on the table. I guess it's going to be the non-mysterious objects, then. I look down at the assignment sheet, feeling confused and unaccountably disappointed.

"I need to show I understand the arrangement of shapes, using objects related to my theme," she says, taking a line from the first bullet point on the sheet. "As well as different lighting conditions, and how essential camera functions complement those conditions."

Bullet, bullet. She has basically memorized the sheet. "Okay," I say, watching the line of her back, still stiff. I lean forward, set my elbows on my knees. The horseshoe, I guess, that's maybe an interesting shape. I try to focus on the light from Kit's window, try to think about the desk lamp she's got upstairs that we can do something with for a nice sidelight, but it all feels blandly unappealing now that Greer's shut me out. "Your theme is luck?"

"Yes," she says, the starch still in her voice. "Because of the lottery, obviously." But something about that box tells me it's got nothing to do with the lottery.

"What—" I begin, but she speaks over me.

"I don't think it'll take long at all," she says, and right then I feel like a window opens, a fresh breeze passing over me. Waking me up.

She's worried I'll leave. Or worse, that I want *her* to leave. That *it's probably boring* for me.

"Greer." I reach out to still the hand she's using to dig back into her shoebox full of mysteries. I didn't think about it, this small touch to the back of her hand, but probably I should have—probably I should have thought about how it'd feel to touch even this small part of her. Soft, delicate skin and the lilting ridge of a vein, a live, lean cushion beneath my fingertips. I clear my throat, draw my hand away from hers. "Thank you."

She turns her face to the side—not quite looking over her shoulder at me, but acknowledging me. There's a pretty blush on her cheeks, underneath her freckles. "It was no problem."

"It was exactly what I needed. The best sick day I ever had."

Now she does look at me, her blue eyes bright again. A memory from Patricia's office this morning comes to me, unbidden. *Complicated is fine,* I'd said.

"Really?"

I nod. "Really." I pause before this next part, gathering some of my courage. "I'm going back to see Patricia. On Friday."

A slow smile spreads across her face, a warm, special secret between us. When she speaks, she does so quietly, as though she's keeping this secret from the house itself. "You won't regret it."

I smile back at her, nod my head toward her camera, and borrow some words from my new therapist. "Let's get started."

Chapter 7

Greer

No surprise: Alex is a better teacher than Professor Hiltunen.

Last night's class had been, for the most part, brutally mundane, organized via a thirty-two-slide PowerPoint that was not made more interesting by virtue of Hiltunen's opening dramatic reading of an excerpt from a Walt Whitman poem that was most memorable for its use of the word *sea-gluten*, whatever that is. When he was finished he'd looked out over the ten of us in the class like we were a sea-gluten of adoring followers. "I'm sure you've all guessed this week that our focus is"—*dramatic pause*—"nature."

For the first hour of class, I'd scribbled notes about Eliot Porter, Carleton Watkins, Ansel Adams, wondering whether you had to have a penis to do nature photography; for the second hour, I scribbled notes about monopods and tripods and wide angle and normal fixed focal lenses and wondered whether all such things were metaphorical penises.

There'd been some life in the last hour when we'd each shared a photograph from the previous week's assignment. Two students had chosen family as their theme—one photographing a collection of her daughter's toys, the other a pair of wedding bands, stacked on top of each other—and Hiltunen had offered vaguely condescending remarks about how "common" themes can still produce interesting photographs. Another student, a man named Gus who had the same model of camera as mine, had picked transportation, sharing an image of the tire of his motorcycle that I'd thought was pretty breathtaking for the way light shone on the black-and-red fender. Hiltunen said it demonstrated "potential."

Seeing my own photograph projected at the front of the room had made my throat go dry, my palms sweaty. It'd felt strangely intimate to show the class the shot I'd settled on—nearly every one of my good luck charms stacked haphazardly on top of a copy of the newspaper Alex had had there. It'd been my idea, to keep the newspaper, and Alex's to use everything from the box, not just the obvious things. "You don't have to tell anyone what they're about," he'd said, and I could tell that *anyone* had included himself. "But the shapes are good, distinctive. Enough textures that the light hitting them will teach you something."

That's what I'd tried to say in class—what I'd learned from the photograph. It wasn't perfect, I knew, but I felt like I'd ticked all the boxes from my assignment sheet. I'd explained each of the settings I'd used, the different types of light I'd tried before settling on sidelighting, encouraged by Alex's spirit of experimentation. I thought about saying why I'd left the newspaper, how there'd been something I'd liked about all that good luck piled against the columns of bad news, but that seemed too private, too unrelated to the assignment. I'd clasped my hands in front of me and waited for the professor to give me a verdict.

"Now remember, everybody," he'd said, "Greer joined our class late."

From the front row, Gus had winced in sympathy.

By the time I got home, Alex had already texted to ask how it'd gone, and I'd managed a neutral reply—*Long, but fine*—focused on how I could do next week's assignment better, or at least more to the professor's liking. After all, he's the guy that's going to decide my fate.

I try to remember that now as I walk toward the north entrance of Hazleton Park, a rope of tension along my weary spine, a ball of nerves in my stomach, and my camera bag pulling tight and heavy across my body. I went to work early this morning, stayed late to make calls for Dennise, who's finally got Mr. Morgan to agree to in-home care. The traffic out to the townhouse had been snarling, a minor accident slowing everything to a crawl, so I'd barely had fifteen minutes to change and grab my camera before coming all the way back downtown, clenching my jaw in frustration the whole time at how far I still live from the things I'm trying to make more central to my life. It's been a six-ibuprofen day and it's not even 3 p.m.

I stand at the tall, wrought iron gates that stay open until dusk in the summer and make a conscious effort to relax my body, to let go of some of the tension I'm carrying. Some of it is from the day I've had, the stress

I feel over how the class is going—and I certainly don't want Alex to see that, don't want him feeling responsible for Hiltunen's hostility toward me.

But some of it, too, is from the fact that I'm here meeting Alex at all—from the way I think about him, late at night.

The way I shift and stretch in my bed, straining to get comfortable in ways that have nothing to do with my body's imperfections. When I'm with him—walking streets I know with my eyes closed, sitting on a couch where I've sat hundreds of times before—it feels like something's changed in the way time moves. Every second is that second before the runners spring off the block at the start line, or the second before the bass drops in a song you love.

He makes the whole world sit in that beat of suspended animation. And every time I'm with him, part of me is always thinking: *Please, please, please. Press Play.*

"Hey there," he says, coming from the other direction, and jeez. I didn't mean *Press Play* for right now. "Sorry if I snuck up on you. We've got to stop meeting this way."

He smiles as though he's nudging me with a small inside joke. He looks good—I mean, he *always* looks good, but today he looks better rested than he did yesterday, his cheeks less drawn. I'm a little annoyed, actually, at Alex showing up looking like he's had a full eight hours and a very productive therapy session whereas at 2 a.m. this morning I was looking to distract myself by mentally counting the bottles of nail polish Ava has on the top of our toilet tank (eight, nine if you count topcoat). This morning when I put on concealer I'm pretty sure my dark circles cackled at me.

"How was it?" I ask him, even though I know it's rude to. What he talks about with Patricia is private, and absolutely no one's business. But I'm so *tired*, and that's at least in part because of him, and this small, petty piece of me wants him to give me *something*.

He looks past the gate into the park when he answers. "It was—okay. Not fun, that's for fucking sure." When his eyes shift back, cast down slightly to meet mine, they're so bright green in the sun that they look like the great swaths of grass that'll greet us as soon as we pass through this entrance. "She gave me homework. A book I've got to read, about panic disorders, and then some—I'm supposed to write in a journal. Keep track of when I've got...you know. The noise."

I nod, not wanting to break this spell.

He lowers his head further, chin dipping almost to his chest, and breathes out a laugh that makes me feel like my clothes have disintegrated from my body.

"I've never done homework a day in my life. But I feel like if I don't do this, I'll go back there next week and she'll make me stand in the trash can or something. She's scary as hell."

We both laugh this time, and there's a new, tentative camaraderie in it. I like having a person in common who isn't Kit—its own kind of intimacy between the two of us. I mean, not *intimacy* intimacy. If my clothes hadn't already fallen off at the sound of his laugh, this would also be a moment where they'd give up the ghost.

"So," I say, eager to get us back on task, "I was thinking, there's an herb garden here, a huge one, and it's got—you know. Herbs. A lot of them. And there's always ladybugs this time of year, which are good luck."

He's still got a crooked smile, a remnant of our laugh, or maybe something new. "Only good luck, then?"

"Uh, *yeah*. Why would anyone take pictures of bad luck things?"

He shrugs. "Variety?"

Variety? What is he, crazy? I'm trying to graduate here, not tempt fate.

"Variety is overrated."

"So's luck."

"You don't believe in luck?"

He laughs again, but this one's different, a sharper edge to it. He runs a hand through his hair, making the black mass of it stick up in all directions. "Not really. My dad was a big fan."

Oh. I know a little more now about Kit and Alex's dad than I used to, know he's got a problem with gambling—a huge source of guilt for Kit after we played and won the lottery. I open my mouth even before I know what I might say to this—before I've decided whether to ask a follow-up, or to change the subject, or, hey, to say something about how his laugh has textile-destroying capabilities—but he speaks before I do.

"We can try a ladybug. Setting yourself a pretty tough challenge there, a little thing like that."

I lift my chin defiantly, but when I look at him again I see he's not saying it as a warning, or as some kind of condescension. No *Greer joined our class late* bullshit from Alex. Only a glinting look of anticipation that's as bad as the laugh for all the things it makes me feel.

"Well, come on then," I say, walking through the gates, muttering the next part to myself. "I need all the luck I can get."

* * * *

The first thing I'd done when we'd gotten to the herb garden was move to take my camera out, but Alex had paused beside me and said, "Don't worry about your equipment yet. Worry about the bug for now."

We'd walked through rows of fresh plants, small placards of identification tucked tidily into the ground at their roots—*Caraway, Angelica, Fennel, Yarrow, Dill*—and each time Alex would ask me questions: Did I like the leaves of this plant? What shape did I like best? Which would I like best for a small, rounded bug? What did the underside of this plant look like, if you took the photo from beneath it? He'd move to stand somewhere different, his long body changing the angle of the afternoon sun, and he'd gesture again—asking, wordlessly, for me to look at the light, to notice how it'd be different. In those moments I'd understood something different about the camera and all its features, even without it in my hand. The picture I'm trying to get—that's got to do with my eye, not my camera. Everything the camera can do is about showing someone else what my eye is seeing.

By the time we've settled on where we want to try for a shot—Alex warning me that we've got to be willing to move, if something changes—I'm oddly relaxed, oddly focused, oddly alert. It's still that second-in-suspense feeling, but now, with my hands on my camera, that feeling is purposeful, necessary. The time's moving slower because I need it to. Because I need to wait for this shot.

We've chosen a spot on the edges of the carefully planned garden, where there are a few long, narrow, weathered-wood boxes filled with dark soil. Set inside are conical, silver-wire towers, like bare Christmas trees, but at their bases there's abundant, early summer growth—mounding plants with leaves flat and round, little botanical dinner plates. *Nasturtium*, the placard tells us. There's only a few flowering blooms—cheery red and orange and yellow—but by the end of the summer, they'll have taken over this metal cone. They'll be people-tall and fully alive, ornamented all over with flowers.

"Here's one." I nod my chin in the direction of the plant in front of me, where a ladybug has just landed on a leaf that's tipped slightly up and to the left, so from where I'm sitting—butt in the grass, legs crisscrossed and back curved slightly to get me closer—I'm looking mostly at her back end.

"Try it," Alex says, his voice encouraging—but knowing too.

"No. I'm going to wait."

This little exchange happens almost without any movement at all, and that's how it's been for the last ten minutes or so—we've got to be still and quiet, and even though I'll pay for sitting in this position later, I have the strangest sense that I'm in my natural state out here. Still and quiet, and for once, that's the exact right thing to be.

"We're close, though." His voice is so low, almost a whisper. I don't think I imagine feeling that whisper alight on the skin of my neck. My palms suddenly feel sweaty on my camera. We *are* close—he sits beside but slightly farther back than me, so his knee is centimeters away from my hip, and whenever I speak—whenever I notice something new about what's in my line of sight—he leans silently to the left so he's more directly behind me, so he can see what I see.

The ladybug's tiny red shell lifts minutely, and I have a split-second feeling of disappointment, thinking she'll fly away, but she settles again, turning her shiny, speckled dome of a body.

"Elbows on your knees," Alex says from behind me, and I follow his directions, a shiver going up my spine. Silently, he moves—it's some kind of magic, the way he must use his hands to lift the weight of his body from the ground and reposition himself. He's behind me now, and I'm trying to stay focused, to keep my eyes on the ladybug's cheerful march around the edge of this leaf. But I'm using all my other senses to determine the shape of him back there—how his body must be bracketing mine, how he's near enough that I can smell his skin, how when he speaks again, I feel that whisper in a way so real that I know I *was* imagining it before.

"Make yourself the tripod. Your professor would tell you someone taking a shot this close would need one, because it's hard to keep your hands steady when you do work this fine."

I nod, not wanting to answer—part because I don't want any movement of mine to disturb my subject, part because I want Alex to whisper to me like this forever. "But remember what I said. Don't worry about your equipment." I suppress another shudder of shameful delight. I'm not thinking about camera equipment at *all*.

The ladybug has turned again; she's moving up the center of the leaf so that her whole body is on display for me. My fingers twitch on the sides of my camera, and I slowly—so slowly that it's almost painful—lift my hands, pressing my elbows more firmly into my knees.

"Wait," Alex says, and I stop with the camera half raised to my eye. "Tell me again what you're using. Aperture."

"F 5.6," I breathe. "Shutter speed, 1/500."

"Good."

Like she's heard us talking about her, the ladybug stills in place. Her tiny body covers the creamy white blot in the center of the leaf, where all the planty veins coalesce. I've got the camera up to my eye, my finger on the shutter release. I think I've stopped breathing.

"Go," he says, a single word that brings me to life, and for what must be only a few seconds all I hear is the click of the camera, all I see is my leaf, my little ladybug good luck charm posing for me, giving me permission, telling me that Professor Hiltunen's doubts, *my* doubts, were all wrong. Inside my chest there's a rising tide of excitement—*I'm* getting *it. Every single one of these pictures is going to be so* good. In my head I'm halfway across a stage, my hand reached out to take my diploma.

But right as I'm thinking it, something changes in the air behind me, and Alex says, "Keep going, okay? Keep shooting." All of a sudden, I feel a warm hand settle on my lower back, placed vertically—I can feel two of Alex's fingers on each side of my spine, strong and purposeful, and maybe it should feel strange, this unexpected touch, right in a place where I've spent my life collecting tension. But it doesn't feel strange at all, not really. He's become part of the tripod I've made. He's keeping me steadier.

Until he does it. Until he presses me forward.

It's a slight push, hardly a fraction of pressure. When he does it, he repeats himself: "Keep going." He's leaning me closer to the leaf, to the ladybug, and as I shoot, my cover is blown—she sees me, hears me, feels me, whichever, and all at once her candy red shell spreads wide, a blurring, black-gray movement beneath. I can't make my eyes work fast enough to see her take flight, and then the moment's gone. *She's* gone. All I can see in my field of vision is the leaf, plain and empty and maybe trembling, ever so slightly, from its runaway guest.

Alex drops his hand, and I try to remember how to breathe normally.

It the quiet I feel as though I'm coming out of a spell—the way Alex had talked to me, those gentle orders. The way he'd touched me too—a different kind of order. The way I'd *liked* it.

"I guess I got enough before she took off." My voice sounds terse, distant. It's suspended animation, again—I'm caught. Part of me wants to stand and stretch, stalk away and look down at the view screen to see if I managed to get something before we lost—before he *ruined*—the moment. But another part of me wants to lean back, see if that hand is still there—to push back into it until it gives, to let all my bones and muscles fold into whatever shape Alex's body has made behind mine.

"You want to get out of here?"

I turn my body without thinking, feel an answering twinge in my neck, and suppress a wince. I hold my camera in one hand, plant the other in the soft, slightly overlong grass, feel it tickle between my fingers as I adjust to face him. And—yeah. I could've folded right into that space. He's got both feet planted on the ground, his knees spread wide, his elbows resting atop them. He uses his right hand to hold his left wrist. I picture him unlocking that gate and letting me in.

"What about the pictures?" I ask.

"I think you got them. If you didn't, we can come back."

"Shouldn't we—" I tip the camera forward, gesture vaguely at the viewfinder. My mouth resets, and I feel the tension there. I don't want to look down yet. I don't want to see the pictures of that empty leaf.

"Better to see these on a big screen, the first time. Trust me."

He moves quickly, almost as though he's trying to keep me on the move too, keep me distracted. He separates his hands, holds one out toward mine, where I'm keeping my camera in my grip, and without thinking, I pass it to him. He stands smoothly, his once-huddled body now a long column, and somehow he's also managed to grab my bag from where I'd rested it beside us on the ground. He's tall and lean, backlit by the hazy summer sun, as relaxed as I've seen him since he came here, strong and flexible and—*free*. Like he could walk right back out of those gates and never come back.

Trust him?

When he holds out a hand to me, I don't take it.

I get up all on my own.

* * * *

After a quick stop at my car for my laptop, we walk three blocks to a sandwich shop Kit loves, a place called The Meltdown where sometimes you've got to ask for less than the regular amount of cheese or else you'll probably have a stomachache for a good twelve hours after. I choose it on purpose, so it feels like I'm doing something for Kit—showing her brother around town, nice and casual—and so it feels like I'm reestablishing a boundary between us. He seems to get it and doesn't argue with me when I insist on paying as a thank-you gesture, sending him to wait at a table while I order.

While I wait for our food, on impulse I take my phone from my back pocket and snap a picture of him—fast and thoughtless, nothing like the tripod-body, held-breath anticipation from the park. When I check my screen I see Alex, the stretch of restaurant between us, his head tipped to the side and slightly bowed as he plugs something into my computer's

USB port. He looks calm and focused, as though he's sat in that booth a hundred times. A regular work spot after a day of shooting.

I navigate to my messages, attaching the photo in a text I first intend to send only to Kit. But then I pause, adding Alex's name as a recipient too. The picture is of him, after all, and I don't want to seem like a creeper. *Ordered your brother your favorite sandwich,* I type, and press Send. I picture Kit, probably somewhere in Italy now, maybe having a big bowl of pasta and a glass of wine—and know it'll make her smile to see it.

When I carry our food over, he's pushed the camera and laptop to the side so there's still a big expanse of table for us to eat. He's got his phone in front of him, and when he looks up at me, there's an expression on his face that's new to me—somehow shy and mischievous, all at the same time.

"Saw your picture," he says, teasing. "Too grainy. Bad light in here."

"Was it okay I sent it?" I ask, feeling unsure now. Maybe Alex is looking to keep his distance from Kit right now, not let her think he's settling in here.

He shrugs. "She knows I'm still here. I spoke to her last night." His jaw tightens slightly, and I wonder what they spoke about—if he's told her about Patricia, if he's told her he'll be here for a week even after she gets back. "They're having a great time," he adds, which I'm guessing means he doesn't want to talk about it.

I nod toward the laptop. "Did you look already?" As soon as I ask, the plates in my hand feel heavy, distracting. I'm nervous, embarrassed, excited. I have to know how those pictures turned out.

"Not closely. They pass over the screen when they import." There's a twitch to his mouth that tells me *Not closely* means something different to him than it does to me. I set the sandwiches on my side of the booth, pushing them almost to the edge. Then I slide into the short expanse of bench that's left on his side, and he immediately moves to give me room.

Not much, room, though. It's a short bench, so my shoulder is against his arm, my thigh against his. Everywhere we touch, something happens to me, still. Electricity. "I need to see before I can eat," I say, trying to keep the moment casual.

He smiles at me, eyes crinkling at the corners, and here's another bosom-heaving moment for the director.

He moves his hand, taps a finger on the trackpad of the laptop, and pulls it closer. In my periphery I see bright green first, and I'm all anticipation—for a second, I watch him, see the green of his eyes take in the green of the photograph.

"Come on, now," he says, gentle and coaxing, same as back in the park, and I let my eyes slide to the screen.

It's *beautiful*, this picture. I must've started slightly off center, or maybe I stayed that way, who knows, but the nasturtium leaf takes up about three-quarters of the image, dark brown soil and the edge of the garden box showing along the bottom of the screen and along the left side. It's nice, how that is—the settings I used have blurred them out, so they're mostly a rich color contrast to the sharp, clear edge of the leaf—so green that it both does and doesn't look like it comes from nature. It's like—the ur-leaf. The Platonic ideal of leaf.

And right there in the center is my ladybug.

Candy-apple red, so in focus you can see every one of her spots—three on each side, and one in the middle, up where the red shell gives way to the jet-black head of her. I see details on her body I've never seen before on an insect—the way her shell curves up minutely, right at the very edges, a little aerodynamic rim, the way each spot is slightly different, like a tiny, imprecise paintbrush dolloped on her back before sending her on her way.

"Oh," I say. Or—maybe I heaving-bosom it, whatever. Alex's finger taps the keyboard, and the next picture is just as good, nearly identical to the first. "I told you I was a good student," I add, and Alex's quiet laugh, released right beside me, feels like the softest caress over my bare skin.

He starts to tap more quickly through, and for the next ten or so photos some of the initial awed pleasure wears off. Aside from a shift in positioning, the pictures are almost identical, and I think my biggest problem will be choosing one to show for my assignment. I'm already leaning toward the first one, like I imprinted on it as soon as it came across the screen.

I can see in the photographs the very second Alex had touched me— the first image is slightly less focused, the leaf grainy and unremarkable looking, the ladybug's shell blurred on one side as it lifts, a sliver of gray peeking from underneath it, wrecking the look of that cheerful, shiny dome. She looks…disturbed, frantic, spooked.

Before he can click again, I lean back from where I'd curved my body toward the screen.

"Wait." He taps again, and again. I'm not watching closely; I've blurred my own eyes a little, wanting to remember that first picture instead. Alex has adjusted his own body at some point—the arm not operating the computer rests along the back of the booth, so once again I'm in the bracket of his body. Anyone would think we're together. *Together* together. "Here," he says, and takes his hand away from the laptop, dropping it beneath the table to rest against his thigh.

And—*this* picture.

She's lifted off, barely, casting a tiny shadow on the leaf beneath her; her shell is spread wide, covering most of that jet-black head. It looks gorgeous that way, spread apart—somehow seeing it in two pieces makes it look harder, sturdier, more like armor than decoration. And beneath are her big, gray-black wings, wings I knew existed but had never even thought of before—thin as tissue paper, veined like the leaf beneath her, wholly transparent in their thinnest spots. And in the middle, her wide, brown-black body, red flanks along either side, ridges stacked vertically. The sturdiest spine you've ever seen on something so tiny.

"That's the one," I say on a gasp. "That's the one, right?" Before I think of it, before I remember how close he is, I turn to face him, to see whether he's as excited about it as I am, but he's not looking at the screen.

He's looking at me.

The light from the laptop screen casts his stubbled jawline in bright, visual echoes of my picture—a little green here, a little red there, and I'd like to trace those colors, see how they feel with the textures of Alex underneath. His eyes are on me—he's cocked his head ever so slightly in a way I recognize from the park, but this time his expression is hooded, less acute and less focused, as he takes me in. When those eyes settle on my mouth, I hear it again, I *feel* it again: *Press Play*. If it isn't my bosom heaving, it's definitely something else. I press my knees together, feel the pulse of desire there, and Alex shifts, his thigh moving so I feel the long, ropy give of his muscle underneath one of my kneecaps, and his blink is slow, concentrated, like in that split second of registering my body against his, he's closing out the world and making a picture of his own, the same one I'm making. The same one where I slide closer, where I give him the same mouth he's made a study of—

Ping.

I jerk back at the sound of a text message, in stereo, both of our phones lighting up on the table surface. In that second, all the suspended reality is gone—it's the same restaurant it always is, the smell of cheese and fried bread, the indistinct folk-rock playing tinnily from the speakers, the white cast from the pendant lights hanging over every table.

From where I sit I can see the name at the top of the message.

Alex clears his throat. "It's my sister." He moves his arm from where it'd been behind me, and both of us lean forward to look at our screens. I read the message at the same time I feel Alex's body turn tense beside me, his breath catching and then quickening. It's not quite like that night in the alley—but it's not all that different either.

Funny, Kit has written. *He looks like he belongs there.*

Chapter 8

Alex

It's not the first time my sister has interrupted a private moment.

The summer I turned fifteen, I had a job doing grunt work for an electrician who was rewiring a local grocery chain's bakery headquarters, the place where they made doughy, pre-sliced bread in bulk. It was a good gig—I got paid under the table and could take damaged goods home with me, loaves that didn't get sliced right or that had too-dark spots on the crust. Plus there was a sixteen-year-old line worker named Tara who flirted with me on lunch break, where she'd eat something her mother had packed for her and I'd eat a Hostess fruit pie from the break room vending machine. Then she'd smoke a cigarette and I'd try to work up the courage to kiss her.

It went on like that for two weeks before Tara found out my address from my boss and showed up at 10 p.m. on a Saturday night. The initial humiliation had been pretty bad, since at that particular time we'd been living in a basement apartment with one bedroom that Kit and I shared, my dad taking the couch on the rare nights he was home. But at least Kit had already gone to bed, so I'd let Tara in, for once letting my adolescent brain—or dick, I guess—do the decision-making. Within ten minutes we were making out on the couch, Tara—smelling faintly of cheap beer in addition to the cigarettes—halfway in my lap while I shoved a hand up her shirt, and I didn't even hear the bedroom door open. I didn't hear anything until my sister said, "Alex?" in a small, confused voice. I'd practically dumped Tara on the shoved-together milk crates we used for a coffee table.

It wasn't just that I'd been setting a terrible example, or that I was opening the door to conversations with Kit I wasn't ready to have, conversations that I eventually stumbled through with help from a set of parenting books in the public library. It was that in the moments following, when Tara was smoothing down her clothes and grabbing her cheap, quilted pleather bag with a gold chain shoulder strap, Kit had looked up at her with hopeful excitement. "I like your purse," she'd said, and in that single sentence I'd heard a whole world of longing from my sister. Starved as she was of women in her life, barely able to make friends for all the times we had to move, Tara had looked to her like a store full of knowledge I could never offer.

That might've been all right had I thought there'd be any chance of our sticking around. Sure, Tara smoked like a chimney and snuck beer from her dad's garage refrigerator, but she was kind and she had a good sense of humor, and she probably could've talked to Kit about all sorts of things that made me feel clumsy and unsure. But there wasn't any chance of that; there never was, and it'd do Kit no good to get attached to any girl I'd bring around.

After that, I'd taken my fumbling efforts elsewhere.

Now, I push myself up a steep, brick-paved hill that's about a half mile from Kit's place, lungs and quads burning, sweat dripping from the edges of my hair and down the center of my back. Usually this'd be the time I'd feel the adrenaline of being almost through it—I've been out here for a good hour, and running's always been a head clearer for me, especially after a long day of shooting. On a bad day, when it feels like all I've seen and shot is the garbage of human life, poverty and fear and despair, a hard run can make me feel like I'm shaking images out of my brain, one step at a time.

I haven't been able to shake Greer, though. Haven't been able to shake those last few minutes we spent together before I'd bolted.

Maybe I hadn't dumped her on a set of milk crates, but what I had done wasn't much better. I'd leaned back from her as if our phones had electrocuted me, shoved a hand in my pocket for a stick of gum that did nothing to stop my churning gut, and asked if she'd mind taking our food to go. The flush of embarrassment that bloomed on her face made me feel about as ashamed as I've ever felt in my whole fucking life. Worse than the basement apartment, that's for sure.

A grunt of fatigue or frustration escapes me as I reach the top of the hill, the row houses on this street bigger, more elaborate than the ones on Kit's, all of them redone and polished to a high shine, whereas the house three doors down from my sister's has a sheet of plywood covering one of the upper windows. Up ahead there's a car coming toward me, slowing as it gets closer, the driver rolling down his window when I'm about to cross the plane of his bumper.

"Excuse me, sir," he calls, and I let out another grunt when I slow down. My legs are so tired that starting up again will feel like hell.

From my spot along the curb, I swipe my sweat-soaked hair from my face and set my hands low on my hips, panting out the worst of that hill. I hope this guy doesn't want to have a conversation, because my lung capacity is fucked. I lift my chin in his direction, a nod of acknowledgment.

"Sorry to interrupt you. But my GPS seems to have stopped working, and these one-way streets are giving me a heck of a time. Can you tell me where to find Bronwen Avenue?"

It's right on the tip of my tongue to say what I'm thinking: *I don't live here.* But even I don't need Patricia to tell me what the fuck that's all about, same as I didn't need Patricia to tell me why I've been finding reasons to get out of Kit's house since I'd gotten back there Friday evening, a greasy bag of food in my hand and her text message flashing in my brain like a traffic sign.

He looks like he belongs there.

I take as deep a breath as my tight chest will allow. "Two streets over." My voice sounds like it's being operated by a rusty old crank in my back. "Stop sign at the bottom of the hill. Take a right."

He looks ahead, nods, and waves his thanks before driving away, and I resist the urge to call out after him: *I only know because I've been running these streets for days!*

I watch until he makes a right at the sign, then turn my back and walk the rest of the way to Kit's, taking in the sounds of a Sunday afternoon in this neighborhood—kids on bikes, someone mowing a small patch of grass in their postage stamp front yard, the faint whir of traffic on the main road Kit walks to get to work, the same road I walked to meet Greer.

Another image of her face comes into my mind—this time, the way she'd looked at the picture she'd taken—her eyes wide and excited, her lips parted and flushed a darker pink than usual. When she'd turned to me, everything around me had gone soft focus, my eye in macro mode. I'd thought, with startling, sharp clarity: *I could look at this face forever.*

On the porch I fumble with the key I've tied in the waistband drawstring of my shorts, wonder whether I ought to try calling or texting her again. But she's already got such a great picture for class next week—that ladybug had been a stunner—so there's no real point for another of our lessons yet. And the apology I'd sent her—short but sincere—she'd brushed off as though nothing had happened. *No reason to apologize at all. Busy this weekend, but will be in touch soon.*

I should be glad about it. I should be thinking that this is the one time my fucked-up brain has done me a favor by keeping me from making what would have to be massive, reckless mistake. Even setting aside that she's my sister's best friend, that Kit'd have us married off in her mind and being her next-door neighbors if we so much as kissed—what about the fact that she affects me like an anchor, making me feel pleasantly, rockingly tethered in this place that sometimes feels like a vast, unpredictable sea? What about the fact that I think about her when I'm supposed to be writing in my goddamned journal for my goddamned therapy; what about the fact that I can't sit on the fucking couch without thinking of her sweet, soft weight beside me?

I should be glad about it, but I'm not.

So maybe that's why I nearly trip over the threshold when I open the door and hear my phone ringing, maybe that's why I make for the dining room table with all the speed I thought I'd used up on my run. I pick it up without even looking at the screen; I'm too afraid of how many rings I've already missed.

"Aleksandr!"

Fuck. I may have only met him once, but I recognize his ingratiating tone immediately. "Peter," I say, my voice as bland as his is enthusiastic. "Hello."

"Glad I caught you." As though he's somehow familiar with my schedule, as though we're jokey buddies who do quick calls like this every day. "Thanks for sending over the picture for the auction."

"Not a problem." I wipe my forehead with the bottom of my T-shirt, eager to hang up. Maybe if I call Greer tonight, maybe if there's more of that cooking show on she'd want to come over....

"I was calling about the class I mentioned. Documentary photography?"

I drag my mind back to the conversation, since I know that it's as much about Greer as whatever I'm thinking about Ina Garten. Judging by the three local interview requests I've already agreed to via email, it's clear Hiltunen's milking this connection for all it's worth, knowing what he's holding over Greer. "Yes. The guest lecture?"

"Is tomorrow evening too soon? It's short notice, but I had an open—"

"It's fine. I can do tomorrow."

I'm only half listening while he gives me the details and offers suggestions about what to discuss, but basically it sounds like he wants an hour of me talking about how I got started, which'll be easy enough though probably not all that helpful for a bunch of kids in actual college, seeing as how I barely graduated from high school. "It'll take me a couple of days to get the honorarium together—"

"No need. If you get one, you can donate it to your department. I'll sign whatever." *But you better give Greer what she needs.*

"That's great, very generous. How about dinner after, or—"

"Probably can't swing that." I'm about to tell him I've got to run when an idea scratches at the back of my mind. I clear my throat. "Listen, is this a public lecture? Or only for your class?"

Hiltunen pauses. "Well, if you don't mind, it'd be great if I could send out an email to the department, or even—"

"I don't mind," I say quickly. I don't mind at all who the fuck is there, so long as one particular person is. In my head, I'm already typing out an invitation to her.

Already telling myself—despite all precedent to the contrary—that I won't screw it up with her again.

* * * *

Of course she comes.

She sits in the back of the lecture hall, tucked into a small architectural alcove most of the other guests avoid. It's a bigger crowd than I'd have expected on such short notice, maybe a hundred guests, and while most of them have the slouchy, dewy confidence of new adulthood, there's also a good deal of people who are either faculty or staff or members of the community. The more people file in, the more I feel the weight of responsibility to get this right. It's not only that I want to keep Hiltunen happy for Greer's sake; it's that I want to do right by Kit, who's an everyday part of this community.

I concentrate on my breathing while the professor introduces me, and wonder—from some detached part of myself—how I'm managing to stay regular nervous, public speaking nervous, instead of panic attack nervous. The book Patricia gave me talked about this, about the unpredictability of panic, about how you've got to celebrate the wins but also be mindful of your behavioral therapy, sticking with your practice even when it seems like you're doing fine. So when I stand from my seat to face the room, I keep that detached part of myself focused on my breathing.

And I look at Greer too.

It's easy, once I get going—I've got slides behind me, arranged chronologically, an exercise not all that different from what Jae's paperwork on this book idea had asked of me. The first few are pictures I took when I was in high school, mostly straggly trees and battered street signs, a few distant shots of street corners where the people are hunched, indistinguishable forms. I talk about how I learned to trust my eye this way, to manipulate the camera so it'd communicate that trust to the viewer. When I shift to the first photos I sold to a paper—stringer work I did for the *Plain Dealer* up in Cleveland—I mostly talk about all the mistakes I made. This problem with composition, that problem with shadow. This time the picture felt intrusive, cruel, that time it felt cautious, bland. Everything from later—the freelancing work that made me a known quantity as a photojournalist—has most of my hallmarks. The focus on people, the trend toward saturated hues, my preference for the sun at a low angle, the way I tend toward chaos in background context—trash in the street, bombed-out buildings, angry mobs at the corner of a frame.

It's comfortable and exposing, all at the same time. It's work, and it's always been easy for me to talk about work. But whenever I catch Greer's eye, I can tell even from a distance she's seeing things in those pictures no one else is.

The Q & A is less about the pictures than it is about me: how I learned and how I got started so young, how I was able to shoot so much in such a short period of time. Mostly I give canned answers that avoid the realities of my younger years. I say vague things about trial and error, about photography being like a calling, that it never felt like I was shooting all that much, that it's a way of life. When it's time for the final question, a student in the second row raises his hand tentatively, looking hopefully toward Hiltunen, who's been making the calls on who speaks up. This time, I take over, nodding toward him in invitation.

"This may not be a good question," he says, shifting his shoulders nervously. "But, um. Don't you ever feel bad? I guess what I mean is— you're in the middle of all this"—he waves a hand toward the screen, but keeps his eyes on me—"this madness. Terrible stuff. Doesn't it feel bad that you're just…um…*watching*? Don't you ever want to put down your camera and, I don't know. *Help*?"

You can feel the change in the room, various adjustments the audience makes for the change in tone. Most people look down—the floor, the desk, their phone, whatever's convenient. A few people seem annoyed, eyes rolling or arms crossing, shaking heads that suggest they don't think the kid gets it. Some sit straighter in their chairs, nervously attentive, probably glad he's had the courage to ask. Hiltunen awkwardly chuckles; from the corner of my eye I see him shift on his feet, as though he's considering shutting this down, but I give a small shake of my head and let my eyes drift to the back of the room briefly.

She's too far away for me to see much about her expression, but she's leaned forward, her body stretching from that alcove, alert in her posture. I can tell the answer matters to her as much as it matters to the kid.

I tuck my hands in my pockets, breathe through my nose. It doesn't bother me he's asked, and it doesn't bother me to answer, but it feels important, heavy, something I want to say exactly right. For the first time I think fleetingly about why it might be nice, someday, to write it all down—to have enough time to really think this part through before communicating it to an audience. But I don't have that time right now, so I do my best with a short pause, a deep breath before I speak.

"I do want that, sometimes. It'd be a lie to say I never have that instinct. But if you do this job, what you've got to remember is that you're one of the few people in the world who can—" I pause again, thinking it over. "I guess who can be a witness to the immediacy of something with your camera. You've got a responsibility to it, to the people involved in it. You've got a responsibility to be the eyes for everyone in the world who needs to be paying more attention. That's the thing you learn, doing this job. You learn—I guess you learn that watching *is* helping."

I think the kid nods, says a word of thanks. I don't take it in, not fully, because once again my eyes are drifting to Greer, to where she's sat back in the alcove again, hidden herself from me further. When Hiltunen invites a round of applause, I give the barest recognition of it; I shake his hand and nod, take a gift bag from him that he proudly announces has a university T-shirt in it. It's harder to see Greer now, members of the audience standing and shuffling out, or gathering in small groups to chat. In front of me there're a few guests who've come up to express praise or thanks, to ask additional questions, a few students who introduce themselves as participants in the showcase I'll be reviewing photographs for. I do my best to pay attention, to shake hands and make eye contact, to tell them I appreciate them coming.

But when I see that Greer's stood to leave, her hand clutched around the strap of the bag crossing her body, I excuse myself hastily. I take those lecture hall steps like I'm a desperate, crushing college kid looking to carry the popular girl's books. Actually I'm pretty sure that's not a real thing in college, but obviously I wouldn't know.

"Hi." I am embarrassingly short of breath. Greer looks up at me, then around at the people still in the room, all of whom I have pretty much forgotten exist. I have the oddest, most unexpected urge—to lean down and give her a brief, closed-mouth kiss, the kind of everyday welcome that'd tell everyone in this room exactly who I came here for. "You're leaving?" "I wasn't sure if you had something after." With her free hand, she makes a small gesture toward the stragglers, as though she thinks I've got some kind of fan club meeting after this. "I don't. I'm grateful you came. It helped, having you here." That tiny line, right between her eyebrows. It slays me. "I was nervous." Her lips tip up at the corners. "You didn't seem like it. You were really good." "Yeah?" "Oh, yeah." She leans forward slightly so I catch a whisper of lavender again. "The girl in front of me put a picture of you on her Instagram. Probably you're trending. Hashtag hot photographer." She blinks. "I—did not mean to say that out loud."

There it is again, that tiny glimpse of what I see in Greer underneath all her reserve. Secret, precious liveliness—sly humor and clear, clever understanding, the sense that she's got some incisive comment on every single thing she's quietly observed throughout her day.

She's probably not going to let me carry her books, but I'm too desperate not to try for *something*, anything that'd keep her close to me.

"How about I walk you to your car?" I ask, for all the world like the desperate, crushing kid I never had the chance to be.

* * * *

We're quiet as we leave the building, as we cross the threshold from the campus to the city that surrounds it. I'm grateful for the few minutes of silence after hearing my own voice for the last hour. When I walked these streets a week ago, coming to meet Greer, the storefronts I'd passed—a tattoo parlor, a few sandwich shops, a used bookstore, a café where through the window, almost everyone had been staring at a computer—had looked blandly, distantly familiar to me from the times I'd come to visit Kit here, always with the chip on my shoulder that I'm only recently starting to acknowledge fully. Now, the streets look lively, interesting, streetlamps twinkling on in the falling twilight, sidewalks busy with people.

"I took some more pictures this weekend," Greer says.

"You did?" I've said it as though I'm surprised, but I'm not, not really. Greer's got a good eye; that'd been clear even before I saw her hold a camera, but once she did I knew she'd do just fine in her course, with or without me. Still, there's an unfamiliar twinge at my breastbone, a feeling I've missed something important.

"Nothing major. But the professor already has future assignments posted on the course website, so I was experimenting."

"What're the assignments?" I'm genuinely curious, and not only because I don't want her doing them all without me.

She makes that *hmm* noise again, the one I like so much, before speaking again. "Black and white. People—a portrait and a crowd shot. I mostly took pictures of my sister, for the portrait assignment. She's—let's say she's camera ready." The smile she aims at the ground is sweet, indulgent. "She's an actress, like my mom."

"She's the one you live with?"

She tucks her bottom lip into her mouth for a fleeting second before she answers. "Not for much longer. I'll move into the city when I graduate."

"How come you didn't—" I break off, cautious now. What I was about to ask, it's probably too personal.

"How come I didn't what?" I've kept my eyes ahead, on the stretch of street in front of us, but I can feel that she's turned her head toward me.

"How come you didn't move here after you won the lottery? With— you know. You didn't want to use some of your money for that, be closer to school?"

I look over to see her open her mouth and close it again, tilt her head slightly, considering. She's arranging something in that head of hers, some version of this that isn't the whole truth. "Well. I have a big family, as you know, and—it was important to me, when I won, to share it with them. I paid off some things for them. So I need to wait until I graduate. Until my job starts."

I still think there's more to the story, but this alone—this is a lot. Kit had wanted the same, to split the money with me. A payback of sorts, she'd said, for my raising her. I'd had such a terrible reaction to it—first, to the implication that she owed me anything for doing the most important thing I've ever done in my life, and second, to the suggestion she'd made that I settle down, stay in one place.

Greer and her family, I'll bet they don't have the same kind of fucked-up baggage Kit and I do. It nags at me somewhere unpleasant, that Greer doesn't seem to have kept enough for herself, but I don't suppose I understand what it's like for money to be something unproblematic, unweighted by addictions and responsibilities and resentments between family members. Maybe it was perfectly natural to her, what she'd done.

"I like what you said," Greer says, interrupting my thoughts. "About watching. *Watching* is *helping.* I've never thought of it that way."

I let out a breath, my shoulders loosening from a tightness I didn't know I was holding, I guess at what she'd thought of my answer. At whether she thought there was something to what that kid had asked me—that maybe I *should* feel bad about what I do for a living.

We turn a corner, down another side street, and I've got to imagine we're close to her car, a fact that fills me with unaccountable dread. Now that the lecture's over, I feel a strange, pulsing weightlessness, not unlike the feeling I get when I've finished a job where everything's gone well. I want to work off that feeling with Greer, and while my ideas about that are mostly of the gutter variety, I'd also be content to walk these streets with her beside me, to get a bite to eat, to talk about her project. Hell, to *loaf around* some more.

Up ahead there's a small group of students gathered, a few of them kneeling on the ground around something I can't see. At the exact same time, Greer and I look at each other with what I suspect are twin looks of concern on our faces, and without saying anything we both pick up the pace, Greer's skirt fluttering at her sides and grazing against my hand.

When we get closer, a peal of laughter splits the air, girlish and uninhibited, and I breathe in relief. We're close enough now to see floodlights on the sidewalk, tangles of extension cords behind them, tilted up to illuminate the brick wall of a building, vast and brutally plain, no windows at all. The students who crouch are gathered around a set of baskets—laundry hampers, I'd guess—some wicker, some plastic, all filled to the brim with...

Water balloons?

"What's this?" I ask, breaking stride to pause at the same time Greer does. There's not much that seems secretive about what this group is doing out here in the encroaching dark; the lights are a dead giveaway, but so are their bold laughs, their called instructions to another set of students who linger closer to the wall, spreading tarps along the sidewalk just beneath it. Whatever this is, it's got to be city sponsored, or at least city sanctioned.

"I'm not sure." Greer looks toward one of the students, who's tipped a plastic bottle into a deflated balloon and is filling it slowly, a bright smile on her face, three tiny hoop earrings piercing her right eyebrow, long braids on either side of her head, reaching almost to the ground. She's got a smudge of bright yellow paint across her right cheekbone.

"You have your camera?" I ask Greer, without thinking.

"In my car." She points up ahead, where her silver crossover is about a half block away. She takes a step forward, and I immediately, instinctively, move to follow. "Excuse me." Her cheeks flush immediately at the way she's said it—a little overloud, maybe. The streak of yellow paint has nothing on Greer's flush. I feel like a magnet's drawing me to her car to get that fucking camera.

The girl with the braids looks up, and Greer speaks again, more quietly this time. "I was just wondering what y'all are doing?"

I must make a small noise, part surprise, part delight, and when Greer looks over her shoulder at me, I smile at her and mouth *y'all?* It's the first time I've ever heard a little of the South in her accent, the native lilt I sometimes hear in Barden, and it sends a shot of heat right through me. She gives me a small shrug in return.

Another student from the group stands, brushes his hands across the sides of his jeans, and sticks one out to Greer. "Hey, I'm Tarek," he says, his eyes on her bright and interested. I'd be jealous, but I fucking get it. Who wouldn't look interested, that's the thing. He uses his other hand to gesture down to the girl in the braids. "This is Britt."

"This is our senior project," Britt says, staying crouched on her haunches while she ties off the balloon she'd been filling. "Guerrilla art, except of course we had to get ten thousand kinds of permission first."

"So it's not really guerrilla," Tarek says. "But it's still cool."

"You're going to—" Greer says, looking down toward the baskets, then toward the tarps spreading ever wider over by the wall. "Paint balloon it?"

"Yep," says Britt. "That's the backdrop. Tarek and I will add more later. But like, this is perfect! Because the whole thing is to have a bunch of people participate? You guys can go in on this! We don't have as big a crowd as we wanted because we weren't allowed to do it during regular business hours. And like, we don't want idiot people who just want to come by and draw a dick and balls, you know?"

"Uh," Greer says. "I—would not draw that. Those."

I bite my tongue to keep from laughing.

"Great!" Tarek says. His eyes slide toward me, maybe noticing me here for the first time. "We're going to start in a few minutes, so hang out if you and your..."—he breaks off, a tiny pause—"friend want to join us."

"Sure," Greer says, watching him walk toward the tarps, her hand squeezing and releasing that strap on her bag.

I clear my throat, feeling awkward. Should've offered to carry her books, I guess. "I could go get the camera, if you want. You probably need to talk to him about permission to photograph." Tarek looks like the kind of guy who wouldn't have a panic attack when he's a hair's breadth from kissing her. He looks young, light, easy, free.

For long seconds, she's staring ahead—after Tarek, at the wall, I'm not sure which, though I know what my preference is. Then she turns and looks up at me, and I have a memory of her outside the tent last weekend. I like Greer in this light, twilight. I like what it does to her skin, like the light curl that twists the short hair by her ears and along the nape of her neck. I like that she seems different at this time of day—looser, closer to the surface.

I shove my hands in my pockets, wait for her to tell me what to do next. Get the camera, get on home to Kit's, get bent.

"I don't want to photograph it," she says, finally. She smiles. Close-to-the-surface Greer. "I don't want to watch it. I want to *do* it."

Chapter 9

Greer

I don't know what's gotten into me.

I'd come to tonight's lecture determined to maintain the distance from Alex I've committed to in the days since our—our *moment* at The Meltdown. Our *Press Play* moment, the one that had almost made me forget the Greer I need to be for the next month—focused, steadfast, serious.

When I'd left Alex on Friday, skin still flushed and tight, lips still sparking in anticipation, I'd driven straight home and marched right past Doug and Ava up to my bedroom, where Kenneth was lying like a gray loaf of bread in the center of my comforter, slitting his eyes open in welcome or in knowing censure. From the same wooden chair that had been in my childhood bedroom, I'd stared down at the surface of my desk, looking to set my eyes on things that would remind me of what's important. My degree application, currently declined, waiting for the exception I need from Hiltunen. My contract to Holy Cross, signed in Dennise's looping script.

My passports to freedom.

What I need, I'd told myself, is to graduate and do well at my job. To stop daydreaming, afternoon dreaming, early-evening dreaming, all-night dreaming about a man who's here to help himself as much as he's here to help me. A man who'll be gone even before I hold that diploma in my hand. A man who might, given the look on his face when we'd parted, already be gone.

For the rest of the weekend, I'd stayed focused. Each time I'd held my camera, I'd thought of Alex, but I'd worked hard to push those thoughts away. I'd read the boring manual about my camera online; I'd studied all of Hiltunen's future assignments. In between, I'd worked on minor tasks related to my thesis, caught up on emails, finished patient notes from work on Friday. I'd had dinner at my parents' house, had gone to brunch with Zoe and Aiden, had taken a long walk through the city streets, quietly pocketing brochures for apartments for rent.

I was sticking with the plan.

Of course, for as long as he's in town, Alex is part of the plan—so when he'd texted to let me know about tonight's lecture, there'd been no doubt that I'd attend. All morning at work I'd thought about it, had told myself that nothing about what had happened Friday had to change the plan. We're friends; he's my best friend's brother. He's a professional who's doing me a massive favor.

But then.

Seeing Alex up there tonight, twelve-foot-tall projections of his genius behind him, his manner easy and graceful, his answers thoughtful and funny and sometimes sad, his sea-glass eyes occasionally seeking mine—something had shifted inside of me. That Alex up there, that was a real and true Alex. But it wasn't the whole Alex, the Alex I'd been getting to know over the last week—the one who gets heroic over a condescending professor, the one who refolds his sister's towels, the one who says, *We can try a ladybug.*

That Alex, it seemed, was only for me, and I had the strangest sensation—that there's a Greer who's only for him.

So I'm still feeling it, that suspended animation. I'm still thinking it, *Press Play.* But this time, I'm not silently encouraging *him.* I'm encouraging myself, first for the long walk out of that lecture hall, and again when we'd come across this crazy, unexpected thing—guerrilla art. It feels as sure as Alex's hand on my back, the one pushing me forward while I took my shots in the park.

I don't want to watch it. I want to do it.

At first he hangs back while I help fill balloons, my hands shaky with nerves and anticipation, and it's almost as if he's standing watch over me, over the whole situation. His hands stay in his pockets, his jaw set, but when I pick up a balloon in my hand, stepping back to the strip of colorful tape Britt and Tarek have placed along the sidewalk—a starting line for the chaos—Alex moves too, grabbing his own balloon and fixing me with the same sheepish smile he'd given me when he'd asked to walk me to my car. The night is warm, and more than a few of these students have come bearing the heavy smell of marijuana. One of them has set his iPhone on top of a newspaper box and he's playing Rage Against the Machine like we're really out here doing something subversive. It is ridiculous and hilarious, and the tiny space between Alex and me is filled with silent, knowing laughter.

Britt stands in front of the wall, her arms spread wide as she tells us to do our best to cover the whole surface, to work as quickly as we can. And when Tarek cups his hands over his mouth to tell us to have fun, Britt whoops loudly and ducks out of the way of at least fifteen airborne paint balloons.

And it's so, *so* fun. It's sloppy and loud and maybe a little pointless given how one splash of color is so quickly covered by the next. We jostle around the hampers for more balloons; we pay no attention to the small crowd of onlookers we've attracted; we make the kind of fast, entirely impermanent friendship that'll only last as long as we stand here cheering each other on.

It must only be a matter of minutes that Alex and I stand beside each other, our increasingly paint-splattered fingers tossing the small, heavy balloons against the wall, laughing as we watch them explode unevenly in great, messy bursts of color. Alex throws high, all his balloons hitting the upper quadrant of the wall, and everyone hoots and hollers every time he lands one. Britt claps him on the back and leaves a red handprint, which Alex either doesn't notice or doesn't care about. I discover quickly that my splatters are bigger, more prominent, when I aim toward the middle of the wall, and when I hit two in a row almost exactly beside each other, like a set of big, bright, watchful eyes—one lime green, one purple—I clap in delight and feel the paint on my hands make a fine spray onto my face.

I've never felt so alive.

I turn toward Alex, catch him right at the moment one of his balloons hits. He looks how I feel, young and surprised by delight, his eyes widening and shining up at the mess we've all made together. He lifts his forearm, swipes it across his brow, but he's not gotten off so easy either, and now he wears a smudge of bright yellow paint at his temple. It tangles with his jet-black hair, an abstract, zooming bumblebee on his skin, and I laugh, a louder sound than I'm used to, at least out here in the open air.

He looks over at me then, catches me watching and laughing—*watching is helping*—and for a few seconds we stand like that, smiling at each other as though we're in on some kind of big, happy secret together. And the thing is—we are. This Alex—boyish and inexperienced, easily entertained—this Alex is my secret. And this Greer—loud and impulsive, quick to laugh—I'm his.

"Your freckles," he says, and before he's even finished, before he's made that last sibilant sound, I've pushed onto my tiptoes, I've leaned forward. I've pressed my mouth right against his.

* * * *

It's sudden enough that it's a little wobbly, off center, and his hands rise to catch me right underneath my elbows. For a split second I think—*Oh God, he's going to push me away*—but no.

No.

Instead he's steadying me, holding me still so he can tilt his head, so he can shape his mouth to mine, so he can make this kiss what I meant it to be—hungry and close and paint-splattered-together—and before I know it he's moved the hands cupping my elbows up to my triceps, gathering me to him. It's nothing at all for me to lean in, to press my whole body against his, to tip my head back, to feel his arms wrap around me and hold me close, hold me up so that my heels lift from the ground again while we kiss. I know there's people and light and color and sound around us; I know there's still that faint smell of marijuana and the angry sound of Rage Against the Machine. But I don't see, hear, smell, touch, taste anything other than Alex. The man I guess I've been waiting to kiss for two whole years.

It's him who pulls away first, and if there's a comfort in that, it's the sound he makes, a protesting grunt that I'm grateful to hear before the other noise intrudes—a loud, deep voice calling out, "That's enough now, time's up!"

I turn my head to see a cop by the floodlight closest to the wall, Britt and Tarek already headed his way to make a protest, and I hope they work it out, I really do—but I also hope I'm not here to see it. I hope I'm somewhere in the dark with Alex, finishing what we've started.

"Let's go," he says, backing away only enough to catch up my hand in his, dipping in one smooth move to pick up my bag from the ground, towing me behind him as soon as he's got it, and this is perfect too—the way his strides eat up the ground, not cautious or tentative about whether I can keep up, not rough but not gentle either, where he grips my hand.

We turn a corner into darkness, the sounds of the group muted now, and I feel a small shiver of fear tracing up my spine at what this will trigger. It's different, this space, narrower than the one behind Betty's, narrow enough not to be a storage spot for garbage cans or HVAC units or some old mattress a tenant didn't know what to do with. It's not *clean*, strictly speaking, but it's free of cigarette butts and beer cans. There's some gentle light, a beam shining from a streetlamp on the sidewalk that led us here.

"Of course it's an alley," Alex says, his voice rough and impatient. When he turns back toward me, his hair fallen over his furrowed brow, I think it's to retreat and quit this whole thing. But instead he guides me back toward the wall, looking down at me with heat in his eyes, keeping a foot of space between us instead of pressing up against me, which is what I really want right now. "This okay?"

Okay? Let's get married in this alley, who cares. "I mean, it's not an ideal location, but—"

"No," he says, laughing softly. "This. You there. Me here."

"Closer would be better."

He doesn't kiss me again, not right away—he steps into me, placing his hands at my waist, his lowered head beside mine, so that his hair tickles my cheek and forehead, his breath soft beside my ear. "Greer," he says quietly against the shell of it, and it sounds like a surrender, as though he's sinking his whole self into my name, and I close my eyes, let that sound shudder through every part of me. He pulls his head back, kisses me softly on the lips, and before I'm even recovered from that first time, he says it again. "Greer. Do you want to open your eyes?"

I shake my head, firmly, my temple pressing against the sharp line of his jaw, his coarse stubble prickling deliciously against my skin. "No," I whisper back, and I can feel his eyes trace over my face as sure as if it were his fingertips. When he moves again, it's to put his lips softly against first one of my closed eyes, then the other.

"No?" He moves his lips to my forehead, a touch that should be gentle, comforting, innocent—but when the tip of his tongue touches right at the arch of my eyebrow, my hips roll of their own accord, and he presses his own into me briefly, too briefly, before drawing back again.

"I just want to—" I pause, take a shuddering breath at the way one of his hands has drifted higher, stroking right at my rib cage. "Feel this. Feel you."

He nods and runs his lips over my temple, down to my cheekbone, and then back over, this time to the lobe of my ear, which he nips once with the edge of his teeth, and I guess I didn't realize that that's where my entire central nervous system was located, because oh my *God.* "Keep them closed, then. Whenever you want, tell me to stop."

"Okay." But I know already I won't be telling him to stop.

He follows the line of my jaw, learning it with his lips, tortuously slow, dragging the full curve of his lower lip up the slope of my chin, and then his mouth is tangling with mine again, deeper this time—a kiss that makes my head tip back against the brick from pleasure as much as from the pressure of his lips, his desire in every rolling, perfect thrust of his tongue, showing me the way he'd move against me, inside of me, if it weren't for these clothes and this semipublic place and the bare, hard surfaces against my back and everything else that's probably going to stop him. His sister, his staying, his—

"Greer," he says again, pulling away from my mouth, as though he heard the drip of cold water thoughts. "Tell me."

"I don't want you to stop." My eyes are still closed, my hands moving up and over the soft fabric of his shirt. The muscles of his shoulders bunch, lean and striated and perfect. The skin on his neck is warm, and I let my palms rest there, linking my fingers at the back and pulling his mouth to mine again. When I swipe my tongue against his lip, he makes a noise, a low grunt coming from his chest, and I press mine against his, trying to feel that sound as we kiss and kiss, and there's no more cold water thoughts after that.

I don't know how long it is before his knees dip slightly, and my breath hitches with anticipation, expectation—maybe he'll press me against this wall with that hardness between his legs, maybe I'll wrap my legs around him, maybe we'll join our bodies the way we joined our hands that first night—

"Feel this?" he asks, bringing me back to myself, stopping me from living in my imagination, and I'm grateful for that, since this is better than anything my imagination does on its own, and that's saying something given my years of practice with it. I realize he's only dipped his knees enough to reach his fingertips against the side of my leg, right above my knee, and when I tip my head down in a small nod of acknowledgment, pressing my lips to his shoulder, he moves again, trailing the rough pads of his fingertips up, underneath the fabric of my skirt. He traces the line of my quadricep in a way that makes me flex in display, in delight. How *strong* I feel when he touches me like that. How beautifully in control of myself and of him.

He moves slow, his breath warm and even against my neck while mine grows shallower. By the time his hand is all the way up, right at the hipline of my plain cotton underwear, I'm practically grinding my forehead against his collarbone, seeing those bright splatters of color behind my eyes while I wait for him. When he teases at the fabric, his index finger tugging the seam minutely away from my skin, I jut my chin forward, scrape my teeth in a light nip against his chest, and he breathes out a quiet, surprised laugh.

"I like that," he says, right into the shell of my ear.

Then he moves, first his mouth lifting to catch the sensitive top edge
of my ear between his teeth, a light hold that feels like the most delicious,
gentle collar to keep me still. His hand shifts to tuck between our bodies,
his fingers dipping beneath the front of my underwear, teasing the soft
skin that's right above where I need him. I move my hips, tipping them
up, but he only presses his teeth down slightly in answer, chasing it with
a soothing flick of his tongue before he moves his mouth back to mine.

I should've known he'd be patient, should've known he'd pay attention to
everything. When he lowers his fingers to touch me, he's soft, exploratory,
quiet at first, listening to the catches of my breath, the whimpering
exhalations that grow more regular when he sets his other hand to my
breast, rubbing his thumb over the most sensitive part, using the fabric
to his advantage. He learns the shapes of me, learns what I like, and once
he's got the knowledge, he uses every bit of it, letting his fingers play
more roughly, spreading the wetness between my legs, dipping first one
and then two inside of me, a move I reward with another scrape of my
teeth against his chest.

He speaks to me then, rough and tender words against my mouth—how
good I feel on his fingers, how wet I am, how much he's thought about
this. "Two days," he says, almost a growl, "two days and I missed you so
fucking *much*," and that's pretty much what does it; that's what makes
my breath come fastest, my hips riding his hand shamelessly as I come,
clenching around his fingers and feeling his free hand move from my
breast to grip my waist tight, pulling me toward him even as he softens
his touch, stroking gently through every last pulse.

"Jesus *Christ*," he breathes, sagging against me, still holding me up.
His forehead is pressed against the brick wall behind me; I'm basically a
pancake between it and him, if pancakes had spectacular, fervent orgasms
in the great urban outdoors.

I slide my hands down his back, tucking my hands underneath his shirt
so I can feel his warm skin, but he reaches a hand around and stills me.
"Better not. I'm—I need to get ahold of myself."

"What about—"

He steps back, a full, deliberate step, and we're back to watching each
other now, both of us breathing heavily—me in aftermath, him in what
I can only hope is anticipation. "Not here," he says, in that same rough
voice. "I can't have what I want here. Come back to my—"

And it's just that quick that something cracks in the air between us,
both of us realizing at the same time what the end of the sentence is. *Come
back to my sister's place? Come back to your best friend's place?* I only

see a brief flash of something in Alex's eyes, but that's all I need to see before I lower my own, staring down at my paint-splattered shoes on the concrete ground beneath me. Maybe it wouldn't be so bad, if I could offer an alternative other than *Come back to my twenty-minutes-away townhouse and listen to my sister's boyfriend snore through the thin walls.*

But I can't.

The alley feels close now, narrowly oppressive instead of narrowly intimate.

A fleeting, perfect moment of freedom, but all of a sudden it feels like Alex and me, we're both trapped again.

* * * *

"I mean," Zoe says, her voice high and annoyed. "You could've gotten a *hotel.*"

Here's a thing most people don't think about: how a granite countertop feels on your forehead after you've been facedown on it for fifteen minutes, confessing to your best friend what you've just done in the dark with your other best friend's brother. It's pleasantly cool, particularly if you make occasional shifts, setting your warm skin on some untouched region, like flipping over your pillow in the middle of the night. But it's also punishingly hard, a brutal reality check for your face, all your bones sharp and jutting and in the way.

"Zoe," I groan, lifting my head and feeling my neck smart in protest. "You're missing the *point.*"

From her spot leaning against her sink, Zoe stares at me, arms crossed, eyebrows raised. "I'm really, really not." She turns, runs a hand towel under a stream of water from her fancy faucet, wringing it out slightly before handing it to me. "Here. You have paint all over your face."

You should see my underwear. "Thanks." I rub halfheartedly—a little wistfully—at my cheeks and the bridge of my nose, a freckled and paint-splattered mess. I'd come to Zoe's right after leaving Alex, who'd walked me back to my car silently and declined my offer of a ride back to Kit's. "Better I walk," he'd said, the tilt of that roguish smile tinged with regret. It wasn't as awkward as what had happened at The Meltdown, but it certainly wasn't resolved either. All that boldness, all that secret Greer come to life—it'd retreated when I'd remembered the limits to Alex and me. The places we didn't have to go, sure, but also the time we didn't really have, and the complication of how we know each other in the first place.

"Kit wouldn't be mad, you know," Zoe says. "She'd love it."

"That's the problem, I think." I look down at the towel I've probably just ruined. There's more paint than I thought on it, rainbow smudges everywhere.

If it bothers Zoe, she doesn't say, taking the towel from me to rinse it again. "What do you mean, that's the problem?" When she gives the towel to me this time, she leans her elbows on the counter so we're across from each other. Her face is fresh and clean from a shower and she's in her pajamas, but I can tell she was working when I showed up, her laptop on the coffee table and a half glass of wine beside it, the TV turned on low volume to a news program I know she wasn't really watching.

"Alex is—complicated."

Zoe rolls her eyes so hard that I imagine them simply falling out of her head with the sheer force of it. "Did he tell you that? Because if so, I'm glad you didn't get the hotel room. Get him a T-shirt instead. We'll have 'fragile' printed across the front."

"No, he didn't." I pause, still cautious. There's nothing I'd say to Zoe about what Alex is going through—the panic attacks, the fear about his work and his future. But of course Zoe already knows about Alex raising Kit; she knows they've fought before about his lifestyle. "Do you remember when Kit told us about her homecoming dance her junior year?"

"Sure. The one where she ironed Schrodinger's equation on her dress? God." She laughs, probably remembering the picture Kit had shown us, her smile huge as she gave a thumbs-up to the camera. "She's such a nerd."

"Right, but—if you remember, she said Alex did her hair for that dance?"

"Oh," Zoe says, furrowing her brow. "Yes, I guess I do remember that."

I can tell already Zoe doesn't remember it as well as me, and why would she? After the first time I met Alex, I basically felt like a freshly plucked string every time he came up in conversation. I gathered details about him like they were lucky charms for my collection. "She said she couldn't afford to get it done the way she'd wanted it, and so he bought a hair magazine and a bunch of bobby pins and did it himself. She said it took him hours. He wanted it perfect for her."

"Uff, that is—yeah. I seriously don't know why this story would make you want to sleep with him *less*."

"It doesn't," I admit. "But Alex fought really hard to be on his own, to get where he is." I think about all the photographs in that slideshow, how terrible and beautiful they were. "I think it's difficult for him with Kit sometimes. I think he still feels—" I break off, think of how I can say something about that moment when Kit's text had come in, when Alex had gone white with anxiety, without saying too much. "The weight of what he had to be for her, when he was so young. If he and I got involved—Z, you *know* Kit. You know what she'd think, or what she'd hope. She'd be thinking Alex would finally settle down, not put himself out there all the time in these dangerous situations."

Zoe's quiet for a minute, clasping her hands together and shifting her weight to her other hip. When she speaks, she looks right at me, serious and calm and no-time-for-bullshit. "Listen, Greer. You are not responsible for Kit's worries about Alex. And Kit's my best friend, and I love her, but Alex is not responsible for living a life that would make her more comfortable, or that would have her worrying less."

She pauses, giving me a long look that we both know the meaning of. There's one other person in this room who lives life a whole lot based on making other people comfortable, and it isn't her. After all, a half hour ago I sat in this kitchen with my phone pressed to my ear and soothed my anxious mother, whose calls I hadn't heard when I'd been splattering paint all over a brick wall and having an orgasm in a back alley.

"Either way," Zoe says, straightening from the counter, "I don't think either one of you is giving her enough credit. She's really dealt with this stuff about Alex over the past couple of years." I look down, blinking at my colorful hands. What Zoe has said—it's true. Kit *has* been different about Alex, and I know that, whether he does or not. "I think you might be using her as an excuse."

"I'm…" *Not going to bother denying it.* My shoulders slump. Maybe I need to get reacquainted with the countertop again. "He makes me feel—a little scared, I think."

Zoe stiffens where she stands. "What the fuck?"

"No," I rush out quickly. "No, jeez. Scared of myself. I had so much *fun* tonight."

"Well that sucks," she deadpans.

"I need to stay focused. I'm so close to everything I've worked for. And he's not a part of my future. He's not going to be here, in the long term."

"Honey." Despite the endearment—rare for her, and I wonder if she's doing her best to play two roles here, hers and Kit's—Zoe's voice is firm. "You know—you *know* I think the world of what you've done since our numbers came up. Kit knew she wanted the house, and she made it happen, but you—what you did for your family, and your schooling—you had a plan, and you've carried it out so beautifully."

"Thanks, Z." More than Kit, Zoe knows all about the work I had to do—with her help—to get the money to my family. The payoff I did of my parents' home equity loan, the mortgage on Ava's townhouse, Humphrey's student loans. All kept a secret until it was done.

"You're right, you are close to everything you've worked for. But there's absolutely no reason why you can't get out of your head and have a little fun along the way. The fact that he's not going to be here in the long term—that's sort of the perfect thing about it, you know?"

I look up at Zoe, and something about her—her confidence in herself, and in me—it gives me a quick-fire stirring of what I'd felt tonight. After all, it's not just Alex who sees other sides of me. It's my friends too—my friends who know me best, who see me as the grown-up, healthy, shy but fun-loving Greer they've always known me as. Maybe Zoe is right. Maybe I could have more nights like I had tonight, with Alex. And maybe the fact that he won't be staying—maybe that's the best reason of all to do this. The least likely to mess up all my plans. Free like this with him for a while, and free like I'd planned all along, after.

"Besides," Zoe says. "At the wedding he looked at you like you were coming out of a clamshell. He's got it bad. He'll probably be a monster in—"

Just then the door opens, Aiden in his dark uniform, his tread heavy in his boots and his eyes going immediately to Zoe, soft and grateful. Talk about having it bad. Aiden looks at Zoe like she invented vaccines.

"Hey, Boy Scout," she says, smiling at him. "Okay night?"

"Busy night." He toes off his boots, walks over, and bends to kiss her lightly, leaning back to smooth a strand of hair from her forehead, and for a quiet second they only look at each other, Aiden's face alight in a way that's so different from his usual stoicism, Zoe's face free of her standard wry humor. Secret selves, that's what Aiden and Zoe are for each other, and I feel an ache that's in none of the usual places. This one's deep in the center of me.

"How's it going, Greer?" Aiden says, turning to the cabinet behind him for a glass. It is a mark of Aiden's extraordinary circumspection that he says nothing about the paint all over me. "Get your project sorted out?"

"Funny you should ask," says Zoe. "She's actually thinking of starting a new one—"

"Ugh," I say, and Aiden looks from me to Zoe. Then he looks back at me and we share the long-suffering glance of two easily embarrassed people.

"I'm sure you'll get it done," he says. "The photography thing, I mean."

"I'm gonna go." I slide myself off the stool and grab my purse. Zoe comes around the counter and puts her arms around me, and I hug her tight, feeling a familiar spring of tears—gratitude for her and this friendship. As odd as it is, given what we've just talked about, I miss Kit too, miss the three of us together. "I'm probably getting paint all over your fancy pajamas."

She shrugs and pulls back from me. "I've got a bunch more just like them." She gives me a narrow-eyed look and pats my shoulder, like she's letting me off easy. But when I'm almost out the door, she speaks again.

"Get the hotel room," she calls after me. "And for God's sake, quit dreaming up shit and have some *real* fun for once!"

Chapter 10

Alex

"Would you say you have trouble letting yourself enjoy things?"

Of course, in response to this, Patricia's chair protests embarrassingly. We're three-quarters of the way through our third session, and I still haven't quite mastered how to keep the thing quiet, even when it feels like I'm freeze-drying myself into immobility. I'm tired, a whole night of restlessness behind me, and since it wasn't panic related—it was erection related—I'm feeling irrationally resentful of Patricia.

"You need a new chair." I sound so grouchy. *Get off my lawn* grouchy.

"Enjoying things," Patricia says slowly, as if I didn't hear her. "Do you have trouble doing that?"

I rub a hand over my jaw, considering. Last night, I'd enjoyed things. I'd enjoyed walking beside Greer, talking to her. I'd enjoyed throwing paint balloons against a brick wall, laughing with her. I enjoyed every hot, perfect second of having her against me. I'd even grudgingly enjoyed thinking about it again later, my hand on my cock, my head full of Greer and the sounds she'd made when she'd come against my fingers.

Of course then I'd been humiliated that I'd defiled my sister's shower, and I'd spent the next twenty minutes scrubbing it, which is probably something Patricia could find a definition for in one of the fancy textbooks on her poorly constructed shelves.

Well, it needed cleaning, anyway.

"Yes," I say. "I have trouble doing that."

"I'm concerned, Alex, that you don't prioritize self-care."

I snort, trying not to think about the self-care I did with my right hand. "Someone else said that to me recently. Greer." *New coping mechanisms. You need them.*

"Ah." Patricia makes a little note on her tablet. "You've been around her quite a bit while you've been here." I look up at her, narrow my eyes, and she puts up her hands in surrender. "You've mentioned her several times." The way Patricia says "times." It sounds like *toimes*, which makes me smile in spite of the fact that she's just pointed out my utter transparency when it comes to Greer.

"She's—a friend."

"Let's talk about that." *Oh, hell.* Maybe Patricia has some kind of divining rod that tells her when I'm being dishonest. Maybe the chair is the divining rod. Maybe when I leave here the chair will tell Patricia about how I've been waiting for Greer to call me, waiting for her to tell me we can finish what we started. "About your friendships, I mean," she clarifies.

"Oh."

"Do you have many friends?"

"Do you want to see my homework? Because I did the worksheets in that book."

Patricia rolls her eyes.

"My agent, he's a friend. I've got colleagues I'm friendly with, other journalists I see on the job. My sister and her new husband, they're friends."

"Excuse me," Patricia says. "I need to find some sad music to put on."

"This is the strangest therapy."

"How would you know?"

That's a good point. I swipe a hand over my face and laugh. Whatever the fuck Patricia is doing, it makes me feel oddly better about the things I tell her in here. It's some strange version of poking a bear and then swatting it on the nose so it'll be too surprised to get angry. I doubt she does it with everyone, but damn if it doesn't work on me.

"I have trouble making friends, I always have. Kit was my best friend growing up. She was enough."

"Kit wasn't your best friend. She was your responsibility."

I shrug. "She was both."

"Alex, what I'm getting at here is that you don't have a lot of mechanisms in your life—human or otherwise—to support the self-care you need more of. You had two years where you were dealing with panic attacks. You told no one." That sounds bad, the way she says it. My neck heats in embarrassment. Patricia stays quiet, knowing the right times to wait me out.

"When I was young, making friends—it was a lot of work. I told you, we moved so much, and the way things were with me and Kit—there just wasn't a lot of time. I still think of it that way, I guess. It's work to get to know people, to have relationships." I swallow, hoping the *r*-word doesn't result in a conversation about my love life, which is basically a series of three- to seven-day-long affairs with women who are as uninterested in intimacy as I am. "And I'm obviously still on the move a lot."

"Does it always feel that way to get to know people? Like work?" I don't know if I'm imagining it, but I think I hear something in how she's asked it, as though Greer—*you've mentioned her several toimes*—is a specter in the room with us.

I lean my head back in the chair, close my eyes briefly, see the constellation of paint and freckles on Greer's cheeks. It'd been a brief moment of shock, right after, when I'd been about to invite her back to Kit's. But it wouldn't have stopped me. I hadn't wanted to leave her. I wanted to spend the evening with her—in bed, sure, finishing what we'd started, but also out of bed. Talking and laughing, looking at those pictures she's taken without me. Intimacy, I guess. I wanted it all, and that guest bedroom at Kit's would've done just fine.

I don't even think I would've felt like cleaning after.

But it had been Greer to pull away this time, and I've been waiting to hear from her ever since.

"No," I answer finally. "It doesn't always."

I hear, rather than see, Patricia make a note on her tablet. "Well," she says, after a few seconds. "Then it sounds like this is an area where we can make some progress."

* * * *

I'm writing in my journal when the text comes in.

I've not had much success writing about the panic attacks, and that's either because it's been a few days since I've had one or because I haven't found a way to put into words what it's really like. I've always been better at pictures, especially for the important things, so mostly I write about those—notes I'm making to myself about the images I'll use for Hiltunen's showcase, ideas about what might work and what definitely won't. It's unexpectedly soothing, looking over pictures I've taken long ago, pictures that have either already been published or consigned to my archive folder. With distance, I see the shots differently; I'm not thinking so much about my audience or about how any given shot will look on a bifold, or online, or in black and white.

Still, the vibration of my phone is a welcome relief even before I pull it toward me from where I've set it on Kit's porch railing to see who's calling. It's after dinner, a restless time for me, and that's even after I've stopped getting anxiety about the contents of the pantry.

It buzzes again before I've set a hand on it.

Moneypenny, the first text says, and yeah. That does it for me.

The second text is an address not far from here, and maybe it ought to freak me out that I know that already, but I'm too busy watching those three little dots that tell me she's still typing.

There'll be a key waiting for you at the front desk, under your name.
Holy. Fuck.

I almost forget to lock the house; basically, I start walking down the porch steps before I get enough sense to think about putting my boots on. Even then I'm doing everything haphazardly, dropping the keys, searching the coffee table for the wallet that's in my pocket, lifting my T-shirt to my nose to make sure it doesn't smell like the pasta I just ate. In my haste I hear the scolding tone of my own voice in my head, the one I used to use on Kit when she was running late for school. *You make more mistakes when you rush.*

God. I was fucking *annoying* when we were kids.

For only the second time since I've been here I take Kit's car, which is basically a dented tin can that she has some bizarre nostalgic attachment to. It makes a series of worrisome noises while I drive to the address Greer sent me, most of which get louder when I slow down in front of the valet stand. Probably the teenager behind the podium smirks, but I'm too busy shoving a tip in his hand and walking past him into the lobby to care. It's weird in here, boutique-hotel weird; the light fixtures look like hanging egg sacs and all the furniture is magenta velvet, but I don't care about this either.

I care about getting into that hotel room.

"Alex Averin," I say to the receptionist, whose lipstick matches the furniture. "There's a key for me here."

She taps on her computer and looks up at me. "We don't have a key under that name."

"Wh—" I pause, blink across the desk at her, and sigh, a smile tugging at my mouth. "Try—uh. Moneypenny." For fuck's sake. When I get up there…

I'm smiling like an idiot when she hands me the keycard, when I'm waiting in the elevator bay, when I'm riding eight floors up to the room

I've been sent to. I'm probably still smiling like an idiot when Greer first opens the door to me, her cheeks flushed and her feet bare. She's wearing a pale yellow dress that shows all of her arms and her legs from the very top of her kneecaps down. It's the fabric she seems to favor, light and delicately layered, a little old fashioned but somehow still dead damned sexy. I stay where I am, right outside the door. "Cute trick with the name."

She smiles up at me, says nothing as steps back and to the side, letting me in.

The room, thankfully, is free of magenta accents. It's spare, ultramodern, and I like the contrast of it—soft Greer inside of all these hard lines. There's only one point of disturbance in the room, but it's a big one, as these things go.

The bed.

It looks like it's been slept in, the bright white duvet half pulled back, along with the heavy top sheet, also white. There are four down pillows askew near the headboard, seemingly punched into various states of disarray. I stare at that bed like it's hypnotized me.

Greer clears her throat from her spot by the small desk in the room. "If you could sit there, please," she says, gesturing to the bed. For the first time I notice her camera's on the desk, and she speaks again. "I won't have your face in it. I know you don't like that."

I cross to the bed and sit, my hands curled around the edge of the mattress, and try hard not to think about the bulge in my jeans, which I would also like to avoid having in a photograph. My heart feels like it's going to pound right out of my chest, but not in the way I've been worried about.

More like in the way I've been waiting for. With Greer, specifically.

"Like this?" I ask her, willing to go along with this, whatever it is. *Intimacy.* She and I, we do it well this way. We don't have to say much at all.

She takes a step away from the desk, cocks her head to the side, her eyes passing over me slowly, thoughtfully. I recognize that look—or maybe I recognize the *feeling* of that look, the feeling of taking in your subject, thinking of how you can adjust it, make it work for you.

"Move to the right," she says. "And lean forward a little."

I do what she says, shifting to the right, and once I do, I know exactly why she's asked. It's a couple of degrees warmer here, a beam from the setting sun shining in from the transom above the bed, heating my back and whitening out the denim on my thighs. When I lean forward, curving my spine, her eyes narrow, and she shakes her head, stepping forward, and I have to curl my fingers into fists to keep from reaching out for her, from running my hands up the sides of her thighs, all that gorgeous, soft skin I felt the other night.

She sets her hands on my forearms, tugging slightly, and nothing in my body resists her. I'll let her do whatever she wants. "Elbows on your knees," she says, the same instruction I gave her out in the park. "Clasp your hands together, loose. Like that." She steps back again, and my whole body heats—not from the beam of light, but from her eyes on me. Making sense of me. "That's good. Stay there."

She turns away, reaches into her bag, her brow furrowed deep, her lips pursed. When her hand emerges, she's holding an old baseball cap, faded from navy, the bill curled so aggressively that it'd have to entirely hide the eyes of anyone wearing it. There's a small lowercase *g* on the lower right side, which I spot when she turns it over in her hands, once, and then again.

"You don't believe in luck, still?"

I shake my head no. I'm caught in time on this bed, waiting for her to come to me.

She steps forward, sets the hat on the bed next to me, and I don't think I imagine the way her hand shakes a little. "Bad luck, putting a hat on the bed. So they say."

I press my lips together. I don't know who these "they" are, but no matter what a crock of shit I think luck is, probably this is the luckiest I'll ever feel in my life, being in this room with her. I stay still, try to keep my breathing regular. It'll make it easier for her to get the shot she wants, whatever it is.

"Line, shadow, shape," she says. "That's what the black-and-white assignment is."

I tip my head forward, the barest nod. Now that she's said it—*line, shadow, shape*—I can see exactly what she's framed up in her mind. The curve of my back, the curve of that hat brim. The shadows on the bed, from all the shapes made by the disordered pillows and sheets, shapes I'm guessing now she made just for this. The V between my legs, the way my arms cross through it.

For the next ten minutes, most of the sound in the room is the shutter release on Greer's camera, occasional murmured instructions she gives me after she's looked down at her viewfinder, her brow lowered, her lips pursed and tucked slightly to one side. At one point, she asks me to take off my shoes and socks, and I know she's close to getting it—that detail will matter. In black and white, my feet will look ghostly pale on this dark gray carpet; they'll connect me to the white of the bed. It'll look private, secret. It'll look like intimacy.

By the time she stills her hands and body, her camera quiet, I'm warm from the inside out—my clothes a weight on my body, my arms tense with the strain of not moving, not reaching for her. I'm half-afraid of what'll happen if she touches me—I still don't know yet what I'm really doing here, but I can't help thinking that this has been the longest, tensest foreplay of my life.

"Alex," she finally says, setting her camera beside her own bare feet. She takes a few steps, and those bare feet are nearly between mine. I let my eyes trace up and up, past where her fingers tangle again in the skirt of her dress, past where her chest rises and falls, past the bare column of her neck, slightly flushed. The smile on her lips is shy, tentative.

"I was wondering," she says, her breath catching when I unclasp my hands, reach up to plait my fingers with hers. She spreads her arms, our hands still joined, almost as though we're both gesturing to this quiet space around us. "I was wondering if we can have what we want here?"

* * * *

In the alley with Greer, I learned that she likes a little indelicacy, a little roughness. I learned that she likes when I whisper dirty things in her ear, when I grip her tight at her waist. I learned that she'll reward me for it with a little roughness of her own, that she'll set the edge of her teeth against my skin, that she'll tangle her fingers in my hair like she does with her skirt.

But, oh, *fuck*. Do I have a lot more to learn. The best homework I've ever, ever had.

As soon as she asks me the question, I let go of her hands and pull her toward me, my hands on her hips. I'm partway to turning so I can roll her beneath me when she stills my shoulders with her hands and climbs into my lap, straddling me, knocking the hat from the bed. I've got to adjust, lifting slightly so we're more centered on the bed and also, frankly, so that the warm space between her legs is pressed right against where I'm rock hard, desperate and hungry for her. When I do, I'm rewarded with a hum of pleasure that comes from Greer's chest, a glorious, in stereo version of what I'd heard in the alley, since now there's not even one part of me listening for distractions or interruptions.

She takes control, her mouth hot and open on mine, her tongue sweeping into my mouth, and I'm worried I'll bruise her, the way my fingertips dig into the flesh at her sides, worried I'll tear this dress right off her body. But whenever I ease up, loosen my hold to make my shaking hands caress her more gently, she rolls her hips, somehow warning and torture and reward all at the same time. We kiss for so long in this position that my own hips seem to disconnect from my brain; they rise and fall in small, pulsing thrusts that I don't want, not really—I want all those thrusts to be saved for when we're out of these clothes, when I'm against her skin or inside her, when I'm not halfway to coming in my jeans like a frantic teenager.

I whisper her name between kisses, and when she pulls back I see that her lips are swollen and dark pink from this, the skin around that gorgeous mouth reddened from my stubble. There's a strange pleasure-pain in that, seeing how I've marked her. I run my fingers over her chin, the small space above her top lip, concentrating on stilling my hips beneath her, and I love the way her own twist and wriggle in frustration. "Your skin here, sweetheart," I say. "I should've shaved."

She shakes her head no, leans forward again to press her mouth to mine, hard and a little frantic, and this time I do turn her; I stand from the bed with my hands supporting the backs of her thighs before I lower her down again. She likes that—her legs stay wrapped tight around me, her hands growing impatient in my hair. Her dress is bunched around her waist, and that's it, I'm fucking done with the dress. I practically hate it now, how wrong it looks on these sheets. I pull back far enough to take the hemline of it in my hands, tugging it up, and she's doing the same, tugging at my T-shirt, and for a minute it's a tangle of clothes—I can't see her skin, can't see the view I've been longing for.

Greer in the twilight.

Taking off the sweet, diaphanous yellow dress reveals that Greer—sensible, shy, quiet—does not have a bra on, and I feel like someone's short-circuited my brain as I take her in, smooth skin dotted with freckles that are abundant along her collarbone, her shoulders, but that fade into a lovely, spare smattering on her small, perfect breasts. Overall Greer's body is short, compact, but her torso is long, the curve of her waist a delicate flare—a whole expanse of beauty for me to set my hands to, my mouth to. I bend my head, lick along the lower curve of her rib cage, and she shudders in pleasure, her pale brown nipples tightening.

"You—" she breathes out. "Um, you have chest hair."

I lift, pressing up on my hands, staring down at her and then, briefly, in a flare of self-consciousness, at myself. "Yes?"

"Like the perfect amount of it." She lifts her hands, sets her palms against me, and now I'm the one shuddering in pleasure as she moves those hands up, across my shoulders, up my neck, her palms tracing the rough, thick stubble along my jaw. "All these textures. They're so...*good.*"

I kiss her again, lower myself so my skin presses against hers. "Good together," I murmur, and after that there's a newness to this, to the way we touch each other. She unbuckles my belt; I tug her underwear down. She tucks her hand down my pants; I bend my head and lick her nipple. She moves that hand beneath my underwear, grips the hot, hard length of me; I take that nipple in my mouth and suck, feeling her hand tighten as she strokes me. When she whispers to me that she brought condoms, I nearly trip over my own feet getting out of the bed, shoving my jeans the rest of the way down as I go. I basically dump the contents of her purse on the desk, and she laughs from the bed, her head tipped back, one hand resting on her chest, the tips of her fingers gentle on her sternum.

I don't so much come back to the bed as dive into it, heedless and half-silly, spurred on by Greer's laugh and my own sense of lightness. I think I bump her slightly with an elbow; she makes a tiny *mmph* at the collision, but before I have the chance to apologize she's pulled me back on top of her, her hands and arms surprisingly strong, one of her legs wrapping around mine to get me back between hers. Her kisses are even hungrier now, her body tight with anticipation, but when I have the condom on I try to slow down. I'm suddenly as self-conscious about my size over her as I was in that moment she pointed out my chest hair—I worry I might seem looming, overpowering, too much. I pull my hips back from her slightly, slow my kisses, use the hand that's not bracing me away from her to stroke her skin gently. *We'll go slow,* I tell myself, ignoring the part of me that's screaming to press forward, *I'll make this so slow and good for her.*

"Don't—" she says, and I stop where I am, pull my hips back further from hers, that word like ice set right against my cock until she quickly grabs ahold of my sides and pulls me back to her, my hardness sliding right against the place where she's wettest. "Don't take *care* of me," she finishes, her voice breathy and frustrated, and oh, hell. Fucking *hot*.

"Don't take care of you?"

She closes her eyes, a beat longer than a blink, her chest rising on a deep, frustrated inhale. "I mean—don't be soft. Take—take care of your*self*."

I lower my head, press my forehead into her neck, groaning in relief as I push into her, slightly at first because no matter what she's said, no matter how wet she is, she's tight here—exquisitely, perfectly so. She makes a noise of pleasure, her hands still greedy on me, shifting to my lower back so she can guide me further into her.

"We take care of each other," I tell her, right against her skin, and after that, it's silence for a while, nothing but the sounds our bodies make, the rough grunt I make when I'm fully inside her, the breathy sigh she exhales against my neck as she thrusts her hips up, pulling me deeper.

I can hear it when she gets close, same as I did the other night, and if I don't want the hair trigger that is my cock to go off before she's done I'd better distract myself with *something*, anything, so I talk to her again, telling her everything true I'm thinking—that I've never had it better, that I can't wait to taste her in that same place that's clutching me now, that she's the hottest, sweetest woman I've ever had beneath me, next to me, within ten fucking miles of me.

And thank God, thank God she comes then, because I don't expect I could've held it for much longer, and for the next few blissful, perfect seconds I'm pushing those last few thrusts against her, her legs around my hips, her nails in my back, her inner muscles clenching around me so tight I feel like I could stay here, stay hard forever. I say one last thing, one last rough exhalation into her neck, and it's so muffled by our bodies and our breathing I don't know if she can hear me.

I tell her no one's ever taken better care of me in my life.

* * * *

Afterward, we lie in the now genuinely rumpled bed, Greer in a too-big white terrycloth robe from the closet that's sliding off her shoulders and gaping distractingly around her legs, her laugh big and full when she tells me that the hat on the bed didn't stop her getting lucky. It's the kind of corny joke—slightly punny, slightly off color—she seems to favor, at least when she feels comfortable, and damn if I haven't made her feel comfortable.

I order her weird, boutique-hotel room service, something called a "deconstructed turkey burger," which is actually just an open-faced roast turkey sandwich served with french fries in a wax paper cone. I rub her back through her robe, which she seems a little stiff and cautious about at first, finally sinking into it when I find a spot on her neck that makes her go limp in pleasure. I look at her pictures, not only the ones she took of me, but the ones she took over the weekend. I tell her every little thing I notice, and she likes it so much; she presses close against me, the smell of lavender mixed with the smell of me, asking questions about composition and light. I answer as best I can until I get too distracted, until I give up and pull her on top of me again, shoving the robe off her shoulders and bringing her body up and over mine, so I can kiss and lick her where she's sweetest and most secret, and she grips the upholstered headboard and rides my mouth like we've got no secrets from each other at all.

Only when it's full dark, after-midnight dark, two-more-times-inside-her dark, do we quiet ourselves, breaking from all the touching but also all the talking we've done—me mostly about places I've been, the photographs I remember most, and her mostly about the classes she's taken, the people she's met at her job. I've got a feeling like we've both had a big, delicious meal—not the weird sandwich, but everything we've told each other, morsels from our lives. Now we have to lie still, digesting it all.

From where I lie beside her—on my back, with her head tucked on my chest, one of her smooth legs set across both of mine, I feel her body get heavier as she drops into a dozing sleep. I think fleetingly about the second night I stayed in this city, the night I woke from a panic attack, and idly hope—with the confidence of a newly quiet mind—that it won't happen tonight.

"Alex?" Greer murmurs, not even lifting her head. I love the way her voice sounds, sleepy and satisfied, and I press my mouth to the top of her head, into the short layers of hair there. "I don't know about the hotel room, like—"

"I'll pay for it," I say, keeping my voice low, careful of our small cocoon.

She shakes her head, tickling my skin, and I feel my cock stir again, surprisingly. Up until today, I genuinely thought I was getting to the age where I needed a nap between orgasms. But I guess I don't feel my age with Greer—or maybe I do. Maybe it's all the other times I don't feel my age right. Maybe I've always felt too old.

"No, I mean—I don't know if they'll have a room again, tomorrow, or—whenever. If you'd want to come back."

I furrow my brow, unsure of what she means.

"Plus," she adds, a pause for a small yawn, "I've got Kenneth at home. He's my cat." There's something different about her stillness now, that sweet heaviness from her body gone now as she's come more awake, and then I remember her question to me—*I was wondering if we can have what we want here.* Away from my sister's place, she means, away from the place she thinks I can't or won't have her.

"Greer." I bring my other arm around her, stroke a hand up her bare spine. I find I care about little else than reassuring her about this. "For as long as I'm here, we can have what we want, anywhere. Anyways we're not eating a sandwich like that again."

She laughs against me, nuzzling her cheek against my skin, but then she stills again, going quiet for a long minute. "She'll be back in a week and a half," she whispers, and I tighten my hold on her, angry at myself for the way I've spooked her about this over and over. The way I spook myself about it.

"She will." I wait, feeling Greer's warm weight against mine, waiting for the tinny sound that's a harbinger of panic for me. There's nothing, at least not yet, so I tell her what I hope is true. "And that's got nothing to do with this."

When she finally falls asleep, I lie awake for a long time, waiting for the noise to come.

But it never does.

Chapter 11

"You aren't the boss of us, Harold."

Beside me at the conference table, Dennise shifts in response, her hands clasping and reclasping atop the padfolio she brings to meetings like these—longer, planned affairs where the patient isn't present. Inside there's probably a fifty-sheet stack of paperwork, filled with hospital policy and insurance claim forms and care facility information, and at any point, she's ready to open that sucker up and distribute the exact right thing, the thing that even the most diligent, well-prepared family member has forgotten about. When things get tough, when families are impatient and overtired, scared and quarrelsome, Dennise is like a superhero bomb defuser. Her secret weapon is her knowledge of bureaucracy. Her cape is—well, mostly it's brightly colored blouses from Chico's, but they work for her.

Right now, though, instead of opening the padfolio and saving the day, Dennise is waiting. For me, specifically.

"If we could pause for a moment—" I say, and already I know I've been too quiet.

The Friedrich family has been at each other's throats for the last fifteen minutes, not unheard of for a meeting like this. Once the white coats leave the room, the mood always shifts. Our job is logistics, and frankly, no one likes logistics. Dennise usually lets some squabbling go on for a while, either because she knows it's part of the process, or because she knows her voice will have more impact when it enters at peak unreasonableness.

"Quit calling me Harold, you know I hate it. The point is, Cathy, if Dad's not going to get better, we need to think about the best long-term-care facility—"

Cathy looks affronted. "I know you're not suggesting that *I* can't provide the best long-term care...."

Things devolve further when Harold's wife, who barely ever looks up from her phone, rolls her eyes at Cathy, and then Cathy's boyfriend, a man named Curtis who Harold obviously does *not* approve of, interjects to say that since he doesn't work full-time, he'd be able to look after Mr. Friedrich during the day. Harold tells him he won't be getting in the will even if he wipes Mr. Friedrich's ass for the next three months, and I can feel Dennise wince beside me. It's never good when a will comes up. Or ass wiping, for that matter.

I sit forward in my chair, trying, as best I can, to remind the family that I'm a meaningful bodily presence in the room. "Hal," I say, using Harold's preferred nickname, my voice firmer now, spurred on by the fear that Dennise will have to take over for me, that she'll see me as too weak to get the job done. "It can be tempting to think of this meeting as a chance to talk about end-of-life matters. But remember, what we're doing here is thinking about your father's life as it will be going forward, for however long that may be."

Hal's eyes track to me, almost as though he's surprised to find me in the room, obviously not an unusual experience for me. *Except when it comes to Alex,* my brain interrupts, and in spite of the fact that I'm 100 percent invested in work right now, I feel my face heat—memories of the last few days swirling inconveniently.

I clear my throat, keep my eyes on Hal's, making sure I assert myself as the person in charge here. I may not have the padfolio, but I spent two hours on the Friedrich case this morning, between looking at the file and talking to the head nurse on the critical care floor. I've researched every available hospice facility Hal and Cathy's father is eligible for, and I know every agency they can rely on for in-home services, if that's the route they decide to go.

I'm good at this part, the part where I cycle through some of their options, alert to the ways Cathy and Hal respond subtly to some of the details. Both seem reluctant about larger facilities that are more suburban, distant from the hospital, and while Cathy looks apprehensive about in-home services, Hal leans in, and I'm pretty sure that'll be the ultimate compromise—Mr. Friedrich at home with Cathy, with professional aides and nurses. I can feel Dennise's approval, and when she takes over to address some of the finer points about the rest of Mr. Friedrich's stay here in the hospital, she pats the table next to her padfolio, a small gesture that tells me I did a nice job.

Toward the end, when I'm making notes about additional information Cathy and Hal want, I sense a familiar shift in the room. It doesn't always happen, especially if you've got a family who isn't close at all, or if the practicalities you've got to solve are far more financially or medically complex than what the Friedrichs are facing. But Cathy and Hal, they've got an eighty-six-year-old father with good insurance, a good pension—and advanced stage lung cancer. Now that they've dealt with enough of the logistics, they feel the full weight of what they're really facing: a goodbye.

"We'll be all right, Cath," says Hal, reaching out to pat his sister's hand across the table, and her chin quivers. Curtis takes off his camouflage-print baseball cap and puts his arm around her as she sniffles. Hal's wife has finally put away her phone, and she's patting Hal's back in a way that feels slightly forced, but at least it's something. My own superhero power—invisibility—comes in handy here, and for a few minutes I fade into the background, making my notes, tuning out the quiet murmurs of the family as they leave.

"That was wonderful, Greer," Dennise says, tucking a pen into her bag. "You get better and better."

"Thank you." I keep my head down, flushing with pride. It's the second time I've felt such a flush in so many hours, since last night Professor Hiltunen picked my ladybug as the class example, and I don't even care if afterward he name-dropped Alex three times. Actually, if I'm counting being flushed from anticipation, from arousal, from Alex all together, then maybe I've spent every day since Tuesday with an entirely different complexion. This morning I'd come to this hospital fresh from a shower I'd shared with him, my hair still damp behind my ears, my mascara a little unevenly applied.

Given the look I got from Dennise when I'd rushed in a minute before my shift started, those Chico's blouses also seem to give her the power of knowing when you've gotten laid.

We pack up our things and move out of the conference room into a sunlit corridor. It's our last case of the day, and we're pushing 4 p.m., my usual quitting time on Fridays, and I feel good—tired, what with how my nights have been going—but all in all, good. I've done something useful at work, accomplished something for a family who needed help. What soreness I have—in my hips, along the insides of my thighs—feels earned, not imposed, a warming reminder of what wonderful things my body can do.

So when I say goodbye to Dennise at the bay of elevators, I'm riding high, maybe even a bit reckless—eager to check my phone for any message I might have from Alex. A small voice warns that this in itself is foolish, dangerous—no version of my future involves getting off work and expecting something from Alex. "For as long as I'm here," he'd said, on that first night we spent together, and even though we've both let go of any anxieties about being at Kit's, spending most of our nights there, it still feels like both of us have tried to run up against the time limit as a reminder of what this is. *We should go to Betty's trivia night, while you're here. I ought to go see Henry, while I'm here. You should go to that camera shop again, while you're here. Might as well see Patricia as much as I can, while I'm here.*

Still, a small-voice-drowning zing of pleasure passes through me when I look down and see his name on my screen. *Call me when you have a chance,* he's written, which is about as banal as a text can get, but I imagine he looked dead sexy when he typed it. I think about his forearms for what I'd guess is the one millionth time today, and forgo the elevator so I can call him back.

"You know there's a bowling alley out on the east side of town called the Lucky Strike?" he asks when he picks up, no greeting, but there's an edge of excitement to his voice, nothing terse about it.

"Hello to you too. Yes, I know about the Lucky Strike. Humph had his fifteenth birthday party there."

"Crowd shot," Alex says, referring to my next photography assignment. "We can get it there, and it'll be on your theme. Let's go out tonight."

Let's go out tonight, I repeat to myself, an adolescent thrill going through me. When I was young, the Lucky Strike was a teenage hangout, a place kids in my class would go with groups of friends. All the muted, complicated flirting from the school hallways during the week would translate into Friday night pair-offs at the old bowling alley, where there were fourteen lanes and six arcade games, a concession counter that let kids mix all different kinds of soda in massive Styrofoam cups. Ava had her first kiss at the Lucky Strike, a fact she'd announced with great pride when my mother and I had picked her up on a Friday night, me ducking low in the front seat, afraid of being seen by all the kids who actually got invited to such things.

I cannot picture Alex bowling, playing an arcade game, or drinking soda out of a Styrofoam cup, but I can absolutely picture myself feeling awesome walking into a place like that with him, no matter that I'm twenty-seven years old.

I open my mouth to agree, but then remember with a guilty sense of deflation that I've got plans tonight. "I can't," I say, not succeeding at keeping this disappointment out of my voice. "I've got a party at my parents' house tonight. It's my mom's half birthday."

"Oh." I try not to smile at the way he's not been able to keep the disappointment out of his voice either. "Her…half birthday?"

I laugh a little as I reach the ground floor, swiping my keycard and pushing the heavy door out, emerging into the bright sunlight of a clear summer afternoon. "She feels strongly that her real birthday in December is too close to Christmas. Thus dulling the impact of the occasion of her birth."

There's only a second of quiet before Alex says, "Okay. Maybe tomorrow."

But I make a lot of that second. I make a lot of Alex alone at Kit's house tonight; I make a lot of the fact that he spent time today looking up a place of business with the name *Lucky* in it for my photography project. I make a lot of how many *for as long as I'm here* days we have left. And I make a lot of the fact that I had a good day, that I just corralled a grieving family into seriously considering options for a terminally ill family member, that Dennise is proud of me and that I'm proud of myself.

I want to see him tonight, even if it's not for the kind of date I never got to have.

I tilt my face to the sun, take a deep breath. "You want to come to my mom's half birthday party with me?"

* * * *

In the hour and a half I have between the time I leave the hospital and the time I pick up Alex, I do a lot of frantic preparation for what is absolutely the dumbest idea I have ever had. I send a group text to my siblings and tell them that I am bringing a *FRIEND* who is *ABSOLUTELY NOT* a boyfriend. I send an additional, separate text to Ava who's not yet home from work and tell her he does not take headshots and she shouldn't ask him to. Then I go back to the group text and add another one: *Don't say anything to him,* and I guess the good thing about our family dynamic is, they'll know exactly what I mean by that.

I call my parents' house, but my mom can't come to the phone because she's got a face mask on, and while I try to convey the importance of "acting normal" around Alex to my dad, he makes a joke about whether it's okay for him to be cleaning his hunting rifle when we arrive. Then he gets distracted by my mom's singing in the other room—I'm pretty sure she's doing her Stevie Nicks voice, which is basically like a siren song for my dad, face mask or no—and makes an unconvincing excuse about marinating hamburger meat for the party. Gross. He hangs up before I feel like I've really gotten my message across.

I also change my outfit six times, less for Alex's benefit than for my family's. Kenneth seems to find this so offensive that he stalks from the bedroom, disappointed with my people-pleasing. I call Zoe and ask her what would look good for showing that I care about my mother's half birthday but that I don't care what my absolutely-not-a-boyfriend will think of my appearance. She has me on speaker phone, and I hear Aiden make the coughing sound he makes when he's suppressing laughter. Zoe tells me to stop being weird but also says showing my legs wouldn't be the worst thing. I hang up on her, but still I decide on a pair of kelly-green shorts and a faded denim shirt that is the exact same color as my eyes.

I'm a wreck.

I gather my things: my mom's present (which required no effort on my part since for every birthday, half birthday, and Christmas she sends me a direct link to exactly what she wants, and then does an elaborately surprised face when she opens it), my purse, and my camera. Whatever else tonight brings, it'll give me an opportunity for a crowd shot, and while it won't necessarily be on theme, I'll still my assignment ready for next week's class. My family will make good subjects too. If nothing else, the Hawthornes—except for me, I guess—are animated, alive in themselves in a way that's transfixing to watch.

Alex had offered to meet me there, to save me the back-and-forth of going in and out of the city, but that seemed risky, Alex getting there before me. Anyways, the drive all the way back to Kit's gives me time to comfort myself about how this will go. The big personalities of my mom and my siblings, the way my dad takes his straight-man suburban normalcy seriously enough that he's as much a part of the performance as they are—maybe it'll be enough for Alex to take in that he won't notice the dynamic I'm most worried about, the one that shows how they all still treat me with kid gloves.

But already the person I was in that conference room today feels like someone else entirely, and I hate, hate, *hate* that I asked him to come.

He's outside when I pull up, not in one of Kit's cherished white wood rockers, but standing on the top step, leaning against one of the big beams that holds up the front porch where I've sat dozens of times, talking and laughing with my best friends. I'd be lying if I said I didn't feel a shudder of discomfort go up my spine, seeing him there, his head tipped down to his phone, his black hair falling across his furrowed brow as he flicks his thumb upward on the screen—forearm, obviously, doing some of its best subtle work. Now I'll probably always associate this porch with him, a probably that turns into a definitely when he looks up, a crooked smile evening out the lines of his brow when he sees me.

"I like those shorts," he says when he gets in the car, his eyes tracing over my bare legs. He looks up at my face, smiles that crooked smile again, and leans over my parking brake to press a firm kiss against my lips. When he pulls back, he sets one big, warm palm against my thigh, and it takes me a few seconds to remember how to operate a motor vehicle. "How was work today?" he asks, casual as you please, as though this is something we always do, provide small accountings of our days. I pull away from the curb and have to remind myself of what the next turn is. I'm navigating these familiar streets like a first timer.

"It was—okay?" No. I'm not going to let my nerves spoil the day I had. "It was actually really good." I tell him about the meeting, about Dennise letting me take the lead, and while he listens he strokes his thumb idly on my thigh, asking me questions about Dennise, about what will happen next for the family. He tells me I must be really good at my job.

When I ask him about his own day, he laughs and says he went to see Bart after his session with Patricia, and he was there for three hours, getting the old FG cleaned but also looking at every used camera Bart has in the shop. "He and Henry have to meet," he says. "I think they'd produce some kind of singularity."

It all goes a long way toward easing my nerves, but once we're on the highway heading west, Friday evening traffic out to the Cherry Hill suburbs heavy with SUVs and minivans, I decide to give him a warning.

"My family. They can be—intense."

"Yeah?"

I look over at him briefly, see if he's got any traces of impending panic. Maybe he was only being polite, saying yes to this. Maybe this—a family party with a woman who's only temporary, no matter how much she's tied up with his sister—is the exact kind of obligation that'll send him out into the night, heart thudding and stomach roiling, feeling trapped and desperate. But his face looks placid, that shovel-sharp line of his jaw not tight with tension as he looks calmly out the window at the slowly passing scenery. I wonder if this is how it is with me and him, if there's some strange seesaw effect between us. He gets panicked; I get calm. I get nervous; he gets restful.

"Like not about who your dentist is or what your credit score is," I add. "But probably not all that different either."

The hand he's kept on my thigh moves, a brief caress up and down that lets me feel the callouses at the top of his palm, that has me shifting my butt in the seat just to get some relief from the pulse between my legs.

"I'll handle them." His voice has notched down an octave, as if that small caress has affected him just as much as it has me. "I'm used to all kinds of people."

And of course that must be true. Of course Alex has been all over the world, photographing families from all different cultures in all different kinds of situations. Of course he knows how to set everyone at ease, to make it so they don't notice when he lifts a camera to his eye and captures the truth of them.

The problem is, that's exactly what I'm so nervous about.

* * * *

"He seems nice, Greens," says Humphrey, setting his plate down beside me before pulling out one of the cheap plastic chairs set out around one of the old, fold-up tables dotting the backyard. Eight in all, each topped with a faded, red-and-white-checkered tablecloth, small metal pails filled with bright yellow daisies in the center, my mom's favorite. It always looks like this for my mom's half birthday, at least as long as I can remember, and back when I lived here it'd been my job to do the flowers, the heavy lifting of the tables and chairs going to my brothers and Ava. When Humphrey sits, the back two legs of his chair sink slightly into my dad's manicured lawn, which he'll probably spend all day tomorrow complaining about to my mother, though he'll be secretly pleased that there were over fifty people here admiring his grilling skills even as they trampled his grass.

"Your standard fare," I say, nodding to his plate, where he's got a bun with no burger—just cheese, lettuce, tomato, and an absurd amount of mustard—and a stack of watermelon that'll probably give him stomach cramps later. Classic Humph. He hasn't eaten meat since he was twelve. My dad took it pretty hard.

"He's handsome too. GQ handsome. Felipe asked him if he uses growth cream on his eyebrows."

"Oh *jeez*," I say, raising a hand to my forehead and looking over toward the deck, where Alex leans casually on a railing talking to Humphrey's husband, seemingly unconcerned about his eyebrows, which are in fact magnificent but I don't think cream assisted. "Everyone's treating him like a celebrity."

Humph shrugs, taking a bite of his meatless sandwich. "He is, kind of. The photographs, sure, but that face, God. Mom asked him if he'd run lines for *Cat on a Hot Tin Roof* with her theater group while he's here."

The theater group in question, actually, is two tables away, and when I look over half of them are looking at Alex like he's a piece of birthday cake they're waiting for and the other half—including Ava, who's already pinched me and told me I have a *lot* of explaining to do—are looking at me like I have already eaten that entire birthday cake. I feel the strangest, most unfamiliar impulse: to smile back at them like I have.

That smugness only lasts for a minute.

"Your boyfriend told Dad that there's a whole day dedicated to grilling in South Africa," Cary says, taking a seat in that loose-limbed, master-of-the-universe way he has, the most like his movie-star namesake than any of us. He's gray at the temples, more wrinkled now around his mouth and eyes, especially now that he and my sister-in-law have two preteens. But still it's usually Cary that the theater group gawks at during these events. "He told him most of them use a Weber but pronounce it 'Veeber.' So now Dad wants to go to South Africa and he wants to give Alex Grandma's engagement ring to propose to you."

Humph laughs, and I put my face in my hands. Cary's probably joking, at least about the ring, but Alex has made quite an impression over the course of the evening. If there's any latent panic, he's doing a bang-up job of hiding it, because all night he's been the picture of casual, friendly interest—the perfect party guest, shaking hands and demurring humbly about his work, shifting the focus of conversations back to whomever he's speaking to. He even talked to Doug about Mass Effect, in spite of the fact that I don't think he knows what a gaming console is.

I'm embarrassed by my brothers' gentle teasing, but if there's one benefit to Alex being such a star, it's that it's been no problem at all for things to turn out exactly as I'd hoped. In the hustle and bustle of the party, in the gathered guests' and my family's curiosity about Alex, it's been easy for me to stay where I'm most comfortable—in the background. I've already taken a few pictures, one when my mother was welcoming some of her guests from the Barden Orchestra with a jazzy rendition of "It's My Party," and another when most of the guests were eating. For the second one, Alex had stood close behind me like he had that day in the park, making himself see what I'd seen. He'd murmured a question about how I'd handle the string of white lights hanging over the deck, and the sound of his low voice had made me hunch my shoulders so no one could see my nipples bead under my shirt. Afterward, I'd given him a scolding look that had made him quirk his mouth in amusement. But in his eyes I'd seen the heat of awareness, of desire.

Since then, we'd both kept a bit of distance.

"So he is your boyfriend, then?" says Cary, and I lift my head.

"No. I said he wasn't."

"Right, but you didn't correct me before. That was a test." His voice is still easy, coaxing, but I can tell by his posture that he's homing in on a familiar big brother routine. Almost like a switch has been flipped, I clam up. I want to make a clever quip, something about how I was distracted by the weird salmon-colored linen pants he's wearing, but instead I roll my fork between my fingers, tucking my lower lip in as I stare at my plate. "He's a little old for you, Greens," Cary says.

You're not the boss of me, I want to say, exactly like Cathy had this morning.

"Lay off, Cary," says Humphrey. "She said he's not her boyfriend."

I slide my eyes over to him, feeling betrayed in spite of what seems like a defense. Like me, Humph was always a little quieter, his fretfulness over me more patient, less bossy, but he's still got protective instincts that chafe. "What would it matter if he was?"

Humphrey blinks back at me. "Oh, I mean. It wouldn't. How much older is he?"

I roll my eyes. "He's thirty-four. Not that it matters."

"Travels a lot," says Cary. "How would that work?"

I set my fork down on my plate, push it away, and lean forward to rest my forearms on the table, clasping my hands on the rickety table in a posture that exactly mimics the stance I'd taken today in that dreary conference room. I wish I had a blouse from Chico's, but even so I feel like I'm the burner on a gas stove, like his words have turned the knob and right now I'm clicking my way to light. "What's that supposed to mean?"

Cary slants a look at Humphrey before he looks back at me, something surprised in his expression. "Nothing," he says, and the uncertainty in his voice sends a little thrill through me. I don't know if I've ever caught Cary off guard. He was twelve years old when I was born, fully a teenager in my earliest memories. He was well out of the house the first time I was admitted into the hospital. In practical terms, he was affected the least by the realities of my sickness, but in some ways that's always made him the most uncomplicated about it. He's never been jealous of the attention I required of our parents; he's never felt slighted or resentful about having to miss a school event or a slumber party or a family vacation. It's simple in his mind: I'm his baby sister, the one who had all the health trouble.

"Do you think I can't travel, Cary?" I ask, and even as I'm leaning into it, I know I'm being unfair. I'm purposely misinterpreting his words, shoving off other irritations onto him. If I was clicking before, I've been ignited now, a big blue flame in my middle.

"No, of course not," Cary says, his eyes soft. "Greens, that's not what I—"

"Because I *can*. Anytime I want." A whole bunch of *cans* bubble up inside me. *I can go for days without doing my PT stretches. I can stay up too late and have one too many drinks with my friends. I can have sex—lots of it—with Alex.*

"Okay," says Cary. "I only meant—"

I stand, cutting him off before he can say what I know he did mean—how *would* it work, long distance, between me and Alex—but that's not what I feel like talking about. It's a nonissue—*for as long as I'm here*—and anyway, I want to savor the tiny moment of victory I've had in standing up to them. I grab my camera from the center of the table and march off, feeling both of them watching me.

I set myself beneath the big silver maple at the corner of the yard, turning on my camera. It's nearly dark now, so I set my ISO higher, change my aperture. I hold the camera near my sternum at first, looking around the yard, tracking the pockets of people who are talking, laughing, eating, drinking. I feel strangely powerful out here, that *watching* is *helping* feeling, and without thinking too much about it, I raise the camera to my eye, pivot so I'm pointing it toward the deck, where Felipe and Alex's conversation has expanded to include my parents and two of my dad's golfing buddies. I put Alex in the center of the shot, and for a few seconds I hold there, appreciating that power I feel looking out at the night this way, looking out at *him* this way.

But as I'm about to take the shot, about to freeze them all in time, a flash of red enters the viewfinder, and I lower the camera with a dull feeling of foreboding settling at the base of my spine.

There's a new guest here, and already I know the night's about to change for the worse.

Chapter 12

Alex

I hadn't expected things to go so well.

On the way here, I could see Greer was nervous, regretting her spontaneous invitation. I'd hidden it well, but I'd kicked my own ass the whole way here, thinking I'd backed her into it. Twice I'd opened my mouth to ask if she wanted to drop me off somewhere, maybe at one of the three Starbucks we'd passed once we'd gotten onto the suburban surface streets off the highway. I'd sit and drink coffee, damn Patricia's advice about caffeine and anxiety. I'd check news feeds, click through some slideshows Hiltunen's upper-level students have sent me for consideration for the showcase. But—but shit, she was pretty. Her smooth, bare leg felt good under my palm. That hair-thin wrinkle between her eyebrows made me want to press my lips to her forehead. I didn't want to leave her, not for all the suburban Starbucks and photo slideshows in the world.

When we'd pulled up to her parents' place, though, some of that desperate need I'd felt to stay close to her had dissipated, and the full weight of what I'd agreed to had started to sink in.

Growing up, Kit and I missed out on a lot of what seemed like rites of passage for other people our age, including heading over to a friend's house for dinner, getting that little-kid sneak peek into how other families operated. Once, when we'd been able to stay in one place for all of Kit's eighth-grade year, she'd had a friend from the math team invite her over on a Thursday night, and when I'd walked to pick her up at a split-level a mile away from our apartment building, she hadn't been able to stop talking about their fireplace. "Well it's really a *hearth*," she'd said, emphasizing the word, like she was speaking in some language she'd never heard. "It's got pictures all over the top of it, on this wood shelf. Family pictures and this snow globe they got in *Alaska*. They went to Alaska. Can you believe that?"

I could believe that. By that point, I'd become acutely aware of all the things other kids were getting that Kit wasn't.

In my job, of course, I visit all kinds of homes. When I first got to New York, barely a year after Kit had left for college, I took most of my pictures on the streets, but I did one series on an abandoned hospital in east Williamsburg, where squatters—"urban homesteaders," they'd preferred—had moved in and taken over, cooking over Sterno burners and leaning against rolled-up sleeping bags, conditions that had made my reporter colleague grimace in disgust and that had left me feeling humiliatingly homesick.

Once I left New York and started shooting internationally, I got even more of an education. I visited homes that were sometimes warm and welcoming and other times cold and forbidding; homes full of food I'd never eaten, clothes like I'd never seen, languages and traditions I was desperate to understand. Homes half-destroyed and stripped of comforts, homes dripping in ill-gotten gains, homes where people laughed at me and spoke to me in broken English, homes where people treated me with cool suspicion, barely enduring the lens of my camera.

But I've never really been to visit a house like this: suburban America, middle class. Wide, tree-lined streets. A mailbox with a little red flag and an *H* stenciled on the side, a lawn that's almost disconcertingly green. Brick with black shutters, a door painted colonial blue, big ceramic planters stuffed full of sweet potato vine and petunias all over the back deck where I've spent most of the party. It looks like a house on a sitcom, a half-hour comedy where even "very special episodes" get resolved before the credits roll.

And yet somehow, I've managed to enjoy myself. Maybe not to fit in, not exactly, since it's clear I'm an object of curiosity around here, almost as though Greer's never brought anyone around, but her family's a trip and basically no one lets you stand still for five seconds without offering you food or a drink or an opinion about the weather, your T-shirt, how young Greer's mother looks, whatever.

"Alex," Susan says now, one hand on my elbow and the other sweeping a gesture to two new guests I haven't yet met. "This is Gary and Bob. They play golf with Michael. Do you play golf?"

Even the thought of it makes me smile as I shake newly proffered hands. Me, golf. "No, I'm afraid not."

Her face falls dramatically, but not in a way that seems serious. It's how all her expressions are—big and communicative, calculated for maximum effect. When we first arrived she'd gasped fully, mouth open and eyes wide, clasping her hands together before opening her arms, a practice perfect but somehow still authentic version of welcome and excitement. If there'd been one inscrutable moment from Susan, it'd been when she'd pulled back from her hug with Greer, her brow lowered as she scanned Greer's face in question, an expression Greer had answered with a frown of disapproval.

"Michael once tried to teach me to play," Susan says, gesturing her husband over. "Remember, darling? I wore those plaid short pants you liked so much."

"Alex, I don't mean to make you uncomfortable," Michael begins, meaning that I'm about to be really uncomfortable, "but my wife in those short pants, she—"

"Hello, Hawthornes," interrupts a new voice, and when I turn I'm greeted by a guy about my height, tan skin with close-cropped blond hair and a red polo shirt that looks like the twin of what Gary and Bob are wearing. Susan seems thrilled, her gasp only slightly less enthusiastic than the one she'd greeted me with.

"Oh, Josh! I didn't know you'd come by tonight!" She leans in to give him kisses on either cheek, then backs away so Michael can shake his hand.

"How's business, son?"

The guy gives an orthodontia-commercial grin. "I'm getting by." There's something a little false in his humility. "Buyer's market, and all that."

"This is Alex," Susan says, gesturing to me. "He's a friend of Greer's."

Just like that, Josh's ultrawhite, ultrastraight teeth go into hiding, a brief second where he blinks in something like shock. He extends his hand, and I take it, trying not to smirk when he squeezes extra hard. I don't know what his problem is, but I'm not about to get into some kind of suburban dick-measuring contest with a guy who's got a tiny sperm whale stitched onto his shirt.

"Alex, Josh grew up next door," Susan adds. That explains a lot, I guess. Talk about a person who looks natural to his environment. Five years and he'll probably have a charcoal grill that matches Michael's, a minivan full of toddlers with his same blond hair. He'll save for their college funds and their braces at the same time. I shift on my feet, uneasy at my own pettiness—old, poor-kid wounds stinging their way open again.

"Good to meet you," I say, watching as his eyes scan the yard. When he looks back at me, there's something flintier in his eyes. I guess he'll be taking out his dick and a ruler, whether I'm participating or not.

"How do you know Greer?" His voice is still in that falsely humble, cheery "buyer's market" register. Michael's turned back to the grill, immune to this little sideshow, but I'm guessing Susan and Felipe and maybe even Gary and Bob are watching close. Maybe he's an ex-boyfriend, maybe he's got a crush on her, who the fuck knows, but I've got a feeling he thinks I belong here even less than I do.

"I'm Kit's brother." I watch his face closely, see a flash of relief.

"Oh, right. That's one of her friends in the city?"

That answer tells me enough about how well this guy knows Greer. Plus he says "in the city" like we're talking about somewhere other than a place that takes twenty minutes to get to, as though that part of Greer's life is entirely unreachable to him.

"Something like that."

"Josh," comes Greer's voice from behind me, slightly breathless, and when I look down at her, her cheeks are pink. An ugly, small part of me hopes that Josh's crush wasn't ever reciprocated, not that it's any of my business. "I didn't know you'd be here."

He shrugs casually, tucks his hands in his pockets, a move that strikes me as an effort at self-control. Hug, interrupted. "My parents are in Denver visiting Jennifer and the kids. I'm checking in at their place now and then. Thought I'd stop in."

"That's nice." There's something anxious in her voice. I look down at her, then back up at Josh, and I feel, rather than see, the weight of history between them. In spite of my determination to be detached from whatever he's trying to do here, my fingers tighten around my sweaty glass, half-full of unsweetened tea. "Tell them I said hi," she adds.

"Graduation coming up soon," Josh says to her, and Jesus, this guy's teeth. They look photoshopped. "Are you getting excited?"

I shift on my feet again, irritated. Something about his tone, I don't like. He sounds like he's asking if she wants a cookie for her efforts.

Greer clears her throat. "Sure." Judging from the way she dulls the sound of her voice, I'm guessing she's noticed the tone too. She's moved a fraction closer to me, a silent answer to the way Josh has subtly shifted his shoulders, blocking me out of the conversation. "Alex has been helping me with a photography course."

Josh turns back to me, that edge back in his eyes. "Is that right? You know, I used to be something of a tutor to Greer too."

"I'm not her tutor."

"Mom," Greer says, looking toward Susan, eyes wide and nervous. I mean, all right, it's tense, but I hope she doesn't expect some kind of jousting situation here. It's only a little male ego. "Don't you think it's time for cake?"

Susan blinks up from her conversation with Felipe, looks out to the yard, where a good number of the guests are still eating Michael's burgers. "Hmm, maybe…"

"Greer missed so much school that I'd bring her assignments every day," Josh says, and Greer stiffens beside me. I know what I should do right now. I know that whatever Josh is doing, Greer doesn't want him to do it; I know this portion of the dick-measuring contest is about him showing me how much he knows about her that I don't. What I should say is, *Good for you*, and then walk away, leave Greer to give him the scolding he's due for.

But I don't. I could talk myself into thinking I'm ten kinds of superior to a guy who looks like he doesn't know other continents exist, but my feelings in the face of that colonial-blue door, this nice lawn, and these pots of flowers, are still right there at the surface. I don't belong here, that's for fucking sure, but not belonging here because I don't know something important about Greer?

That's a punch to the gut I don't see coming.

"Josh—" Greer says, but she's spoken softly, too softly for this guy's intentions.

"Even when she was in the hospital I did it." The iced tea, the burger—all of it turns to lead in my stomach. *Greer in the hospital.* "We did our best to keep you caught up, huh, Greens?"

Beside me, Greer's shoulders have dropped. For the first time I notice she's got her camera in one hand, and now she looks down, idly runs her thumb over the mode dial. "Yeah," she says.

Josh shrugs. "Anyways, we didn't quite make it, but we eventually got there. Long road to recovery."

Greer looks up at him, and there's anger in her eyes, disappointment. I don't know what I want more, her to slap his face or me to clasp a hand around his neck and throw him over the side of this deck railing. It's not like it's a far drop, but it'd send a clear message: I don't give a fuck about the size of his dick. I wait, my whole body tense, but eventually Greer drops her eyes again. She looks small, sad, resigned. I set my tea on the deck railing.

"I need to go take some more pictures," she says. "I'll see you guys later."

I watch Josh watch her, see a look of longing there. I'd feel bad for him, maybe, if he hadn't just tried to stamp a *Mine* sign on Greer's body by revealing something about her she obviously didn't want me to know. He opens his mouth to speak to me, but I give him a hard look. My head, my body, everything about me is desperate to go after her, to find out what this guy is talking about, to soothe myself about her health. To hold her body against mine and feel her breath against my neck, to kiss her and touch her until she gives me all her secrets.

Instead I look at Josh and give her the respect she deserves. "Save it. If she wants me to know, she'll tell me herself."

I walk away, out into the warm night and noisy party, and feel a pit of dread yawning open inside me.

* * * *

We don't talk on the way home.

For the rest of the party, Greer avoided saying much of anything, to me or to anyone else. When the cake finally did come out—a big rectangle with white frosting and icing-piped yellow flowers—I'd taken advantage of everyone's singing distraction and leaned into Greer to ask her if everything was all right. She'd moved away from me like I'd shocked her, had barely shifted those big blue eyes to mine before looking back to where her mother sat beaming down at her candles.

Greer's lips had hardly moved when she'd finally answered me. "I'm fine," she'd said, basically through clenched teeth, and then she'd walked away—again—to retrieve the present she'd brought. It'd been almost rude, the way she'd crossed to her mother, setting the cheerily wrapped package down, the newly blown-out candles on the cake still smoking, and Susan had looked up at her with another one of those inscrutable expressions. Only a couple of minutes later, when Susan was cooing over the *Costumes of Old Hollywood* book Greer had given her, Greer had leaned down and whispered something, giving her mother a quick kiss on the cheek before walking back toward me. "I'm tired," she'd said sharply. "We're going to go now."

I'd barely had time to raise a hand in goodbye to everyone.

When we'd pulled away from the curb, I'd made my first and last attempt to start a conversation.

"Greer. He didn't—" I'd begun, hoping to tell her that Josh hadn't said anything, at least not anything that matters. But I'd been almost glad she'd cut me off with a shake of her head, a snapped remark about how she didn't want to talk until we were back at Kit's. What I'd been about to say, after all, was a lie: he *had* said something. Something that matters to her.

I'd sat in the seat next to her, felt my fingers twitch with the need to touch her, soothe her like I'd done on the way here. But the way she'd set her jaw, her eyes straight ahead—cocooning herself, it seemed, in a separate place, somewhere icy and hard and impenetrable—told me to keep my hands to myself.

Outside of Kit's I'm afraid she'll leave the car running and pull away once I've climbed out. Instead she exits the car before me, and I hustle to follow; she walks up the front steps with a sort of grave, focused march. She stands with her hands at her sides, her eyes on the dark street, waiting for me to open the door. Inside, she still says nothing. She walks straight to the dining room, flips the switch that turns on the old chandelier Kit loves so much, sits down in the exact same spot she sat in the first night I'd met her, and clasps her hands on the table. And somehow, I know exactly what she wants me to do.

I sit right across from her, like I did that night. I push the copy of the *Times* I have stacked there out of the way. I wait.

"First," she says, her eyes on her hands, her voice quiet. "I want you to know, I didn't lie to you about Humphrey. He did have panic attacks."

"Okay," I say, wholly confused at what the fuck this has to do with her brother who seemed nice enough even if he did look a lot at my eyebrows.

"But Patricia was my therapist too. When I was young."

"Okay," I repeat, and wonder if this'll be the only thing I can say for the entirety of this—whatever this is. Everything about Greer's body right now tells me I'm meant to stay quiet. Stay out of her way until she's done. That asshole stole something from her tonight, and right now, she's on a mission to take it back.

"My parents and my teachers at school, they thought—" She breaks off, her hands clasping tighter. "They thought I had a problem with telling the truth. That I was—that I was a hypochondriac, or that I was making some things up about being sick because I was shy. Because I didn't want to go to school a lot of the time."

I bend my head, and my own hands feel useless, clumsy. I don't think I'm breathing.

"And Humph, he was a bit like that too. Kind of a nervous kid, and he got pushed around a lot. I think my parents figured it was the same for me. And I didn't always—I wasn't always good at telling them how I felt."

I hear her inhale, remind myself to breathe too. "So I went to Patricia, and—well. I *am* shy, obviously. As you've probably noticed."

I look up at her, think of how quiet she was sitting in that same seat two years ago. "You don't seem shy to me. You seem—separate." She winces slightly, and I rush to say it better, what I mean. "You seem strong, in yourself. Comfortable in the quiet. Watchful."

She looks back at me for a long moment, her blue eyes soft, contemplative.

"I wasn't a hypochondriac," she says, slowly, seriously. Something hot and unpleasant moves through my body, a wave of foreboding that's all at once entirely similar and entirely different than a rising tide of panic. "I was not well. My—the things I had, headaches and unsteadiness on my feet, and some other things too—they were not in my imagination."

My imagination—it's a dense storm of chaos right now. I'm thinking terrible shit—cancer, a brain tumor, something deadly and invasive, something that must still stalk Greer, no matter that she looks healthy to me now. Every observation I've ever made about her takes on new meaning— the way the skin under her eyes purples at night with fatigue. The way she adjusts her body sometimes, like she can't quite get comfortable. The way she stretches when she rises from the beds we've shared together, less luxuriating than—than correcting, I guess.

"I had something called Chiari malformation." I don't know what the fuck that is, maybe it's a kind of brain tumor. "It's a birth defect, where—I don't know. I don't know what you want to know about it."

"I want to know everything," I say, immediately. I'll get my panic attack journal and take fucking notes. I can tell already what I'll do when she leaves here tonight. Now that she's told me, now that she's let me in—I'll look this thing up online until I know every goddamned thing about it.

She unclasps her hands in a deliberate, focused effort. "Basically it's— ah. As I grew up, my brain tissue—" She closes her eyes, like this is the hard part to think about, to talk about. I sympathize. She said *brain tissue* and my heart stopped beating. "It sort of extended out of its appropriate area. It has to do with the shape of my skull."

"Jesus." I'm guessing she's given me the most dumbed-down version of this possible, but it still feels complicated, unknowable.

"It's not that uncommon, the kind I have. Type 1. Some people have it and don't even know. They live totally regular lives, and maybe have a car accident or a minor fall, and they find out then, and there's no need to really do anything. But I—that's not how it was for me. I started having the headaches when I was about fourteen, and that's not so unusual. That could have been anything. Hormones. Stress. Anything."

I know what she's doing with this, with this *That could have been anything*. There's a gossamer thread of defensiveness there on behalf of the people I've just spent the last few hours with. I've heard Kit do it on my own behalf, thousands of times. *That's no big deal*, she'd say, when I couldn't get a turkey for Thanksgiving, when I couldn't make enough money to cover a science camp she wanted to go to. *Turkeys are full of chemicals, anyway. I can do the stuff from the camp on my own.*

"Sixteen, when I started going to Patricia—I'd had more issues. The headaches were unmanageable. Sometimes it felt like I couldn't swallow, which maybe seemed like anxiety. My ears would ring. I had trouble sleeping, and so I'd miss my alarm for school, or I'd be asleep on my desk by ten a.m."

I have a flash of Josh's red polo shirt, the pride he'd taken in telling me he'd helped Greer with school. I'm irrationally angry about it, that he didn't notice more. Bringing her fucking worksheets but not getting her to a doctor. It is entirely beyond my capacity to remember that he would've been a kid himself at the time.

"Greer." I hope my voice doesn't sound as choked as it feels. "You don't have to tell me this if you don't want to."

"It's fine." The same *fine* she'd used earlier. She shrugs, falsely casual, and I wonder if she knows she did get some of her mother's acting skills after all. Her voice changes, growing flippant, impatient. "Patricia told my parents that they needed to do some more investigating before she'd see me for more sessions. You know how she can be." For the first time, her mouth eases, a tiny smile at the corners, not unlike the one she'd had when she'd first told me about Patricia. But it fades quickly. "A few scans later and we had a diagnosis. The first surgery didn't take, but the second one did. Turns out, my type 1 was more like—a type 1.5."

I've got about 1.5 million questions right now, 1.5 million frantic thoughts about Greer getting her fucking head cut open. Greer sick and ignored. Greer scared and alone. Not one but two surgeries, and I know there's a lifetime of experiences she must've had during both, in between both. I stand from my chair because—because I worked hard enough staying away from her after Josh, after that scene on the deck, after she made clear she didn't want me around. I've got to get close to her again.

"Don't," she says, and I freeze. "Let me finish."

I stay still but don't sit back down. I wonder if she can see the way I'm breathing, the way it's too fast and too frantic.

"I didn't graduate from high school, not until later. Obviously college wasn't an option, and when it was—well, it's expensive to have this. To be sick, to do the physical therapy you need to recover. My parents were going to send Ava to New York for a year; that had been the deal, so long as she saved up for a year after she graduated from high school. But then they couldn't, so Ava stayed here. Humphrey, he took a semester off college. My mom quit her job to stay home with me, and my dad took out a loan on the house. I tried to work, to pay back some of the—but, you know. I had trouble finding good jobs."

I'm trying, I'm trying so hard to listen. There's all sorts of dots to connect: what Greer had meant, when she'd said she "shared" her lottery money with her family. What Susan had meant, looking at Greer that way. But my head is so full of noise I can barely think straight. Greer's *brain.* Brain *surgery.* "But—you're okay now?"

She ignores me. "And of course everyone felt guilty. Everyone worried. Still worries. They look at me like—" She looks up at me, a long and steady look that opens up that pit of dread again, even wider now. I've fucked up just standing here; I can tell already. "They look at me like you're looking at me now."

"Greer, no. I'm not—"

"You know Cary thinks I can't even travel. He's not wrong. I *can't,* that's the thing, or at least everyone thinks I can't. Every time I want to, my mom asks me something about what I'd do if I had an accident, if I had to see a doctor in some other country, because—because I'm high risk. Simple injuries could be complicated for me."

How complicated?, I want to ask, because I want to know everything about this, about her. But she doesn't break stride, doesn't even take a breath.

"Or she reminds me that I get migraines when I experience air pressure changes, that my neck and back ache when I don't get good sleep, or when I push myself too hard. It's not just the money that keeps me living with Ava. It's that my mother made herself sick crying when I suggested living alone. We talk every weekday morning at six thirty and every weekday night at eight, which you may have noticed because that's when I try to duck away to the bathroom in hopes you don't hear. If I don't answer I'd better call her back within fifteen minutes or she'll call Ava or Kit or Zoe, or she'll send my dad over to the townhouse. He'll pretend he came to check on the leak in our sink, or to drop off a new privacy window-cling film, but we both know he's only there because my mom won't relax until she knows I'm okay. Josh and I broke up when I was twenty years old, and he's still got no doubt I'll marry him by the time I turn thirty, that I'll come around and realize I need to go back to someone who takes care of me like he did."

That makes my knees feel weak, that casual mention of Josh taking care of her, of the two of them married. They'd probably have a backyard wedding, not unlike the party we just came from. Josh would find them a great house in the buyer's market he's so fucking excited about. The minivan full of toddlers would be *theirs*. And why, *why* should I even give a fuck about that?

I sit down again.

"The good luck charms—that's because of this too. When I was fifteen I went through a phase where I was obsessed with astronomy. I learned all about the planets and their moons and constellations. My dad took me out one night to see the harvest moon and we saw a shooting star, and for three weeks afterward I didn't have a single headache. And I got—I got sort of obsessed with good luck charms, good luck omens. I'd play these little games with myself. Don't look at the clock during the thirteenth minute of every hour. Save the heads-up pennies you find on the ground. Avoid stepping on cracks in the sidewalk."

Her face is pink now, her voice thin. If she cries I don't know what I'll do, probably crumble up into dust. She clears her throat, rallying. "I know they don't really work. I know it doesn't make sense. But they made me feel—in control, I guess."

I think about that, Greer feeling in control from luck. It'd always been the opposite for me, I guess. My father's luck—good and bad—had determined the entire shape of my young life. "Lucky break tonight," he'd say, dumping a wad of cash on the counter, swaying pleasantly from side to side and tossing me a wolfish grin, proud and undeservedly confident. Other nights he'd come in empty handed, the swaying unpleasant, vaguely threatening. He'd say his luck ran out. He'd say he'd try again tomorrow. He'd throw up in the kitchen sink and pass out on the nearest soft surface. It was all the same to me, the good luck and the bad. Some mess I'd have to clean up.

I swallow back the unpleasant gorge that rises in my throat at the memories—too much in combination with the hot slick of fear in my stomach from this new information—and scrub a hand down my face. When I look over at her, she's watching me, and I guess it was the exact wrong moment to think of some terrible garbage from my childhood. Her face is set in a mask of neutrality, but it's the eyes that give her away. They're wide and clear.

Heartbroken.

"Greer." But I know it's too late. I'm betting that even if my subconscious hadn't just punched me in the gut, she'd still do what she's doing now— standing up, holding the strap of her purse where it rests across her chest.

She never even took it off. She was always going to say this and go. "You can't leave," I tell her, and our eyes lock, both of us hearing the echo at the exact same time.

She clutches the strap tighter, her knuckles going white, a tense contrast to the shrug of her shoulders she serves up next, the sad, soft smile that curves her mouth. I already know what she's going to say.

"I can," she whispers. Then she turns away from me, and walks out the door.

Chapter 13

Greer

"So—what, you're afraid he's never going to have sex with you again?"

"Zoe. For God's sake," I say, tightening the knob on my handlebars and giving an apologetic glance to the rider on the bike next to me. She's either not listening or pretending not to listen. "Be quiet."

"Oh, no one can hear over this—" She looks up and shouts across the room to the instructor of our early morning spin class. It'd been my idea, a change from our usual weekday routine. Six a.m., Saturday morning, why not? It always makes me feel good to come. Makes me feel strong. "What is this song again?"

A cheerful but terrifying coed named Gabby looks over at us, one of her hands adjusting the mic she'll wear once class begins. She's a sports management major at the university, and she wears a different pair of disarming screen-print leggings every time she teaches a class, as though you're going to forget that she's going to ask you to do hill climbs that feel like someone is murdering your quadriceps. This morning's pair is covered in what I'm pretty sure are different-colored skulls, though it's hard to tell in the weird purple light that's supposed to give us "warm-up" vibes.

"It's not even a song," she yells back. "It's just like, electronic noises. To get you excited."

"Right, I'm excited about these electronic noises!" Zoe calls. She looks back at me, lowers her voice again. "I'm getting too old for this shit. Anyways, so you told him. I mean, it sucks that Douchebag Chad is the one who let him in on the secret, but it's not the worst thing."

"It's Douchebag Josh," I say, and then wince. "*Not* Douchebag Josh. Regular Josh." But he *had* been kind of a douchebag last night.

Zoe shrugs, snaps one of her feet into her pedals. "I always forget. He feels like a Chad to me. Did he freak out? Not Chad, obviously. He probably went home and flexed his tiny muscles in the mirror and looked at your homecoming photo. I mean Alex."

"We didn't go to homecoming." I was too sick, the first surgery unsuccessful, the wait for the second one painful, endless. "And no. He didn't freak out." Though even as I say it, I have a disturbing flash of Alex's face when I'd told him. He'd turned pale. He'd looked like I was bringing on one of the horrible panic attacks that I'd stupidly, irrationally, started to think of myself as some strange cure for, no matter whether I know the exact lecture Patricia would give me for thinking in such a reductive way about mental health. "Or if he did, he waited until I left."

Zoe stops her warm-up pedaling. "When did you leave?"

"Uh, you know. After."

"After you had more sex?"

The rider beside me has definitely heard that. She's tucked her chin into her chest to hide a smile, pretending to stretch.

"No," I loud-whisper, the best I can do with this—God. This music is the *worst*. It's so aggressive I'm hearing it in my teeth. "Just after I told him. Like, right after?"

"Are you asking me a question?" says Zoe, her tone slightly scolding. Yikes. I knew it was risky, asking her to leave a warm bed with a hot paramedic on a weekend, but she showed up punchy this morning.

"Kit would be nicer about it," I say, a half mumble. I'm positive she won't be able to hear me.

"Kit wouldn't talk to you about her brother's penis. This is a one-woman job, Greer, and I'm your woman. So basically, you dropped a big bomb about your past and then ran out of there like you have something to be ashamed of."

"We're not talking about his penis!" Even Gabby hears that. She looks up from her iPhone like she's never seen me before, in spite of the fact that we've been coming to this studio for years. "Anyways, I'm not ashamed." I lean forward, grip my handlebars under the auspices of checking their stability. But really I'm squeezing out my frustration, and—yeah, my shame. I can feel Zoe watching me.

"If he loses interest in you because you were sick, that sucks. But if you didn't stick around to find out, that sucks too."

"It's not like I'd expect you to understand."

I regret it as soon as it's out of my mouth. I told Zoe about my Chiari at the same time I told Kit, when Zoe had found a coupon for a boxing class and they'd both been browbeating me endlessly about joining. I'd used all kinds of excuses: I couldn't get Thursdays off at the telemarketing gig I'd had at the time, I was pretty sure someone got murdered in that boxing gym back when it was a billiards hall, I objected on moral grounds to combat sports. Finally, after two margaritas and Zoe's laughing threat to send the instructor—who called himself Ribeye, in case I was wondering—to my job before the next class, I'd caved. I'd said, "I cannot actually risk blows to the head and neck," and then I'd blurted the entire thing. Kit had cried (she'd had four margaritas) and for weeks afterward she'd do this *isn't she brave* smile when I did anything requiring bodily movement: walking through a door, climbing stairs, holding a bag of groceries.

But Zoe had sobered up almost immediately. She'd listened to me talk, her face serious but not sad. She'd said, "Well, that's horrible," and ordered me another margarita, then she'd told Kit to go to the bathroom and clean herself up. She'd looked back at me and asked if I could do the boxing class so long as no one tried to hit me in the face.

"I'm sorry," I say to her now, but it's drowned out as the warm-up electronic music shifts into prepare-to-die electronic music, and Gabby's on her bike, shouting about whether we're ready for this. When she tells us to set our intention for the workout, I choose the same thing I always do: *feel strong.*

But it doesn't work the same as it usually does. For the next fifty minutes, following instructions to sprint, to add on, to get out of the saddle, to jump and tap back, I feel weaker and weaker, smaller and smaller. I try catching Zoe's eye, but she's focused, her jaw set—not just against the struggle of this workout but against me and the way I'd cut her off. By the time we segue into the congrats-you-didn't-die song that Gabby's chosen for cool down, I think *I* may well burst into tears, no margaritas necessary.

Out in the lobby, switching out of our cycling shoes on one of the teak benches, I lean into Zoe, nudging her shoulder with mine. "I'm sorry. I know you're trying to help."

Zoe sighs, big and gusty—probably part in frustration with me, and part in fatigue over what we've just been through in there. It's not even seven in the morning yet. "Greer. I know I can't understand what it was like for you. Of course I know that. And I know your family doesn't help, acting like you need to be vacuum sealed with packing materials every time you go outdoors. But I've been your friend for a long time now, and the thing is—" She breaks off, shakes her head, pulls a thin, long-sleeved shirt over her head, her blond ponytail dark with sweat.

"The thing is what?"

"The thing is, you can't freeze people out because you're afraid they'll treat you differently. They might treat you differently, at least for a while. It's new information. It's scary information."

"You weren't scared."

She laughs. "Are you kidding? I paid a paralegal at my firm a hundred and fifty dollars to write me a report on Chiari malformation. I called a friend from college who's a pediatrician and made her answer about six thousand questions. I just have a good poker face."

"Oh." I'm probably not crying because there are no fluids left in my body, but I'm confident that I would be in any other circumstance. "That's nice."

"I'm nice," she says, defensively. "Anyways, my point is, at least give him the chance to disappoint you." She stands, sets her hands on her hips, looks down at me.

"I liked how he saw me," I say quietly, tilting my chin up to see her better. "You're right, I know. But—I liked how it was with us. How he never thought twice with me. I'm not someone he has to take care of, be responsible for, be careful of. He never—" I lower my head, flushing. I'm thinking about a lot of things between me and Alex, all the time we've spent together even before it got physical, but I'd be lying if I said that wasn't at the forefront. Zoe's no prude, and neither am I, but we are in the lobby of a cycling studio, and since I haven't had any stories to share in this regard lately, I feel sheepish now. "He never asked me if I could do something, you know? He always assumed I could. That's over now."

She's quiet for a long moment, looking down at me until I meet her gold-brown eyes again. Then she shrugs. "You're probably right, Greer," she says, never one to sugarcoat things. She reaches down to the bench, picks up the pair of shoes I've set there, and tosses them in the studio's rental return bin, making a metallic clamor. "I guess the question is whether you're interested in starting something new."

* * * *

I'm home and showered by nine. It's unusually quiet in the townhouse, Ava having left for an early rehearsal. She's left me a fresh pot of coffee, a new box of Cheerios, and a sticky note with a cartoon heart on it, stick legs and arms and a goofy, smiling face. Underneath she's written: *I already called Mom for you.* Last night, she'd come back from the party without Doug, which I'm guessing means the whole family had a conversation about my hasty exit and she'd been instructed to check on me. She'd tapped once on my bedroom door and asked if I wanted to use one of her bath bombs. That's really saying something too, because she hoards those things like they're made of fairy dust.

I'm soaking up the quiet and these small acts of care from my sister, listening to Kenneth purr steadily from his sunny spot on the arm of the couch. But I'm also tapping through images on my laptop from last night, the conversation with Zoe knocking around in my head endlessly, obnoxiously. The gallery of pictures on-screen isn't helping either. Maybe a few are interesting, especially the ones I took from the deck, but all in all it's not a good showing, and I think I was probably too hasty, trying to get ahead without the actual lessons. There's definitely nothing as striking as the ladybug, nothing as curious as my heap of lucky charms, nothing as personal as the picture of Alex.

There's difference too, in these pictures. I don't know how I know, don't know if I understand enough about the art to even say what I see. But there are pictures before that moment on the deck with Josh, and pictures after, and they're not the same. At first I tell myself it's the light—waning sun at first, fading into bluish twilight, every shot illuminated at least partially with something from nature. After, the porch light by the back door so bright and fluorescent, the white twinkle lights giving off tiny, garish halos that infect every image.

But of course it's more than the light. It's me; it's the way I'd stopped watching, really *watching* for the shot. I let the camera do all the work for me, not thinking about the settings I could control. Not moving my body to see things differently.

Alex would hate these pictures.

It's not as simple as Zoe made it sound, that's the thing. Maybe she's right that I overreacted, that I'm too sensitive about my illness and what it's meant for me and my family. But starting something new? Something where Alex has to adjust to this new knowledge of me? It's not really an option, not with him leaving so soon. What we're doing—casual, fun, temporary—doesn't really hold up under the weight of a chronic illness I hid from him. I already feel like an obligation to a lot of the people I love most, and I certainly don't want to add Alex to the list.

Of people who are obligated to me. Of people I love most. I don't think I'd survive it.

When a sharp knock comes on my door, I'm so lost in my thoughts that I startle and almost drop the laptop on the floor. Kenneth makes a *mrrr-ow* noise and darts off the couch as though I've thrown the computer at his face. This early, it's probably my neighbor from across the street, Joyce, who runs the neighborhood watch and posts complainy comments on the Listserv when the mail gets delivered after 3 p.m. She thinks cats are "nature's prostitutes" (a memorable Listserv rant) so I make sure I pick Kenneth up before I answer.

"Oh." It's not Joyce, but she's probably looking out her front window right this second, staring at Alex's broad back, the way it tapers to a lean waist. As for me, I'm staring right at his *GQ* face, his green eyes bright and piercing, the way they always are when they take me in. In spite of the heat he's wearing a black jacket over his faded gray T-shirt, the material thick, sturdy.

The strap of his canvas pack shows olive green over his shoulder.

For a few seconds I can't do anything but blink at that jacket, that strap. Of course that's what this is. Of course he's leaving. He'll come in, tell me he's taken a job. He'll tell me he's had fun, that nothing I said last night matters to him, but it's time for him to go, that's all. He's doing well—barely a whiff of an attack in days, and way more than one session with Patricia. He'll tell me he's written a charming fob-off to Hiltunen. He'll give me a kiss goodbye—something gentle, sweet. No tongue, I'll bet. We could take care of it right here, one of nature's prostitutes squirming irritatedly between us.

"Greer," he says quietly, and my stomach seizes. *Here it comes.* "I was wondering if you'd want to go on a trip with me."

"A what?" But obviously I heard him.

"A trip. Just tonight, we'll come back tomorrow. I know you've got work, and I've got—I have a session with Patricia."

There's a pause while I use a second, less sophisticated stalling trick—sort of a blank stare situation—and after a beat of silence Alex shifts on his feet, a slight repositioning that feels so soft and vulnerable to me that I instinctively open the door wider, though I don't take a step back from the threshold. Kenneth leaps away from me, probably running upstairs to hide under my bed.

"You don't have to do this," I say finally, happy at how level and unbothered my voice sounds. "You don't have to prove anything to me. I know it's different now."

"Tomorrow's Saint John the Baptist Day." That—does not have anything to do with anything, so far as I know. I blink up at him, confused. "It's a tradition for some cultures to—well, you spend the evening at the beach, the night before. And then at midnight, you go in the water. You splash away your bad luck. You get good luck."

"Oh," I repeat, dumbly.

"Six years ago I photographed it in San Juan. It was beautiful. You wouldn't believe the crowds."

"I already got a crowd shot," I say, not bothering to tell him that most of my photos from last night are trash.

He shakes his head. "There won't be a crowd where I'm taking you. It's not really—it's not a thing around here, I guess. I looked into it. But we—we don't have to shoot it. We can just—do it."

I don't know whether to laugh or cry. I'd thought he was *leaving.* Again. "You don't even believe in luck."

He looks at me for a long time. "I don't," he says, simply, a small shrug of his shoulders. "But I believe in you."

* * * *

"I'm not going to be able to stay up," I whine, collapsing back onto the blanket we've laid out on the cooling sand. We've been on the beach for a few hours now, coming here after the four-hour drive and a check-in at the small, careworn bed-and-breakfast Alex booked here on Turner's Point. Even though it's peak season, this place is sleepy, a little run down, a few miles north of the strip of barrier island towns that each offer their own brand of tourist appeal to East Coast travelers. My own family has vacationed four towns over for years, at least during the times I was in good enough shape to travel, but I don't tell Alex that, at least not yet. I want him to feel like every part of this is new to me, because every part of it is.

"Want something else to eat?" he asks, nudging the cooler he'd packed my way. He must've stayed up late, planning this, preparing it—the reservation, the rental car, the food, the blanket, the LED lanterns he's tucked partway into the sand. He even brought a small speaker for his phone, which right now pipes out some kind of Spanish guitar music that gives me acute pants feelings. If the words he said on my doorstep—words that had lit me up from the inside, a million shooting stars of good luck in my joints, up and down the column of my spine—were intended to prove something to me, then the trip itself has been designed to break me of any sensible caution I've been applying to this situation. One look at the convertible he'd parked in my driveway for this trip—a convertible!

My mother would have a heart attack—and I'd quit lying to myself: I am absolutely in love with him.

Not that he needs to know about it.

"No. I don't want to get cramps in the water."

He snorts, looks down at his watch, the hands of it glowing ice blue in the dark. "We're not going swimming, sweetheart. Just a little splash. Anyways you've got twenty minutes."

I make another groan of fatigue. "Up so early today," I complain, but it feels *good* to complain. It feels honest, and true. It feels like he won't hold it against me. I snuggle myself closer to where he reclines, elbow bent and head resting on his hand, his smile indulgent as he leans down to kiss me.

"I'd like to see you do one of those bike classes," he says when he pulls away. "Bet you get all sweaty."

"You're gross." He laughs, but when he quiets, there's something heavy to it, a trail-off that feels acute. "What?" I say, knowing already where this is going. "You can ask."

He clears his throat, lifts his free hand, and traces his index finger along my hairline, a delicious tickle I feel right between my legs. Too much of this plus the guitar music and I'll probably embarrass myself. "The physical stuff," he begins, and I guess the cycling classes are going to be a handy smokescreen here. "It doesn't bother you?"

I shrug my shoulders against the soft blanket. "Not so much. The second surgery—it changed my life. Before it, sometimes even laughing would give me a headache like you wouldn't believe. Or coughing, my God." I wince at the memory of getting bronchitis in between the first and second surgery. "I still get headaches sometimes, tension and soreness in my back and neck from some misalignment, damage to my musculature. I do exercises to help."

"I'd like to see those too," he says, but when I look up to chide him about how his weird sweat kink doesn't apply to isometric exercises where I basically push my head around using my palms, I realize he's not kidding. He's got a look on his face like he needs to know this information for future reference.

"Stick around," I say teasingly, trying to get that seriousness out of his eyes. "I don't get much longer than a week without them."

"Yeah," he says, but—oh, of course. "Stick around" is a pretty awkward thing to say, given the situation. I try to think of a way to change the subject, but he's still touching me, his fingertips trailing down my cheek, the side of my neck. He pauses at my sternum, a gentle touch that I recognize—I often set my own fingertips there when I'm lying down.

It feels better when he does it.

"What was it like?" he asks, after a minute of my simply breathing, my chest rising and falling under the measured weight of his hand. "To be sick like that?"

I look up past him, at the midnight-blue sky, unevenly dotted with pinpricks of starlight. There's a bank of clouds rolling in, dulling the moonlight, but the ocean whirs calmly, evenly in the air. Part of me doesn't want to answer, doesn't want to do more of this with him. Fragile, delicate, weak—it's not what I want to be to him. But didn't I want Alex to know my secret self? Didn't I want to know his?

I spread one of my arms out, let it reach past the edge of the blanket so I can dig my fingers into the sand. "It was a little like this." I keep my body deliberately still. "It was me, looking up at a ceiling, or at a wall, or out a window. It was a lot of waiting. For the pain to pass or subside."

He leans down, kisses my lips again, the line of my jaw, my cheek, and then my forehead. It's as though he means to mark me in every place he can, to leave a trace of his body all over mine.

"I mean," he says, feathering his lips along that spot of my hairline he'd touched before, "what was it like in here?" *Inside you.*

When he pulls back to look down at me, I feel a gentle smile curve my mouth, my little secret self, and he leans down and kisses me again, taking what he can get of that privacy. When I make a small humming noise, the fingertips he's rested on my sternum twitch slightly, gentling into a stroke. I feel like he's drawing my heart right out of my body.

"It was sad," I say, after a few seconds. "Sad and boring and frustrating. Crazy making, some days, which is probably why I have the weird, elaborate imagination I have." I shift my eyes from the sky back to him, smiling as I think of every imaginary scenario I've put him in. I could never have imagined this one. On a wave of relief or gratitude or crazy-making love, I say something else. "It was the loneliest thing, to be in pain like that."

"Greer," he breathes out, the sound of it focused, purposeful. My name like a mantra.

"I think maybe it changed me, made me different. Remember what you said, about me being separate?"

"I didn't mean—"

"I think I am, a little. In my job, when we're talking to patients about facilities they might go to, they're just coming around to that idea, that loneliness. The realization that no matter how much family you've got, no matter whether you've got a spouse or a kid who comes three times a week, or even just a really good caretaker on your ward—when your body's failing you, you're alone. No one can do it with you. No one can feel the pain with you, feel it right alongside you. I realized that early. We're all a little alone. A little separate."

His face looks so stricken that I feel a pang of regret or guilt or maybe—maybe, like Zoe suggested—some shame. I roll toward him, tucking my face into his chest. His T-shirt smells like spice and sea air, Alex far away and Alex right next to me.

If he's put off he doesn't show it physically; he wraps an arm around me and gathers me closer, the move forceful in a way that soothes me, makes me feel strong. For long minutes we're quiet, drawing ever closer to this good luck ritual he's only doing for my sake. When he speaks again, his voice is low and rough.

"I always thought I liked being alone. Times in my life, I would've given anything to be alone, just for a while." I know he's thinking of Kit, of his dad. The pressure he must've felt, all the time, being present for them. I shove one of my legs between his, tangling us up more. "The worst panic attacks I have—they're when I think other people will see. All I can think about is getting to a place where I'm alone again. Where no one can see it."

I saw it, I think. *I* knew *it.* Talk about something to be ashamed of, feeling proprietary over someone's private struggles. I stroke his back, a silent apology for something he doesn't know I've done wrong.

"But when you say it, Greer," he begins, his voice even lower now, well into a register I recognize only as the one he uses when he's inside me, or close to being so. Those dogs in Pavlov's experiment, I sympathize. I start to wonder whether Pavlov had long eyelashes, but the next thing Alex says wipes my brain of all coherent thought.

"You say it, and I feel like I want to drag you back to that room I've rented. So you remember what it's like to be together. Not separate at all."

We almost miss it, the stroke of midnight. I push Alex onto his back, so he's only half on the blanket; I straddle his hips and lean down to kiss him; I move my hips across the bulge in his jeans—frustrated, hungry, *separate*. He grunts his impatience, his fingers digging into my hips, but eventually he lifts himself, the lean, strong core of his body jackknifing up as he shifts his hands to my ass. It's a little clumsy, the sand underneath us soft and shifting, but eventually he comes to his feet, me wrapped all around him as he walks forward.

"Eleven fifty-nine," he says to me between kisses, taking us to the water's edge. I'd planned to take off my sundress, to go in in the bathing suit I'm wearing underneath, but I don't care now. "You almost missed your luck, sweetheart."

I shake my head, moving my mouth back to his, feeling the fine spray of saltwater on my feet, ankles, shins as Alex continues wading us forward. This is supposed to be a cleansing ritual, that's what Alex said—wash away your bad luck, splash on some good. But when Alex is up to his knees, his lips still dragging across mine, I start to think of this ocean as something else—a vast, endless wishing well. When he dips down, the water swirling around us both now, we're the coins—plain copper pennies about to be turned into something special and precious and memorable. Maybe he's making a wish on me, and I'm definitely making one on him.

A big, bold, unlikely wish.

When we stop kissing long enough to laugh, to splash ocean water on each other and run back onto the shore, our clothes and the sand sticking to us uncomfortably as we race back to the blanket, I think about telling him. About throwing caution to the wind and saying aloud every big, bold, unlikely part of that wish.

But of course I don't.

Of course I know that your best chance of having a wish come true is to not say anything about it at all.

Chapter 14

Alex

"You're telling me you can fix this camera?"

"That's what I'm telling you, old man." Bart turns the Lubitel over in his hand again, bends his head closer to where he's popped off the camera back so he can look at the take tip spool. He and Henry Tucker are the same age, I think—Henry might even be a little younger. But since this is maybe the third time one of them has laughingly called the other one old in the forty-five minutes since we've been here, I'm guessing this is some kind of local small business owner friendship ritual. Both of them seem to have thicker southern accents now.

"Fix it so it takes pictures?" *Pitchers*, that's how Henry says it. Bart looks at him across the counter like he's nuts.

"What else would I fix it for? I'm not selling decorations over here."

Henry takes the ball cap off his head and runs a hand through his blond-gray hair. He looks a lot like my new brother-in-law, and for some reason I take this as a comfort on behalf of my sister, like I'm judging Ben's fitness for staying healthy as the years go by.

"You know it's funny you should say that," he says, settling the cap back on. "I got a whole table full of old cameras and I get these kids coming around, real tight jeans on, you hear? Flannel shirts when it's this kind of hot. They buy these cameras and I'm telling you, it's for decoration."

"Oh, I know those kids," Bart says, but listen, I don't think they mean kids. Probably they mean people in their twenties and thirties who've got a thing for vintage home design. There's a whole show about it on Kit's cable TV; Greer and I watched an episode last night. Or I guess I watched, and she fell asleep, her hair tickling my beard pleasantly and the smell of lavender infusing me with drowsy calm. The lavender, I've learned, is from a little bottle of oil she keeps in her purse. When she feels a headache come on, she rubs a small amount right behind her ears, then she does some of those exercises she told me about that night on the beach.

We've been together every night since our trip, and in that time—only a few days, but we spend every minute we can with each other—I feel like I've been collecting small intimacies like this about her: the kind of toothpaste she uses, how long it takes her hair to dry when she gets out of the shower, the difference between the voice she uses when she's on the phone with Zoe and the voice she uses when she's on the phone with Susan. She likes a lot of milk in her coffee. She thinks ginger tastes like soap. She keeps cough drops in her purse all the time. She hates the sound of ice being put into a glass.

Mostly we've been staying at Kit's, though on Tuesday we went to Greer's townhouse, a comfortable but stale place that—other than Kenneth, who had a real fondness for my right thigh, kneading it with his paws like it was a slab of bread dough—doesn't seem to have any meaningful trace of who Greer is. We eat out or in; we choose photos for her class and for my part of the showcase; we talk and sleep and make love like we've got all the time in the world.

We don't, of course. Greer's got her second to last photography class tonight, and in just over a week we have the showcase that's my last official obligation here. On Tuesday Jae emailed me—not for the first time since I've been here, but it's the first time he's mentioned anything other than the book idea in weeks—asking whether I've got any interest in heading to Syria for a story the *Times* is doing, working with a journalist I've partnered with before. *Only if you're feeling up to it,* he'd added. And all this is to say nothing of the fact that my sister and Ben get back tomorrow, an eventuality that Greer and I have avoided discussing with surgical precision.

But this morning I'd woken up in Kit's guest bed, Greer sleeping soundly beside me on her stomach, most of her bare back exposed to the morning light coming in through the window. I'd let my eyes trace over the freckles there, memorizing them like they were a map home. And then I'd thought: *Maybe they are. Maybe they could be.* I wanted to say something to her about that, to talk to her about what possible future we might have, given my work and her life here, given the way I'm obviously still dealing with the shit that brought Greer and me together in the first place.

But at 6:30 sharp her phone had started vibrating, her mother's daily call startling her out of sleep, and it'd been time to start the day.

"Say, Count Dracula," says Henry, snapping me out of my thoughts. Count Dracula is his nickname for me, I guess because of my black hair, decided sometime between when I first met him a couple of years ago and the rehearsal dinner. He's got a lot of these nicknames in his back pocket, I've learned, all of them a genial form of affection. "Me and your photograph friend here, we're gonna do a little business about all those cameras I got at the yard."

"Great." I feel a blooming sense of satisfaction at setting up this meeting. Bart's a good guy, a bit isolated since his wife died two years ago, and I get the sense he's had trouble keeping up with his business. I've been bringing him film from the FG, pictures I've started to take over the last week when Greer's at work or in her class. He knows more about cameras—digital or otherwise—than any single person I've met, and every hobbyist and professional in this city should be coming to him. I even sent Hiltunen and the showcase students an email about him two days ago.

"You walk here?" asks Henry, peering over my shoulder to look out the window, where a soft rain has started to fall. "Find something to do for a half hour, look at these fancy"—he gestures to the far wall, where Bart's got a display of leashes and pro clips and cuffs—"whatever this weird stuff is, and I'll give you a ride back to Kit's."

For a second my mind stutters over this, a benign offer of extra care from someone I hardly know who is also, strangely, something of a family member to me now. He lives in this town with other family members I have now. My new brother-in-law, sure. But also my new brother-in-law's stepmother, and mother, and stepfather. They're all connected to me, however distantly. I'm connected to Bart, and now I've connected him to Henry. Little dots everywhere, all over this map.

I wouldn't say it feels good to me, not like waking up next to Greer feels good. I suppose it's too new for that, or I'm too unpracticed at it. I clear my throat, look down at my watch, grateful that the time's syncing up right, both for this specific moment and for the one I'm staring down more generally. The one where I try to figure how to keep Greer in my life, even when I'm thousands of miles away from her.

"Thanks, but I've got an appointment. You kids have fun."

* * * *

I stop and get two coffees, but I still make it over to Patricia's office early, the extra-dark roast I brought for her almost eye stinging in its strength as I walk into the waiting area, empty again with a note leaning against the salt lamp. *GO ON BACK*, it reads, and I'm starting to think the receptionist either doesn't exist or hides in a secret compartment when people come in.

As I make my way down the hall, I can hear Patricia's brash voice, and I hang back, worried I'm catching her at the tail end of a session. In the lag I think through what I want to talk about today. I'm nervous enough that I rehearse it a little: *I've been thinking about what I need to work on so I can be in a relationship. So I can be in a relationship and not feel so much pressure, so much obligation.*

It's not long before Patricia sticks her steel-topped head out of her door, her phone handset up to her ear and an annoyed expression on her face as she ushers me in.

"Put your wife on," Patricia says into the phone, taking the coffee from me and raising her eyebrows in thanks. "I like her better."

I hitch a thumb over my shoulder, gesturing back down the hall. I can look at that Bowie poster or any of the other weird shit that's plastered out there while I wait. But she points at me and then points at the chair, a look on her face like thunder. I sit and feel bad for the wife, whoever she is.

"I'm coming on Saturday," Patricia says into the phone, no gentle greeting if she's got a new audience on the other end. "I'm happy to babysit but not for more than six hours. Much past that and I'm liable to drop him off at the fire station."

There's a screechy sound I can hear on the other end of the phone.

"Oh, relax. You're just as bad as my son. Have a sense of humor. All right, give that baby a kiss for me. I'll see you soon."

She hangs up, and I don't imagine she's waited for a sign-off from the person I'm guessing is her daughter-in-law. She lets out an exasperated sigh and pulls the plastic lid off the coffee, taking a gulp that would burn a human woman's throat. Patricia, obviously, is superhuman, part of an alien race that is comfortable not wearing shoes at their places of business.

"You don't get a discount for bringing this."

"I figured you didn't work on the voucher system." I settle further into the chair. I know how to move in it now so that it doesn't make any gruesome noises. "So you've got kids?" I ask her without thinking, gesturing toward the phone.

"Just the one." She grabs her iPad off her desk, settling it in her lap while she takes another drink of coffee. "I worried about raising a kid here, you know. He's had it so easy! My grandkid'll probably operate a cell phone before he talks. They live way out on the far west end of town, one of those big McMansions. Becca—that's the wife—she wears stretchy pants every day and she's got this ponytail that goes *swish swish swish*"—Patricia reaches a hand up to do an elaborate *swishing* gesture behind her head—"I guess because she wants to work out enough to get her 'postbaby body' back."

Two weeks ago I might've shifted awkwardly at this point, but I know this is how it goes with Patricia at first. Three to seven of our fifty minutes are going to be spent on her being bizarre enough that there's not much I can say that feels like oversharing.

"I've got news for her about what's happened to her cervix, I'll tell you what." *There it is.* "You want kids?"

I don't think before I move, and the chair breaks wind at me. I can't believe I walked into this trap. "No."

"No? You've never thought about it?"

Things have shifted so rapidly I feel like I'm getting the bends. I try to recover my plan—*I've been thinking about what I need to work on so I can be in a relationship*—but probably Patricia's done some sort of fancy psychology training on me over the course of our sessions so I can't avoid her questions.

"I've—no. I've *done* it." I've got a memory of changing Kit's diaper when I was six years old that's so acute it has an aromatic component. I open my mouth to get back on the plan, but Patricia speaks before I can.

"Do you think you'd be a good father?"

I clear my throat. "I don't know. I don't suppose I know much about what a good father is." Henry, he seems like a good father. Greer's dad too, even if his jokes are truly terrible. I swallow, stay still. There's a packet of gum in my pocket that's calling my name.

"Right, you mentioned your first panic attack was when your father was ill."

Fuck it. I set aside my coffee, get out the gum. This is the shit no one understands about panic until it happens to them. That sometimes you're just panicking about panic, about the thought of panic, about the memory of panic. It fucking sucks.

"That was more about—it's like I've told you. I get stressed when I feel stuck somewhere. Actually that's what I wanted to—"

"You don't think you had a reaction to your father having a stroke?"

"We're not close." That's an understatement, obviously. I've spoken to him one time since the wedding and it was about whether I could float him a thousand bucks for a new transmission on his old Chevy. Since that car gets him back and forth to the only steady job he's held during my lifetime, I'd wired it the next day, before he could even think of bothering Kit about it. "We're nothing alike."

Patricia makes a note on her tablet.

"We're not," I repeat.

For a few seconds it's quiet, and I'd like to try again, to get back on track with my plan, but I've got a feeling if I do, it'll seem suspicious somehow. It'll seem like an admission of guilt for a crime I don't even know if I've committed. When Patricia speaks, she does so carefully, extra calm. Suspicious calm.

"You mean because you don't share in his more reckless behaviors?"

I snort dismissively. When I answer her, I have to try hard to keep my voice level, to keep my back against this chair. My instinct is to sit forward, to drive this point home with a voice like the ice I feel in my spine at this comparison even being suggested. "I've never gambled, not even once. You should see my savings account. Even that feels risky. If I had a mattress to stuff all my money in, I'd probably do that instead of take the chance that the bank goes under. My retirement plan is so conservative that my accountant gets indigestion when we talk on the phone every year."

"Okay, so you're careful with money."

It's clear she's not getting it. "Every drink I've ever had put in front of me, I've only taken two sips of, and that's out of politeness. I hold my breath when someone near me smokes. I broke my collarbone in Namibia and didn't take a single one of the painkillers I got prescribed."

Patricia purses her lips, and I know that's because we've had a version of this conversation about meds once before—my first session here, when I said I wasn't ready to try anything pharmaceutical for the panic. She'd made a note about it on her tablet.

"So you don't have your father's addictions," she says, finally, and it's irritating how calm she's stayed, when I've grown increasingly agitated.

"I don't have any addictions."

"You don't think your work is an addiction?"

I blink. "No."

"You don't think there are any addictive qualities to your work?"

Blink, blink. "Like I'm an adrenaline junkie? No. I told you. My shoots aren't all that dangerous."

"You ought to judge that on a sliding scale. But anyways, it's not necessarily adrenaline that you'd be—"

"Let's skip this part, Patricia. What do you think I'm addicted to? I want to know what I need to feel terrible about on the walk home from here."

She only looks at me, a long, steady look, and I feel something heavy settle on my shoulders, a weighted cloak made up of a patchwork of memories. Just then, just with that swiping, thoughtless, dismissive remark, just for a moment—I sounded like my father.

"I'm sorry," I say, scraping a hand through my hair. "I'm sorry. Please go on."

"Let's think through it." Her voice is still entirely calm, entirely unbothered. She holds up a loosely clenched fist, raises her thumb in the air. "You say you have trouble turning down work when it's offered to you, even when you're sleep deprived or ill." Her index finger. "You feel that situating yourself in a single city as a home base would compromise your ability to travel as frequently as you do now." Middle finger. "You admit to compulsively checking news feeds, and you have trouble accepting the quality of your work even after it's published." Ring finger. "You become irritable when someone suggests you take on fewer projects." Pinky finger. "Your work has compromised important relationships in your life, including the one you have with your sister."

There's a dim light of recognition at that word, *relationships*, but I doubt I could get back to the plan if I tried. I'm in pure survival mode now, my mind racing to figure out the right thing to say so we can move on, so we can end this session. "So I'm a workaholic? That's what you're saying?"

She lowers her hand, shrugs. "There's no real medical definition for workaholism. Certainly it's possible to have addictive behaviors associated with work."

"I don't have addictive behaviors." But even as I say it, I'm thinking about every single thing I've ever read about addiction. I'm thinking about every single time my dad thought he could stop after five dollars, ten dollars, twenty dollars. I'm thinking about every time I said, *One more shot, one more job.* I'm thinking about the way I feel when I'm out in the field, when I know I'm getting good pictures. I think about the way it makes me feel as though I could put off sleep for days and days.

I want out of this room like I've never wanted anything in my life.

But Patricia, she only raises a steel-gray eyebrow at me, and I know I'm locked in.

* * * *

Here's what I thought the plan would be for the last night Greer and I have together before Kit gets home and we have to take this thing wide:

First, I'd stop at the grocery store on the way back from Patricia's and buy ingredients for dinner, maybe some kind of pasta dish or a nice piece of fish if they had it.

Second, I'd get back to Kit's and tidy up, light a few of the candles she keeps on her mantel, right underneath that big picture of mine she's got hanging up.

Third, I'd make the dinner so it'd be ready when Greer gets back from her class; I'd have a glass of wine poured for her and the table set.

Fourth, I'd tell her about whatever plan I'd come up with for the two of us going forward, the one Patricia was supposed to help me figure out.

Fifth through tenth was, in short, all sex related.

Instead, when Greer comes in through Kit's front door I'm lying on the couch, no food or wine in sight, no candles lit, no attempt made to clear the half-read newspaper from this morning off the coffee table.

No plan.

"I'm *pretty* sure," Greer says, her voice cheerful behind me as she drops her bags in the foyer, "that Hiltunen has some suspicions about that black-and-white picture, like he recognizes your bare feet, somehow? But actually the lecture he had on photographing people was—" She breaks off, coming into the living room. "Oh."

I sit up, scrub my hands over my face and through my hair. I'm sure I look like shit, which is appropriate given how I feel. I can't quite say what I've done exactly in the hours since I left Patricia's—a long run, an extended amount of time staring at that email from Jae, a shower that did nothing to calm me down or refresh me. I thought maybe I'd try for a nap, stretching out here on the couch while the sun went down, but mostly I just stared at the ceiling, and now I feel worse than I did when I started these feeble efforts at—what was that word again, from Patricia? *Self-care*?

"Hey." My voice is scratchy, thick. "Class was good?"

"Alex. What happened?" She's already come around to the couch, and when she sits, it's right up against me, her leg pressed to mine. She's wearing another pair of those tight, cropped jeans, these a pale pink color, soft and pretty in the light from Kit's chandelier in the dining room. I set my hand on her knee, my eyes down, and think about lying to her.

Nothing happened, I'd say. *I have a headache, is all.*

Instead I ask her if she's hungry. "I could make something. I meant to pick something up."

"No, I'm not hungry. What happened?" She's focused, undeterred. I've got a feeling that if I lie to her now, after everything she and I have told each other—after everything she's told me about something that's awful and painful for her—we won't make it much further than next week, whether I've got a plan in place or not. The fact that I'd even consider insulting her by suggesting I have a headache, of all things, makes me feel guilty, uncomfortable.

I press my palms to my eyes, feel the weight of her hand settle in the center of my back, right between my shoulder blades. She strokes up and down slowly, waiting.

"Patricia wanted to talk about my father today. About whether I've got some of the same problems as my father does."

"Yikes," Greer says, and I don't know why, but that little *yikes*—it strikes me so funny, goofy and sweet and disarming. I look over my shoulder at her, and my mouth somehow—it's unbelievable, really, given the way I feel—tips into a smile. "I mean, not *yikes*, like there's a spider in your cupboard. I don't know why I said that."

I squeeze her knee gently, shrug my shoulders. I'm used to this too, now, about Greer. She's got an imagination like nothing I've ever heard of in my life. Sometimes she tells me about the elaborate, saga-like dreams she has, but only after breakfast, because talking about dreams before breakfast, she's told me authoritatively, is bad luck.

"It's okay. Is that the noise you make when you find a spider?"

"I do it shriek-ier. Not for nothing am I the daughter and sister of actresses." She rubs my back again. "You want to talk about it?"

"Maybe." But as I lean back, settling myself into a more comfortable upright position—Greer moving her hand and turning sideways so she faces me—I realize that yeah, I do want to talk about it, or at least I want to talk about it with her.

It takes me a good while, almost as though I need to work up to it. At first we simply sit in the quiet, only old-house noises surrounding us, and I imagine us back on that beach at Turner's Point, the shoreline empty except for us, the clouded night sky a blanket above us. Somewhere along the way I realize this is what my panic attack book would call *visualization*, and damn if it doesn't work in terms of calming me down enough to get the words out. I start small—first I tell her about the meeting with Bart and Henry and she laughs; she tells me I did a good thing, and she shifts to lean against me, tucking into the spot underneath my arm that I've come to think of as hers. She rests her hand over my heart while I talk.

I tell her everything Patricia said, everything I said. I tell her about how frustrated I am, that I go in there for panic attacks and we talk about those, but then also it's all this other—*shit*, shit I don't want to think of or look at or talk about. I tell her I know what Patricia says is right, that it's complicated, but that—even though it makes me sound like a petty, whiny baby—I don't *want* it to be complicated. I tell her I want it to be fixed. I tell her I chewed three pieces of gum in Patricia's office, that I had to do some of those breathing exercises right there in front of her while sitting in that fucking annoying chair, and the damned thing didn't even have the courtesy to stay quiet during my struggle.

What I don't tell her is about the plan, or the lack of a plan, the plan I wanted to start figuring out before the subject of my father came up. But for some reason, as we've talked here, I feel like—I don't know. I feel like maybe *this* is the plan, or at least part of it, maybe this is what I'm working on so I can be in a relationship. Maybe that moment, where I set my hand on Greer's knee and *didn't* lie to her, is part of what it means to let go of feeling trapped, feeling obligated.

"I can't believe she still has that chair," Greer says, and both of us laugh in something like relief at having gotten through it.

I don't know how long it is that we sit there, my head tipped back against the cushions, my eyes closing easily now. I think about reaching for the remote, wherever it is, turning on some Ina Garten. That ought to put us both in the mood to eat. It's late, but maybe we'll still light those candles. Maybe we'll talk about the plan. I've got a dim idea forming about finding a hotel for the next week, up until the showcase, but I decide the idea will keep until tomorrow. Maybe we'll simply fall asleep here, a different night than what I'd imagined, but all right in its own way. Necessary in its own way.

It must be that we doze off. It must be that I'm more tired than I thought. It must be that I really wore myself out today.

Because the next thing I hear is my sister's voice.

"Well, well, well," she says, and I can hear her big smile even before I open my eyes. *Oh, fuck.* "Isn't this just the best thing I've ever seen?"

Chapter 15

Greer

I wouldn't say, in general, that there are a lot of advantages to having a chronic illness as a teenager. Or at all, really, but the point is, as a teenager, there's something specific about the way information regarding your health gets communicated to you, two filters that color every single one of the exchanges. The first filter has to do with the nature of being a minor—when the doctors come in, they're as likely to talk to your parents as they are to you, and sometimes, when you wake up from a deadened, surgical sleep, you might find that it's your parents who are the ones communicating the information about your procedure. They've already heard a whole host of information from surgeons and nurses while you were trapped in a dreamless void, and they're going to filter it in the way they see fit.

And the way they see fit is almost always through the second filter, which I long ago named the "Everything's Fine Face." The Everything's Fine Face is often accompanied by the Reassuring Hand Pat or the Bedtime Story Voice of Placation, but even without these accoutrements, the Everything's Fine Face is designed to inform you that circumstances are absolutely questionable but that you should absolutely not worry about it. You might use the Everything's Fine Face, for example, when you say, "The scan turned up something unexpected," or "Our procedure simply wasn't as effective as we'd hoped."

The important thing about the Everything's Fine Face is that there are degrees of difficulty and capability. My mom's Everything's Fine Face is the worst; even when she tells you your surgical staples look a little inflamed, she delivers the news like you've got five minutes until the atomic bomb in your head explodes. My dad's is pretty good, but he has trouble with maintenance—you might catch him, only a few minutes later, blinking glumly out into the middle distance, his shoulders slumped in defeat. Out of everyone in my family, Cary's Everything's Fine Face is the best, the most natural. He's got a smile that looks authentic, sympathetic, and conspiratorial all at the same time. *This sucks,* that smile says, *but no way will we let it be a problem.*

Of course as I got older I realized that the Everything's Fine Face translates to many situations outside of hospital rooms and doctors' offices, such as when your mechanic finds out what that distressing rattle is, or when your friendly neighborhood computer tech tells you the hard drive has failed, or when a member of your group project realizes, two hours before a deadline, that she in fact did not "understand the assignment."

Or, as I'm realizing now, when your best friend walks in on you sleeping with her brother. With her brother, *on* her brother, whatever.

All four of us are doing it now, with varying levels of success. Ben is definitely the winner here, since he pretty much always looks like Everything's Fine, and coming off three weeks of a European honeymoon, he looks like Everything Is Literally the Best. Now that the initial shock has worn off—now that Alex and I have leapt up and apart—Kit is also turning in a commendable performance, pretending this isn't that unusual after all. "I guess I should've called! We got rebooked on an earlier connection, so—"

"Of course you didn't need to call," Alex says, and jeez. His Everything's Fine Face is not good right now. Not as bad as my mom's, but you definitely wouldn't want him telling you about your hard drive. "Let me help you with your things." He looks quickly around him, gestures vaguely at the coffee table, where he's got a newspaper and his FG, his laptop with the lid closed. "Obviously I'll clean up. I'm sorry for my—"

"You don't have to apologize," says Kit, and this is it, the moment her Everything's Fine Face cracks, seeing how uncomfortable her brother is now in her house. She looks at me, her dark eyes wide behind her glasses, and I'm guessing my face isn't cooperating either.

"Kit, this is—" *Exactly what it looks like?*

"Alex," Ben says, saving me from myself. He hooks a thumb over his shoulder out to the porch. "I could use a hand bringing in some of our stuff."

"Yeah, sure." Before he moves, though, Alex looks to me, a question in his eyes—something sweet and genuine and protective breaking through the initial shock, and I appreciate it; I really do. But also I think this initial awkwardness might be better managed in pairs rather than as a stunned, tentative foursome. I nod my head, and can feel Kit looking back and forth between us.

I know I only have a couple of minutes, depending on how committed Ben is to stalling out there, but as soon as he and Alex cross the threshold out to the porch I look back at Kit and try again. "Alex has been helping me with a photography course, and it—um. Took a turn." *Into the naked.*

"Yes," says Kit, looking at the couch. "I could see that. Are you—"

"It's not serious," I blurt, a knee-jerk, protective lie on behalf of Alex I already hate myself for, at the exact same time she finishes her sentence with an "okay?"

"Am I okay?" I repeat back to her. The discomfort I read on her face before—now it seems that it wasn't directed so much at Alex as it was at me. Maybe it's not so much discomfort as it is—concern.

Already I can hear movement outside again, Ben's and Alex's voices and the sound of Ben's truck door slamming. Kit shifts on her feet. "He's not—he won't be here long term. He never is. I shouldn't have said that, what I said when I came in. I'm jet lagged, and it was a surprise. I just don't want you—"

Oh, God. She's *warning* me. It's kindness, genuine kindness from one of my dearest friends, maybe even more so because it's coming at the expense of her brother, the person she's loved the longest. But kindness and doubt—they've always been two sides of the same coin for me.

Greer, you're not cut out for this kind of thing

Greer, you always take on more than you're capable of

You have to be careful of pushing so hard

"Oh, I know," I say, waving a hand. I am now doing the best Everything's Fine Face of my whole entire life. "It was only for while he's here." I smooth down the front of my shirt, wrinkled from where it was pressed to Alex while we slept. I look up at Kit again, and the expression on my face feels frozen, uncomfortable. "Obviously I know we'll have to talk, you and me, and I'm sorry about this. I didn't think I should call while you were away, and—"

"You don't have to apologize. I always had a feeling he—"

The screen door opens then, Ben first, hauling a huge suitcase that I'm sure Alex, experienced world traveler with a duct-taped rucksack that he is, finds vaguely ridiculous. Alex has a duffel over one shoulder and a laptop bag over the other, and his eyes immediately go to me when he's in the foyer.

"I probably should go," I say, smiling falsely. I picture myself humbly clutching a Best Actress Oscar to my chest, dabbing gently at my smoky eye makeup while I thank the assembled crowd for honoring this very difficult performance. "I have work early tomorrow, and you all should catch up."

"Greer," Alex says, and he's not even bothering with Everything's Fine anymore. But what's he going to do, ask me to stay? It's not his house; we were just *playing* house here, and he can't very well grab his bag from the guest room and come back with me to the townhouse five minutes after his sister's come back from a weeks-long trip. I give a minute shake of my head, another silent message that he seems to hear. "Give me a minute. I'll walk you to your car."

Once we're outside—bags carried upstairs, hugs all around between me and Ben and Kit, whispered promises to *talk soon*—Alex and I stand awkwardly on the curb where my car's parked, me clutching the strap of my purse at my sternum and Alex keeping his hands in his pockets. He mumbles something about that "being worse than the milk crates," but I'm pretty sure I'm not meant to hear.

"Alex, don't worry about this, okay? I told her it wasn't serious." Now I picture myself playing the world's tiniest violin. What am I trying to do, martyr myself out here on the sidewalk? This is like the time my mom told my dad that she really *did* like the toaster he got her for their fortieth anniversary.

Alex looks up at me sharply, apparently unimpressed with my impressive self-sacrifice. "I told you, she's got nothing to do with this. It's just unexpected, that's all."

"Right, yeah. Obviously you'll talk to her, and I'll talk to her—and it'll be okay. She'd love to come to the showcase. I'll tell her about that."

Alex steps into me while I'm gearing up for additional babbling, setting his big, warm hands on either side of my neck, his thumbs teasing the line of my jaw. I shift on my feet, conscious of the window at the front of Kit's house, but Alex leans down and presses his lips against mine, and as Everything's Fine efforts go, this one's pretty good, the kiss soft and unhurried. When he pulls back he keeps his hands and eyes on me, his expression serious, full of the effort I can see it's taking him to stay calm.

"I'll look into a hotel room or short-term rental tomorrow. Something so we'll have a space of our own until I go."

Until I go.

An hour ago, when Alex and I were cuddled together on the couch, maybe this would've seemed like the perfect offer, the perfect solution for our last week together. Some breathing room, some freedom for the two of us while he's here. Maybe we might've even talked about what comes next, *if* something comes next after he goes. But in the face of Alex's shocked expression and Kit's gentle warning, it only seems like we'll be trapping ourselves in a box of our making, ensuring that these final days are going to be one long, painful goodbye.

"Sure," I say. "That sounds absolutely fine."

* * * *

Five. Freaking. Days.

That's how long it takes for Alex to find someplace to stay in the city, probably because of my stupid, reckless hat-on-the-hotel-bed bad luck. First it was a cycling race over the weekend, and then a pharmaceutical sales conference at the start of the week, both of them clogging every downtown hotel and affordable short-term rental. Without a car of his own, staying in the suburbs or out by the airport didn't seem like a viable option, and anyways, when he'd suggested it, he'd told me that Kit's face had fallen in disappointment at the thought of him being so far away. "I get it," he'd said to me later that night. "I'm not here that often, and she just got back. I don't want to hurt her feelings."

That had seemed—enlightened. Certainly more enlightened than the Alex of two years ago, and even than the Alex of a few weeks ago, when he'd stood outside Kit's wedding tent and looked pained at the thought of her knowing he planned to stay in town at all.

But as the days wore on, I could feel Alex grow more tense, more restless—on his laptop more, or worse, on his phone, once or twice picking up calls and having clipped, focused conversations about a job in Syria he's only told me he's still "thinking about." He goes to see Patricia, but returns quiet, thoughtful, something closed off in those sea-glass eyes that keeps me from pressing, from taking the kind of chance with him that had felt easier when we had more privacy.

On Sunday, in a fit of what must have been post-honeymoon optimism or delirium, Kit had asked me and Zoe and Aiden to come for dinner, and while Alex had greeted me with an un-self-conscious kiss on the cheek, I'd noticed the difference in the way he moved in the space—tentative, unobtrusive, compact. On the first floor, there was no record of him—no newspapers left out, no laptop, no FG, no nothing. After dinner, excusing myself to the restroom, I'd made my way upstairs, unable to resist peeking into the guest room he'd been sleeping in—that *we'd* been sleeping in—and my heart had clutched when I'd seen the bed made so crisply, his rucksack stuffed full in the corner, as though he was planning to leave at any moment.

On Tuesday, he'd come to the townhouse, an alarmingly lifelike mouse toy for Kenneth in one hand and a bottle of rosé for Ava in the other. "Good news," he'd said, his brow smooth and untroubled for the first time in what had felt like days. He'd told me about the studio he'd be checking into the next day, and late at night—once we'd heard Doug's gentle snoring through the thin walls—we'd turned to each other, Alex rolling me beneath him and whispering hot, filthy instructions about how quiet I needed to be, how slow I needed to move. When I'd been close to coming, the silence and slowness making my whole body heat and tense in postponed delight, he'd looked into my eyes and set the heel of his hand to my mouth, giving me something to bite down on, and that's what had done it, another secret Alex unlocked about me as my body spasmed beneath his.

But afterward, he'd slept restlessly beside me, and when I'd woken in the morning—6:27, back to normal—he'd been on his back, an arm thrown over his eyes, as though he'd only succumbed to a short, unplanned nap somewhere inconvenient.

Trapped, I'd thought, watching him. *Not enough freedom here for either of us.*

As for me, I take photos like I've got something to prove, anytime I have a chance—some for my assignment, some not; some that borrow from the class lessons I've learned, and some that are uncalculated, sloppy experiments. I pore over them, desperately focused on the showcase, on the letter I need from Hiltunen, on my graduation. Last night, while Alex had finally been checking into his new place, I'd met Kit and Zoe at Betty's, determined to capture a new portrait and a new crowd shot in the bar where we'd decided to take a chance on what turned out to be the luckiest ticket of our lives. I'd stayed late—late enough that it was easy to make an excuse to Alex, to tell him I'd see him at his new place tonight instead, once I finish my final class with Hiltunen.

"This one's nice," says the professor now, his arms crossed over his chest as he looks up at the screen at the front of the room. For our last session, Hiltunen's asked each of us to show up at scheduled times across our normal three-hour window, so he can help us make our final selections for the showcase. I watch him take in a photo from last night—Betty close up, the almost blue black of her blunt-cut bangs striking against her skin, one eye closed in her signature wink, a lucky benediction, the other open in all its blue, heavily eye-shadowed and winged-line glory, her nose scrunched, and her red lips exaggeratedly puckered in an air kiss. It's loud and fun and vibrant. "Good color, good light. Is it on your theme?"

"Yes," I say, but don't bother clarifying. I'll save it for the small caption I'm meant to write for each photograph I choose.

He clicks his remote again, which brings him to the ladybug from our third session. Bright and taking flight, it still makes me smile to see her. "Obviously you'll use this one."

"Yes. Obviously." The colors from the photo project onto Hiltunen's tiny-plaid shirt, and I look away from him, suddenly picturing Alex beside me at The Meltdown, when we'd looked at this picture together. I regret not going to him last night, not taking advantage of every second I have with him.

I shift on my feet, anxious to get this meeting over with.

"You've certainly got your four for the showcase," Hiltunen says, clicking back through, his brow furrowed. He's been mostly vague like this, carefully neutral, not giving me any indication about where I stand with his letter of support. Probably he wants to make sure my association with Alex pays off for him, that his showcase goes off without a hitch.

Behind me I hear the next student come into the room, and again I feel unreasonably restless, conscious of my photographs still on-screen, no matter that whoever it is has probably seen them before. I murmur my thanks to Hiltunen, eject my flash drive from the computer. The student who's come in is one of the women working on a family theme, and she looks restless too, probably nervous about whether the professor will make another asinine remark about babies being "dull subjects, usually." I give her an encouraging smile.

Outside the classroom I readjust my bag clumsily, my footsteps quick as I make my way down the hall. It'll be easier with Alex tonight, in a space of our own. Maybe tonight, we can finally talk—about those work calls he's been taking, about what it's been like for him, here with Kit, about how it's been going with Patricia. I can show him all these new pictures I've taken. I can tell him about this meeting with Hiltunen, about my day at work yesterday.

I can ask him, maybe, about what comes next.

By the building's front door, there's a student standing in front of a large bulletin board. She's holding up a poster-size sheet, her movements hamstrung slightly by the roll at the bottom of the thick paper, which keeps curling as she tries to put a tack in one corner.

"Need some help?" I ask, tamping down my desire to leave here, to get out into the open air and back to Alex.

She turns her head to face me, palms pressed against her poster. She's on the older end of the undergraduate population, maybe a junior or a senior, probably taking summer classes or doing an internship. She's got the effortlessly cool style of many of the students I've seen around this building in the weeks since I've been coming to class here. Her heeled combat boots—worn with short, frayed black shorts—are a red ombré that matches the ends of her hair. I'd probably have to sit with a heating pad for two days if I attempted those boots.

"Thanks." She moves over slightly, and I take the box of tacks from where they rest on the ledge of the bulletin board. "You're coming from the adult ed class?"

"Yeah, last one. Individual meetings tonight."

"I'm Peter's research assistant." She drops the hand that had been holding up the corner I've just tacked. "Doing some last-minute publicity for the showcase around campus."

"Oh." My thumb slips slightly on the head of the tack I'm adding. "That's—" I break off when she takes a step back, smoothing her palms down to unroll the poster. The first thing revealed—big, bold print, headline font—is a name.

ALEKSANDR AVERIN

I barely process what's beneath—a smaller, italic font that's got words like *world renowned* and *National Geographic* and *of a generation*. It's all important, I'm sure, all true, and all likely to make Alex set his mouth in a tolerant but embarrassed expression.

But I'm too busy looking at the picture beneath.

It's Alex—Alex's silhouette, I guess, the long line of his body as he stands on the cement block sill of a huge, glassless first-floor window—bombed or broken out, not even a frame remaining. Beneath the sill there's rubble—hulking, cement pile shapes, rebar sticking out and up haphazardly—but all of it has the effect of looking like a fire set beneath him, banked up either to keep him warm or keep him in place. All of his shapes are familiar to me—the boots on his feet, the utility pants that loosely cover his leanly muscled legs, the gorgeous curve of his back, only slightly compromised by the bulkier vest he wears over his T-shirt, his arms and hands held exactly the way he showed me on the day of our first lesson. The camera itself hardly matters—I've seen his Nikon before, inside the bag he usually kept on one of Kit's dining room chairs, though never with this long lens on—but the way it looks like an extension of him does, the way he's got his whole body held in relation to it. The spot in the center of him, the one he'd slapped his palm over—*Stable here; In, out*—is the dead center of this photograph.

"Wow," I breathe, the only appropriate ending to my aborted sentence. I feel like someone's punched me, right in my dead center.

"I know, right? Last year the guest artist was the engagement portrait photographer for the *Barden Dispatch*. I can't believe Hiltunen got Aleksandr Averin to come."

I got him to come. I guess if I were feeling normal I'd appreciate the double entendre potential of that thought, but I'm absolutely not feeling normal. I'm feeling like this poster is reminding me of all the reasons Alex has had, over the last week, to look tense and restless. And all the reasons I've had not to press him, not to push my luck. Even when I sat in that lecture hall, weeks ago now, the first night Alex touched me, I hadn't really gotten it. I'd known, in the abstract, that Alex had taken those photographs—beautiful and terrifying and *watching*-is-*helping*. But I hadn't really been able to picture it, hadn't been able to picture him *doing* it. Not like I can now.

I clear my throat, take a step back from the bulletin board.

"Good picture, right?" she continues, bending down to reach into a paper grocery bag at her feet. "I found it on Google. There's not many of him out there, but this one's a doozy." She comes up with a single sheet, handing it to me, a reprint of the poster in flyer form. "I can't *wait* to meet him. You want to take a few with you, hand them out to friends and family?"

I'm still blinking down at the one in my hand when I answer her. "No," I say finally. "No, I think one's enough for me."

* * * *

I walk five blocks to the address Alex texted me yesterday. I recognize the building, an old wholesale textile factory that was converted a few years ago into trendy, loft-style condos. When I get to the entrance, I stand and look up to my left and in the distance see the white neon cross of the hospital; to my right I can see the clocktower from the campus quad. Tucked right between two places that are sending me on to freedom.

I take the stairs, three flights, all the while conscious of the flyer I folded in half and tucked inside my bag, the picture of Alex living behind my eyelids like a double exposure—his silhouette stuffed full with images from the last month, of the two of us together. When I get close to the door I hear the sound of music, Spanish guitar again, and I'm already taking a deep breath, knowing another metaphorical punch to the center of me is coming.

Inside the unlocked door it smells like basil and lemon, the light low and a set of candles lined up on a narrow strip of polished concrete that serves as the studio's only eat-in space. Alex stands in a tiny galley kitchen, a white towel over the shoulder of his black T-shirt, his hair messy and his stubble thick like it always is by the end of the day. Another silhouette that makes my heart seize. Big print above: *ALEX, THE LOVE OF YOUR LIFE*. Small print below, Kit's words: *He won't be here long term.*

I think, briefly, about backing out and running right back down the stairs.

But then he turns and sees me, his eyes light, his mouth curving into a smile, the set of his shoulders looser than it's been for all the week we've been kept apart.

"How was it?" He takes the towel and wipes his hands as he crosses to me, leaning down for a kiss—a *welcome home, how was your day* kiss.

But just now, with those twin silhouettes behind my eyes, it's the kind of kiss I'm afraid of, the kind of kiss I don't want to get used to. As soon as his lips touch mine, I curl my hands into his T-shirt, pulling him closer to me, opening my mouth and tracing my tongue over the curve of his bottom lip, a move he answers with a soft, surprised grunt of pleasure. Within seconds his arms are around my waist, lifting me from the ground so I don't have to tip my head back to kiss him the way I want, hungry and open mouthed and hurrying. He starts walking toward the bed but pauses, pulling his mouth from mine briefly. "The dinner," he says, and I like the way his voice is, slightly breathless, needy in sound the way I am in my heart.

"Will it keep?"

He doesn't answer right away, licking into my mouth again, taking another step toward the bed. "I guess I don't care." The quiet laugh that follows rumbles against my chest.

I wriggle away from him, turn us so I'm pushing him toward the bed until the backs of his calves tap the mattress and he sits, his hands going back to brace himself, his knees spread wide apart, making a space for me. I could lift the fabric of my skirt, tuck my hands beneath and shimmy out of my underwear. I could get a condom while he unzips his pants, takes himself out, waits for me to straddle him in the way I know he likes so he can guide himself into me, so he can grab my hips and feel the rhythm I set for the both of us.

But I want something different, something new between us, something I've never—maybe surprisingly, maybe not—done before. Not with Alex, and not with any of the few men I've been with before him.

I kneel between his legs.

"Oh, *Christ*," he whispers, shifting his hips even as I'm reaching for his belt buckle. This part is familiar from the days and nights we've been together—the way he lifts his hips to make it easier, the way he's hard and hot already in my hand, the way he likes a tight, rough stroke. When I lean in, moving one of my hands to tuck under his shirt, stroking the skin along his side, he shifts forward, bringing himself closer to me. It was this part, always, that kept me from trying this before—my head bent like this, the nape of my neck exposed, the white line of my scar visible and the threat of pain if it went on too long, if I couldn't shift and move the way I needed to.

"Greer, you don't have—"

But the rest of it is lost on a groaning exhale as I cover him with my mouth. For the first few seconds, I feel awkward, unsure of the best way to move, what to do with all the parts of myself involved with this—my hand, my tongue, the suction of my cheeks. But even this, the simple act of the attempt, seems wildly arousing to Alex, who thickens in my mouth and grunts out an expletive. Within seconds he guides his hand to that soft vulnerable place on my neck. "Okay?" he asks, because he *always* asks, every time we're together, every time he touches or moves me in a new way, and it's never about condescension or knee-jerk concern.

It's always only about consent—perfect, adult, decide-for-yourself consent, and that alone makes me hot enough, confident enough to keep going with a brief nod of my head.

He shows me with gentle pressure on my neck, with the sounds he makes, with quiet instructions to do it *harder* or *faster*, and within minutes he seems to have lost all the slow control he clings to when he's inside of me, waiting for me to come. He gently squeezes my neck once, a warning, whispers my name. "I'm close," he says, but I stay where I am, taking him as deep as I can. When he stiffens and takes his hand from my skin, moving it to grip the covers in his fist, I feel his release pulse onto my tongue, the taste new and unforgettable, the most intimate thing I've ever done with this man, *any* man.

"Holy shit." His chest is heaving, his hand shaking as he reaches out, pulls me from the floor, and gathers me onto his lap. He laughs softly into my neck, his breath warm and arousing against my skin. "Give me one second, sweetheart. I think you made me forget my own name there."

I wrap my arms tight around him, press my forehead hard into his shoulder, my eyes shut tight against that big, bold font, probably all over campus by now. *ALEKSANDR AVERIN.*

ALEX, THE LOVE OF YOUR LIFE.

Chapter 16

Alex

She's trying to kill me.

The dress is blue, waiting-for-midnight-on-the-beach blue, so unlike the delicate pale blue of her bridesmaid's dress from a month ago. It's also polished and professional and modest in cut—sleeveless, but with a high neck that covers the pale line of her throat, form fitting, but with a low hemline that stops just beneath her knees.

When she turns, though, everything about this dress feels like sin to me—the slit that's barely visible at the back of the skirt until she takes a step forward in the silver heels she's wearing, the same ones she wore at the wedding, the close fit that hugs the curve of her ass, the keyhole cutout that starts beneath the closure at her neck and fans out slightly, like a teardrop, to the middle of her back, showing the gorgeous, strong column of her spine.

If she'd let me get close to her, I'd set my hand right there. I'd place my fingertips on the tiny map-marks I've been studying for weeks, feel steady in the way I haven't been able to in days.

"Aleksandr," says Peter, for probably the thirtieth time tonight. I turn to the latest guest he's brought to me here at the showcase, a tall, white-haired woman who has the same moneyed look as most of the people I've spoken to. Donors, I'm sure, every one, and Hiltunen is using me like a carrot on a stick. "This is Kazuyo Segawa. She's on the university's board of cultural arts."

I shake Ms. Segawa's hand; I smile and answer her questions about the photographs that are hung on the largest gallery wall behind me—but all the while I feel my eyes drift to Greer across the length of the room, standing in front of her own quarter wall, the rest of which she shares with three other students from her class. They're cramped over there, the adult ed contingent. The rest of the space—a vacant storefront rented out along a hip shopping district adjacent to the university—is taken over by my display and the displays of the art students. Hiltunen had boasted about it to me when we'd toured the space yesterday, letting me know that the bigger venue was a gesture to my "high profile," and the students setting up their work not far from mine had looked wide eyed with pride, excitement. It'd made me feel good then, but now, with Greer's class added to the mix, I feel guilty, uncomfortable. Her work is getting dwarfed, her bright, thoughtful pictures and her small explanatory placards drowned out by the crush of people that all seem to push down to my end of the room.

I swallow, take a sip of the water I've held in my hand for the last hour. I nod my thanks to Ms. Segawa as she moves on, take a step back, and try to look remote for a few minutes so I can focus on my breathing.

So I can focus on her.

It was smart, of course, that Greer hadn't wanted to come together, that she doesn't want Hiltunen knowing she and I are anything more than friends. "It's bad enough, the way I've used you for this," she'd said, and that had been—unpleasant. Too casual, too simple, too crass for what Greer and I have been to each other over the last month, but I hadn't wanted to press her, or maybe we haven't wanted to press each other. Since my sister got home, everything between us has been more of a negotiation—how to navigate the time we spend together, where to spend it, who to include— and I'm trying, I'm trying so fucking hard, but I'm terrible at this type of negotiation. Too new and too tentative, unsure of how my old life can work with this new one.

I've been in a holding pattern—unwilling to commit to the job in Syria, unwilling to book the studio I've rented past Sunday, unwilling to talk to Patricia about anything more than how best to manage the anxiety for this night, this showcase, this promise I've made.

That Greer has been different all week—differently shy, differently separate, and now, even differently *dressed*—it's kept me off kilter, bad off enough that once, in a moment of embarrassing, unpracticed weakness, I'd asked Kit if she'd noticed anything unusual about her.

"It's probably not a good idea," my sister had said gently, "for me to be involved with you two."

So. It's definitely not her fault I'm fucking this up.

But I'm resolved. After tonight, after she seals the deal on this thing with Hiltunen, Greer and I will have a chance to turn the corner, to get out of this holding pattern. I'd thought Thursday might be the moment, my plans from the week before finally coming to fruition in a space we could call our own, but after a surprise blow job that had basically made my brain go absurdly, deliciously blank—Greer had turned quiet, had told me the meeting with Hiltunen hadn't been ideal. She'd wanted to go through her pictures again, and so that's what we'd done over dinner instead of what I'd hoped to do—to talk about the two of us, about what happens after this showcase.

Across the room, Greer lifts her eyes to mine briefly, sends me a soft smile before returning her eyes to the person in front of her, a fellow student pointing happily at one of Greer's photos—the black and white, which I try to blur my eyes to, lest it gets me thinking about that hotel room, the one where we first had each other. Took care of each other. I swallow back a fresh wave of nerves, of restlessness, let my eyes drift to the clock on the wall. One hour to go. One hour more I need to be in this hot, crowded room, everyone watching me.

"Alex!" It's Kit's voice, high and excited, and I find her not far from the gallery entrance, one arm in the air waving at me, the other linked with that of the man at her side. There's lots of guests here for Greer tonight—Ben and Zoe and Aiden, Humphrey and Felipe, a woman in a very loud blouse who I think must be her boss from the hospital. At any moment I expect her parents to arrive, her sister and Doug, maybe even Cary and his family.

But this guest is for me, or more specifically, for Kit and me together. I recognize him from his website picture as Dr. Singh, the advisor Kit had all through her master's program, and still her most frequent collaborator. I put up a hand in greeting, nodding a smiling excuse toward the guests closest to me who've been angling for a better view of my gallery wall, and try to make my way to them.

It can't be all that far, maybe thirty feet between us, but it feels like it takes me hours to get there—bumping into other guests, getting stopped, shaking hands, taking compliments, answering questions. All of it should be flattering, bracing, encouraging, but of course, for me—the anxiety of the past week and of being here tonight already at a low simmer—it's not, and I can feel the way my thoughts start spiraling away from me, chastising me for having the anxiety at all, for not being able to do my job, for being unable to enjoy the simple pleasure of being admired for my work. Behind me, I can hear Hiltunen call my name again—"Aleksandr!"—and

I pause in my progress toward Kit and her colleague, frozen, momentarily, between what I know, I *know*, are two relatively small obligations: to meet whomever it is Hiltunen wants to impress, and to meet and thank the man who's been part of my sister's surrogate family here for years.

But they feel huge, impossible. *You're panicking,* I think, feeling the sheen of sweat on my lower back, the roiling heat in my stomach. *They'll notice. You'll ruin this for Kit, or you'll ruin it for Greer.* I swallow, too many times, clutch my water, grateful that I've kept it with me but strangely unable to lift it to my mouth.

"God, it's so crowded in here," Kit says, laughing as she makes the final step to me, navigating around a small crush of people. Dr. Singh doesn't look like he enjoys crowds much either, but he certainly doesn't look as though he's on the verge of a medical event, which is how I feel right now.

"Dr. Singh." My voice sounds hollow and strange to my own ears, though he and Kit don't seem to notice, both of them smiling up at me as I shake Dr. Singh's hand. Immediately I worry it's a mistake, that he'll be able to feel the clamminess of it, the way I've gripped slightly too hard, everything about my body disobedient. "It's nice to finally meet you."

"He was so excited to come," says Kit. "I always show him your photographs."

I nod, my head feeling heavy, outsized for my neck. "I've heard a lot about you over the years," I say, tucking my hand back into the pocket of my dress pants. They're the same ones I wore to the rehearsal, and I have a strange thought, obviously Greer inspired: *Maybe these are bad luck pants. Panic attack pants.* I clear my throat, afraid the pauses to regulate my breathing are too long, awkward. "Thank you for everything you've done for my sister."

Has it come out too fast, overly hasty, insincere sounding? Again, Dr. Singh doesn't seem to notice. He smiles and tells me Kit was first the best student and now the best colleague. Kit shares with me a degree of sheepishness about compliments, and she's turned away slightly, a flush on her cheeks as she shakes the hand of a student I worked with last week, a talented photographer who sold an image to the local paper last month.

"I must say," says Dr. Singh, looking over my shoulder toward my gallery wall, "I always look for your photographs now. I'm quite a consumer of news."

Behind me, I hear Hiltunen's voice again, calling my name.

"I've always wondered how it works," Dr. Singh says, and I try to keep my focus on him. His voice sounds so quiet in this loud room, or in comparison to the noise kicking up in my head. "Do you pick your own stories, or does someone tell you where to go next, or…?"

I don't know if he finishes that thought, if there are more options he offers. I get stuck on the first two, thinking of how I'll answer through this panic, and then when I realize he's stopped speaking and I've said nothing, I feel a new, hot rush of it, my eyes darting to Kit, who's now deep in conversation, to her friends on the other side of the room, to Greer. *Oh, God.*

Everyone will see.

"Dr. Singh," I manage, and for the first time he maybe looks as if he knows something's wrong, though I can't focus enough to be sure. "I apologize. Would you excuse me?"

There's people between me and the glass door, the dark rectangle to freedom I need to get to, and I move as quickly as I can, leaving my glass on a high-top table and muttering more apologies as I go. If Hiltunen's still calling for me, I can't hear it. I can't hear anything over the noise in my head, the endless loop of anxiety that's punishing me with a thousand ugly, upsetting thoughts and only one comforting one:

Just make it to that door. Make it to that door, and you can be alone.

* * * *

Once I'm outside I turn left, walk down a few storefronts so no one inside the gallery will be able to see me out here. I lean one shoulder against the hard, ridged iron of an old-fashioned lamppost, my body sagging into it like it's a soft, reliable friend. At first the panic rises slightly, a tiny crest—here I am, out on the street, *illuminated*, for fuck's sake, where anyone walking by can see—but through my breathing I remember Patricia's reminders over the past week especially. "It only feels like you're the center of the universe during one of these," she'd say. "But mostly, people are going about their business, fighting their own battles. Focus on your own self-care."

So that's what I do. Propped against the unforgiving metal at my shoulder, basically a spotlight shining down on me, pedestrians passing me on the sidewalk, I close my eyes and imagine myself on that dark beach at Turner's Point, Greer next to me on the soft sand. I turn the sound of passing cars into the sound of gentle waves. I breathe in, counting for four, pausing slightly before I exhale, counting for eight. When I feel my unruly thoughts spiral—*What if Kit comes out here, what if everyone inside notices I've left, what if the therapy hasn't helped at all, what if I never get better, what if my career is over, what if I fucking am just like my father*—I do my best to follow the advice of Patricia, of my book. I confront every one of those thoughts; I'm kind to each one of them in a way that would've made me roll my eyes a month ago. *If Kit comes out, she'll be surprised, but she's an adult and she'll understand. If everyone inside notices, you can say you didn't feel well, and everyone knows what that's like. Therapy takes time, and you've made progress. If you never get better, you'll figure out how to manage this. Your career will wait, because you've earned this time.*

You probably are a little like your father, but you're working on it.

It isn't like any of this is a magic bullet. At one point I lose track of the breathing, and I'm sucking wind hard enough to hunch over; I clumsily take a piece of my gum from my pocket and chew hastily, desperately, terrified of getting sick on the sidewalk. After that I basically have to start over—the breathing, the visualizing, the patience with a whole fresh hell of terrible thoughts, coming so quick it's like being in a sandstorm.

But eventually—I don't know how many minutes later—it feels as though the worst of it has passed, my breathing more regular and the tightness in my chest gone, the nausea resettling into something less immediately threatening. My shirt clings unpleasantly to my sweaty back, but the unbearable flush of heat seems to have faded. My hands still shake with the rush of adrenaline, but they'll follow my commands now, and I run them through my hair, smoothing it back into what I hope is something less haphazard.

"Alex?" Greer's voice is breathless, and I feel her hand settle on my back even before she's fully beside me. "I'm so sorry I didn't see you'd come out. I got stuck talking to—"

I take her hand in mine, pressing our palms together and breathing out another gust of air. "It's all right. I think—shit. I think I may have actually handled that one."

She squeezes my hand. "Yeah?"

I nod, already feeling the exhaustion build, the muscles in my legs shaky with the same fatigue I feel after a hard run. "Did—did everyone see?" I ask her, quietly.

She squeezes my hand again. "No. It's so crowded in there. Kit thinks you went to the bathroom to avoid Professor Hiltunen."

"Would have done. He's relentless."

"He's like Mr. Collins." Greer pauses. "I don't know if you've ever read that book, *Pride and Prejudice*? But trust me. Mr. Collins is—not great." She swings our hands a little, and it's nice, this comedown. The first time Greer stood with me for one of these, I'd only felt I'd pressed Pause on the panic, wrestled it into submission for long enough to finish out the rehearsal.

"I'll have to pick it up sometime." I feel myself smile. It's a thin, cautious thing, but it's there nonetheless. A little sliver of hope. "I'm glad you came out. I was missing you in there. Missing you for the last couple of days."

She furrows her brow, makes that hair-thin line appear. "I've been around."

I squeeze her hand this time, only slightly embarrassed at how slick mine must feel. "Been hoping we could talk about things. About what's next."

She avoids my eyes, looks down the street. Her hand now feels stiff, heavy in mine. "I guess we'll see," she says.

We'll see?

I should leave it. I know I should. My head's not right, my body still processing the shock of adrenaline from the panic. There's another forty-five minutes of the showcase, and it's the most important thing right now, not whatever Greer and I have to figure out between us.

But my tongue is loose, my body and mind tired, and I speak without thinking.

"I don't want to just see about it. About us. I want to talk about it. I want us to—I want us to do it."

She takes her hand from mine, moves to delve her fingers into the skirt of her dress. But this one, it's too slim cut, too fitted to her curves for that, and she looks disappointed as she simply smooths them over her hips. There's a long pause. Too long. Endless.

"Alex," she says with a sigh, now lifting one of those fidgeting, frustrated hands to her brow, tracing her fingers across her temple. "I don't know. I don't think it's a good idea."

I blink down at her. "You don't think what's a good idea? Talking about it? Or..." I trail off, not wanting to finish that thought. I want to take this back, this moment of weakness where I brought it up—it was stupid and selfish. I want to give her only the least painful option, the one where we talk about it later. The one where we go back into the showcase together, by each other's side with an unspoken promise to figure out this thing between us after.

She clears her throat. "It's just that—my life is here. And yours is—everywhere. You've never wanted to stay."

"I can make changes to my life," I say. "I can."

"I'm sure you can." She takes a step back, so there's a square's worth of sidewalk between us. "But I—I'm not going to be the one who traps you here. I mean, look at—" She's swept a hand between us, gesturing at me, and I stiffen in shock, in sick surprise.

"Look at what?" I say it quietly. But angrily too. "Look at what, Greer?"

She shakes her head, looks down at her feet. "I only mean that this is a struggle for you, being here. I can see it—how you feel when you're stuck."

Jesus. Bad enough how I've made myself feel about these panic attacks. This hurts like an unexpected blow to the face, Greer seeing one of them as a reason not to be with me. I don't know what expression must move over me, but in response Greer squeezes her eyes shut tight before reopening them, her hands clenched into fists at her side.

"That's not what I meant," she says.

"It is. It's what you meant."

"Alex, I—"

"Listen, I shouldn't have brought it up." I tuck my hands in my pockets, *panic attack pockets*, and try to look unaffected. For myself, for her. "You're probably right."

"No, I'm—" She raises a hand to her brow again, looks over her shoulder back toward the door of the showcase. "Let's talk about it."

"Greer, please," I say, my voice firm, distant, calm. I am such an *asshole*. "I'm sorry I said anything. Go back in, all right? I'll be in right behind you, and we'll finish this."

Finish what, I don't know. I only know I want what I wanted when I left that room, and that's to be alone, to collect myself. For a few seconds, Greer stares across the sidewalk at me, her blue eyes looking darker than usual under the streetlight, against the fabric of her dress, and she's so beautiful, so *necessary* to me that I drop my eyes, stare down at my own feet against the concrete, already rallying my thoughts to go back inside. *It'll be fine. Less than an hour.*

It's why I miss what comes next; it's why I don't see Greer turn away. It's a split second of movement—all that's necessary, really, for my heart to stop beating—Greer turning to go back inside, a shouted, too-late warning, the skid of a tire, the gasp of shock followed by the brief, aborted scream.

And the sick, thudding sound of Greer's body hitting the ground.

* * * *

"She'll be all right, man."

Aiden's voice is a quiet rumble beside me, a gentle giant comfort that's so different from how he was—fast, efficient, emotionless—in those first minutes on the sidewalk, after he'd run out to where it'd happened, to where I'd knelt on the ground beside Greer, the barely even bruised cyclist frantic next to me, to where Greer—

I bring my hands up from where they rest between my legs, press my palms against my eyes, trying to get the image out of my head. Greer on the ground, her body tangled with the frame of a bicycle, blood on the sidewalk, enough of it that I hadn't been able to tell, at first, where it was coming from—a gash across her forehead, one on her leg, a long, ugly scrape from her elbow to the palm of her hand. All of that I could've handled, maybe. All of it would have been easier if she'd opened her eyes. If she'd moved at all.

"They put her—" I say, my voice shaky, my throat clogged with terror even at the thought of it. "On that board." The one they'd strapped her to, calling instructions to each other about staying steady, not moving her head or neck, keeping her as still as possible.

"Not uncommon," Aiden says. "She's high risk, but she was awake in the ambulance. She passed all her pulse, motor, and sensation tests. That's a good sign." Aiden's put his hand on my shoulder, squeezing slightly. We're seated on a row of chairs in the lobby of the emergency room, slightly apart from the rest of the group—Greer's siblings and their respective partners, Zoe and Kit and Ben, even Greer's boss, whom I've learned in the last hour of waiting is named Dennise. She sits a little apart too, her head bent and her hands clasped, as though she's praying.

Greer's parents are with her, rushing into the hospital two hours ago, Susan's keening cry audible even before they passed through the doors. When they'd gone back, welcomed through the swinging double doors by a nurse, I'd felt the same powerful but utterly useless anger and frustration that I'd felt when they'd put her in the ambulance, when Humphrey—her brother, of course her brother—had been the one allowed to ride with her.

I nod at what Aiden's said, desperate to believe him. But I saw her, I *saw* her there, pale and motionless and cut up; I'd been all of fifteen feet away from her and I hadn't been able to stop this, to keep her from this. He could tell me she was dancing a waltz back there, swimming laps, what the fuck ever, and none of it would help until I get some picture of her in my mind to replace the one that's haunting me. *Please,* I think, looking over at Dennise, *be the kind of person whose prayers get answered.*

There's a melodious chime that makes me raise my head instantly, spots from the pressure dancing behind my eyes as I look toward the double doors. It's Michael there, his face drawn but relieved, and he puts both his hands up as we all stand at once, making our way toward him.

"She's okay," he says, and that's the first time I realize Aiden must not have taken his hand from my shoulder, because he squeezes it again, shaking slightly, like he's making sure the news connects, making sure I feel it through my body. Beside me, Kit takes my hand.

"She's got a broken wrist, and sixteen stitches in the cut along her calf, from where she got caught up in the bike chain. Also—uh—" He raises his hand, touches the exact spot on his own forehead where Greer had been cut. "Some glue for the injury here."

"Thank God," someone breathes, maybe Cary's wife; I'm not sure.

"Her CAT scan was good. No skull fractures. No bleeds." He takes a shaking breath. "No damage to her vertebrae."

It takes me a second to realize the noise I hear comes from me, a groaning sob that I have to place my hand over my mouth to stop. Other than the firm pressure from Kit's hand, I've got no idea if anyone else notices; most everyone is breathing out their own relief, putting arms around each other or clasping hands together in gratitude. "Please," I say, grateful to be standing close to the front of the group. "Please let me see her. I—"

Michael looks to me, and I hold his eyes. Maybe I should feel embarrassed. Maybe I should feel like the outsider here. Of everyone out in this lobby, I've known Greer the shortest period of time. I've got the most tenuous connection to her life here. But in the look I give him, I'm trying to tell him that I know Greer just as well.

That I love Greer just as much.

"He was with her," Kit says from beside me. "When she got hit. Please, let him go back."

Michael shifts his eyes to the whole group. "She'll be up in a room within a couple of hours, and then you all can take turns." He looks back to me, giving me a brief nod. "I'll take Alex with me now."

I sag in relief and gratitude against Kit, who's reached her other hand across her body to grip my forearm above where she holds my hand. Aiden gives me a firm clap on the back, and—yeah. He's basically the nicest fucking guy I've ever met, or at least as nice as Ben, as Henry, as Bart—another dot on the map I've made here. I'd hug the hell out of him if I wasn't so busy catching up to Michael.

It's louder behind the double doors, more beeping machines and ringing phones and shuffling feet. When we're halfway down the hall, Michael stops and turns to me. "They gave her something for the pain. She's always been sensitive to opiates, so she—she's not awake right now. Don't let that scare you." He's got a gentle, understanding look in his eyes, beneath all his own concern. "It'll probably be a long wait."

I think about that as we make our way down another hall, past several curtained bays, past a couple of empty gurneys along the walls, past a few medics leaning in doorways, heads bent over clipboards. Years ago, on one of my first freelance jobs in Argentina, I'd met a photographer for Reuters named Oumar who'd watched me shoot a protest in Buenos Aires, masses of young people holding signs and raising fists in the air. "You don't understand the light," he'd said to me, telling me I had to learn to wait for it. I'd argued—I had to get the shot in the moment, when the news was happening. But he'd stuck to his guns. "They'll be here for hours. You'll get a better shot when the light changes. Wait for the light."

I'd taken some of my best pictures later that afternoon, and from then on, I'd done my best, whenever I could, to wait for the right light, to watch it move across the landscape, my eyes chasing it, chasing that moment where it'd give me the right illumination.

So when Michael pauses before another curtained bay, his hand pausing briefly before pulling it back, that's what I steel myself for again, the waiting. I've been waiting for the right light my entire adult life. Chasing it.

I know the light.

And Greer—Greer is the light.

Chapter 17

Greer

Ten years ago, when I had my first surgery, I'd woken slowly to the sounds of my family. Too tired, still, to even open my eyes, I'd merely basked in their collective noise—their messy, amassed effort being quiet. Ava's ridiculous stage whisper, and Cary's deep rumble of a voice, a vibration you can feel even when you can't fully decipher his words. Humph's paper-shuffling in the corner, the crisp way he'd turn the pages of a magazine he wasn't even really reading. My dad's occasional cough, more of a throat-clearing, a nervous habit I recognized from every single doctor's visit he'd ever sat in on. My mother's dramatic sniffles, the almost comically timed gusty sighs, always followed by a muffled patting sound—my father's hand on her knee, tapping his solace onto her. I'd drifted in and out to that noise, appreciated its rising clamor when a nurse would arrive to check on me, the murmured *excuse me*s and sliding chairs, the clicking sounds of monitors being checked, adjusted, updated.

I'd thought, dreamily, in my anesthetized stupor, about how lucky I was.

But after the second surgery, not even a full year later, something had changed about me. I'd grown weary of my family's cacophony, had heard it not as the sound of my own good fortune in having them, but as the sound of their bad fortune in having me. It'd be hours, I'd recognized, even in my drugged state, before I would be alert enough to open my eyes fully, to reassure at least some of them that they could go home, that I'd be fine, that I didn't want to cause any more trouble.

Until then, though, it'd felt like being trapped in a glass cage, beating my wings bloody against their shared concern, their *fear*, their mounting certainty that I'd need more protection and more care than ever.

It's achingly, perfectly quiet now, though, a soft landing out of what I'm experienced enough to recognize as a chemically assisted sleep. Memories of the time before this—a shouted warning, a chaotic tumble to the ground while tangled up with metal and rubber, a long, burning slice against my calf—all of it feels wispy and indistinct, like a dream I'm trying to hang on to before it tucks itself away in my subconscious.

I'm not as tired now as I was after that first surgery, but still I have to work hard to bring my other senses online. Unlikely I'll get my eyes to open—the lids feel heavy and swollen, and even a minimal attempt to flutter them apart has my eyelashes tangling stickily together in a way that makes me think I've been out for a while. But with no cannula pressed against my nostrils—a good sign—I can smell the room. It's antiseptic, mostly, but to my left there's something richer, recognizable, something I've had close to my skin for weeks now. I'm so desperate to get closer to it that two of my fingers twitch against the cool sheets, a jerking motion toward the source of that perfect, longed-for smell.

"Greer." Alex's voice, softer than I've ever heard it, and for the barest, briefest second my heart tells me the same thing it did ten years ago, when I woke to the symphony of Hawthornes around me: *I'm so lucky. I'm so lucky he's here.*

But then I remember. Before the warning, before the tumble, before the slice. Alex hunched in panic. Our strained conversation on the street. *I'm not going to be the one who traps you here.*

"Greer, sweetheart," he repeats, and in those words I hear a world of concern and desperation, and then his big, warm hand comes to rest on mine, his index finger curling over the top of those two fingers I'd managed to move, hugging them in the only embrace my prone form will likely allow.

I work forth a raspy noise deep in my throat—no chance of getting a word out yet; I'll need more sleep and something to drink to get that done, I'm guessing. But the noise is enough to get Alex talking again, and he speaks quickly, almost apologetically.

"Everyone's here, just down in the cafeteria. Your family and also Kit and Zoe and Ben and Aiden. Dennise went home, but she'll come visit you soon. She said not to worry about anything, that it's no problem about work." He pauses, and I hear him take a shaky breath. "You seemed—you were a little restless, with all the noise, so I—well. I'm still pretty good with managing difficult family members, I guess. But I can go get them, if you'd want that." I feel the soft touch of his fingertips along my hairline. "Do you think you'd want that?"

I do my best to squeeze his finger back, to let him know, in the only way I can, that no, I don't want that, not yet.

"I'm so sorry this happened," he says, his voice strained, muffled now, and that's because he's moved his mouth closer to my hand. When he finishes speaking, he presses his mouth against it, his warm lips on my knuckles, and I feel a shudder move through his body, feel the breath he exhales when he raises his head again. I feel something small and warm and wet track between my fingers, and I think, in that muddleheaded, slightly nonsensical way of half consciousness: *Good thing I'm in a hospital. Good thing, because my heart just broke in two.*

I don't know if I fade out again, don't know if time passes in silence or only in this drugged sleep, but when I register noise again it's still only Alex I hear, that same soft, low voice. Alex's hospital voice, I guess, and it's beautiful. Beautiful and terrible, all at the same time.

"When you get out of here, Greer, I'll find us a place to stay, the two of us. Somewhere close to here, so it'll be easy to go to work. I'll—" He breaks off, a pause while he strokes the skin along my arm, stopping when his finger meets the limit of the new, stiff cast that covers almost to my elbow. "I'll get a car, and I can take you back and forth, because the cut on your leg, I don't..." He doesn't finish that thought, only trails off and starts again. "And the showcase, I'm sure it'll be fine; I'll call Hiltunen tomorrow morning. You'll graduate. We'll make sure you graduate."

He talks, so softly like that, all through my feigned sleep, making promises and plans—how he'll take care of me, how he'll handle me, how he'll shape his life to mine. And I know he means to make me feel better, stronger. I know he means to make me feel cared for, cherished. I *know.*

But right now, lying in this hospital bed, even my own damned eyelids not doing my bidding, all I can think is that these are the secret selves I never wanted Alex and me to be to each other: me in this cage, weak and trapped, and him outside—like everyone else who's ever loved me—never wanting to let me out.

* * * *

"You're very lucky, Greer," says Dr. Farroukh, draping her stethoscope back over her neck, her eyes on me as her nurse comes around to the other side of the bed, rearranging the sheet and blanket that had been disrupted during her exam. It's not necessary, really, for Dr. Farroukh to have come by; the doctor who'd treated me overnight has already been by once to check in and give the okay for work to start on my discharge papers, but Dr. Farroukh is the neurosurgeon who did my second surgery, and the one who's overseen all my checkups and physical therapies since. Since it's a Sunday morning, not even 10 a.m., I'm guessing this was a special trip—a call, perhaps, made at the insistence of my mom, who'd been begging nurses for her number last night.

"Yes," I say. "I feel very lucky."

"Still feeling a little woozy from the meds?" Her brow furrows, and I guess I wasn't all that convincing with my tone.

"Just—um. Sore, I guess. All over." *On the inside of me. In my heart.*

"I think they should keep her here another night," says my mom, from a chair in the corner of the room. God knows how Alex got her to go even to the cafeteria overnight; maybe he shot her with a short-term tranquilizer dart or something. Since I've been awake this morning, she's been like a hovercraft directly over my face. She's only in the chair because it was hard for Dr. Farroukh to do her job with such limited access to my body. "Don't you think they should keep her another night? Because I read something about brain bleeds, how they can show up days after a fall—"

Dr. Farroukh smiles at me first, a knowing commiseration that we've formed over years of our doctor-patient relationship, and then turns to my mom. "Very unlikely here. As Dr. Charles said last night, it's pretty clear that the knock to the head was minimal." She taps my cast, whisper soft, with the tip of her pencil. "That's why she's in this thing for a few weeks. Broke a bone, but also broke her fall successfully."

My mom wrings her hands, her eyes brimming with tears. Her liner looks spectacular, though. Maybe she got it tattooed on for her half birthday.

"I'm okay to go home today," I tell the doctor, who turns back to me.

"I think so too. But I think we'll want to do some extra physical therapy in the coming weeks. That soreness—it's going to chase you for a while."

"Yeah. I'm sure."

We're going over a few things—when I can start PT, whether I should add back in some muscle relaxers for a few weeks—when there's a soft knock at the open door and Alex steps in cautiously, holding a tray full of to-go cups in his hand. I'd been wondering if he'd gone—if I'd maybe dreamed him here last night—but seeing as how he's wearing a version of the same clothes from the showcase, a tear in the knee of his dress pants, a white T-shirt that he must've been wearing as an undershirt beneath his now-bloodied dress shirt, and seeing as how his stubble is thick again, the skin beneath his eyes darkened, I'm guessing he slept here, either in this room or in one of the small family lobbies nearby.

"I can wait outside," he says, taking a step back, but my mom stands from her chair, holding her arms out for a hug as though he's a long lost friend she hasn't seen in years. For a second, Alex's widened eyes track to mine in an expression so comically startled that I smile, feeling a discordant note of lightness, looseness.

Dr. Farroukh takes advantage of the hug and coffee delivery to lean down slightly, speaking only to me. "You really are fine, Greer. The most important thing is to rest, okay?" She sends a speaking glance my mom's way before looking back to me. "Whatever that means to you."

I nod, making an effort to keep my expression neutral, realizing immediately that nodding is a real bad idea for the foreseeable future.

When she's gone, my mom moves to resettle back in her chair, moaning over the first sip of the large latte Alex has brought her. "Mom. Do you think you could give me a few minutes? With Alex?"

"Oh." She looks wounded, runs her finger around the top of her coffee lid. "I suppose I could go find your father."

"Why don't you go home and get showered, or take a nap? Ava's bringing me a change of clothes."

"Greer, I'm not going to leave you here alone."

"I'm not alone. Alex is here."

"Kit and Ben are still here too, Susan," Alex says. God, his voice. He wouldn't even need the tranquilizer dart. He should be a hypnotist. An audiobook narrator. "They're with Michael in the family rest area down the hall."

"Mom, please," I add.

It's five minutes before she goes. She's got a lot of things to do, such as to feel my forehead as though the problem with me is a fever, to add another blanket to the foot of my bed even though I've already complained of being hot, to adjust the water bottle, tissue box, and bottle of lotion that have been left for me on a rolling tray that she insists on placing over my lap, and to stand by the bed with her hands on her hips, looking down at me with tears in her eyes as she tells me how glad she is I'm all right.

By the time she's left the room, I'm hot faced and humiliated, feeling childish and pathetic, and it gets worse when Alex takes the blanket and the bed tray away, smiling crookedly as he pulls the chair closer to the bed, sitting beside me. "She's a lot," he says, but it's not cruel or judgmental. It's an effort, I'm sure, to defuse the tension and shame coming off me. "I brought you some tea, if you'd like that."

"No, thank you." I make a move to push myself up more, giving Alex a sharp look when he reaches forward, attempting to help me. "I'm fine."

"Okay," he says quietly, sitting back.

"Alex, listen. I wanted to say, I'm sorry about last night. About what I said."

"Hey," he says, reaching out and setting a warm hand over mine. "There's nothing to be sorry about. I should be apologizing to you. I can't believe I didn't see, Greer. I can't believe I didn't stop—I'd do anything to go back and stop it."

"No, please. Don't do that, okay? I don't want that, for you to apologize. It was an accident. Bad luck, that's all." He takes his hand away, runs it through his hair.

I let my eyes stray down, taking in the hospital gown I'm wearing. I wonder if Alex recognizes it, the pale blue fabric with the tiny gold stars. The same type of gown I woke up in after my second surgery, the one that worked. I can feel him watching me.

"I'm sure you understand," I say, my voice careful, slow. I hope I'm not slurring anything, conscious of the aftereffects of the meds. "I'm sure you understand why I'd like you to go."

From the corner of my eye, I see his body startle in his chair, a small, sharp movement. "No. No, I don't understand that."

I clear my throat. "Well, I think you can—" I gesture in the direction of the door my mother just went out of. "You see I have a lot on my plate here. Enough people I'll have to manage. Enough people to take care of me."

"I'll manage everyone. You don't know how good I am at that. And I'll take care of you."

God, he sounds—he sounds *scared*. I risk a glance over at him, see he's sat forward in his chair, his hands clasped together tightly between his knees. If it hurts this bad to see him this way now, when he's wanting to stay, I hate to think how bad it'll hurt to see him this way when he's wanting to go. When he's trapped in this new place he imagines getting for us, when he's driving me back and forth to work, when he's answering phone calls from my worried parents, when he's watching me with my head in the toilet, sick and silent with a migraine.

When he's desperate to go, to get back out there to the thing he waited for his whole life.

Big bold font, right at the top of the page. *FREEDOM.*

"I know it wasn't right what I said, about the panic attacks. I know it's more complicated than what I—implied last night. But I still think it's better if you go."

"You don't get to make this decision for me, Greer. I'm telling you, I don't want to go. I want to stay here, with you. I love you."

I have to swallow the catch that bounces up my throat, the beginning of a sob. I concentrate on the room around me—the antiseptic smells, the low hum of the monitor that's on the IV pole, the dry erase board across from me that has my name written on it, followed by the nurse's name on duty. *Fall Risk*, it says. I wish I'd told Alex before, that I love him. I have a feeling that if I had—if I'd told him that night Kit came home, the night he'd had that spooked, wary Everything's Fine Face on—he would've been gone long before this showcase, long before this accident. He never would have said it back, and definitely not this way, when I look like this. When I feel like this.

"I don't—" I raise a hand to my face, rub my hand across my forehead, feel the stiff residue of the glue that holds my cut together. "I don't want to argue."

"Sweetheart," he says, and I—I have *got* to get him out of here. I'm hurting and I'm tired, and I don't want to do this with him, not now. Not ever.

"The thing is, I do get to make this decision," I say, bracing myself to look right at him now. "I want to be alone, and I know you understand that, at least. I told you before. You can't do this with me, and the problems we had before this are the same problems we'll have after this."

It's too much, to see the hurt and confusion on his face. I drop my eyes again.

"We don't *have* problems." He stands from his chair, moves to the foot of the bed, so it's harder for me to avoid his eyes. He waits and waits, until I look at him. Now he looks coiled, tense, frustrated. He *hates* being told what to do. He hates not being in control, having his fate decided for him. He hates being stuck. That's all this is, this fight he's putting up.

"Alex—"

"We have a—*relationship*," he says, emphasizing the word, as though he's been practicing it. "I told you last night, I can make changes to my life, to the way I work. To the way I *live*. It's what I want to do. I can do a hundred other things with my life. I don't care if I never take another fucking photograph."

For a long moment, I let that sit in the air. What a ridiculous, offensive lie—a swatting, aimless, feckless attempt to get what he wants from me in this moment. What a show of all the things he hasn't truly thought about, if he'd actually propose giving up his career. Not even his career—his calling. A part of his soul I've seen in those pictures. It's an absolute, dead-end confirmation for me. If this is what Alex is thinking about his future, about our future together, we'd never, ever make it. Not even for the time it'll take for these bruises to heal, for this cast to come off.

I look back down at my hands, one curled into the cast, one spread over my gown and the textured white blanket atop it. I worry I'll lose my resolve, that I'll look at him—see the face that's smiled at me, the arms that have held me, the hands that have touched me—and say, *Stay*, and that afterward, I'll always wonder if this is it between us, that we trapped each other. That he stayed to take care of me, and that I—in spite of everything I've worked for, in spite of all the freedom and independence I've been chasing—let myself be taken care of, again. Always.

So I look up at him, making my eyes and my voice as vacant as I can, and say the words I know will work.

"I don't believe you."

Chapter 18

Alex

Kit finds me in the hospital cafeteria, at a table that's empty of everything except for my phone.

I don't notice her coming, because I've been staring at that black screen for the last hour, since Greer sent me out of her room with a look final enough to convince me that it'll never light up again. I feel formless, fatigued. There's a distant ringing in my ears. My elbows, resting on the slightly sticky laminate surface, each weigh ten tons; they're pulling my entire upper half down, curling my spine, and if I didn't hear Kit's voice interrupt me, I'm pretty sure I'd lay my forehead down right onto that shiny, black, rectangular void in front of me. I'd disappear there, hoping, hoping, hoping she'll call me.

"Alex." Kit slides into a chair across from me, lets out a gusting sigh of relief that I feel brush across my knuckles. I curl my fingers in, thinking of how Greer's hand had held mine overnight, how cool her fingers had felt. "Are you okay?"

"No." There's a new reflection on the black screen, a winking light from Kit's glasses in the upper right corner.

There's a long, strange pause—the time when anyone else might say, *What can I do*, or *How can I help*, but of course Kit must not be thinking of any of that right now. Greer's her best friend, after all, so she's probably not okay either. I look up, finally, because it's still there, that instinct—to make sure my sister is all right, and I see her tuck two fingers underneath the right-side lens of her glasses, pulling down and to the side, the same way she'd do when she was a kid, tired and upset.

"I'm sorry," I say to her, though I don't really know why. Maybe I'm sorry for not being okay.

"Sorry for what?" she says, lowering her hands, setting her elbows on the table too, so we're mirroring each other. "It was an accident. It's just that for Greer, an accident is bad news."

"They say she'll be fine." I'm trying to mimic the conviction the doctor seemed to have.

"Yeah. She—" Kit's voice catches; her chin quivers for a second. "She looks terrible. It's scary."

I lean back, sick to my stomach, entirely unable to comfort her. When I close my eyes, I see Greer in that bed, stiff and bruised and pale, and I feel like I won't ever sleep again.

For the first time I notice that Ben's here too—over by the counter, filling up Styrofoam cups of water and setting them in a cardboard caddy. I wait for him to come over, try to come up with some bland greeting that'll conceal the fact that my heart's broken inside my body. But once he's done stocking up he only nods my way, a look in his eyes that makes me think he can see what I'm trying to hide, anyway. A quick wave from Kit and he's gone, heading back, I'm guessing, to where everyone waits for Greer's discharge to come through.

There's something familiar about the quiet in here. Inside this cafeteria, Kit and I are basically alone—there's a couple in the corner who sip coffee and look at their phones, nothing unusually urgent or sad about their postures. All around us, though, is noise—voices, elevator dings, PA announcements, muted rings and beeps from phones. What I can't hear I can feel: the chaos of a hospital, people sick and in crisis, family and loved ones desperate for answers and reassurance. Doctors and nurses, all kinds of caretakers, stressed and fatigued, hustling from one task to the next. Kit and I never spent much time in hospitals before, at least not before my dad's stroke. But finding quiet in chaos? Making a safe space out of just the two of us?

That's right in our wheelhouse.

"Kit," I say now, fractionally calmed by the familiarity, but tentative about trying something else with it. I've never been the one to look to her for help, and I've done it twice now, about Greer. I take a deep breath before I continue. "I don't know what to do."

I meet her eyes—those black pools of light I know so well—and see something change in them. A trace of something like resolve, something like—pride, maybe. Gratitude that I've asked. "Tell me what you need," she says, her voice serious and calm and...familiar. It's *my* voice, really. It's something I've taught her.

"She doesn't want me here. She asked me to go."

Kit gusts out a sigh, rubs her eye again, and nods. "She doesn't much want us here either. She's never liked people knowing she was sick."

"I don't care that she was sick. I don't care if she's sick now."

"I know you don't." Something's changed in her posture. She's got her head cocked slightly to the side as she looks at me. "But Alex, she is going to be okay. All of us are here to help her, and watch over her. And you were—I mean, you were leaving anyway, right?"

I look up at her sharply, like she's just done something simultaneously incredibly stupid and incredibly smart—like she's tested my boundaries in the same way she used to. Taking apart our dad's old weather radio, laying out tiny pieces all over the floor to test herself for reassembly. Making dry ice with a plastic bag and a hallway fire extinguisher. Growing rock candy on a skewer inside a jar—a development that'd near given me a heart attack, thinking Kit had somehow found her way into the world of manufacturing hard narcotics at the age of eleven.

"I'm not leaving her," I say. "I'm in love with her."

There's a long stretch of silence. The couple at the other table gets up, clears their trays. The lone cashier's turned on a television set in the corner, and I recognize the urgent chords of the intro that plays on the local news station I've been watching while I've been in town. Breaking news, maybe, and I have never cared less. Kit folds her hands, one on top of the other.

"Alex." It sounds like my voice again, a version of it that I'd use on her. A thread of discipline to it. "You're always leaving. I love you, and it's okay with me that you leave. I'm fine with that now—it's who you are. But Greer—" She breaks off, takes a deep breath before restarting. "What happens when she gets better? You love her, okay. But you'll leave again."

For the first time in years, there's no accusation in what Kit's said about me. It's been a tender spot for us ever since she settled here, ever since she'd started to make herself a true home—her need for me to want one too. Holidays, short visits, whatever, it was always the same: Kit pushing me to stay. And me desperate to go.

"It's not who I am. It's what I *do*."

"Okay," she says, sort of drawing out that last syllable. Like she's not really clear on the difference. Like she's just indulging the semantics.

I'm worried about what I need to tell Kit about this, to make her understand. I'm worried it'll hurt her feelings, make her feel somehow like

Greer's been more to me in the course of a few weeks than Kit was for her whole life. But Kit—Kit's a married woman now. Kit's lived a whole life here, learning what it means to belong somewhere.

"I don't want to leave her. I didn't want to leave her before this. I hadn't slept in days before the showcase, thinking of how I could stay with her."

"Weren't you already booking a—" Kit begins, but I shake my head no, cutting her off.

"I hadn't booked it. I didn't want to book it until she and I—"

Something blinks alive in my memories then, fleeting at first—a late August day in northeast Ohio. A pickup truck I borrowed from a buddy at the paper. A Soundgarden song on the radio. It feels so important that I close my eyes, trying to catch the rest of it.

When I do, I lean back in my chair, almost as though I've been pushed. "Holy fuck," I breathe out.

My first panic attack. I remember it.

"What?" Kit asks, her voice concerned, higher pitched than usual. "Alex?"

"I have panic attacks," I say, bluntly, loudly. Probably the cashier's heard it. "An anxiety disorder."

Kit stares at me, her mouth slightly open. "You—?"

I stand from my seat, grab my phone in my hand. Press the button on the side to light up the screen, in case there's some minuscule chance I missed a message while I had my eyes closed. Some chance Greer has changed her mind. But I know already she won't have. Why would she? When have I ever shown her I was the kind of man who'd stay, who'd *really* stay in the ways that matter most to her?

Kit stands too, her brow furrowed. If she's still shocked, she's covering it well; she's pure concern now. "Are you having one now?"

"No. But I need to step outside for a minute. I'll stay right by the front doors. Can you call me if—" I scrub a hand through my hair. *If Greer wants me,* is how I want to finish that sentence, but I saw the way she looked at me. I saw how determined she was. I know I'm going to need to have something real to tell her if I want to change her mind. "Will you call me?"

"Yeah, sure. But, Alex—what are you going to do?"

I swipe a hand over my face, feel the way my beard's grown in. "Well, Kit," I say, a strange, breathy laugh escaping me. "This is going to sound pretty fucking surprising to you, I guess, but I'm going to start by calling my therapist."

* * * *

Thirty minutes later, I'm pacing outside a long panel of sliding glass doors that lead into the hospital lobby, my phone in my hand like a crutch. While I've been waiting, I've used it for three things: First, to text Jae to tell him I'm not taking the job in Syria, but that I'll call him soon. Second, to frantically tap out what I remembered in that cafeteria, a poor substitute for my journal. Third, to cling to the relentless, stubborn hope that I'll be needed.

"You look terrible."

I stop midpace, turn to face Patricia, who's wearing track pants and a Yale T-shirt, a pair of huge, teal-framed sunglasses pushed onto the top of her head, her steel-gray hair curling riotously around them. "I slept here. Thanks for coming."

She nods, her face grim. "Is she all right?"

"They say she'll be fine," I answer, feeling slightly guilty. When I'd first called Patricia, I'd figured I'd probably catch her voice mail—I'd tell her I'd remembered something. I'd ask her if I could get in first thing Monday. I'd wait for her to call me back. But instead she'd picked up on the second ring, and I'd been so relieved that I'd blurted out, "Greer was in an accident." In my haste I'd forgotten. Patricia, of course—Patricia who's half the reason Greer's as healthy as she is today—would care about that news.

"I'm sorry you had to come all the way down here on a Sunday."

She shrugs. "I was only cleaning the bathroom. Let's go for a walk." She gestures over to where there's a concrete embankment a few yards from where we stand, a couple of hospital visitors and an orderly smoking cigarettes. "The smell is giving me an old jones."

I look over my shoulder toward the doors, shuffle my feet uncomfortably. I don't want to be so far from her.

Patricia rolls her eyes. "Listen, pal," she says, lifting her left wrist and shaking her Fitbit in my face. "I need to get my steps in. There's a track two blocks away. Your phone'll work there."

I type out a text to Kit, let her know where I'll be, and follow Patricia.

On the way we're mostly quiet. She asks me a couple of questions about what happened with Greer, and I answer them briefly, quietly, not even wanting to release the terror I'd felt into the air, more bad luck superstitions rubbing off. On the track, though, Patricia moves fast, her steps churning up the springy, orange-and-white surface, her face focused in the same way it is in her office. "So you said you remembered something." Her breathing is deliberate, her eyes straight ahead.

"Yeah." I take a few seconds, match my breathing to hers. It'd been a relief to remember this, back there in the cafeteria; it'd felt like a breakthrough.

But now I'm afraid of what Patricia will say when I tell her. I'm afraid she won't see it as the answer I think it is.

She turns her head, cuts me a look. "I'm thinking of charging you double for this, so get a move on."

"The first one was the day I dropped Kit off for college."

In the quiet Patricia leaves there, I tell her what I remember. I'd been excited that day—really excited, and not just for Kit. I'd been searching classifieds for apartments in Cleveland, something that'd put me close to the paper. I'd been kicking around the idea of going to Columbus, where there was more political work. I'd made a plan: New York City by the next January, when I knew Kit'd be settled.

Kit had ridden next to me in that borrowed truck, a new backpack I'd bought her tucked between her feet for the entire forty-five-minute drive from the dingy suburb we'd been living in for her last couple of years of high school. I'd carried everything we'd brought with us up three flights of stairs to her dorm, trying to ignore how much less Kit had in comparison to her roommate, a girl named Megan who looked at me like I was a dessert that had arrived at her dinner table. I'd shaken the hands of other parents, and I'd thought of how far I'd come. I felt like a man there, dropping off my brilliant sister whom I'd raised. I'd taught her what she needed to know. I'd leave her there and she'd be fine, and I'd finally, *finally* be free.

Then I tell Patricia about what happened when I got back in the truck to drive home.

"I thought I was just sad. A little choked up, you know? She'd cried when she'd hugged me goodbye, so—you know. I figured it was hard driving away from her."

"Sure," says Patricia, a matter-of-fact agreement that seems based in experience. "They ought to hand out benzos at college drop-off day."

"Maybe." For a second I'm back in that truck, thinking about the way I'd pressed my foot more firmly on the gas, turning up the radio. "I wasn't choked up, though. I was—I *choked*. Couldn't breathe right. Chest in a vise. It'd never happened before that. I know because I was so freaked out I pulled the car over."

I'd gotten out. I'd leaned over the guardrail at the edge of the highway and waited for a sickness that never came. I'd barely heard the cars speeding by, my heart beating so hard, so loud in my ears. I'd watched my hands tremble every time I'd try to lift them from the hot, sunbaked metal.

"Must've been scary," says Patricia.

I nod. It had been scary. "I thought about driving to the hospital. I kept thinking I'd die. I thought—" I break off, allow myself a slow breath through my nose. "I thought maybe my sister had been the only thing keeping me alive."

"Hmm," Patricia says, her pace quickening.

"So that's it, right? I don't have panic attacks because I feel trapped or stuck. Maybe I have them because—because I don't always know where to go."

I'm a couple of steps ahead before I realize Patricia's stopped on the track, so I turn to face her. She's got a sheen of sweat on her forehead, the hair at her temples damp. I must've been talking for a while. "So you think you've solved it, huh?"

She's said it in the way that you know means you have not, in fact, solved it. If we were in her office I'm sure the chair would've made its feelings known.

"I was scared to death for Greer. I'm still scared, all the way into the center of my bones. But I didn't panic, not once, not the whole time I sat beside her in that hospital room. I don't feel like panicking now, and I've got no intention of leaving her. I'm *staying*, and that doesn't bother me at all. I'm supposed to be here with her."

"Greer's not the answer to your problems. She's not medicine for you, and she's not a test you pass." Greer's words, from a month ago, echo back to me. *It doesn't work like that.*

"I didn't say—"

"Alex, I told you from the beginning. Anxiety is complicated. *You're* complicated. You want to make this about one thing."

I shove my hands in my pockets, stare across an expanse of the track at her. "I want it *fixed*," I say, through gritted teeth.

"Okay, sure. One month and we've worked out the fact that your mother died before you could remember anything about her. We've worked out that you lived with an abusive, addict father who put you in the direct path of danger since you could walk. We've obviously solved the problem that you parented a sibling when you were a child yourself. And let's not forget when we tackled the last decade of your life, where you pathologically sent yourself into the center of chaotic, devastating humanitarian crises all over the world. I should charge you triple."

I feel the way my jaw has set in frustration. I don't want to do this right now; I don't want to go over it again. I want back in that room, where I left everything about me that matters.

"She thinks I only want to stay because I feel sorry for her. She thinks what I've wanted all along is to get back out there and now I won't because"—I pull my hand from my pocket, gesture toward the hospital—"because of *this*."

"So what do you want, a doctor's note? You want me to write her a letter and say you're all better, that you won't have any more panic attacks from sticking around? That you're not staying here out of obligation?"

Not a bad idea, a really dumb part of my brain tells me, the part of my brain that's exhausted and lonely and terrified of losing Greer. Instead I say, "No." But it sounds sullen. It sounds like I've been caught out after curfew, not that I ever had one of those. It sounds like I'm telling her I wouldn't jump off a cliff if all my friends did.

For a good half minute, neither of us says anything, and in that time all the hope and adrenaline of my memory seems to drain out of me. I feel it pool at my feet, feel my body sink by degrees into it. I think of Greer in that bed, her already blackening eye and her braced wrist, the tight line of her mouth as she'd turned her face from me.

"She kicked you out, huh?"

I nod, keeping my chin down. My throat is tight; my eyes are wet. I don't think I've ever wanted a hug so bad in my life. It's humiliating, what I'm thinking right now. Unprofessional and probably disrespectful.

I'm thinking about what it'd be like to have someone like Patricia for a mom.

"You know that's not necessarily about you, right? Her telling you to leave?"

"I know she doesn't like me seeing her this way. She's—" I pause, think it over. I want to use the exact right words. "She's proud of herself, for being as strong as she is. It's hard for her to have a setback."

It's Patricia's turn to nod, and I know I've put her in a tough spot here, or at least I know we've put each other in a tough spot, sharing Greer between us. I may be Patricia's patient, someone who pays her for her services, but Greer's more than that to her.

When we're moving side by side again, Patricia takes a deep breath. "I'm sure it's hard for you too. You finally figure out you can stay somewhere, and once you do, you're not needed anymore."

"Jesus, Patricia. You want to kick me in the nuts while you're at it?"

"Again with this drama. You can take it. But you can't sit around outside the hospital and wait for her. It's not good for either of you."

"I want to show her that I can be here for her. Not just that I can be. That I want to be."

Patricia doesn't look over at me, but I can feel her thinking, turning something over in her mind. "I'm not charging you for this," she says, a blunt, brook-no-argument tone to her voice. "This isn't me giving you therapy, okay?"

"Okay."

She stops again, puts her hands on her hips as she looks up at me, her serious face almost funny in those big blue sunglasses, if I were in the mood to find anything at all funny.

"I need to try and say this in a way that's professional." She looks down, takes in her track pants and T-shirt, and shrugs. "Imagine you're a person," she finally says, choosing her words carefully. "Imagine you're a person who had years—painful, scary years—when people weren't hearing what you told them. About how you felt."

Except you, I think, and nothing about Patricia is even almost funny now. She should be standing there with some kind of medal around her neck, for saving Greer. For hearing Greer.

"And then afterward, everyone who's ever loved you said you weren't strong enough to do things on your own. Can you imagine it?"

She's asking it rhetorically; we both know I can't. It may well be the biggest gulf there is between me and Greer. No one's ever taught me I wasn't strong enough. No one's ever taught me there was an option to be anything but on my own. So I don't say anything at all. I wait for her to finish like I'm waiting for a verdict.

"I know you don't want to hear it, Alex. But maybe the way you show her is to go. Maybe you leave, and she'll know you believe she's tough enough to take it."

Chapter 19

Greer

"Mom," I say, my voice croaky and slightly impatient, my fingers clenched around the phone. I repeat it when she doesn't seem to have heard me—when she continues right on, reminding me for what must be the hundredth time about "the scare you gave the whole family."

"I've taken a Xanax every morning since the accident. I don't see why you won't come here and stay with us."

From my spot on the couch, I lift my still-heavy head from where it rests on two pillows I've stacked behind me and peer past where Kenneth's perched at my feet. Outside the front window I see the tidy post light that stands between our townhouse and the neighbor's, the orangey glow that lights the pond's geyser-like fountain. Every once in a while, a beam of light crosses through the room, and I hear the gentle swish of tires moving slowly through the neighborhood, no one ever going faster than the prescribed, frequently posted 20 mph, lest they attract Joyce's Listserv wrath. I close my eyes and think about the city—noise and light and open all night, and so far away right now I don't ever feel like I'll get back there.

"Because I'm fine," I tell her. "I don't need to be staying with anyone."

"Ava says you kicked her out."

I sigh, set my fingers against my sternum, feeling it fall with my exhale. "Mom, you know she didn't say that." When Ava had come to the hospital Sunday morning, a small backpack of my clothes in her hand, I'd asked her to help me change in the bathroom, away from the prying ears of my mom, who'd done a *very* authentic shocked face when she'd returned to find Alex gone. "Please, Ava," I'd said to her, my chin wobbling. "Please, just let me have a few days to myself." She'd hugged me when I cried, had helped me wash my face and comb my hair into something presentable. She'd told me she'd stay at Doug's place, and I'd said, "Who even knew Doug had an apartment," and both of us had laughed before I started crying all over again.

She left me all her bath bombs too.

"Well," my mom sniffs. "She doesn't like it at Doug's. Doug doesn't like it at Doug's. He played a video game here yesterday! Your father thought we were having a military event in the house."

Normally I'd laugh at this. Maybe some part of me is laughing, but I can't get to that part, not right now. I'm tired and sad and in a stupid amount of pain. Getting hit by a bike, for God's sake. Maybe I'd laugh at that too, if I were literally any other person. If I had any other body. Instead I say, "Yeah. His video games are pretty loud."

"I asked Humphrey to stop by there after work yesterday. But he said no. He said we should give you some space." I shift against my pillows, my face heating. I'll need to apologize to Humph. He'd stopped by here before work yesterday, on his own accord, I guess, bringing a loaf of banana bread Felipe had made me. I'd accused him of doing Mom's bidding, coming to check up on me, and even after that, I'd *still* taken the banana bread.

I am a jerk of the first degree.

"He's right."

"You're still weak," Mom says, and I know she just means from the accident. My wrist in a cast, my brain foggy in the mornings from the muscle relaxers I take before bed, the cuts on my head and leg alternately burning and itching, my whole body tender from bruises I didn't even know I had. But of course that's not what I hear, and right now, I'm too tired, too frustrated to manage my response.

"I'm not weak," I snap at her, and I hear her intake of breath through the phone.

There's a few seconds of silence while my mom probably does one of two moves. Either a dramatic gathering of courage—chest expanding, chin raising, eyes steeling—or, if my dad's nearby, a subtle but effective crumpling—shoulders curling in, lips trembling, brows furrowing. "I guess you don't need my help, then," she says, so it was definitely the crumpling move. She sniffles again, and my heart clenches.

"Mom, I'm sorry." I pinch the bridge of my nose, then jerk my hand away when I feel the soreness there reassert itself. By Sunday afternoon, what I'd thought would just be some slight bruising around my eyebrow had developed into a full black eye, and the only good thing about that was that Alex had been gone by the time it'd looked its worst.

"I know you're just trying to help. But it—" I pause, resettle my head on the pillow, try to think of how to say this in a way that won't be hurtful. "It feels better to be by myself right now. It makes me feel stronger." *Sort of,* a voice in my head adds, the same voice that practically screamed out a Susan Hawthorne-inspired *Noooooooo!* as Alex had walked out my hospital room door.

Almost a whole week ago now. Forever ago.

"I don't mean to smother you, Greens." Her voice is softer now. "I know you don't like it."

My head fills with old memories. My mom lying next to me in a hospital bed, gingerly placing herself so as not to disturb all the things attached to me, telling me ridiculous, surely embellished stories about her time in New York, making me laugh so hard that she'd have to pat my arm to settle me, to keep me from disturbing some of those things myself. Directing my brothers and sister like a small army of caretakers, the look of icy warning she'd give any one of them if they acted—even for a second—like I was an inconvenience. Her mask of genuine, devastated shock when my first neurologist had told her about my diagnosis.

"You don't smother me, Mom." I curl my toes against the arm of the sofa, a tiny reaction to a tiny untruth. Kenneth stands from his bread loaf position and sulks away.

"You know I love you."

I'm doing a pretty good crumple myself right now, actually, hearing those words—*I love you*. I've heard them a lot, over the last week—my mom and dad, my siblings, Kit and Zoe. *I love you; won't you please come home with us? We love you; we just don't want you pushing yourself. I love you, but I think you're being stubborn. I love you, but you absolutely need a shower.*

I'm so—I'm so *lucky* to have all this love. So why do I feel so bad?

There's a knock at the door, and I close my eyes in fatigue and frustration. "I know, Mom. I love you too. I'm going to get some rest, okay?" I say it quietly, hoping my guests—and I know it's guests, *plural*—won't hear.

When I hang up, I stay comically still. Mummification still. I could do this all night.

Another knock, and then Kit's muffled voice: "I brought Ben's toolbox."

Zoe shouts, "I watched a video on how to pick a lock!"

Kit: "*I* watched the video."

There's a slight scuffle, a squeal of surprise, and I swing my legs—gingerly—onto the carpeted floor. If I don't open for them, Joyce will call complex security, which is basically comprised of a guy named Darryl who wears what looks like a UPS uniform while he rides around the sidewalks on a Segway. Zoe always says he probably stole all the badges on his sleeves from a Girl Scout.

"I'm coming." I hobble toward the door, not because of my injuries but because I've been lying around so long. I flick on the dining room light as I go, because I don't need them to know the full extent of my weirdness, that I've been in the dark most of the night, thinking and crying about a man I sent away.

"Whoa," Zoe says, when I open the door, her eyes widening as she takes me in.

Kit's holding her tricep, rubbing her palm over it. "She pinched me." She looks up, her face transforming from surprised indignation to surprised concern. "Your hair."

I reach a hand up, encounter a tuft that must be sticking out dramatically from the side. I don't bother fixing it. I should have had Ava stay, just for occasions like this. Maybe she could've finally taught me what contouring is. "I've been sleeping."

"Okay, well," says Zoe, all business. "Wake up, because we're tired of getting bland texts from you."

Kit holds up her phone, lit up to show our long-running group text, and points to it. My most recent one says: *I'm fine.* I shrug, and try not to wince. Zoe moves past me, a box of pizza balanced on one palm, six glass bottles of my favorite fruit soda clinking together in a crate in her other.

"Ava said you can't have alcohol until you're done with your meds," she says, setting both on the table. "Or else this would've been enough wine to make you tell us your feelings."

"You called Ava?"

Kit passes by me too. She actually does have a toolbox in her hand, but when she sets it down next to the pizza and opens it, it looks like she's replaced all the tools with Saran-wrapped cookies.

She catches my eye and smirks. "Ben was not real happy about this."

"I'm not hungry," I say, but it's a lie. That whole pizza can get in my face. A muscle relaxer chaser and I'll be asleep within an hour.

Ten minutes later I'm sitting at the table, plates and napkins set out by Zoe, fruit sodas opened by Kit, meowing soundtrack provided by Kenneth, sullen face pulling courtesy of yours truly.

"Sooooo," says Kit. "How're things?"

Zoe snorts. "Let me guess. They're—fine?"

"Ugh. Just let me eat my pizza in peace."

"Did you hear anything about your showcase?" Kit asks. "Your graduation?"

Jeez, with friends like these. "Not yet. I got a nice email from Professor Hiltunen, asking how I'm doing. Nothing yet about whether he'll write the letter." *Smarmy bastard,* I think, the thought so uncharacteristic that I pick up my napkin, wipe my mouth. "He's got a few days to decide, I guess."

"He'll come around," Kit says. "Your pictures were amazing. The best of the bunch. Everyone said so."

I take a sip of my soda, and for the first time since the showcase, one week ago, I remember that part of it—the part before everything had happened with Alex, the part before I'd been hit. People *had* loved the photographs. They'd looked for so long, had said how interesting they were. They'd asked questions—why a hat on the bed, how did I get the ladybug so close up, what *were* all those objects on top of the newspaper. I'd felt so good, standing in front of them, those sparkling, good luck memories of the past month. Before I'd noticed Alex had gone, before I'd seen him hunched against that lamppost, I'd felt a blooming sense of hope. I'd thought maybe—

"Have you called him?" Zoe says, getting right to the point.

"No," Kit answers. "She hasn't." I shoot her a look, and she puts her hands up in something like surrender. "It's not like I don't talk to him, Greer."

For a minute, it's nothing but Kenneth's begging meows, a chilly, awkward silence sprinkling over us like a snowfall—Kit, probably angry at me for what I've done to her brother. Me, jealous that she's talked to him, curious about everything—where he is, what he's said, how he feels. Zoe, stuck in the middle.

I reach out, past my stubborn, wounded pride, past my sad, self-imposed isolation, and take Kit's hand. "I'm sorry. I'm so sorry if I've messed things up with us, getting involved with him."

Kit looks up at me, her glasses a little smudgy, probably with pizza grease. She *is* messy, just like Alex said, and I feel my heart squeeze in affection for them both. She gives me a watery smile. "You didn't mess things up. You could never. You're like a sister to me, you know that." She shrugs. "I'm sad, that's all. For both of you."

I lower my eyes, feel tears press there. "Me too."

"Okay but," Zoe says, her voice loud, annoyed. "You could *call him.*"

"Z, come on." I shift in my seat, unsure of how much to get into this with Kit here, but then I remember the night she came home. From the start, she hasn't shied away from the truth of it. "He's not cut out for this, a relationship. He never stays in one place, not for the long term."

Kit takes another piece of pizza, stuffs a big bite into her mouth.

"You're doing it again," Zoe says. "You're making excuses. You did it the first night you guys fooled around—"

Kit drops her pizza, puts her hands over her ears, and calls out "*La la laaaaaaaa*," even through her big mouthful of food. Kenneth runs away, and Zoe's lips twitch in a half smile. After a few seconds, Kit lowers her hands, narrowing her eyes across the table at Zoe while she chews.

"I'm not making excuses."

"You are. You thought he'd be too afraid to be with you, because of Kit. Well, he wasn't. You thought he'd bolt when he found out about your Chiari. Well, he didn't. He took you on a trip and gave you the best s—" Kit yelps, and Zoe redirects. "You spent half the time he was here expecting him to leave, and he didn't. So he's got a job where he travels, big deal. So does Kit, these days. You could've tried to make it work. You sent him away because you didn't want him seeing you like this. You didn't want to give him a shot at figuring out whether being with you long term is what he wants, now that things have gotten hard, now that there's not an automatic expiration date on the whole thing. *You're* the one who didn't stay."

"Uh," Kit says, because that was—quite a speech. I feel like I got hit by the bike again. I wonder if I should look down, check for blood on the carpet. Kit shifts in her seat, fidgets with a piece of pizza crust on her plate. "I think—to be fair, Alex is—" She rolls her lips inward, looking pained. "He's not always great at expressing himself. He's defensive." *I don't care if I never take another fucking photograph.*

This time, a tear does spring out, gratitude for Kit's generosity.

"She can take it," Zoe says, keeping her eyes on me. "You told us yourself, Greer. You're the tough one. You always have been." She stands from her chair, brushes a crumb off her shirt like it's business as usual. "I have to pee."

If the awkwardness was a snowfall before, it's a snow embankment now with only me and Kit at the table. It's the North Pole of awkward.

"Well," Kit says. "She certainly has opinions about this."

I stare down at my plate, a piece of half-eaten pizza there. Zoe is right, and I...I *hate* it. I hate that she's right. I hate that I'm so scared and I hate that I didn't trust him or myself. I hate that I treated myself like an obligation, that I let old wounds and old shame force him out of that room with me. I hate that I didn't try harder for my freedom. Not the freedom I've been working for, with the money and school and my job, but the freedom I felt with him, the freedom of being myself.

Also I hate that I ate so many pieces of pizza.

"Greer," Kit says quietly, and I look over at her. She and Alex, they don't look much alike other than the jet-black hair, but now that I know them both, I can see so clearly how they're family. I can see, like me and my siblings, all the subtle, unassuming ways they resemble and relate to each other. The way they both pronounce their *o*'s, short and flat. Kit's messiness and Alex's fastidiousness.

"Yeah?"

"It doesn't matter to me, either way. I love you no matter what. But— but if you did want to call him, he'd answer. Sometimes he can't always, depending on where he is and what he's doing, but he always calls back, no matter where he is in the world. He always, always calls back."

She stands then, gathering up her plate and mine, walking into the kitchen and starting to rinse dishes. The bathroom door opens and Zoe emerges, joining Kit and opening the dishwasher. They work silently beside each other, doing this small act of care for me.

Waiting, now, for me to figure things out on my own.

* * * *

It's three days before I call him.

On Sunday morning I call Ava and ask her to come home. Doug comes with her, bringing a box of Cheerios and his gaming console, his eyes shifting and uncomfortable when he takes in my bruises. But he says how sorry he is that I'm hurt and he promises to keep the games on mute. While Ava unpacks the small bag she'd had at Doug's, I tell her I'll be moving out next month, and I gently suggest that she make Doug pay rent when he inevitably moves in.

She drives me over to Mom and Dad's for Sunday night dinner, letting me stop off first to buy a bouquet of flowers for Mom. Mom cries and hugs me too hard, and Dad points at my fading black eye and says, "You should see the other guy, right?" and he hugs me too, gentle but long, pressing a kiss to the top of my head before he lets me go and heads out to the grill, probably reassembling his Everything's Fine Face over a hot flame. I apologize to Humphrey and Felipe, and later I call Cary at his house, giving him the update on my health he's been asking me for for a week, leaving me voice mails and sending me text messages every morning. He asks whether "that boyfriend of yours" is taking care of me, and I don't even bother trying to pass the test this time. I only tell him that Alex isn't in town anymore, and when I hang up I stare at the ceiling of my bedroom for a pathetically long time, wishing it was the night sky over the ocean.

On Monday I go to work, which Dennise clearly does not approve of at first, but maybe she sees something in my face when I stand in her office, my tablet held to my chest and my jaw clenched tight, because she takes me with her on patient visits all morning, her steps a little slower as we walk beside each other, her glances toward the chairs in the hospital rooms pointed and directive. I sit and take my notes, but at noon my head is dully throbbing, and I tell her so, my face hot and my hands clenched around the tablet. "Get some rest," she says, handing me a manila folder. "You're handling that case Wednesday morning." She gives me a superhero smile before she walks away.

But on Tuesday morning, I find an email in my inbox that makes me press my hands to my face in happiness, a laugh caught in my chest that I don't want to let out, not yet. I take a quick, haphazard shower, nearly forgetting the bag I have to put around my cast, scrubbing too hastily over my stubbly leg, the one with all the stitches. I put on terrible, comfortable sick-day clothes: an old sports bra that doesn't have a clasp, difficult to manage with my wrist, a faded navy tank top, a pair of baggy cropped jeans that I roll up almost to my knees so they don't scrape against my cut, and my ugliest, most beat-up pair of sneakers, the ones I still have an expensive pair of orthotics in. I drive all the way to the city; I park two blocks from Boneshaker's just so I can walk a little in the noisy morning air. I order coffee with lots of milk, sit at my favorite table, open my laptop again, and stare at the email. I hold my phone in the palm of my hand for a long time.

He doesn't say hello when he answers.

He says, "Greer." That low-smooth voice, a single word that sounds like a whole dictionary of relief. I swallow, reopen my eyes from their closing at hearing him say my name.

"Hi. I wasn't sure you'd answer." I wince with an unpleasant thought. "Is it very late where you are? Or...very early?"

There's a long pause. Briefly, I hear voices in the background—a woman's laugh that I try not to let pierce me to my very core—but then there's silence before he speaks. "It's—neither, really."

"Right, okay. Well, that's good."

"Are you doing okay? You're...well?"

The part of me that's still in that hospital bed—the part of me that'll probably always, a little, be in that hospital bed—winces in fear and frustration, the same fear and frustration that I'd used to drive him from my room a week ago.

But that's not the part of me I want to listen to anymore.

"I'm doing okay. A little sore. Still feel tired in the mornings." For a second, I think about the mornings I woke up with Alex—how alive I'd felt in my own skin. How I'd wanted him to touch me, to see if he could feel it too. How he'd always seemed to know that, running his hands over the curve of my hip, the soft skin of my inner arm, the ridge of a spine that had always felt temperamental, separate from me. Under his hands, though, it'd felt perfect. Strong and sturdy and beautiful.

I worry I might cry.

"I'm glad," he says, and it's so—*bland*. It's nothing like before. It's not the Alex who'd ask twenty questions about even the smallest, most insignificant detail. He's protecting himself from me. Small, quiet, invisible Greer. Look how strong I am. Look what I'm capable of now.

It's the worst feeling I've ever had.

I clear my throat, turn my head toward the wall my table is up against, hoping no one can see the way my eyes are welling up.

"I wanted to tell you," I say, stopping to clear my throat again, to get the tears out of my voice. "Hiltunen is going to support the exception request. He's written—" I pause, thinking back over the attachment in that email. *Greer showed exceptional dedication to her work, a tireless commitment to getting the most out of the experience.* "A very generous letter of support. So I think I'll make it. To my graduation."

"Ah, Greer," he says on a sigh—neither surprise nor relief. "I knew you would. You've got such a good eye."

"You can't know how grateful I am." As soon as I say it, I know it's the wrong thing. I am grateful; of course I'm grateful. But I've made it sound like a transaction, as though the days we spent together were nothing but this project.

He's going to say it again—he's going to say that he's *glad*. I think if he does, whatever frayed strand of thread that's holding my heart together will rend for good. Alex will be lost to me. He'll go back to being the man I avoid seeing, my best friend's brother, who makes me feel terrified—full of that swirling, uncontainable energy I only ever knew how to live out in my imagination, until I'd been with him.

You said it yourself, Greer. You're the tough one. You always have been.

A fat tear splashes onto the tabletop in front of me. "Alex," I say, speaking over him, stopping him from finishing what I know is coming after the *I'm* he's started with. Another tear, this one hitting the knuckles of the hand I have raised to my face. Everyone will see, I'm sure. Everyone will wonder what's wrong with me.

You're the tough one, I hear Zoe say. I hear *myself* say.

I take a deep breath. I tell him the hardest thing. The toughest thing.

"I miss you." My voice cracks at the end, but I keep going. "I shouldn't have sent you away. I'm hurting, and—" I break off, sucking in the gulp of air I need for the sob I can't stop. The man at the table closest to me shifts uncomfortably in his seat, pulls headphones from his pockets. *You're so weak,* I think, but what's funny is—for once, I realize I'm not thinking it to myself. I watch the man stuff the earbuds in, watch him hunch forward in his seat. He'd move tables if it weren't so obvious, I'm sure. *It's only a few tears.* "I can't believe I sent you away. I'm so sorry I sent you away."

"Don't—"

I cut him off again, before the crying gets so I can't say anything at all. "I know you're gone. You're probably a million miles away, and that's okay. That's your job, and I don't ever want to get in the way of your job. But I wondered if—"

"I'm not a million miles away."

"Okay, I know that it's an exaggeration, but—"

"I'm at a hotel out by the airport. By your airport."

"You—what?" I should be crying less, but I'm pretty sure I'm crying *more* now. The barista just gave a *this is awkward* look to the guy with the headphones.

"I just ate a bowl of dry cereal and I'm on my third straight episode of *Barefoot Contessa*. She's making an anniversary cake for Jeffrey. Guess what she's wearing."

"Is—" Something like a laugh emerges. Sort of a phlegmy snort. "Is it a blue shirt?"

"Got it in one."

The barista comes over and sets a stack of napkins on the table and gives me a slightly quelling look. I blot my face, which is wet enough that I'm reasonably sure a piece of the cheap brown paper has torn off and is sticking to my cheek, like how my dad used to come to breakfast after shaving, a red circle of blood gluing toilet paper to his chin.

"Greer," Alex says quietly, so quietly that I almost don't hear him through my sniffling. "I didn't want to be so far from you. I tried to go, but I didn't make it very far. I wanted to make sure you were okay. I know you don't need—"

"I love you." There's a sort of—wet hiccup after that. I am the least invisible person in this café right now. I'm pretty sure there's someone watching from the street, actually. If I weren't so busy blotting I'd wave at her, a small social gesture of the hysteria that's taken over. I take a shaky breath, the deepest one I can manage, and say it again. "I love you. I don't need you, but I want you, and that's—that's even better. For me, that's—that's the best thing."

As soon as I've said it, I feel something loosen inside of my body—this body that I know so well, that I've been doing inventory on every day of my adult life, every hour of it—sometimes, during the worst times, every *minute*. I go still in my seat; I make myself a statue, and now I must look even stranger to everyone around me. But I'm searching for the source of that loosening. I'm scanning myself from top to bottom. My neck and shoulders where I always hold so much tension, where I've been extra sore since the accident? My lower back, which ached enough two nights ago that I'd slept on my stomach, a hot water bottle—a poor substitute for Alex's big, warm hand—resting there, my pillow wet with tears? The space behind my right eye, where a migraine will usually start?

But no.

It's none of that—it's the same body, the same one I'll always have. The same one that's betrayed me and bolstered me in a thousand tiny ways. This loosening is different.

This is head, heart, gut. This is my soul.

There's a rustle on the end of the phone, bedsheets or clothes or I don't know what. "Where are you?"

I wipe my face again. Excellent decision, not bothering with makeup, or else this would be a real sad clown situation. "I'm at Boneshaker's." *Where I've made things very uncomfortable for everyone.* "But I should probably—"

"Stay where you are. I'll come to you."

He hangs up, and for a second I only sit there, the phone pressed to my ear and another cheap napkin pressed to my face.

Then I set my head down on the table and let out a laughing, sighing sob of relief.

And I don't care who sees or hears me.

Chapter 20

Alex

It's the longest car ride of my life.

My driver is a man named Lamar; like Greer, he's lived here his whole life, but unlike Greer he's entirely uncomfortable with silence, and for every one of twenty-nine minutes it takes to get to Boneshaker's he talks. As we make our way through the outskirts of the city, he talks to me about a new overpass that wasn't there when he was growing up, about a now-empty shopping mall that he used to go to every Friday night, about the minor-league baseball stadium where he once ate fourteen corn dogs over the course of seven innings. In the backseat I make murmured sounds of assent and acknowledgment, but I also set my hands on knees, gripping tighter and tighter in frustration. I try to keep in my head the sound of Greer's voice.

I love you.

I could've stayed at Kit's, of course, or I could've found a place in the city. But when I'd left the hospital that day, Patricia's words ringing loud in my ears, I'd thought to leave entirely; I'd taken her advice seriously. I'd gone back to the studio apartment, the sheets still smelling like Greer—soft, skin-warmed lavender—and I'd packed my things, my headphones in my ears as I'd called Jae. "Not Syria," I'd said to him. "But I can't stay here."

I'd flown to New York that night, had slept in Jae's guest bedroom—or had attempted to sleep. Mostly I'd stared up at the ceiling, picturing Greer's face in my mind, feeling so alone and so separate that I thought I might simply disappear, that Jae would open the door to that room the next day and find no trace of me at all. But in the morning, I'd still been there, something inside me different after the long, lonely night. Something full and heavy and—strangely pleasant, strangely grounding. Something true. Something made up of all the things I'd thought about Greer, about me, about the two of us together.

Over a breakfast of fat, decadent pastries ordered from a bakery two blocks over, tiny cups of too-strong espresso sitting in front of us on the narrow breakfast bar of the apartment, I'd told Jae what I wanted to do about my work.

By Tuesday night, I was back in Barden, the airport hotel room a concession to the distance Greer had asked for. I'd made Kit swear not to say a word. I'd alternated between hope and doubt, confidence and despair. I'd had two panic attacks, one in the breakfast room of the hotel lobby and one inside my room late at night, when I was just dropping off into sleep, and both of them were fucking awful, absolutely the worst, but at least I hadn't spent days afterward berating myself about it. Instead I'd gone to see Patricia, conscious and careful on the streets that I'd see Greer somehow, that I'd run into her and lose her trust by not doing what she'd asked of me. I'd written in my journal; I'd taken pictures with my FG, exchanged a few emails with Bart, had dinner with Ben and Kit and Sharon and Henry at a chain restaurant near my hotel.

Self-care, self-care, self-care. I'd waited and waited. I'd waited even when she'd called, when I'd pressed the phone to my ear like it was the camera at my eye. *Light, light, light,* I'd thought, and then she'd said she loved me. A whole entire sunrise of light, all over me, no lens on earth that could capture it.

Before we're even all the way to the curb, I'm on my phone, adding Lamar's tip—large, because however much he talked my ear off he still got me to the woman I love safely—my head down and my heart pounding in anticipation. I pat the pockets of my jeans, making sure I've got my wallet; I raise my hands to my hair and smooth it the best I can, wishing I'd taken an extra minute to look in the mirror before I left the hotel. I take a deep breath, and Lamar looks at me over his shoulder and says, "Good luck, man," and for the first time in my life, I thank someone for the sentiment.

When I step out onto the sidewalk it's a tiny shock of surprise to look up and see her there, standing under the café's awning, her bag slumped on top of the same table where I taught her how to hold a camera. She is an absolute mess, her cheeks splotchy and her eyes red from the tears I heard her crying, her clothes rumpled and too big, her clunky sneakers distressingly dirty.

And the injuries—Jesus *Christ*, the injuries. The cut across her forehead looks shiny and tight, probably itchy as all hell, same as the scraped skin I know is under her cast. She's bruised all the way up to her shoulder on that side, faded purple and greenish yellow, same as the one on her face, swooping underneath her eye and across her cheekbone. From where she stands I can see the very top stitches from the slice on her leg, the ones that curve slightly toward her shin.

She is perfect.

Still, I'm cautious as I approach her, remembering every small but important detail I've learned about her over the month we've had together. I'm keeping in my mind the last morning we spent together in that hospital room, the day she sent me away. I'm wary of doing this wrong, of scaring her again. Of getting sent away again. Of being alone, separate.

But when I'm close, only a table-length apart from her, she shocks me again, opening her arms wide before she—she *falls* into me, a deliberate, thoughtful fall, one it seems like she's been waiting for. A big sigh of relief exits her body as she presses her face—the unbruised side—against my chest, her arms coming around my waist and squeezing, the stiff line of her cast pressing against my lower back, and it's all I can do not to squeeze her back, not to press against any of the parts of her that are tender and hurting. I bring my arms around her gently, one hand smoothing up her back until I reach the nape of her neck, and that's what I wanted—there's where I wanted to touch most, that place on Greer that's most vulnerable, the one she wears exposed to the world—small, private defiance of everything that slowed her down, kept her trapped. I use my thumb to stroke her skin there—too relieved, too overwhelmed, too happy and grateful to say anything at all.

So it's a good thing she speaks for us both, saying the hardest, most secret thing. A thing she knows I won't hold against her, and a thing she'd never hold against me.

"Take care of me," she whispers, and tightens her arms around me even more.

* * * *

At first it's all I focus on: what's immediate to her, what she wants, what she needs for me to take care of her. She doesn't want to go home yet, doesn't want to go back to my hotel, doesn't want to be indoors at all, and other than the fact that I'd like to feel all of her skin against mine, that

I'd like to stroke my hands all over the places I've missed and missed, it's what I want too after the days I've spent cooped up in that hotel. Warm sunshine and open air and her beside me.

So I take her back to the park. She's got a blanket in her car, the one I bought before I took her to the beach, and I walk with it underneath one arm so I can hold her hand, my other one holding a bag of food and bottled water we stopped off to buy her. I choose a spot set apart from the planned gardens, beneath a vast, ropy black locust tree. I spread out the blanket and lie on my side next to her, and within ten minutes she's asleep beside me, as though this exact blanket, this exact tree, this exact day is what she's needed to rest.

She doesn't sleep for long, maybe a half hour, but while she does I imagine I can hear her healing on the inside in the same way I feel like I'm getting put back together, all shaken up and cut apart since that night at the showcase. When she wakes up her eyes look less puffy, her complexion clear of the splotchy redness from before, her freckles prominent across her nose in spite of the shade we've stayed under. I don't think about it; I only lean down to her mouth and kiss her, and right away she lifts her uncasted hand, tangling her fingers through my hair, opening her lips against mine, and I don't know, maybe outside was a bad idea after all. Probably getting arrested wouldn't be good for the panic attacks.

"Ooof," she says, pulling back after a few seconds, slowly lowering her head back to the ground. She takes the hand from my hair, moves it across her body to rub at her shoulder. "I have to be careful."

"Shit, I'm sorry. I got carried away." Some caretaker, Jesus.

She smiles up at me, her face clear and untroubled. "*I* got carried away." Her smile turns a little more rueful as she looks up at me. "But it—it'll probably be a while. I'm doing a lot of PT, but the—I've got all this tension, and then I get headaches. Plus the muscle relaxers I take at night, they make me tired, so—"

"I don't care. I've got all kinds of time, Greer. I'm not going anywhere."

At that she lowers her eyes, and it's the first time since I saw her this morning that I really remember I've got more to focus on than what's immediate to her, than what she wants and needs. If it's going to work between us, we've got to talk about everything else, about what both of us want and need.

"About that," she says, and pushes herself up to a sitting position. There's a moment where she struggles, wanting to sit crisscross-style, the way she did that day in the herb garden, but the cut on her leg makes it impossible. She pushes her back against the tree instead, her legs stretched out in front of her, crossed at the ankles. She gives me a shy look from beneath her lashes and points at her injured calf. "Say anything about my leg hairs and you'll walk back to that hotel."

I laugh, lean down again, and press my lips to her shin, feel the prickly, unfamiliar texture. "I don't mind."

When I look up her cheeks are flushed, but her expression has turned serious. "Alex. It won't work, if you try giving up your job. You know it won't. What you said in the hospital—"

I sit up now so that I'm facing her, my legs drawn up and my elbows resting on my knees, my spine curving uncomfortably given the uneven ground beneath my ass. I don't expect either of us will last much longer out here, but for now, it's okay. It's right, even, a little bit of discomfort for this part.

"I was lying," I tell her. "You know I was."

She nods, keeps her eyes on her lap.

"I wasn't lying about us, about wanting a relationship with you. And I wasn't lying about making changes to the way I work. But of course I'd care if I never took pictures again. I was just—" I look down, shake my head at myself. "I was scared, I guess. Lashing out. Saying stupid shit. It's something I need to work on."

Greer shrugs. "You should've seen me last week. I asked Humphrey whether he was wearing a wire to spy for my mom. I was only half joking." She makes a grimace of embarrassment, and it's so fucking adorable that my fingers twitch where they dangle between my knees, wanting to touch her.

"James Bond," I say, and she laughs softly. I clear my throat, shift against the ground. "After I left the hospital, I went to New York for a couple of days. Met with my agent."

"Oh?" she says, that single syllable full of such practiced casualness. I've got to scrape my hand across my jaw, my mouth, to hide my smile.

"I am going to take some time off." Her eyes snap to mine, wide and— fuck, I don't know. Wary, cautious. Suspicious. I hate that, but I hope what I tell her chases that look away. "And I would've done that whether you'd wanted me or not. I'm not better—" I pause, reconsider the way I've started. "I haven't learned to deal with the panic yet, so I need more time. More therapy. And I'm going to do this project with Jae, a—well. A book, I guess, though we'll see where it goes."

Her eyes light immediately. "A book? That's amazing!"

"It's...I don't know what it is, yet. I started thinking about it before, when I was putting together the guest lecture, and the showcase. The past couple of days, I've looked into a few online courses for—uh. Writing. Obviously, I don't have a lot of experience with that, other than captions."

"Jeez," she says, blinking innocently. "Bet you wish you knew someone who went back to school as an adult who could help you with this."

I nudge her foot with mine, both of us smiling. Jesus, it feels good to be with her again. "I'm going to do domestic work for a while, no more than a couple of shoots a month. Then we'll see how I feel come the fall."

For a few seconds, we're both quiet, and I can see Greer turning something over in her mind, tracing a fingernail over the ridges on her cast. "So you'll do all that...from New York? And maybe visit here, in between your shoots. That would be...good."

"No, I—" But now I'm unsure, that holding pattern feeling again, the one from the week before the showcase. I'm so—I'm so *terrible* at this. I fucked it up before, mentioned it at the wrong time and made her so upset that she'd turned from me and then—*this*. Her accident, our fight, the time we spent apart. I rub my hands through my hair, and I'm sure it looks ridiculous now, as messy as I feel on the inside.

But I've been a mess in front of Greer before. And if it's going to work, I'm sure I'll be a mess in front of her again. I love her and I want to try with her. I want to try with her forever, if she'll let me.

"I thought I'd be here. As my home base. And I won't—listen, you've worked really hard, to be on your own. To live on your own and do your work and arrange your life in exactly the way you want it. I'm not going to get in the way of that. Whatever your plans were, you should—do those plans, and I'll be a part of whatever you want me to. If you want me to."

"If I want you to?"

"Anyways my sister is here. And Patricia. She'd probably mail me a horse head if I went to someone—"

"Alex," Greer says, a smile in her voice. She leans forward, taps her uninjured hand on my wrist, then on the inside of my leg, subtle directions that tell me she wants me to open up, to make room for her, so that's what I do, my heart still in my throat, my neck still warm from embarrassment. She moves—cautiously, of course, more careful with her body than usual—to straddle me, her ass against my thighs, her forearms—one casted—resting on my shoulders. Wisely, she keeps a distance between her groin and my lap, because when it comes to Greer, I can absolutely still get a hard-on when I'm nervous.

"Ow," she says, making a subtle adjustment, the smile in her voice now on her lips. I put my hands at her waist, steadying her. Closing my eyes to take in the feel of her, the smell of her. "Alex," she says again. "I definitely, definitely want you to."

I open my eyes. "Yeah?"

She moves herself the tiniest bit forward, glancingly shy of where I want her most. "Remember that morning at Boneshaker's? Two years ago?"

I smile, lower my eyes. "Oh, man. Yeah. I thought you hated me."

One minute shift closer. "I did, a little. Because I'd had this dream about you, the night before. I woke up from it."

I can't help but laugh. "I've had those kinds of dreams about you too, sweetheart."

"No, I mean—" There's that blush, the one beneath her freckles. "Well, yes, it was that kind of dream, partly. But also it was—it was this dream, where we were like we are now. I was this Greer, and you were this Alex. Not the Greer who was so shy and closed off that first night we met. And not the Alex who was so—I don't know—confident and charming and worldly. Not the Alex who'd have his freedom at the expense of everything else."

I can't help but wince at this, at this being the way she's seen me. At the fact that she hadn't even been wrong. But in the weeks since I've been with Greer, I've realized she knows more about freedom than I ever have. It doesn't depend for her on how fast she can pack or how few people are around to ask things of her. It depends on how she feels about herself. She doesn't have it just right yet—that's what she's been working on, but watching her I know. I know she's right there on the cusp of it, and I want to be there to see it. To share it.

"Listen," she says, the fingers of her uninjured hand kneading the muscles of my neck. "In the dream, we were the perfect match. We were just together, as easy as anything. I felt so—I was completely myself. More myself than I was awake."

Fuck it, I pull her closer to me, so everything about us is lined up, fitted together. When we're like this her chin lines up to my forehead, my lips to the base of her throat. I feel—overcome. Ready to cry or laugh or some combination of the two. I kiss her soft skin, rub the stubble on my chin gently back and forth, a move that releases the gentle *hmm* Greer makes sometimes, my favorite sound.

"Sounds like a good dream," I tell her, my voice quiet, strained. Damn, maybe it's closer to crying.

She moves her head so her mouth is right against my ear. "The best dream," she says, placing a soft kiss there. "A dream come true."

* * * *

While Greer works the next day, I check out of the hotel, go back to the studio I'm able to rent for the next month. I call Kit, and she takes a half day so she can go with me to some massive store not far from Greer's parents' house where they carry everything from clothes to housewares to groceries. She makes a list on her phone of all the things I'll need that aren't included with the place—obvious shit like extra toilet paper and hand soap and laundry detergent, but also stuff she seems to recognize as necessary even from the cursory glance she takes around the unit when she picks me up. An extra dish towel, a rubber spatula, coffee filters, a better set of pillows for the bed. I get sweaty inside the store, seeing the cart fill up; I tell her I don't know what I'll do with all this stuff, after the month is up. That Greer and I, we haven't figured out everything about what's next yet, only that we'll be together.

She shrugs and says, "I can use it all at my house, if you don't end up needing it." Then she puts her small hand on my back and pats me lightly. "Okay?" she asks, and I don't even mind. My baby sister, taking care of me.

We stuff her tin can car full of everything we bought, and I buy her the fanciest fucking lunch we've ever eaten together, some restaurant where the menus are printed on vellum and kept in soft leather booklets. She tells me more about her honeymoon, about a trip she's got scheduled next week for work, about a new paper she's working on with Dr. Singh. I tell her about Patricia and the book, the classes I might take. When she's taking her last bite of crème brûlée I set my elbows on the table and tell her what I should have the day she got married.

"Kit. Remember at your wedding, when you said that I gave you good things when we were growing up?"

She blinks across the table at me, the spoon still halfway in her mouth when she nods. When she pulls it out she points it at me. "I said you'd given me *every* good thing. Every one. I don't want you ever to forget it."

I clear my throat, look down at the white tablecloth, the glass bowl filled with crystal clear water, delicate pink flower blooms floating on top. Who would've ever thought, me and Kit, in a place like this. "I wanted to say that it was the same for me. Everything good I had back then, it was because I had you with me. It's you who kept me from turning out like Dad."

Kit's still holding the spoon in the air, like she's been frozen in shock. "That's not true."

I smile at her. "It is. Or at least it's mostly true. You were the biggest part of that for me."

She swallows thickly, tears springing up. She's always been quick to cry, Kit, at least around me. "Well, thanks. Thank you."

"But after that too. You gave me a lot of good things all these years I've been gone, and you always made sure I had a home with you if I needed it. You always called, emailed. You always cared about everything I did. So I'm thanking you for that. And I'm thanking you for Greer. For knowing Greer, and for—being okay, being supportive of this thing with me and her. It's the best good thing you've ever given me, and that's a long list, Tool Kit."

"I'm going to make a mess of this tablecloth, Alex," she sniffs.

"Well, I'm probably going to make a mess of a lot of things over the next few months. I'll probably be a gigantic pain in the ass while I figure all this out." I make a vague gesture around the room, meaning—being here, in this city, making a life. A new home base.

Kit smiles at me, big and bright, black eyes shining. She's still got the spoon in her hand when she shrugs. "That's okay," she says. "It'll be my pleasure, cleaning up after you for once."

And after that, for the first time in my life, I let my sister drive me home.

Where I wait for the love of my life to share it with me.

Epilogue

Greer

They make me wear my robes and the hat to Betty's.

It's a big group, this "they"—my whole family, immediate and extended, sure, but also Kit and Zoe and Ben and Aiden, Henry and Sharon, a few of Aiden's crew from his rescue squad, Patricia and Bart and Dennise and all my colleagues from Holy Cross. It's the second time in as many months that Betty's shut down her place for one of us, and right now she's behind the bar, filling glasses from a tap and keeping an eye on the phone screen my dad's holding up for her, playing the video of the moment where I walked across the stage to get my diploma.

Greer Garson Hawthorne. Lots of cheers and shouting from the audience. Cary smuggled in an air horn, and for the rest of the ceremony the campus police made him wait outside.

Last week Ava had encouraged me to practice a wave as I went across the stage. "Like this," she'd said, and done a beautiful, smooth walk, the top half of her body perfectly turned out as she raised a hand in the air. "Mom'll love it."

"I'm—just going to try to stay upright," I'd told her, and thank God I had. I thought I'd have a stroke, walking across that stage. I was so nervous that I'd said, "You're welcome" instead of "Thank you" when the dean handed me my diploma. It could've been worse. The dean looks a little like Santa Claus, and I'd almost said, "Merry Christmas." Good thing none of this was captured on the video.

Still, in my apartment last night, trying on the robes I'd had hanging from my closet door, I'd shown Alex the wave, the same way Ava had done it, and he'd laughed and laughed, pulling me onto the bed and kissing me, telling me he imagined I was a princess in another life, a queen, a famous movie star.

Across the room, he stands with Bart and Dennise, his head tipped to the side slightly, his shoulders hunched in deference to their shorter statures. Even from here he looks calm, perfectly at ease, a crooked smile transforming his face at something Dennise says to Bart. I don't want to speculate, but I think Bart likes Dennise's blouse, and also her face and her whole self. If those two get together I will plan the wedding. I will moonlight as a romance novelist so I can write their story. I absolutely have the imagination for it.

Shocking exactly no one except him, routines seem to have helped Alex with the panic attacks—getting enough sleep, eating regular meals, runs in the early mornings, a session with Patricia every Friday, three online class sessions a week, which he usually walks to Boneshaker's to do. He talks to Jae every Tuesday and Thursday. Last month, we'd gone to New York for a weekend to attend a party Jae invited us to, and I'd been loudly hailed as the best thing that'd ever happened to Alex, since he'd finally responded to an Evite. All night, Alex had stood beside me, his hand occasionally coming up to rub the skin across my shoulders. "This is Greer Hawthorne," he'd say, introducing me to journalists, photographers, artists, authors. "She's a social worker."

He's done one job in the time since he's been back, five days spent in California covering wildfire damage, flying back late on a Thursday night and knocking softly on my new apartment's door before using the key I gave him, crawling in bed with me and falling asleep with a satisfied smile on his face. Two of his photos were in the *Post* the next morning.

"One more picture," says Zoe, handing her phone to Aiden and coming to stand next to me, waving Kit over with her other hand. They're both wearing the promised T-shirts, white with a big square covering the whole front, my smiling face in the center.

"Hold up the diploma," Kit says. "Like right in front. Wait, should we get our signs?" They're referring, of course, to the two signs they'd each made to hold up when my name was called. One said, *GREER, WE LOVE YOU*, and the other was a huge print—done by Bart—of my ladybug, so it'd be easy for me to find them all in the audience.

"Don't get the signs," says Zoe. "We want the diploma to be the focus. Aiden, make sure you can see the part where it says summa cum laude."

"Tiny print, Zo," he says, squinting at the phone screen, probably trying to remember where to press to get a picture. Aiden is terrible with phones. Every once in a while I'll get a photo message from him that's just a black screen and then a while later he'll text, *Sorry, sat on it.*

"Let me," says Alex, stepping beside Aiden. He's got the FG in his hand—which he still uses around town here, sending a roll of film a week to Bart—and a smile on his face. He's also got one of the T-shirts on, and it's ridiculous, sweet and absurd and lovely, and he keeps patting at the chest of it, like maybe everyone at the party hasn't already noticed he's wearing my face on himself. Kit rolls her eyes when he makes us move, getting us in better light, and it's at least a minute of him moving himself, figuring out where he wants to stand.

"Say, Count Dracula," shouts Henry from down the bar. "It's not the Sears catalog. Get on with it."

All three of us laugh—Kit's with a small snort, Zoe's big and bold, mine not much more than a quiet chuckle—and that's when Alex gets the picture, probably the perfect picture. Probably I'll have it framed and on my mantel by the end of the month.

Alex comes over, takes my diploma, and sets it on the table behind me, placing the camera beside it, leaning down to kiss my cheek. "Mind if I steal you away for a minute?"

Thank God. "Please," I whisper to him. "This is—so many people here."

Alex smiles down at me, takes my hand in his, and leads me through the crowd, stopping by the bar and taking a covered basket from Betty—who gives the both of us a wink—before he leads me down the hall. When he pushes open the back door, he takes his hand from mine and gestures for me to go ahead of him, bending to prop the door open with a wooden block he's taken out of the basket.

The basket, the block—it's only the first clue to what's obviously been carefully planned. Betty's back alley has been transformed as best as a back alley can be. There's one of her two-top tables up against the brick wall, a few lit tea lights in the center, two chairs pulled out already, one with a hulking bouquet of fat red roses resting on the seat. Above us, tiny white lights have been strung between Betty's and the adjoining building, a stringed canopy that does a lot to make the place look dreamy and romantic, even though there's still a dumpster not all that many feet away. But someone—probably Alex, probably this is the errand he had to run this afternoon—has made an effort to clean up, the ground beneath my feet swept clean, no cigarette butts or bottles or wet, discarded paper anywhere. It smells like someone went berserk with a can of spray air freshener.

"I'm not going to propose," he blurts.

I press my lips together, tamp down my smile. God—this Alex. This Alex who gets flustered, unsure of himself. I love him so.

"I figured not. It's pretty early on in this thing." Two months since my accident. Two of the best months, together.

He reaches into the basket, takes out two flutes and a small bottle of champagne for me, a small bottle of sparkling water for him. Even in the low light from the candles, from the stringed bulbs above, I can see there's a flush high on his cheekbones as he opens them both and pours for us. His eyelashes are still, obviously, stupidly, offensively long. Two weeks ago at dinner Ava asked if she could touch them.

"I wanted to do a toast. For your graduation." I take the glass he holds out to me, but lean in first and press my lips to his. When I step back, he runs his hand through his hair, picking up his own glass. "I know you wouldn't want a big scene. A bigger scene, I guess, than what's already in there."

"You know me pretty well, I guess." My smile feels so big, huge for a moment between only two people.

He clears his throat, rubs his hand across my face on his chest again. I think he's—I think he *practiced* this, same as Ava wanted me to practice the wave.

"Since we got together, Greer—I've been rethinking my position on luck."

I raise an eyebrow at him.

"I've decided that I'm a really lucky person. Lucky I survived all those years on my own. Lucky nothing serious ever went wrong with Kit. I'm lucky I got that FG, and I'm lucky I got to meet a lot of people on the way who were willing to take a chance on a bad attitude kid with a good eye. I'm lucky I never died doing any of the stupid shit I did, chasing this career. Lucky my sister never gave up on me, even though I probably deserved it. And I'm so lucky you're her best friend. That I got to meet you, and that I get to love you. I've got the best luck of anyone I know, I've decided."

"Cheers to that," I say quietly, smiling and raising my glass, my eyes all welled up.

"No, wait," he says quickly, before I can take a sip. "What I wanted to say is that you've convinced me about my own luck. But I hope you know that this, today—your graduation, it wasn't luck. It was only you and your hard work and determination, and you would've done it whether you'd gotten that ticket or not, even if it would've taken you longer. I wish I could've seen it from the beginning, you doing all this, but I—" He breaks off, swallows, and clears his throat again. "I'm glad I got to be here for this part. And I can't wait to be here for the next part. All the parts, really. Whatever you do next." He raises his glass. "Congratulations, sweetheart."

He's hardly finished before I step into him again, kiss him hard.

"We forgot to clink our glasses," he says, a few minutes later. "Probably that's bad luck, huh?"

I shrug. "Probably." I lean back, staying within the circle of his arms, and tap his glass with mine. "Good thing you've got the best luck of anyone you know."

He laughs, leans into me, and sighs, making goosebumps rise on my neck. The party inside is loud, laughing. Just a few more minutes here with Alex and I'll be ready to go back in, to celebrate myself and this massive accomplishment. In two days, Alex and I leave for another celebration, a trip I planned over the last month, staying up late to do research on my computer, checking out guidebooks from the library. A flight out to Seattle, a rented car for us to drive over two weeks all the way down to Big Sur, stopping along the way to visit all sorts of places I've always wanted to go. My mother will probably need a whole bottle of Xanax, or maybe she won't. Maybe everyone in that room is finally getting used to the Greer I've always been.

After a minute, Alex moves, putting his mouth against my ear before he whispers to me, a secret even from the privacy of this alley, from this night sky.

"Just so you know, Greer. I am going to ask you someday. If you won't mind being stuck with me forever."

I squeeze him tighter, smiling into the kiss I press against his neck. Stuck with Alex—what a thought. What a thought, when I always feel so free with him beside me. I nip lightly at his skin before I whisper back.

"Just so you know, Alex," I say, kissing him again, feeling my whole heart expand. *I can, I can, I can.* "I can always ask you first."

Acknowledgments

The first and forever thanks go to you—readers, reviewers, and bloggers—for reading! Whether this is your first book in the Chance of a Lifetime series, or whether you've been one of the lovely people following Kit, Zoe, and Greer from the beginning (and writing reviews and spreading the word!), I'm so grateful to you for taking the chance on a new series, and I hope you loved Alex and Greer's story as much as I do.

From the very first day I started thinking about this series, I knew it would conclude with Alex and Greer—and many eagle-eyed readers noticed their charged first meeting in *Beginner's Luck*. But as well as I thought I knew Alex and Greer and where they would end up, they surprised me as I wrote their story, and they put me through my paces too. As I worked to give them the happily ever after I'd always imagined for them, I relied on a lot of wonderful people to help me along the way, and I'm so glad to have the opportunity to thank them here.

At a particularly fraught point in the drafting of this book, my agent Taylor Haggerty listened patiently while I talked/emailed through the sticking points, and her guidance and encouragement gave me the strength to keep trying. Taylor, I adore you and I'm so glad I get to work with you.

A dear friend, the lovely and talented author Olivia Dade, read early pages of this manuscript and pinpointed exactly what needed to change to keep the story going forward. Her keen eye—not to mention her generosity, her patience, and her unfailing kindness and emotional intelligence—is a chief reason this book got finished, and I'm so grateful to her.

I've said it before and I'll say it again: I'm supremely, endlessly lucky to have had Esi Sogah as the editor seeing me through this series, and I owe her an immense debt of gratitude not just for the shaping of Alex and Greer's story, but for all the stories in these three books. Esi, thank you It is a gift of my life to know you and to work with you.

This book is a lot about older brothers, and though mine doesn't have much in common with the ones I've written here, he deserves my forever thanks for being such a force in my life. When I told my family I wanted to try writing fiction, it was my big brother who bought me my first Scrivener program, and it's him I'm still always hoping to make proud.

Much gratitude goes to the network of family and friends who support and sit tight and sometimes slap me in the face (figuratively, of course) when I'm writing. You are all heroes for putting up with me. Special thanks to my parents (who have had to deal with my whining over the course of many… months. Let's say months), to my dear friend and champion beta reader, Amy (who does the greatest live-text responses as she reads), to Elizabeth (who even flew into town so she could listen to me ruminate over Alex and Greer's first kiss), to Jackie (who has been my best friend and lucky charm forever), and to every one of the writer and reader friends I have been so fortunate to connect with over the course of this journey. I am especially grateful to Katharine Ashe, Emma Barry, Adele Buck, Jen DeLuca, Mary Chris Escobar, Eloisa James, Elisabeth Lane, and Ainslie Paton.

Thanks to the team at Kensington that helps bring these books to life, especially to Michelle Addo and Lauren Jernigan for their terrific publicity work, and to Tammy Seidick for her gorgeous cover, and April LeHoullier for her copy editing.

Finally, for my husband—in the very final stages of drafting this book, you literally took care of every single thing so I could write. Food preparing, dog walking, blanket and pain reliever providing, household maintaining, whatever. And the very best thing about that is that when I thanked you, you only reminded me of all the times I've done the same and more for you. Thanks for being my partner and my friend and the love of my life, and thanks for whispering to me that I am "the best ever" even when I feel like the worst.

Readers, if you'd like to keep up with news from me, please head over to kateclayborn.com and sign up for my newsletter!

Meet the Author

Kate Clayborn lives in Virginia, where she's lucky enough to spend her days reading and talking about all kinds of great books. At home she's either writing, thinking about writing, or—during long walks around her fabulous neighborhood—making her handsome husband and sweet-faced dog listen to her talk about writing. Kate loves to hear from and connect with readers—follow her on Twitter, on Instagram, and on Facebook. Visit her at www.kateclayborn.com to sign up for her newsletter.

Love Greer's story?

Don't miss the rest of the
Chance of a Lifetime series

BEGINNER'S LUCK
And
LUCK OF THE DRAW

Available now from
Kate Clayborn
And
Lyrical Press

Luck of the Draw

Buying a lotto ticket with her two best friends didn't change Zoe's life. Only following her heart would do that . . .

Sure, winning the lottery allows Zoe Ferris to quit her job as a cutthroat corporate attorney, but no amount of cash will clear her conscience about the way her firm treated the O'Leary family in a wrongful death case. So she sets out to make things right, only to find gruff, grieving Aiden O'Leary doesn't need—or want—her apology. He does, however, need something else from her. Something Zoe is more than willing to give, if only to ease the pain in her heart, a sorrow she sees mirrored in his eyes . . .

Aiden doesn't know what possesses him to ask his family's enemy to be his fake fiancée. But he needs a bride if he hopes to be the winning bid on the campground he wants to purchase as part of his beloved brother's legacy. Skilled in the art of deception, the cool beauty certainly fits the bill. Only Aiden didn't expect all the humor and heart Zoe brings to their partnership—or the desire that runs deep between them. Now he's struggling with his own dark truth—that he's falling for the very woman he vowed never to forgive.

Beginner's Luck

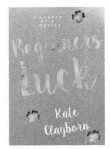

When three friends impulsively buy a lottery ticket, they never suspect the many ways their lives will change—or that for each of them, love will be the biggest win of all.

Kit Averin is anything but a gambler. A scientist with a quiet, steady job at a university, Kit's focus has always been maintaining the acceptable status quo. A sudden windfall doesn't change that, with one exception: the fixer-upper she plans to buy, her first and only real home. It's more than enough to keep her busy, until an unsettlingly handsome, charming, and determined corporate recruiter shows up in her lab—and manages to work his way into her heart . . .

Ben Tucker is surprised to find that the scientist he wants for Beaumont Materials is a young woman—and a beautiful, sharp-witted one at that. Talking her into a big-money position with his firm is harder than he expects, but he's willing to put in the time, especially when sticking around for the summer gives him a chance to reconnect with his dad. But the longer he stays, the more questions he has about his own future—and who might be in it.

What begins as a chilly rebuff soon heats up into an attraction neither Kit nor Ben can deny—and finding themselves lucky in love might just be priceless . . .

Printed in the United States
by Baker & Taylor Publisher Services